My
Mama's
Waltz

Ellie and her mother splash together, Lake Champlain

Sharon's mother, age 18, holding her newborn daughter, Sharon

My Mama's Waltz

*A Book for Daughters
of Alcoholic Mothers*

Eleanor Agnew
and Sharon Robideaux

Foreword by Dr. Robert J. Ackerman

POCKET BOOKS
New York   London   Toronto   Sydney   Tokyo   Singapore

POCKET BOOKS, a division of Simon & Schuster Inc.
1230 Avenue of the Americas, New York, NY 10020

ISBN: 0-671-01385-8

First Pocket Books hardcover printing April 1998

10   9   8   7   6   5   4   3   2   1

POCKET and colophon are registered trademarks of
Simon & Schuster Inc.

Printed in the U.S.A.

For our mothers

Jessica Agnew
&
Ora Cockerham

whom we've always loved.

The waltz ended too soon
and not soon enough.

Acknowledgments

We are greatly indebted to the following people for their advice and support in the preparation of this book: our editor at Pocket Books, Nancy Miller; her assistant, Dan Slater; our agent, John Ware; and Dr. Robert Ackerman, who wrote the Foreword. We are also grateful to our Chairs and colleagues at the University of Missouri at Columbia and Georgia Southern University for their continuing support. We must offer special thanks to our husbands, Doug Robideaux and Liberto Chacon, and to our children, Derek, Shawn, Paul, Stephen and his wife Heather, and Daniel. And we would like to thank our sisters, Diana Agnew, Sheila LaCroix, and Sally Joiner, who are not only daughters of alcoholic mothers and participants in this book, but also the women we turn to most often whenever we need to talk about our mothers.

But most of all, we will never forget the wonderful women who wrote to us, who talked to us, and who met with us, whose stories are in this book along with ours.

Sharon Robideaux
Columbia, Missouri
September 1997

Eleanor Agnew
Savannah, Georgia
September 1997

Authors' Note

Inasmuch as memories can be truth, all the stories within this book are true, but due to the intensely personal and sensitive content, we have changed most, if not all, identifying characteristics (names, occupations, home states) of the women who tell the stories. The exceptions are the events related by Ellie and Sharon themselves, and even then, we have taken the liberty of changing certain names and characteristics of loved ones in order to protect their privacy.

We also wish to remind the reader that memory is its own fact. If one feels something is true, then it is true for that person, regardless of how differently another close to the scene may remember it. After all, no two of us ever dance the same waltz. In life, as on the dance floor, someone always gets stuck dancing backward in uncomfortable shoes.

Contents

〜

Part IV

Foreword

Secrets between mothers and daughters are rarely shared with others. These secrets often build a bond between the two of them that is never broken. They help to build a relationship that the daughter can call upon later in life to provide security, knowledge, and wisdom. However, if the secret is painful and destructive, it becomes more than a secret; it becomes a burden. This is especially true when the secret is that your mother is an alcoholic, and as her daughter you are the one who not only knows the secret but also lives with it.

Having an alcoholic mother always means having more—more secrecy, more social stigma, more family responsibilities while growing up, more worrying about your mother, more self-doubt about your own behaviors, more confusion in your home, and more unanswered questions about being a teenager and a young woman.

Eleanor Agnew and Sharon Robideaux have done a magnificent job in helping us not only to understand what happens to daughters when their mothers are alcoholic, but also to offer tremendous insight so that adult daughters of alcoholic mothers can better understand themselves. And, more importantly, they show daughters how to let go of their pain and to discover the many strengths and capabilities that they possess as women today.

It is an honor for me to write this foreword. I have had the privilege for the past twenty-five years to be involved with children of alcoholics of all ages. I have seen a movement created to help those living in alcoholic families, groups started for children and adults, and I have seen people get better. I am also aware, however, that much remains to be done. Issues still need to be addressed about how to better understand the dynamics of having an alcoholic parent/parents.

Eleanor and Sharon asked me to write the foreword for their book because of the work that I have done with children of alcoholics, and especially because of my research that led to the writing of my book, *Perfect Daughters,* in 1989. In reading *My Mama's Waltz,* it has been a joy to see them go beyond what has been done and to offer the kind of insight for adult daughters that has been missing. This book not only teaches, but it also touches. It offers not only interviews. It also offers the passion, compassion, fears, strengths, doubts, desires, dreams, and hopes of so many women who have endured not only an alcoholic mother but also the burdens of self-doubt that were created during her childhood.

This book is filled with feeling, and it comes forth on every page. This is a book that tells you what it is like to have an alcoholic mother and what her daughters were feeling while trying to survive in silence. It allows us to become part of what it was like for many women to travel through the rites of passage as a teenager and a young woman without a supportive role model. It shares with us the struggle of many women who want it to be different for themselves and their own families, but who are always asking themselves the question, "How do I do this when I've never seen it done?"

Eleanor and Sharon help many daughters not only to unlock the secret of having an alcoholic mother, but also they show the way to share this secret and no longer feel shame, stigma, or the burden of silence. The greatest discovery, however, in this book is not the secret of their mothers but the secrets that many of the daughters have about themselves. The core of these secrets is self-doubt and the feeling that somehow adult daughters of alcoholic mothers are totally different from other women. The authors kindly and compassionately show women how to face their secrets, work through them, let them go, and begin the journey of healing and taking care of themselves.

This is not just a book that tells adult daughters of alcoholic mothers that the keys to recovery are inside them. It's great to know that you have the keys or the abilities inside of you to change your life. But they are useless unless you know something else. Eleanor and Sharon also show adult daughters where their locks are in order to use their newly discovered keys.

Thank you for allowing me to be a small part of this great contribution for adult daughters. I hope that these pages will show women who were raised in alcoholic families that they are so much more than adult daughters of alcoholics. I hope that they will be able to say, "I am an adult daughter and I am becoming . . . and becoming . . . and becoming . . ." I wish you well.

—Robert J. Ackerman, Ph.D.

Preface

They made a strange couple, the eleven-year-old girl with stocky tanned legs extending from beneath her floral baby-doll pajamas, and her mother, bosomy in her stained nightgown, as they box-stepped across the linoleum.

"Whoops!" laughed the woman as she accidentally swung her chubby daughter against the refrigerator. "Well, while I'm here anyway . . . ," she said, reaching into the white box for another Schlitz. She pulled an opener from off the counter and punched a triangular hole into the top of the can, then tilted it back for a long swallow. She set the can down and seized her daughter's hand once again with her own beer-clammy one.

"Here we go, now watch my feet, see, back one-two, slide one-two, no, damn it, not that way!" She dug nicotine-hardened fingernails into her daughter's arm, not noticing when the child winced and pulled back slightly. "You gonna learn how to dance if it kills me, and it damn well might, clumsy as you are. God, how inna world a young'un of mine could have two left feet . . . It matches your tin ear, I reckon. You and your sister neither one cain't carry a tune in a bucket."

She pulled the girl closer, pressing her daughter's face against her bosom. Trapped against the sour smell of the pink rayon, the girl made a face into her mother's cleavage. Above her head, her mother began to sing along with the record in her pure alto voice, only slightly slurring the words.

"Hah! We got better things to do than shleep, don't we? I'm teaching my bee-you-ti-ful li'l girl how to dance, ain't I? You so precious to me . . . Damn! That was my ingrown toenail you went and stepped on, you bitch! When they handed out brains, you thought they said rain,

and you ran. Don't make me have to whip you again. Now, listen to the music. Okay, now, up one-two, slide one-two . . ."

Sharon's memory of learning to dance with her alcoholic mother is a feminized counterpart to a famous poem that inspired our book's title, *My Mama's Waltz.* The poem, "My Papa's Waltz" by Theodore Roethke, one that we have often taught in our college classes, is about a little boy being waltzed around the room by his drunken father. For this boy, as for Sharon above, there is no gaiety in the dance—only humiliation, horror, and desperation. Sharon's dance serves as a metaphor for the psychological waltzing that millions of us have been forced to go through with our alcoholic mothers. We daughters have had to "dance" carefully forward and backward in our relationships with our mothers, reaching out for them but then recoiling as we tried to love them but simultaneously feared and hated them.

All family members must "waltz" carefully with an alcoholic, but this sinister dance is particularly terrifying for children because they are still financially and emotionally dependent. Speaking as women whose mothers were alcoholics, we know that we who were forced into this dance, though we were innocent bystanders, were the ones most irretrievably wounded by the experience.

Robert Ackerman, author of *Perfect Daughters: Adult Daughters of Alcoholics,* estimates that there are now over twenty-two million adult children of alcoholics, eleven million of whom are women. In his study of daughters of alcoholics, Ackerman found that 40 percent of the women had either two alcoholic parents, or an alcoholic mother only. Applying this percentage to the current female adult children of alcoholics population, we can estimate that there are about nine million women today who are daughters of alcoholic mothers. Dr. Ackerman's book looks at the effects upon the daughter when both parents are alcoholic; the purpose of our book is somewhat narrower—to explore the unique effects that having an alcoholic mother has upon her female children.

When we decided to write this book, one of the first things we did was to search the bookstores and libraries. What we discovered was that almost all the significant literature dealing with children of alcoholics was written by specialists in the field, who certainly had *intellectual* knowledge of the problem, but whose *emotional* connection did not seem strong. Additionally, it did not take long for us to realize that most studies about alcoholism tended to study primarily male alcoholics and their effects on their families, and to generalize from those results about the impact women alcoholics have on their families. As Alan Leshner, director of the National Institute on Drug Abuse, has said, "Historically, drug [including alcohol] abuse research has focused primarily on men, as has most health research." This is true, he adds, even though such abuse "may present significantly different challenges to women's health, may progress differently in women than in men, and may require different treatment approaches." We feel that there are different effects, as well, upon the offspring of a female alcoholic.

Our in-depth studies left us feeling that there seemed to be nothing written specifically *for* daughters of alcoholic mothers, *by* daughters of alcoholic mothers, expressing the special relationship between mother and daughter, which psychiatrists from Freud to the present have noted. While Hope Edelman's *Motherless Daughters* includes the alcoholic mother among her models of physically or emotionally absent mother figures, Edelman's primary model is the deceased mother, who is, of course, consistent in her absence. The alcoholic mother, on the other hand, is usually *inconsistent* in her behavior, personality, and emotional availability. And when she dies, she leaves far more emotional baggage on her daughter's shoulders than a "normal" mother does. (Some of us openly admit that we would have preferred it if our mothers had been deceased. At least that way, we could have romanticized her. It is difficult to romanticize a mother who passes out on the floor in front of our friends.)

As daughters of alcoholic mothers, we found that, aside from Dr.

Ackerman's book, there was little out there that addressed *our* specific problems and questions. So we became experts ourselves. After all, both of us had had decades of experience in dealing with the silence, secrecy, and shame of our mothers' drinking. We had learned from years of living with our alcoholic mothers that the silence and secrecy are direct results of the shame that both Mother and we felt. We knew from watching our mothers' daily lives that they felt humiliated and so tried to hide their drinking by lying to us and to our families. In our own shame, we lied for them and about them, something we noticed didn't seem to be happening so much in families where Dad was the alcoholic. Not surprisingly, even as children we concluded that having an alcoholic mother was somehow worse than having an alcoholic father.

Our feelings, we discovered, were quite common, as numerous sources proved. For instance, Curt Krebsbach, a counselor at a drug and alcohol abuse treatment center in Missouri, notes, "If Dad drinks, it's considered acceptable, but it's not acceptable if Mom does, even if they exhibit the same behavior."

Yet we recognized instinctively that we needed to counteract these feelings of shame that daughters of alcoholic mothers disproportionately feel. In the course of our research, which included interviews and correspondence with more than two hundred women, we found strong evidence that women were still much less willing to talk about their alcoholic mothers than about their drunken fathers. We were not surprised. Both of us remember that when we were growing up, we wouldn't have had the courage to discuss our alcoholic mothers with anyone, not even with other daughters of alcoholic mothers. (The secrecy was such that we hardly knew others like us existed.)

Nevertheless, despite the culture of concealment, we still had a strong need to find others like us, to hear the voices of others who had lived and were still living similar lives. We found that other women, other daughters of alcoholic mothers, had that same need. Over and over again, the women we interviewed told us, "I'm so glad you're doing this. I've needed a book like this for a long time. This is going to be so helpful." They had the same questions that we had: how should I feel about myself? In what ways have I been scarred? Have I coped appropriately? With a mother who was deeply involved in her own problems, how did I learn to become the woman I am now? With whom are my relationships today? What are these relationships like? What echoes of my tumultuous love-hate relationship with my mother still linger in me, even as an adult? What have I done, and what can I continue to do, to create a happy and mentally healthy life for myself?

Because of our own husbands' and sons' responses, and even the responses of our friends, relatives, and colleagues, we know that our research will also be helpful to people who live with, work with, and interact with daughters of alcoholic mothers.

This book is our story, and the stories told by over two hundred other women, of what it is like to be the daughter of an alcoholic mother.

Prologue

Sharon

Autumn 1966: Olla, Louisiana

It was nearly dusk. Mama was passed out in the sour air of her bedroom, snoring in that choking way she had when she hadn't removed her dentures, and Daddy was pulling up fall turnips in his garden at the back of the house. Quietly, I gathered the three notebooks, wrapped them in layers of red-and-blue Holsum bread wrappers, and tied strings around the bundle. Taking the big steel kitchen spoon to use as a trowel, I left through the front door and crossed the dirt road separating my house from the woods.

The shadows were long already, and the ground was damp with early evening dew. Just inside the dark cover of the trees, I hesitated. I'd never outgrown my childhood fear of the dark, but if I waited until morning, it might be too late. Beneath one of the many sweet gum trees, I began to dig, gingerly brushing aside the peculiar prickly balls that my brothers and sisters and I used in war games with one another. I raked through the dense layers of pine needles. The swampy ground smelled of decaying vegetation, and with crackly, whispery noises, little bugs scurried with each scoop of earth I dug. Finally, I had carved out a damp rectangular hole about six inches deep. Then, holding my diaries—my painfully recorded tales of the last two years of my life—I placed them into the hole and covered them, carefully rearranging pine needles and sweet gum balls on top.

Now I could relax, my secrets safe.

After burying my diaries in the woods, I quietly entered the house. I realized that Mama was still asleep; the door to her bedroom was shut. She'd be passed out probably till morning. I could hear Daddy in the backyard washing the turnip greens with the garden hose. In one of the bedrooms, my sister Sheila was tending to Sally and Delmer, the babies; but Curtis, four years younger than I, was off somewhere. Mama's scenes distressed him so much that he had gotten good at disappearing when it got too chaotic. He'd probably sneaked off, only to reappear at the supper table when Daddy, silent and tired, would dish up the turnips cooked with fatback. I'd need to start on the biscuits soon.

Autumn in Louisiana is not a pretty time, with hardly any beautiful red and gold leaves to delight the eye. Instead, because the temperature change is so gradual, leaves simply turn brown and are blown from the trees during the many rains of winter, leaving a spongy mat underfoot and a landscape of evergreen pine trees punctuated with a few stark branches from the hardwoods. Tonight, wind was whipping those branches about, implying that rain was on its way. If it rained hard, Daddy wouldn't be able to work tomorrow.

As much as we needed the money, I secretly hoped that he'd be forced to stay home. If he was home, Mama would have to stay sober, and maybe I wouldn't have to cook supper and wash dishes before starting my geometry homework. If Daddy was home, Sheila wouldn't have to leave school early to come home and baby-sit the little ones. If Daddy was home, I could make it through the school day without fearing that Mama had burned down the house with one of her many Winstons. Lit and forgotten on a wooden windowsill or clumsily knocked into the bowels of the old couch, they might sit and smolder before incinerating the house and my family at some point during the night as we slept. I wouldn't have to worry about Mama being gone when I got home from school, only to have her dragged drunk to the door by Dale Bradford, the sheriff's deputy and father to my classmate, Jay, who sometimes looked at me in knowing ways across the classrooms and halls of LaSalle High School.

I shrugged those thoughts away—after all, what could I do about the weather?—and went into the kitchen. Daddy was standing in front of the stove, putting the greens on to cook. He was a massively muscular man, a log cutter, one of those rugged men we now hold responsible for decimating forests of oaks, elm, and ash and replanting with the boring pine saplings that seemed to dominate the woods in which I grew up. My beloved Daddy usually smelled like those woods, with his pants cuffs full of sawdust and his workboots crusted with leaves and the dark, rich Louisiana mud. Our small house was wood, made of boards cut from trees my father himself had felled, its exterior walls covered with that black roofing paper known to us as tar paper. Our house was a tar paper shack, by even local standards.

Looking back, I realized that our quiet lives had been turned upside down when Mama started to drink. She became ugly, coarse, abusive, sometimes violent. Although she used to be so beautiful, with perfectly coiffed blondish brown hair and impeccable makeup applied to flawless pale skin, now she often spent the day in her thin rayon nightgowns, sometimes not even bothering to cover the stained and torn fabric with her cheap cotton housecoat. Today, her drink-reddened eyes had peered out at us angrily from behind her matted hair, and her foul drinker's and smoker's breath had stunk. But the days she got dressed and put on makeup were worse. Then she took off in the car, leaving us children frightened and forced to fend for ourselves until Daddy came home.

It seemed to us that now that Mama was in her early thirties, all she did was moan about all the injustices of her life—our unending poverty, her own lack of education, her husband who was over two decades her senior and who no longer wanted to go to parties or socialize with anyone but his relatives, and the sudden drowning death of Geneva, Mama's much-loved younger sister. It seemed that Mama also counted her five children among her injustices. I thought how much a burden we seemed to her. I knew she didn't love us; after all, didn't she tell us often enough that we kids were what was keeping her from enjoying life?

Just yesterday, I'd watched Mama rock in the rocking chair on the screened porch, her favorite brooding place. She'd rocked slowly at first and then faster as her turbulent feelings mounted, and as she rocked and drank, she muttered to herself, re-creating conversations, inventing retorts she wished she'd made. There had been a time when Mama used to sit and drink coffee while she watched her children play, but now, the many cups of coffee had become cans of beer. Instead of helping ease the tension, though, the beer only made her more angry and depressed. Sometimes, like yesterday, the rocking and drinking would begin as early as dawn, after Daddy had left for work. During the day, as she rocked and drank and grew angrier, I'd had to care for the younger children, watching them and feeding them.

Lying in bed later that evening, thinking of the diaries I'd buried just a few hours earlier, I wanted to cry. But I had had to get rid of them. In Mama's hands, a secret was a weapon, an instrument of blackmail; and if that didn't work, she'd use it to torture us, belittle us, shame us in front of other people. Even if one of us had a crush on a schoolmate, instead of treating our feelings tenderly, she'd sing vulgar songs about it in a taunting voice. All of us, even the little ones, had learned to hide our emotions, to keep everything inside. It was so much safer that way.

I never retrieved those diaries, in part because I could never find them again. In the growing shadows, my heart pounding with fear, I hadn't marked my hiding place. Later all the sweet gum trees had looked alike, and all the places that seemed to indicate disturbed earth were only places where squirrels had dug for acorns or where possums had rooted for tender grubworms and beetles. After a while, I convinced myself that the plastic bread wrappers had probably failed to keep the Louisiana rains from soaking the cheap paper, so I no longer continued to search. And eventually I grew to accept that mine was not the only house where some secrets were best deeply buried so that they could not be used as weapons.

Ellie

Spring 1962, Highland Park, Illinois

Ice cubes clinked in glasses. I stood at the entrance to the living room watching the doctors and their wives gather into little semicircles, drinks in one hand, cigarettes in the other, murmuring in that same pleasant professional voice my father always used. Occasionally, someone's low-key laugh would punctuate the gentle buzz of conversation. Every few minutes, the doorbell would ding-dong in the background. My father, handsome in his navy blue suit, would open it and greet the newcomers.

"Ellie, why don't you show Dr. and Mrs. Herman into the living room?" he would ask politely as he handed their coats to my younger sister, Diana.

At the age of thirteen, I loved it when my parents had people over. Slipping unnoticed through the crowds of grown-ups, I inhaled the smell of aftershave and perfume, studied the women's outfits and accessories, and overheard tidbits of adult conversations.

"—and I explained to him what the best alternative was—"

"—very paranoid, almost delusional—"

"—and I said to Harry, 'That's it; we either send Lloyd to Bell Academy or I'm leaving you!' Ha! Ha!—"

I scooped a few salted peanuts from a silver bowl on the coffee table and meandered through the crowd, looking for any adults who might be available for conversation. I got a kick out of querying grown-ups about themselves, and they always answered my prying questions courteously.

My father stood nearby conferring with a fellow psychiatrist. Extracting his pipe from his breast pocket, he dipped it into the pouch of rich-smelling tobacco that he kept in the other pocket. Tamping it down with one finger, all the while listening intently to his colleague, he placed the pipe between his lips, struck a match, and cupped the flame at the pipe's bowl, inhaling in little breaths. The flame reflected momentarily in the lenses of his tortoiseshell glasses. Delicate white clouds puffed out from one side of his mouth.

With his warm, happy-go-lucky manner and his love for hearing people's stories, my father was a natural-born psychiatrist. This three-

story house in the suburbs was testimony to his continuing professional success. Mother loved the house—nobody had been more excited than she on the day we moved in. Yet despite her burst of enthusiasm—she was always excited whenever we moved into a new and better house—I had sensed over the past few years that all was not well with her.

I had started to notice subtle changes in Mother several years earlier. One day I came home from school for lunch. She sat at the kitchen table, her auburn hair rolled onto sponge curlers and wrapped in a scarf. Silently, she spooned in her soup, her face hard. When the clinking of her spoon stopped abruptly, I looked up. Her face was red and twisted. She was sobbing, her shoulders shaking. I particularly remembered watching the tears stream out of her green eyes and splash into her bowl of soup.

"What's the matter, Mother?" I asked with alarm.

"Oh, nothing," she sobbed, dismissing me with a wave of her hand.

Another time, I came home after school to an empty kitchen.

"Mother!" I called, searching through the silent living room. Alarmed, I ran upstairs. The door to the master bedroom was closed, so I pushed it open without knocking—Mother never shut it, even when she was dressing—and walked in. The light from the hallway fell onto the bed. Her form lay beneath the covers.

"Mother?" I asked. "What are you doing here?"

"I was taking a nap," she responded irritably.

"When are you going to get up?" I persisted.

"When I feel like it," she snapped. "Now will you please go do your homework or something and let me rest for a few minutes?"

But I swiftly disregarded her occasional dissonant behaviors—the naps, the fuzzy eyes, the angry outbursts, the crying jags.

Now, two years later, as I stood in the living room among the guests, I wondered where Mother was. Earlier that evening, I had sat on the bed watching her apply the finishing touches in front of her dressing table mirror. She was wearing a dress of her favorite color: tangerine orange. She leaned forward into the three-way mirror and carefully smoothed coral lipstick onto her mouth, pursing her lips and then blotting them with tissue. She patted powder over her face, sprayed a few whiffs of *perfume onto her neck, and then clipped on the pearl earrings that matched her beads. Stepping into her heels, she stood before the tall mirror on the back of the door and said proudly as she turned back and forth, "Not bad, huh?"*

Where was she now?

"Ellie, would you go to the kitchen and get Mrs. Silvers a glass of ginger ale?" asked Diana, who was now standing by my side with a bowl of peanuts in hand. Weaving through the crowd of adults, I left the living room, walked to the other end of the first floor, and pushed open the white swinging door into the kitchen.

I froze. Mother was futilely grasping the open refrigerator door as she slid downward, her thin legs crumpling beneath her. She moaned, making a strange, animal-like sound as she lay on the floor. Her glazed eyes had a faraway look.

I was stunned, my vocal cords paralyzed. Before I could speak, Dad swept past me. His face a mask of tension, he bent over and lifted her bony frame from the floor into his arms. Carrying her in a fireman's carry, he opened the door that led to the back stairs. Her arms bobbed limply against his navy blue back as he disappeared around the bend of the stairs, which creaked as he ascended to the second floor. I could hear his footsteps above moving down the carpeted hall toward their bedroom.

My heart was hammering. When Dad returned, smoothing his suit, I asked in a frightened voice, "Daddy, what's wrong with Mother?"

Unflappable as he was, the only indication of any distress was the tightness in his voice. He answered calmly, enunciating his words. "Nothing's wrong, honey. Mother just had a beer on an empty stomach and it affected her." He went back into the living room to join his guests and apologized on Mother's behalf, saying that she was a little under the weather and would not be joining them.

A creepy feeling settled into me. I felt scared, as though I was about to fall from a great height. The next morning, I waited for Mother to awaken, pressing my ear against the door. Finally, at midmorning, I heard her footsteps moving toward the bathroom. When the bed groaned as she climbed back in, I walked boldly in. She sat against the wooden headboard, her face swollen and indignant.

"Ellie, will you bring me my cigarettes and matches from the kitchen table, and also two aspirins and a glass of water?"

"Mother," I began haltingly. "Last night . . . you . . ." I breathed heavily, unsure of what exactly I was trying to articulate. "You were lying on the kitchen floor last night when all those people were here!" I blurted out. "Daddy carried you upstairs—"

"He did not!" she snapped. "What makes you say a stupid thing like that?"

"Because he did." I breathed shakily. "You were lying on the kitchen floor!"

"Whhaaat?" she cried indignantly. "That is not *true! Why in the hell would you say something like that!"*

"Because it's true. Ask Daddy."

Her face flushed and her eyes narrowed to slits.

"Why, you little bitch," she hissed. "You are a goddamn liar to say such a thing about me! How dare you make up lies about me!"

"It's not a lie!" I yelled.

"Why, you nasty little brat!"

She threw back the sheets. I backed away, terrified of the blows she knew how to inflict when she was in a bad mood. I left the room before she could get close to me, but I could hear her yelling as I hurried down the hall: "Goddamn it, come back here, right now!"

That morning, I learned the first of many lessons that I would learn about the world of alcoholics. I discovered that the logic of the sober world—such as, "How do you explain why you don't remember *anything about the previous evening, if you* weren't *drunk and unconscious?"—does not apply in the world of alcoholics, which has its own set of bizarre rules. But like every child of an alcoholic, I learned the new rules fast.*

Part I

Chapter One

Introduction

"My father never knew. I don't think he believed me when I told him about my years of torment."
— *Beverly Hendrix, fifty-three, salesperson, Baton Rouge, Louisiana*

On the face of it, we are quite different, hardly twins separated at birth. Ellie is slender, blond, the oldest child of a well-educated, middle-class psychiatrist and his wife, who was almost as well educated and who met him in medical school. Ellie is married, the mother of three sons, and is a college professor, a transplanted New Englander who has come to love the South. Sharon is a natural-born southerner from Louisiana, the overweight, brunette oldest daughter of an uneducated manual laborer and his waitress wife. Sharon is also married, the mother of two sons, and now lives in Missouri, where she has almost completed her doctoral degree in English.

To see the two of us huddled together, usually a stack of papers between us and cups of hot tea or coffee within reach, a stranger might wonder, How did these two women ever become friends? What kind of bond could they have?

Ellie is energetic, a morning walker, a drinker of coffee, an owner of pets, a lover of movies and books. She is usually optimistic, sometimes mystical. This marriage is her third, this time to a man a good bit younger than she, who was born in another country. Her older sons are grown and live far up the East Coast, and her youngest son, on the touchy cusp between childhood and adolescence, loves and rejects her equally. Ellie is a tenured professor who loves her job and particularly enjoys the travel, which is a perk of the profession.

Sharon is less physically energetic but a great storyteller. She's a poet and an artist who walks only when she must, hates flying, consumes far too much black coffee, is owned by cats, and is a lover and writer of mystery novels. She is sometimes pessimistic, seldom mystical, and can be more antisocial than reserved. Her only marriage has endured for over twenty-five years; her husband, also an academic, is a fellow southerner. One of her sons is a recent newlywed; the other is a high school senior. Sharon loves teaching; like Ellie, she loves the students, and she loves the written word.

We met in 1989 when we were both employed at the same southern regional university. What really unites us, though, is not our similar careers nor our similar ages, both mid- to late forties. It is not that we both are married or mothers of sons, or that we both love animals. What connects us is a not-so-tiny detail that has affected almost every facet of our lives. Both of us are daughters of alcoholic mothers, mothers who were far easier to forgive than they were to understand. We know, because we've spent our lives trying to figure out how to become the kinds of women, wives, and mothers that ours were not. It hasn't been easy. Both of us can testify that we've made many false steps.

Over many lunches at our favorite off-campus diner, we began to share our respective pasts, rather like unpeeling a multilayered and particularly pungent onion. (You can only do so much before the tears fall.) We discovered that, despite our outward differences, there was commonality in the pain we have carried inside and still carry today, decades later. We discovered that the background and setting are irrelevant: whether she is a manual laborer's wife who washes the clothes by hand in tin tubs, or a doctor's wife whose home is cleaned by "merry maids," an alcoholic mother creates special problems for her daughter.

We knew we were not alone, that there were many other

daughters of alcoholics out there. When we decided to write this book, we set up an 800 number and placed ads, mostly in local newspapers, across the country, requesting daughters to phone us if they would like to fill out our eight-page questionnaire. As soon as the first ad appeared, our "hot line" began to ring . . . and ring and ring. Within a few months, over three hundred women phoned in, and soon we had more material than we could handle in one book. We mailed out questionnaires to the women who requested them, and to our delight, about two hundred took the time to fill them out and return them. Even though the questionnaire was lengthy, many women wrote additional pages of material. (Months after the last ad ran, we still get calls, and questionnaires still come in.) One woman penned in the margin that it had taken her four hours; she was not unique. "This questionnaire has been difficult for me to fill out," wrote Donna Cartee, fifty, a sales representative from Canaan, New Hampshire. "I avoided it for two days! It has brought so many painful memories to the surface."

We were indeed touched that so many were willing to contribute their stories to our project. Despite the thoroughness and complexity of the questionnaire, virtually all the women who returned it said they would also like to be interviewed. In fact, some women who had not filled out a questionnaire called us and begged to be interviewed. We would have loved to talk to everyone but were only able to phone about sixty women. We also met and interviewed a number of women in person. Hearing from and talking to all these wonderful, intelligent, strong women will always stand out in our memories as a life-changing experience.

Through the questionnaires and interviews, we learned that most other daughters of alcoholic mothers have been affected in the same ways we were. They too are suffering from lack of self-esteem, problematic relationships with friends, family, lovers, and spouses, memory gaps about significant childhood events, and insecurity about themselves as women. "I really don't have much self-esteem," admits Marta Hendrix, thirty-two, a chef from Burlington, Vermont. "I have just recently discovered how much I turn to others for their approval. I have always been concerned with what others will think."

"Much of my childhood is a blank," says Jackie McClain, fifty, a nurse from Dallas, Texas. "But I find pictures of myself as a child to be very revealing: I can see the sadness, hurt, and pain reflected in the eyes of a four-year-old."

"I like to forget my earlier life with her," says Lucy Smith, fifty-seven, a physical therapist from Pittsfield, Massachusetts. "I feel that I could have been more successful and had better relationships, if not for the past. Many of my memories are too painful to talk about. She was very abusive and often embarrassed me. I have good health, but I'm often depressed."

Rachel Addington, forty-eight, a typesetter from Jeffrey City, Wyoming, remarks, "I see myself as a dog who scratches on the door wanting to get in, and as soon as the door opens, my mother slams it in my face. I want to love her and be a part of her life, but she won't let me in."

"When my mother was drinking, most of the time you were not aware that she had even had a drink," recalls Virginia Matthew, forty-six, a college professor from Albany, New York. "The general misconception of alcoholics is that they must be stinking drunk and lying in filthy clothes in the gutter somewhere. My mother functioned as any other mother would. She was a homeroom mother, baked cookies, bought Christmas and birthday presents. She gave great parties, enrolled us in summer camp, and wrote us letters to keep us from being homesick, the usual 'Mom' things. Those are the memories that I cherish and keep close in my heart to pull out and bask in. Then there are the not-so-happy times: the arguing late at night, the criticisms, the critical review of my appearance. . . ."

The statement of Lauranne Seiner, thirty-nine, an insurance adjustor from San Diego, California, just about sums up the feelings that all the rest of us have for our alcoholic mothers: "I loved my mom very much. I also hated her."

We, as well as many of our respondents, grew up in the 1950s and 1960s. The fact that our mothers had drinking problems was never even acknowledged, let alone discussed, in our homes. Mothers were simply not alcoholics! So how could we share the "dirty family secret" with others? Other readers who are baby boomers will recall that intimate topics which are now flaunted flagrantly in public were *never* discussed openly back when we were coming of age. People took great pains to hide any family aberrations from outsiders. Thus, we—and, we suspect, millions of other women—carried our shameful, guilty secret inside, like an unseen wound, and grew up feeling ugly and full of self-loathing.

Even in today's secret-spilling, talk-show-based society, most daughters of alcoholic mothers feel just as we two did. Even now, Mother's Alcoholism is still a touchy subject. A double standard endures as much for alcoholism as for sex. Throughout history, in fact, female drunks have always been shunned and condemned far more than male drunks. Mark Lender and James Martin, authors of *Drinking in America: A History,* quote a source from the seventeenth century who says, "It was a great shame to see a man drunk, but more shame to see a woman in that case." It was "a social catastrophe" for a Victorian woman to be called an alcoholic, the authors continue, because alcoholism for women was considered a state of "extreme deviance." The caption on a photograph of a nineteenth-century celebration reads, "Temperance workers frowned on such celebrations. For solid citizens—especially women—to drink enthusiastically in public . . . set a deplorable example for the rest of the nation."

Women who get drunk are still looked upon with more disgust than men who get drunk. Amanda Smith, a consultant to industry and education who helps train men and women to work better together, states that for many people the very term "woman alcoholic" will "conjure up [the image of] a maudlin floozy in a bar." Elizabeth Ettore, author of *Women and Substance Abuse,* agrees: "There is a real social stigma attached to a woman who drinks too much." As Jean Kirkpatrick explains in her book *Goodbye Hangovers, Hello Life,* "The stigma of the woman alcoholic still remains, despite some very forward strides made recently by prominent women publicly announcing their alcoholism. Betty Ford, Joan Kennedy, Elizabeth Taylor, Liza Minnelli—all have brought some 'class' to women alcoholics, but not quite enough. . . . Public attitudes change very slowly, and the feelings toward women alcoholics have been negative for many, many years. Society's desire for women to be 'pure' continues strong and unabated."

The film industry has also gone a long way in reinforcing society's double standard. In *Hollywood Shot by Shot: Alcoholism in American Cinema,* Norman Denzin points out that since the 1940s, female alcoholics have been portrayed very negatively in the cinema. A woman's alcoholism "is used to turn her into a doubly disgraced object: a woman who is a drunk. Cast in this identity, her inferior status as a woman is further degraded by her disease of alcoholism. The male alcoholic in the early modern films simply got drunk. His female counterpart . . . gets drunk and sexual. Sexuality and alcoholism were negatively joined in the female alcoholic film."

Thus, the societal and cultural message persists: a female alcoholic is indeed a "fallen woman" of the worst sort.

When that fallen woman happens to be our own *mother,* most of us feel understandably hesitant to discuss it with outsiders. As Judith S. Seixas and Geraldine Youcha observe in *Children of Alcoholism: A Survivor's Manual,* "hiding becomes a way of life" for all children of alcoholics. Yet we daughters are more likely to hide the shame of having a gender role model who is considered disgusting in the eyes of society. Part of the reason is that we identify with our mothers. Linda Tschirhart Sanford and Mary Ellen Donovan, authors of *Women and Self-Esteem,* write that it is far harder for girls than boys to reject their mothers because doing so forces the girl "to include in her own self-concept a 'despised feminine self.'" Furthermore, the authors say, while boys "are encouraged to fight back when others try to violate them . . . girls . . . are encouraged to do nothing . . . [P]assivity seems the only way to handle problems." Finally, they point out, girls fear confiding in outsiders about family problems because they sense that others will not understand, "especially when the source of information is young and female." Instead, we daughters internalize the pain of "Mother's little secret."

Adding fuel to our pain is society's presumption, reflected in everything from print to television, that a mother-daughter relationship is always close and mutually fulfilling. Stores still stock cute sets of matching mother-daughter clothing. Mother's Day cards meant to be given from daughters to their mothers are the most sentimentally sweet ones on the shelves.

A mother's alcoholism is a crucial social issue because it is so often kept hidden. More women than ever are drinking and taking drugs, according to an in-depth report issued in 1996 by the Center on Addiction and Substance Abuse at Columbia University. Yet "female alcoholics more often experience less obvious symptoms" than men and "are more likely to have mental health disorders, such as depression, in addition to their addiction." Laura Lindsteadt, a therapist at the Arthur Center, states that while men often drink more publicly, at parties, bars, or business lunches, women's drinking tends to be more private. She points out, "A lot of the time their spouse or significant other isn't even aware they have a problem."

Because a woman's drinking is so often done surreptitiously, many people don't realize how much a mother's alcoholism can destroy the family's ability to function adequately. Beverly Hendrix, fifty-three, recalls, "When my son was about three or four, I corrected him at my parents' apartment with a swat on the butt. My dad said, 'Don't do that to that child. We never spanked you.' I can still hear him say that twenty-eight years later! (I was *shocked*.) You can't even imagine how surprised I was to hear this. My mother *beat* me so terribly and would threaten me with 'when your father gets home, he'll give it to you worse.' My father never knew. I don't think he believed me when I told him about my years of torment."

Whereas alcoholic fathers affect families due to their lost wages and possible violence, alcoholic mothers have those same effects and more. After all, women have always been considered the center of the family, since they alone can give birth and breast-feed infants. And, until the 1970s and 1980s, the vast majority of women remained at home as mothers and homemakers. Although the number of women in the workforce has risen dramatically in past decades (about 60 percent of all women are now employed outside the home, as opposed to less than 35 percent in the 1950s), mothers still remain the primary caretakers of children. Dorothy Schneider and Carl F. Schneider state in *Women in the Workplace,* "Overwhelmingly, Americans still assume that women bear the primary responsibility for the care of house and family. . . . Certainly men also work in their homes and in their communities. Women, however, still bear most of the burden of child care, of cooking, of housework."

Susan Faludi, author of *Backlash,* agrees: "Nor do women enjoy equality in their own homes, where they still shoulder 70 percent of the household duties—and the only major change in the last fifteen years is that now middle-class men *think* they do more around the house. (In fact, a national poll finds the ranks of women saying their husbands share equally in child care shrunk to 31 percent in 1987 from 40 percent three years earlier."

Linda Sanford, a licensed psychotherapist, notes that most of her patients believe that their mothers, rather than their fathers, have had the strongest impact on their lives:

Mothers stand as the primary role models for young female and male children alike. . . . Because of our social arrangements, Mother rather than Father traditionally has been the one to spend the most time with infants (regardless of gender) during the earliest years. When we were infants, it was Mother who most often fed us, nursed us, changed us and cuddled us, and in many cases she was home with us most of the time, whereas Father was absent. Even mothers who worked outside the home probably spent more time with us than did our fathers.

Traditionally, or at least mythologically, a mother is indeed the glue that holds the family together—until she becomes an alcoholic. Then she tears it apart. As Signe Hammer asserts in *Daughters and Mothers: Mothers and Daughters,* our relationship with our mothers lays the foundation for our healthy psychological development. Without a solid mother-daughter relationship, our well-being is indeed compromised.

Obviously, daughters of alcoholic mothers cannot stake a unique claim to pain suffered at Mom's hands. Many of us have brothers, and yes, these brothers are also wounded by our alcoholic mothers, perhaps as deeply as we are—but wounded *differently.* As we researched and read and talked with hundreds of other daughters of alcoholic mothers, we have become convinced that the legacy of an alcoholic mother affects more areas of the lives of daughters than of sons. First, evidence is mounting that male and female children are programmed differently from birth: girls really *are* more sensitive. According to a 1991 study by the Institute for the Study of Child Development, female babies even as young as two to six months old are more likely than male babies to become sad in response to negative events. Further, according to a study by the American Association of University Women, young women are more likely than young men to have low self-esteem and to attempt suicide.

Additionally and perhaps more importantly, sons never have to look to Mother in order to learn how to *be.* They do not need her as a gender role model. They do not have to deal with, "Oh, God, I'm bleeding! What's wrong with me?" Sons do not have to learn to become mothers themselves. They either have Dad there to teach them to be men, or if Dad isn't available, they at least have the comfort of knowing they are not *supposed* to be like Mother. The guru of child care, Dr. Benjamin Spock, upon whose advice many of us, along with our mothers, have relied, tells us that little boys want to grow up to be like Daddy, but for a daughter, "it's the other way around. She yearns to be like her mother—in occupation and in having babies of her own." How can any of us admit that our mothers are flawed if we are destined by biology to be just like her?

In our culture, and we suspect in most other cultures, if there are both sons and daughters in the family, sons are seldom the ones who undress the drunk mother, put her to bed, and mop up her vomit. It is we, the daughters, who do that. It is we, the daughters, who are expected to fill in for mothers who are either not there or not functional. As a result, sons, though wounded, may still have more freedom to interact with others outside the home, to participate in after-school activities, to explore healthy relationships. We daughters (seldom sons) are expected to do both our own schoolwork and the family's housework, as well as take care of other children in the family. Sometimes we are even expected to replace our mothers emotionally in the eyes of fathers and siblings. As a result, we daughters become overburdened physically and emotionally and often escape the home at too early an age; we may become self-destructively rebellious, addicted to alcohol, drugs, food, or shopping; we may become sexually active at an abnormally young age; or we may remain trapped with or near our birth families until the deaths of our mothers.

Even in adulthood, we daughters, much more than sons, are affected by our alcoholic mothers. Sons are seldom the ones who care for aging, infirm parents. According to Francine Klagsbrun, author of *Mixed Feelings: Love, Hate, Rivalry, and Reconciliation Among Brothers and Sisters,* "Just about every study made on the care of aging parents has found that the burden falls most often on daughters (and sometimes daughters-in-law). To be specific: daughters outnumber sons by three to one among children who care for their parents." Therefore, our interaction with the family unit is usually of longer duration than that of our brothers'. Even popular proverbs remind us of this lifelong bond that *we* have, from which our brothers are released: "Your son is your son until he takes a wife. Your daughter's your daughter all of her life." (Sharon admits that she would break out in a cold sweat whenever her mother chanted this ditty. "After all," says Sharon, "if my sisters or I didn't take care of her, who would?")

Sons can leave their alcoholic mothers behind, relatively guilt free. As Sanford and Donovan note, both sexes of children are supposed to reject Mother as a step in their maturations: "But this rejection of the mother is often far less difficult for a son than a daughter. Boys, after all, were never supposed to identify with the mother." But as daughters, we carry her with us even after she is dead, in the very echo of her body in our own. We daughters are the ones who look into the bathroom mirrors and are shocked to see our mothers' faces looking back at us. We hear our mothers' voices when we scold our children. We smell our mothers' breath when we have a drink at a party. We fight our mothers' demons, carefully disguised as demons of our own invention: weight problems, sexual problems, relationship problems, self-image problems. Without question, many of the problems we daughters deal with on a daily basis have their origins in our turbulent relationships with our alcoholic mothers.

In the upcoming chapters, we examine such issues as body images and sexuality; weight problems, eating disorders, and addictions; our relationships with our siblings, our fathers, our husbands and partners, and our children; and, of course, the underlying theme of this book, our complex relationships with our mothers. In the last chapter, we look at the many ways in which we have worked to make our lives happy.

But we want to emphasize now, and throughout the text, the purpose of this book is not to bash mothers. As mothers ourselves, we are acutely aware of how difficult the job is and how little appreciated mothers are, not only by their own offspring but also by society at large. And we know all too well how selective a child's memory can be and how unjustly negative, so we have tried to be as truthful about our memories as we can possibly be.

We also know that memories of the same incident or even of the same family life can vary widely. Typically in a family, one sibling remembers one thing; another, being either younger or older, having a different role to play in the family dynamics, will have an entirely different perspective. And not all of us daughters, even of the same mother, deal with the memories in the same way, as we discovered during extensive conversations with our sisters. One will remember each detail, replaying the scenes over and over in her mind; the other will have forgotten because it hurts too much to remember. As Klagsbrun notes about alcoholic and dysfunctional families in *Mixed Feelings,* "The more disturbed a family, the more likely are the children within it to insulate themselves emotionally, each finding a separate corner in which to curl up, heads down, hands over ears, cut off from one another and the outside."

If our memories seem exaggerated and too negative, then we, as well as the women we interviewed, are all exaggerating at the same rate and remembering roughly the same kinds of abuses. That's hardly a likelihood. Daughters of alcoholic mothers remember varying degrees and types of abuse: neglect, emotional abuse, verbal abuse, physical abuse, and sexual abuse. But the kind most of us recall the most vividly is verbal abuse—constant sarcasm and belittlement, almost total destruction of self-esteem. Most of us also remember some type of abandonment, either while our mothers were off drinking, passed out, or engaged in extramarital affairs. We also recall the violations of our own privacy, a kind of emotional rape that has lasting repercussions. And last, none of us will ever forget the bitter details of our mothers' humiliating public scenes.

Like other daughters of alcoholic mothers, when we were younger, it did not occur to us that there was any connection between our mothers' alcoholism and our own adult problems—until years later, in the 1970s and 1980s, when the taboo topics of the earlier era came bursting out of the closet with a vengeance. We then learned that the presence of an alcoholic parent indeed has a profound effect upon the offspring, that the presence of our alcoholic mothers had a profound effect upon us, as women.

Ellie buried her alcoholic mother twenty-six years ago, when Jessica Agnew, barely fifty years old, died mysteriously and unexpectedly in her sleep. Sharon's alcoholic mother, Ora Cockerham, feeble and homebound for years after bouts with emphysema, facial cancer, and heart disease, and even resuscitated back from death three times, died during the writing of this book at the too-young age of sixty. But these two women are still very much a part of who we have become.

Daily, sometimes even hourly, we waltz with Mama.

Chapter Two

Mother at Her Best

~

"She was a bright light. When my mom wasn't drinking all the time, she was fun, loving, kind, witty, and insightful. She was happy, vibrant, and smart."

—Mary Garfinkle, thirty-nine, hospital administrator, Hanna, Wyoming

~

She was the only woman in the classroom full of men.

Dad sat down in the chair beside her. Turning to her, his blue eyes flirtatious behind his tortoiseshell glasses, he asked with mock seriousness, "Did you know that women who go to medical school stand a forty percent lower chance of ever being married?" Knowing Dad, he probably made that up, but it got her attention. Always outrageously warm and open, Dad loved to strike up conversations with strangers so he could hear their stories and file them away, as though he was compiling a mental anthology of people's lives. Maybe that's why he later specialized in psychiatry.

Four months after they'd met, my parents got married. Mother walked down the church aisle in a white satin wedding gown that she had made herself. In those days, nice girls waited till the wedding night (which explains why they got married in such a hurry; Mother confided later that she had indeed been a virgin at the altar). In the wedding photos, she stands on Dad's right side, her left arm draped through his. She carries a small bouquet of lilies. Her hair is parted on the side and clipped far back from her forehead; two long sausage curls flank her smiling face. On the back of one photo she has written, "Is it my imagination or do we look pretty pleased with ourselves!" She adds, as an afterthought, "Isn't Paul a darling!"

She never returned to medical school. Giving up her dream of becoming a doctor in order to marry one seemed like a small sacrifice. Nine months after their wedding, I was born. Two years later, Diana arrived, followed by our younger brother. We lived in a modest rented house on a narrow gravel road, with two towering maple trees in front. The huge backyard was my paradise, with its goldfish pond, clusters of peonies, and large weeping willow tree.

During the early years, I always felt secure and well loved. There was no indication that Mother wasn't happy. I remember her as a tall, red-headed figure in tan shorts and sneakers, moving tirelessly through the house with baskets of laundry or bags of groceries. Her bare legs were long and slender as she stood at the kitchen counter peeling potatoes, washing dishes, or mixing homemade Play-Doh. I remember following those shapely legs through the grocery store as she filled the cart with vegetables, fruits, meats, and the corn flakes Diana and I were always nagging her to buy because of the convincing TV commercials, and besides, we wanted the Captain Midnight mask. I remember the back of her auburn head above the driver's seat as we drove around town doing errands.

One time, Diana and I stood nearby as Mother sat at her sewing machine making curtains. Suddenly, the machine stopped. Mother looked up, wide-eyed, and said, "Listen!" I listened but heard nothing. Mother pushed back the chair and hurried out of the room. Diana and I followed. She ran to the cellar door. It was open. At the bottom of the stairs lay my little brother, screaming bloody murder, next to his dented tricycle. He was okay, as it turned out, but I'll never forget how impressed I was with Mother's superhuman hearing. I hadn't heard a thing!

Mother also had a sense of humor. When Katherine, a visiting pregnant friend, realized that she'd forgotten to collect her morning *urine sample for her doctor's appointment that afternoon, Mother patted her on the shoulder and said, "Don't worry." Her green eyes twinkling, she got a jar from the cupboard, took Diana into the bathroom, and made her pee into it. She called me in, and I peed into it too. Then Mother herself, who by now was laughing like crazy, made her contribution. Finally, Katherine, howling with delight, added to the jar. Between the four of us, we produced a large enough urine sample for Katherine's testy ob-gyn, who hated women and exploded at any who'd forgotten their samples.*

"Trust me," winked Mother, handing the full jar to Katherine. "He won't know the difference." And she was right. As a former nurse who had worked in the maternity ward at a metropolitan hospital, she knew about these things.

Many evenings in the twilight, Mother, Diana, and I would sit on the back steps. The frogs croaked from the fish pond, and lightning bugs flashed. Mother brushed my long blond hair first, and then Diana's short curly blond hair. My father worked long hours at the hospital, and my brother, still a baby, was often asleep, so Mother, Diana, and I shared a special camaraderie, which did not include the males of the family.

I remember the day that Twinkle, my cat, was scheduled to come home from the vet, where he'd been staying with a kidney problem. I hurried home from school. Mother stood in the living room, coat still on, her face pale. "Where's Twinkle?" I asked happily. Her mouth quivered, then her whole face crumpled as she burst into tears. "Twinkle died," she wailed. With a scream of anguish, I threw myself into her waiting arms. For a long time, we cried together in a warm embrace and wet each other's faces with our tears. Later, she told me that she'd taken the subway to the vet's office to pick up Twinkle, only to learn that he had died unexpectedly. On the return trip, she sat alone, staring sadly out the train window, watching the skyscrapers, slums, and factories rush by. She thought about how devastated I'd be, and her heart ached. The tears slipped freely down her cheeks. Embarrassed at crying openly in a public place, she struggled to hold them back. But every five minutes, she would burst into loud, renewed, choking sobs as the other stone-faced passengers pretended not to notice. "I'm sure everyone on that train must have thought I was totally insane," she told me wryly, blowing her nose.

In the evenings, she sat on the couch, one slender leg crossed over the other, with a thick new best-seller open on her lap. Her pack of Winstons and book of matches lay nearby, as always, in the glass ashtray. Behind the closed doors of the nearby den, my father cleared his throat as he reviewed his patients' charts for the next day. The rich smell of his pipe wafted into the room. Mother, totally absorbed in her book, turned the pages with her left hand and absently scratched her hair with her right. Diana and I settled on the couch next to her. Reaching over to the coffee table, I picked up her latest issue of Ladies' Home Journal and read an article about a woman who'd undergone some new, breakthrough gynecological operation. When I finished that story, I flipped over to "Can This Marriage Be Saved?" By the age of ten, I was already well versed in the dramas of marriage and childbirth. Diana thumbed through Dad's medical journals, cringing at the close-up color photos of advanced malignancies and skin burns. Occasionally, Mother burst into a scale of musical laughter, never taking her eyes off the page. She reached over to her pack of Winstons, placed one in her mouth, lit a match, and touched the flame to the cigarette, all without looking up from the book. A deep draw. A soft exhale. The cigarette lingered gracefully in her right hand, unnoticed, as she read. Two pages later, after one final drag, she crushed it out in the ashtray.

She picked up a glass of Ballantine ale on the table and took a demure sip. Charcoal hopped up onto her lap. He was the special cat she had selected from the millions of unwanted animals at the Humane Society. It was a tough choice, but Charcoal had recruited her as his owner while she stood peering into cat cages in the Lysol-smelling jungle of animal noises. Mouthing soundless "meows," his yellow eyes begging, tiny Charcoal had walked boldly over the backs of the other sleeping cats to follow Mother along the length of the cage. She fell in love immediately and adopted him. Every week, for the rest of his long *life, she bought fresh chicken livers at the A&P, boiled them, and crooning idiotically, served them to him on the kitchen counter. As Charcoal nestled into Mother's lap, the other cats, Casey and Catherine, batted catnip balls along the floor.*

We three females felt connected. Though Diana and I were still children, we were quick little studies, bright and articulate enough to be pleasing company for our sharp-witted mother, who was always full of juicy conversational tidbits.

"There were good times too," Ellie's sister, Diana, had insisted, a trifle defensively, when told the subject of this book. For most of us, that's true. As Ackerman notes in *Perfect Daughters,* "No dysfunctional family is always negative or without some good times." Cherishing any good memories is an important step for all of us as we work to rebuild our self-esteem. We know that our alcoholic mothers did not drink because they were weak or evil; they were warm, loving human beings who became overpowered by the grips of chemical dependency. Gretchen, a college professor, summed it up well: "I admired how hard she tried, and I grieve for her failures. She was a woman . . . like the rest of us."

For us authors, unearthing the good memories from the emotional rubble has been healing. Like most daughters of alcoholic mothers, we grew up burdened with a hideous mixture of love and hate toward them. The two emotions have always battled and clashed, and often, the hate overpowered the love. The mother who threw things at us or mocked us or emptied our bureau drawers all over the floor could not help but inspire hate; in fact, the depth of our hatred was sometimes frightening. When we prepared to write this book, the bad memories flooded back easily. Yet as we foraged through the past, forgotten memories of happy times gleamed at us like tarnished diamonds in a dark mine. Revisiting those good moments was therapeutic, as though we could immerse ourselves in that long-lost mother love. As Ackerman adds, "You may feel contempt for the alcoholism but love the person."

Many of us *did* have happy moments (days, weeks, even years) to remember, either before our mothers began to drink or even after their alcoholism set in. Seixas and Youcha state in *Children of Alcoholism: A Survivor's Manual,* that women usually "start drinking later and move on more quickly to late-stage symptoms." Sixty percent of the women who participated in our study reported that their mothers began to drink most heavily when their daughters were between the ages of eleven and fifteen. Therefore a good number of us had relatively happy childhoods before our mothers started to drink.

And even after the drinking began, we may still have had the occasional good time—at unpredictable moments. Even full-fledged alcoholics typically have lulls, downtimes, intervals of sobriety, sometimes for years at a stretch. During these interludes, their finer qualities and good natures reappear, like patches of blue sky breaking through the clouds. As Camille comments, "In fact, my mother was overly nice at times. I guess she was trying to make up for the bad times." Janet Woititz, author of *Adult Children of Alcoholics,* confirms that these surges of kindness are very typical of alcoholics. "In her sober moments, [an alcoholic] mother [tries] to make up for what she lacked."

Samantha remembers, "When my mother wasn't drinking, she had a sense of humor, was very fair, honest, caring, and loving. She would really try to take care of her personal hygiene, do her nails, dye her hair (to cover the gray), clean the house, cook something good for dinner, go job hunting. She'd work for a while and do great. Then bang! Something would happen, she'd buy beer or vodka, and she'd go into a slump again." Woititz points out that this too is very common: "There might have been long periods of time when [the alcoholic mother] delayed her drinking to try and keep the home in order."

In addition to being loving and lovable, many of our mothers were strong, independent women before they began to drink. When Sara Jo Kea's mother was pregnant with her, she chased a door-to-door newspaper salesman down the street for being rude. When Sara

Jo had a problem at school, her mother would be there to fight on her behalf. "She was strong," remembers Sara Jo. "You can see it in her eyes in her old photographs. She was like a splendid pioneer woman in a novel—colorful, strong, and down-to-earth—but with an artistic, intellectual streak and a regal quality—intelligent, classy, and fearless. She is so much a part of who I am."

Crystal Inman remembers her late mother, a bank teller and bookkeeper, with admiration. "I consider my mother a very brave woman. She divorced my natural father in the late 1950s when it wasn't fashionable; she had to move back, with me, into her mother's home and hear a never-ending litany of 'I told you so's.' My mother taught me to be independent, self-reliant, literate, and always to *try* first and not give up!"

"My mother, who died just recently, was one of the first black RN's to work at the hospital here," says Olivia proudly. She describes her mother as "a tall, brown, beautiful woman, always smiling. She knew what to say and when to say it. She could have talked with a bum on the street and then to the president. Not only did she skip from fifth to seventh grade, she was the valedictorian of her high school."

Many of us remember our sober mothers as smart, well-rounded women who had many interests. Rae Carlson says that she is a literate person today because her mother, who was intelligent and well read, took the time to read to her every night and taught her to read before she started school. "My mother is still very intelligent and loves to read," she adds.

Charlene has happy childhood memories of lying in bed with her mother, who would recite "The Owl and the Pussycat" from memory. "Her intense eye color would change with the mood. Most of the time, Mother was a giving person and gave love through the magnificent meals she always prepared. She also enjoyed parades, the arts, Broadway shows, her favorite and last show seen being *Showboat*. She accepted all people equally, from the very rich to the homeless drunkards. My mother was respected by the entire town."

When sober, many of our mothers can be responsible caretakers who enjoy doing motherly things. Jody Macolly's mother is sober frequently enough so that she and Jody are able to keep up the relationship. In fact, they have some wonderful times together. "We like to read the Martha Stewart magazines, and every Christmas, we have a project that we do," says Jody. "We make these pretty wreaths that we saw once. We've also got some ideas for Easter, just crafts and little projects. That's where she and I get along, when we do that kind of stuff. If she's off work one day and hasn't been drinking, then we might go out to the craft store and buy up some stuff and do some little projects. So it is nice," Jody says wistfully.

Antoinette Turner's mother, Brandy, was a waitress, a beautiful southern belle who turned heads and got the best tips at work when she was sober. She was also a wonderful caretaker. "I remember being sick with chicken pox, and she nursed me through," recalls Antoinette. "She was there when I drank bleach, and later at the hospital. I have one fond memory of my mother as she was oil painting, using a paint-by-number kit. She asked me if I cared to learn how, and she taught me how to complete the painting. I remember her embroidering on table runners and pillowcases. Here again, she taught me. She shared her talents with me, like a mother is supposed to."

Mary Starr, the youngest of four children, grew up on welfare with her single alcoholic mother, who herself grew up in a poor family of eleven siblings. "We didn't have much," says Mary, "but I do know that when I was sick, my mother took care of me. She even shoplifted a piece of steak one day because she wanted us to eat protein. Unfortunately, she got caught."

Karisa says that her mother's concern after Karisa's childhood go-cart accident probably saved her life. Riding the go-cart with her father, Karisa was thrown against the steering wheel when the go-cart hit the side of the track. When her father brought her home, she was crying, scared, and in pain.

"My mother said, 'Why don't you try to go to the bathroom?' "

remembers Karisa, now twenty-four. "So when I went to the bathroom, it was just pure blood. That's when they took me to the hospital. They had to take sixty percent of my pancreas out, and my appendix, and I had to be fed through IV's for a couple of months. If my mother hadn't questioned me—'Are you sure you feel okay? Do you have to go to the bathroom?'—if she hadn't made me go to the bathroom and seen that there was blood, I probably would have died. This," she adds, "was about the only time I can remember that I felt my mother really loved and cared for me."

We understand that our mothers drank to numb their pain, and we sympathize with their struggles. Jocelyn Pratt says, "My mother was a beautiful woman who was very, very intelligent. But she was never acknowledged for who she was as a child. She should have had a successful career."

Lucy Clarke recalls that her mother's drinking never interfered with her ability to give positive support to her and her sisters. Her mother would tell all three of them how smart and beautiful they were. She also insisted that her daughters get an education and be able to support themselves because she herself had been raised to be an ornament on display and had never learned to cook, iron, or support herself. Lucy is sympathetic as she recounts the tragedies that she believes precipitated her mother's drinking: a nervous breakdown, her husband's suicide, and a car accident, which disfigured her beautiful face. "For six weeks, the doctors wouldn't let her see her face," says Lucy. "She had no insurance or money to pay for plastic surgery, and this made a bad situation worse. I told this story to an AA counselor once and was told it was the worst story she'd ever heard."

Linda Hanson understands her mother better, now that she is a parent herself. "When my parents were first married, they lived in a little cabin they'd built on my father's family's property on Long Island," says Linda. Her mother became pregnant almost immediately and felt sick a lot. In addition, she was far away from her own family.

"My father worked nights, and she felt afraid living in that little cottage in a remote area that was really woodsy," says Linda. "It was like being out in the middle of the woods, and you hear all the night sounds. She had trouble sleeping, so she would drink a little at night. Then she had this baby, and babies *cry,* and babies just aren't all cute all the time, and I can certainly see why she might have felt perplexed and frustrated and not known what to do, really. Apparently the drinking started, as a matter of fact, when I was quite young."

Louisa McQuaid's mother married at age eighteen to a domineering man and had five children. "She had a rich fantasy life through reading and imagining herself in a different situation, but I think she felt trapped in her life and unable to change it," Louisa explains. "She could have been anything, but wasn't."

Jo Ann Stills attributes her mother's decades of drinking, which began when Jo Ann was under five years of age, to earlier sexual abuse by her stepfather. "To hide her shame and her feelings, she has always been a drinker, smoker, free with herself sexually—a rebel," Jo Ann says. "But I know she always loved us even though she tried to hide whatever she was feeling. I know that she did love us. She honestly wanted and still wants to be a good mom, but she doesn't know how."

Kitty Dellinger's mother was a waitress and bartender for thirty-eight years. Divorced six times, she gave birth to six children, including one child who later committed suicide. Kitty understands her mother's reasons for drinking. "I wish I could turn the clock back for her so that she could change the things in her life that she felt responsible for," Kitty remarks. "I wish I could take her pain. I think my mother always felt very much alone in life. I wish others would stop hurting her and causing her to suffer for her past. She has hurdles that she has not been able to overcome. I pray for victory. I want her to feel loved and secure, someone for herself to call her own."

"My mother could have been a high achiever if not for her

circumstances and her drinking," says Gretchen Abraham. "She was 'picked on' as a child by an older brother—her parents didn't stop it. Also, as an adult, her first love cheated on her. She was an abused wife, a single mother at one point who put her kids ahead of herself. Maybe these incidents contributed. I loved her very much. She was smart (all A's in high school), friendly, liked to chat with others, and giggle. She was kind and helpful and volunteered at the Battered Women's Shelter. She was an immaculate housekeeper. She also got good secretarial jobs at schools and hospitals . . . but didn't keep them."

"I feel very sad about my mother's life," admits Nichole Von Bergen, whose mother is now recovering from years of alcoholism. "She wanted so much and settled for a lot less. She has never been in love with my father and finds him crude, abusive, unfaithful, secretive, highly manipulative, and controlling. He ruined her life in many ways. She is an extraordinary person—talented, sensitive, bright, and could have been a successful artist if she hadn't let family concerns overshadow her own desires. She had a lot of ambition that was not realized. My mother is my best friend, except for my husband. She is a lovely, charming person, but lonely and afraid. Fear is one of her most common complaints. She is afraid to drive a car, afraid of making mistakes, and afraid for her family. She has a lot of regrets about the choices she's made in life."

Mama was beautiful, despite her poor teeth, a legacy of poverty, and an accident when she was a child. Born in 1933, a child of the Deep South, her skin was cool, fragile, and perfect, her hands delicate and long-fingered. Intelligent and talented, she could sing, dance, and tell jokes. Until she began to drink, she always was clean and fragrant. She could draw and sew. She was funny and witty, full of homespun sayings and tales.

She had suffered during the Depression and World War II and had seen her family's poverty as her own burden, so when a handsome older man showed interest in her, she saw marriage both as a way out of poverty and as a way to benefit her family—the proverbial "one less mouth to feed." Mama was only fourteen when she married my thirty-six-year-old father. She seemed to be full of courage and energy then—such a different woman from the one I came to know as a teenager.

My earliest memories of Mama are of the times before I started school, when we were living in Olla, Louisiana, a small town in the central part of the state. While I can't be sure, we seemed happy there. In the summers, an ice-cream truck drove by our rented ramshackle house (not so affectionately known as the "chicken-coop" house, for its small size and poor construction). One afternoon Mama, who loved Fudgsicles, bought them for all of us. I was happily enjoying mine when my bare foot caught a huge splinter from the old porch. As I cried and wriggled, Mama patiently removed the splinter. Afterward, my foot didn't hurt, but my feelings did—my Fudgsicle, dropped onto the sun-baked wooden porch, had melted. Mama gave me hers, which she had been planning to save for later.

Mama often begged Daddy to let her sleep late on those Sunday mornings when he didn't work. We were too little to go to school, but generally, Mama got up with Daddy, made his coffee, cooked his breakfast, and if he was working, fixed his lunch—egg or bologna sandwiches wrapped neatly in waxed paper. But seldom did Mama get her wish to sleep in. No matter how quiet he planned to be, no one could sleep once Daddy was up. His natural exuberance made him a very loud presence in our tiny little house.

One Sunday, Mother's Day, Daddy's plan was to do something nice for Mama by taking his three children out for a drive so she could sleep late. He piled us into the black 1953 Ford, and we headed east on the blacktop that ran in front of the house. It was a beautiful day; buttercups lined the road. We stopped and picked some for Mama. Sheila Jean, her shining blond hair vying with the flowers, raced our brother Curtis, who had named himself "Hambone," after a favorite song on Captain Kangaroo's television show. We didn't have a television, but Curtis had heard the song when we'd been at our grandparents', and he was so taken with it that he sang it constantly. He was only two years old, and his slight stutter added charm to the lyrics: "Hambone, Hambone, where you been? Around the world, and I'm going again. What you gonna do when you get back? Take a little walk by the railroad track. Hambo-o-o-nnne . . ." The part he loved best was tilting back his head and howling the word Hambone as though it were a train's soulful whistle.

We knew all about trains. The train track ran alongside this very road, across the street from our house. Behind our house, though, was the town cemetery, just over the fence, where we could watch whenever anyone was buried. We didn't like to look, and so we usually just pretended that it didn't exist. Daddy knew better than to take us there, though wildflowers grew abundantly among the headstones.

When we'd tired of picking flowers from the ditches lining the road, we brought them home to Mama. She met us on the porch, her ruddy face creased with concern. "I been worried sick, Calill. How come you to go sneakin' out of the house with all my babies?" Then she admired the flowers and put them in a jar of water so we could have them on our breakfast table. Daddy insisted that she let him cook, so she sat with her children as we drank sweet coffee-milk, our once-a-week treat. Daddy whipped up his special ninety-nine bubble pancakes on the old cast-iron griddle, and we ate them hot, topped with margarine and sugar cane syrup.

A few years later, when Daddy began to build the house that we were to move into at the end of my first grade year, Mama was his primary helper. She held heavy sections of Sheetrock for him to nail and pounded nails herself with true aim. She cooked the huge meals he wanted and probably needed in order to sustain energy for the manual labor he did.

For years we lived in this four-room shack, its wide rough-planed boards insulated only by tar paper nailed onto the exterior walls. It wasn't a lot better than the chicken-coop house; it didn't even have a bathroom, only an outdoor toilet. There was no running water, so Daddy installed a pump in the kitchen. As the green wood dried, the knots in the floorboards fell out, leaving holes about an inch or two in diameter, through which we could watch the chickens or the dogs scrabbling about *in the dirt beneath the house. (Sometimes I'd lie awake at night, the cold sweat of abject terror pouring from me, as I imagined snakes and spiders crawling into my bedroom from the holes in the floor.)*

Despite the occasional fear, life was good in those years before I turned thirteen. Daddy worked hard in his job as a log cutter, while Mama stayed at home with us. In those happy years, she took us to the library to check out the books we couldn't afford to buy, though she didn't read much herself. I grew from a little girl whose S was written backward into a good student whose report cards were filled with A's. In fact, one spring my father responded to my pleas for a bicycle with this promise: "Sharon, I'll give y'all a quarter apiece for each A you make on your report cards. You can put that money on a bicycle and I'll pay the rest." My report card that year was extraordinarily good. I loved that bicycle.

During my childhood, Mama did her laundry using an old wringer washer and two tin tubs. It was hard work, but Mama didn't complain. The only part of it that she didn't like was hanging out clothes, since she had a horror of snakes. Our property line was a small creek; to our delight, it was full of minnows and crawfish, but water snakes loved it too. As a result, Mama had taught us about snakes—which ones were poisonous, which ones had to curl up before they struck. So when I, happily playing with my siblings and my neighbor Perry, spied a water moccasin at the base of a large oak tree, I knew what to do, but I simply couldn't run. With my foot only eighteen inches from the reptile, I was frozen in fear. Like an avenging angel Mama, her full-skirted housedress billowing around her legs, ran toward me. She was brandishing a garden hoe. "Aunt Ora," Perry finally said shyly, "you can stop chopping that snake now. He's dead. You done turned him into hamburger meat."

Despite what was even then an extraordinary collection of fears, Mama seemed very happy as a young housewife and mother. But I remember clearly the day her happiness ended: July 4, 1964. I was two weeks shy of my thirteenth birthday. Mama was hugely pregnant with the baby who would become my second brother. My family of six had just gotten back from a holiday visit with my beloved Aunt Susie, Daddy's baby sister, when the phone rang. Daddy answered it. Mama's father—my Papaw—was calling from Houston to tell us that Geneva, Mama's baby sister, had drowned that day. We could not go to the funeral. The baby was due in only five weeks, and Daddy could neither let Mama travel that far, nor leave her alone while he himself went. Had Mama been able to go to the funeral, perhaps things might have been different. Maybe something more healthy would have come from her grief, I don't know. But whenever I try to figure out why my beautiful, gentle mother became the vicious alcoholic that she was to be within two short years, the only thing that makes sense is Geneva's death.

Still, that can't have been all. I can't believe that one event alone could have changed a woman so much. But somehow it was the catalyst that unleashed all the bad things Mama had ever stored inside, and those things grew until we five children and our father were forced to live daily in our own private hell.

Chapter Three

Mother at Her Worst

⌒

"*She was a very beautiful woman—I used to think she looked like Barbara Eden. Now when I look at her, I see a bag lady, stooped over, no teeth, swollen stomach, rags for clothes. I can't see my mother's face in this woman anymore.*"

—*Susie Abell, thirty-nine, dentist, Des Moines, Iowa*

⌒

We have pictures of Mama taken when she was young. One, when she's only fourteen, shows a girl who looks far more like a grown woman. A taffy blond in a puffy-sleeved dress, she sits demurely on the grass, legs tucked under her and out of sight. In another early photo taken when she was still a teenager, she stands with Edna Mae (relative, friend, and later drinking buddy) beside a rain-slicked road. Clad in jeans and saddle oxfords, she is skinny, except for the beginnings of a belly. Given the time period, she may already be pregnant with me; I hope not, though, because in her right hand, she holds a cigarette. In another photograph taken at about the same time, she hugs my father as they stand together in the snow. They seem very much in love.

And then there is the photo of Mama, age eighteen, holding her newborn daughter—me. She seems awkward, as though she'd never held a baby before, though, as the oldest of seven children, she no doubt had held many of her siblings. One of my legs sticks stiffly out of the blanket; one of my arms sticks up, almost in a "don't drop me" pose. Mama is incredibly skinny here, grinning shyly into the sun, the shadow of a tree covering half her face, causing her to have a strangely harlequin appearance, which seems, looking back, an omen of her two personalities, drunk and sober, to come.

Fast-forward past many of the drinking years. Mama is heavy in this next picture, sitting in her favorite spot at the kitchen table, in the corner. She is on the phone and appears ill at ease. The drinking has left her socially paranoid, and she hates to answer the phone or go out in public anymore. You can't see the scars that she carries on her face from one of her drunk-driving accidents, but clearly visible is the skin cancer, the size of a small grape, beneath the right corner of her mouth. She doesn't go to doctors anymore. Not visible in the picture, either, are her ever-present cigarette and cup of black, bitter instant coffee.

The pictures taken at the end of her life show again a skinny woman, shrunken, the life easing out of her ounce by ounce. The ash-brown hair of her middle age has turned into gray. An oxygen tube is in her nose. Her once clear green eyes are dull and milky. She no longer smokes or drinks, though not by choice. If she could coerce anyone into buying cigarettes or booze for her, she would do it, even knowing that she'd die if she started smoking and drinking again. Not that it would have made much difference. Though her heart is still beating at the time the photos were taken, these last pictures show a woman who has long ago stopped living.

Describe your mothers, we asked. Some of the answers were loving, tender, complimentary. But most of the answers were uncomplimentary, negative, critical. In *Perfect Daughters,* Ackerman notes that there is a difference between daughters of alcoholic fathers and daughters of alcoholic mothers in the way these women describe their drinking parent; adult daughters of alcoholic mothers are more "attacking" in their comments than are daughters of alcoholic fathers. He also notes that daughters of alcoholic mothers are more likely than daughters of alcoholic fathers to express anger at the drinking parent.

Most of the women from whom we heard are old enough to be able to look back, honestly and reflectively, at their lives with their mothers, but we did notice that the younger the respondent was, the more likely she was to present an uncritical portrait of her mother, or to make excuses for her. "Okay, she did it, but she couldn't help herself. It was someone else's fault." Many of the younger daughters would list atrocities that their mothers had committed while drunk, only to follow that description in the next sentence with something hopeful and optimistic, such as "but she's really wonderful, deep down, I know she is!" Once a woman has reached a certain level of experience, however, and especially once she's had children of her own, she is more able to compare the mother she had with the mothers other women had and with herself as a mother. It is often only then that she is able to paint an accurate portrait of her mother's behavior and of her childhood and adolescent reality. It is also then that she grows angriest. At that point, when she envisions the mother she *could* have had, she feels desperately cheated, and she grows disappointed and sometimes enraged.

Those emotions find their way into these portraits. For example, Camille Robbins, a sixth grade teacher, says her mother is "angry at the world. She is lonely, self-destructive, never happy in her marriage of forty-one years. She has dark circles around her eyes that make her look evil. And she never has anything nice to say." Rachel Addington describes her mother as "a bitter, resentful old woman who thrives on hurts from the past and won't let go. She is a person who needs to seek help but refuses to—who would rather wallow in her own self-pity than let in the people who want to love her." S. Jae Austin paints a despondent portrait of her mother in monochromatic grays: "She is a pitiful, childlike, dependent, overweight gray creature with a neon sign saying 'Please, someone, take care of me. I don't know how.'"

Ronda Davidson, a New Jersey teacher, says that her mother "was hateful and disgusting when she drank. She swore using unbelievable filthy phrases. She would start fires, walk around just in panties, and urinate on the floor. She would spit on me and say horrible things to me. She would call people on the phone and harass them. She would argue with neighbors and yell at my father all night long till someone next door would call the police."

Nancy Codgill adds, "My mother was *not* a happy drunk. She was filled with anger and resentment, about which she was very verbal. She almost enjoyed stirring people into a frenzy, and I took the hook all the time. She would shout for hours (and years) to us and the neighborhood about her superiority, how different she was, and how others failed to understand her or measure up to her expectations. This was drummed into us nightly for weeks, months at a time, and I, as a youngster, bought it. Naturally, there wasn't much room in her life for a husband, son, and daughter. There was very little nurturing and no emotional support. Mom was the needy child, and I became the unpaid help."

The descriptions these women provide of their mothers are harsh, cruel, perhaps reminiscent of a kind of antipathy toward our mothers that we don't want to hammer home too deeply. After all, our research reveals that almost all of us loved our mothers, and most of us have forgiven them. But these are pictures of reality. They are not the spoiled whinings of little girls who haven't grown up and are getting revenge against Mommy because she didn't buy us the Barbie doll of our dreams, or didn't let us eat ice cream and cookies instead of making us eat broccoli. Nor are these merely the portraits that victims have painted of their victimizers, because daughters are first and foremost survivors of their mothers' addictions. Rather, these descriptions are the manifestations of years of abuse.

Our respondents report having suffered, sometimes literally, several kinds of abuse at the hands of their alcoholic mothers: neglect, abandonment, physical abuse, sexual abuse, emotional abuse, and verbal abuse. Because these types of abuse overlap so much, it is almost impossible to neatly categorize them as separate and discrete experiences, since women who suffered one type of abuse suffered several others as well. For instance, a woman might report being physically abused, which causes emotional pain that is also abuse; or, a woman might have been both beaten and sexually molested. In almost no cases did our respondents indicate that only one type of abuse occurred.

Neglect

I was still awake, keenly aware of what was missing. My little sister Sally, whose warm, plump body was usually curled next to mine, was gone. My little brother Delmer, a skinny toddler who usually slept with my sister Sheila, was gone. In her room adjoining mine, I could hear Sheila crying, a whimpering, sniffling noise. She was scared. We both were scared. I was sure that my brother Curtis in his bedroom was scared too, but being a boy, he wasn't going to admit it. But it was my job as the oldest child—it was always my job—to comfort the younger kids, so I called out softly, "It'll be okay, Sheila Jean. Daddy'll find 'em. He'll get 'em off the bus and bring them home."

Mama had left Daddy that day, something she did sporadically, and she had taken our baby brother and sister with her. She was drunk—as usual—and we hadn't even known she'd gone until, in a fit of guilt, the woman who'd helped her get away had called.

"Calill," she'd said to my father, her voice slurred, "this is Lottie Fae. I just thought I ought to tell you that Ora and them two little ones caught the Continental Trailways bus for Houston today. She told me she was tired of it and was goin' back to her Mama and Daddy's. I drove her down to the bus stop this afternoon, so she ain't been gone but about two hours." Lottie Fae, a widow (or so she claimed), had had eyes for Daddy ever since she'd met him years ago, and no doubt she was happy to have Mama out of her way. But Daddy loved Mama, drunk or sober, and he loved his children. He was going after them.

After calling the bus station to find out as much information as he could, Daddy took off in our old family car. Before he left, he told me, "Sharon, I ain't sure when I'll find 'em and get back home. You make sure Sheila and Curtis get their homework done and y'all get yourselves something to eat." His face was pale beneath his log cutter's tan, his blue eyes like ice.

It was now very late. We three oldest kids—I was about fifteen, Sheila thirteen, Curtis eleven—had been in bed for a couple of hours. But we weren't asleep, so when the car drove up, we jumped out of bed and ran to the living room.

I keep trying to remember, but I can't, who Daddy brought to the door first, the two sleeping children, or our mother. I took four-year-old Sally from him, and Sheila took our two-year-old brother Delmer, and we brought them to bed. Sally was wearing only a pair of panties and a strange old full slip that was obviously for someone much older than she was. Someone had hemmed it up so she wouldn't trip. Delmer had on a too-small stained pullover shirt and a very, very wet diaper. We washed them and changed their clothing. Neither of them even woke up.

Daddy had had to drag Mama out of the car, through the yard, and into the house. She was kicking, screaming, and cursing, "Goddamn you, Calill Cockerham, I ain't never gonna let you get away with this! I'll kill you, goddamn it, that's what I'll do. You just wait and see if I don't, you bastard. I ain't gonna live with you no more. I hate your goddamn guts, you asshole."

Mama's thin knit pants were covered in blood. I was horrified; had Daddy hurt her? And then I realized—she had started her period and hadn't even known it, she was so drunk.

The next day, my little sister told me, "Sharon, we was so cold on that bus. Mama put Kleenex on us to keep us warm, but they didn't help much. And we was real hungry." Then she smiled. "The bus driver bought me some candy. M&M's with peanuts. I ain't never had none of them before, and they was good. I liked them."

Curled up on my lap, she sighed in her wise little way. "I was just so happy when I saw Daddy get on the bus, I liked to have cried. Then he *picked me and Delmer up and carried us off and put us in the backseat of the car. Then I just felt safe all over."*

One of the most common ways in which alcoholic mothers harm their children is through neglect, physical or emotional. They don't pay attention to the child's basic needs for food, clothing, shelter, and love. Their children are poorly fed, clothed inappropriately, or sent out to play in horrible weather so Mom can sleep off last night's drunk. The children, worried and upset by quarrels and shouting, awakened for no reason at all in the middle of the night, often don't get enough sleep; their health care is neglected; and they number among the most often absent at school. Even worse, these children are not hugged or listened to. "What happened at school today" remains the child's untold story. The bully who is beating her up on the bus never gets dealt with because "Mom has a headache. Don't bother her now. Go play." Unless the father is still in the home and is himself not an alcoholic (or is not too passive to interfere), this child has no advocate. She may have a caretaker sibling or mother substitute, if she's lucky. But no one can make up to her the loss of her mother as her champion, as the person who thinks she's wonderful and interesting and worthwhile. Her mother's neglect and indifference to her needs will mark this child; she will become, in her own heart and mind, one of the unwanted.

Sharon says, "I was talking to Sally, my youngest sister, recently, and we have the same memory—Mama never hugged us or cuddled with us. Even once we were adults, her hugs were stiff, uncomfortable moments, initiated by her children and never by Mama herself."

Children who are not physically caressed by their mothers are suffering from neglect as much as if they were being deprived of food and water. Sometimes they even die; it's called "failure to thrive." Many daughters describe just such neglect. Others describe neglect in terms of not having sufficient food, clothing, and shelter, or medical care, not even for emergencies. They describe being left alone for long periods of time to fend for themselves and to protect themselves from whatever might harm them.

Georgina Iler's mother, for example, barely functioned at all. After Georgina brought her a cup of morning coffee, she was able to get up and make breakfast, but by the time Georgina left for school at 8:50, her mother would be asleep on the family room couch. When Georgina returned from school, she'd still be there, asleep. Every evening, her mother fell asleep in front of the television by 10 P.M. Needless to say, she did not do much housework or cooking. "My sister and I often washed out our own underwear to dry by the water heater overnight," remembers Georgina. "God knows what my brother did."

Krista Moseley, an office assistant from Georgia, remembers how her mother would prepare meals ahead of time and freeze them so that when she came home late and passed out, Krista would have something to eat. Nan MacGregor's mother often sent Nan over to the neighbors to eat so that she could go out and drink.

Marta Hendrix's mother used to forget to pick Marta up from after-school activities, such as ballet or French lessons. Marta would wait and wait, shivering in the cold as she sat on the curb, watching the sky grow darker and the streetlights come on around her. She didn't dare leave the area, for that would make her mother angry. When her mother finally did remember and pulled her car up to the curb, she would yell at Marta for being so much trouble. Marta comments wryly, "I guess it's no surprise that I dropped French and ballet."

Susan Steffen's mother was openly negligent about her daughter's health care. Once, as a child, Susan had been chewing on a stick. She bumped it by accident and sent it halfway down her throat. It sliced the roof of her mouth and part of her throat. Even with all the blood spurting out, she was terrified to tell her mother, who she knew would be angry. So she told her grandmother, who tried to convince

Susan's mother to take her to the hospital. "My mom was so pissed that she told me how stupid I was and that I didn't 'deserve' to go to the emergency room," says Susan, thirty-three. "My grandmother took me, and I ended up having to have stitches in my throat. My mom was quite shit-faced when we got home, and she wouldn't talk to either me or my grandmother for days. I kept thinking that I couldn't be that important to her."

Abandonment

Some alcoholic mothers carried the neglect to an extreme by leaving us unattended for the evening while they drank at bars; others left for weeks, months, or years.

June Godfrey's mother would disappear for unpredictable stretches of time, calling home only when she was ready to be picked up. "Not to say we hadn't already looked for her in every bar in town in the meantime," says June.

Sharon recalls her mother's late evenings in the local bars. "I remember many nights when Daddy and I went out looking for Mama. Usually we'd find her at one of the bars she frequented, but sometimes we wouldn't be able to find her. I don't know if she would be spending the night with some drinking buddy or some man. I just remember feeling frightened and lonely. Daddy's feelings didn't make it easier. He'd be feeling so lost that I knew that for a little while, I wouldn't have either parent."

Some alcoholic mothers stayed away for much longer stretches than just an evening. Because they were abandoned, a number of daughters in our survey were raised by relatives other than their mothers.

Marla Venerable, a writer from Indiana, never even met her mother until she was eleven years old. Her mother had abandoned her at the age of three months, so Marla lived with an uncle, then a grandmother, and finally, in an orphanage. Marla wept openly as she described the pain of having been abandoned: "Even back then as a child, I felt like I had nobody to rely on, I had to rely on me." Then, for reasons unknown to Marla, her mother reappeared in her life, ready to take her back. But this was short-lived. For the next nine years, Marla never lived with her mother again for more than two years at a stretch.

Financial Irresponsibility

Another form of neglect is financial irresponsibility. Ginny Durden's mother let the family car get repossessed and the family business go bankrupt so she could use the money to drink. Rose Habegger remembers how her mother and a boyfriend drank away a $25,000 inheritance in six months. Some daughters must become so ultra-responsible about the household finances, knowing their drunken mothers are incapable of handling them, that they take them over themselves. Such a one was Olivia Reinheimer. "She made the money, good money and all," she remembers, "but I was the one who had to catch a cab and go around town to pay bills."

Money was also a problem for Clara Wilson. "I can remember as a teenager, my sister and me looking for change for cat food because our mother was at the bar. We also looked for money to feed ourselves." Having enough money was also an issue for Abby Giles, who recalls, "We were on welfare when I was small, and sometimes I would have to go and trade food stamps for money so she could get something to drink. I remember I didn't like my childhood too much."

Physical Abuse

Alcoholic fathers have long gotten well-deserved criticism for their violence in the home, but alcoholic mothers, too, do their share of hitting, slapping, scratching, punching, and even burning.

"We'd all start to shake automatically when we'd hear her wake up, or come home, or when we were on our own way home from school," states Michelle Polinsky. "She's put my sister in the hospital and didn't know it till a week later; then my sister got in trouble for causing trouble. Mom's had many blackouts, then denies it. She's beaten up my sister for not saying hello when she came home from school. She was both physically and mentally abusive almost twenty-four hours a day, seven days a week. I've lived a life of complete fear."

Hair pulling was only one of the types of abuse that Dale Waters suffered at the hands of her mother. "If she felt like pulling your hair out of your head (which was her favorite), she did it. If you ever reacted—watch out! She'd make you bald!"

Laditea Sanders, age twenty-nine, remembers the beatings she got when she confronted her mother about drinking. "The older I got, the worse the beatings got, until at the age of twelve, I finally ran away."

"When my mother was drinking, it unleashed the monster within her even more," reports Kimberly Franks. "She was more rageful and brutal in her beatings after drinking. She would hit until she passed out. She would beat me awake if I fell asleep at night while she was out. The most important feelings associated with my mother were hatred and fear."

Sandra Peabody says, "My mother poured hot coffee on me—a potful. She once tried to strangle me, once hit my head against a brick wall. She made me eat when I did not feel well. I vomited and she tried to make me eat *that*. She said I was only doing it to get out of eating."

Jane Howard's mother shot herself in the abdomen when she was three months pregnant with Jane "because my dad didn't think I was his. And she hung my baby sister over a balcony to get more beer from my stepdad."

"While taking diet pills, she would beat me senseless over the smallest infraction," says Gail Ricker. "She was constantly feeling left out, passed over, or underappreciated. She nagged on and on over insignificant incidences and imagined slights. She would humiliate family members by berating them in front of others."

"She would be extremely belligerent and argumentative and would become violent and slap me with her fists clenched," says Leigh Vives, forty-six. "She didn't care where the punches landed. Once she hit me across my back with a mop handle and also pushed me into my closet, where I fell back and hit my head on the wall."

Sharon recalls the time her drunken mother almost killed her sister:

I don't remember what it was that Sheila said that could have set Mama off; usually, Sheila was the one who acquiesced and said nothing at all. But Sheila had said something to Mama that day, and in her usual fashion, Mama did nothing about it immediately. She just went and sat on the back porch in her rocking chair and rocked and drank. As she drank, she would always stew over whatever infraction it was that someone had committed against her. Now, she was a real chicken with people she couldn't control. If a store clerk was rude, or if the banker smarted off at her, she'd sit and rock and drink and invent retorts she wished she'd made, but she wouldn't do anything about that. But with us kids, it was a different story.

Sheila, who was about twelve at the time, if that old, had forgotten the number one rule of survival in our house: if you make Mama mad, she is going to get revenge. Not immediately. Never immediately. She was going to wait until you no longer expected her to do anything; then she'd strike. But Sheila had forgotten this, or maybe was just hoping she'd get lucky this time, and she'd gone into the living room to watch television. I was just coming in the living room door when I saw what was about to happen. My mother was coming up behind Sheila, who sat unaware on the sofa. In Mama's hand was a heavy cast-iron skillet. She was raising it back, like a giant black tennis racket, and Sheila's head was her target.

I can see that so clearly—Sheila sitting there, a smile on her face from the cartoons she was watching—and Mama aiming that big black skillet for Sheila's little white-blond head. From out of nowhere—I hadn't even known he was in the house—my father appeared, and just as my mother began to swing the skillet forward, Daddy caught her arm and twisted the skillet from her hand.

Indirect Forms of Physical Abuse

Smoking and Fires

Most (85 percent) of our mothers smoked, so our fears of fires were quite justified. How many of us have not had close calls with a passed-out mother's lit cigarette as it burned its way down to the sheets or the couch? Many daughters told us of cigarette accidents in their houses.

Tracy Barnwell's mother would often put her head down on the kitchen table and fall asleep, lit cigarette in hand. Marie Willow's mother, on the other hand, would drop her lit cigarette when she passed out at the table. Every night, Marie waited up until her mother passed out so that she could snuff out the burning cigarette.

Morgan Landry adds, "My mother would pass out in the home, leaving candles burning, lights on, appliances on, TV on, doors unlocked, cigarettes burning. She would burn food and burn herself."

The family of twenty-four-year-old Iris Sheffield was forced to endure a near tragedy because of her mother's drinking. While Iris and her husband were out, Iris's mother, who was visiting, got drunk and left food cooking on the stove. The house caught fire and burned down. Though none of the family was killed, they lost everything, including the family cat.

Drunk Driving

One area that concerns not just the children of alcoholic mothers but also the public at large, is drunk driving, a tragic national epidemic that took more than 17,000 lives in 1995 and led to 1.4 million DUI arrests. (Those numbers, of course, reflect only the drivers who were caught.) Another national survey estimates that in the United States in 1993, 123 million incidents of drunk driving occurred.

Of course, fathers also drive drunk, but mothers who drive drunk often have the kids or grandchildren in tow. It's usually the mother in the family who drives the car pools, drives the children to after-school lessons, picks them up from day care or after-school care, takes them along on the family errands. As a result, for many daughters one of the greatest fears is their mother's driving while under the influence of alcohol and drugs. They worry that she will kill or injure herself, other people, or her children.

Donna Cartee remembers her mother peeling away into the night after a quarrel with Donna's father. "It terrified me," says Donna. "I can still hear the sound of tires screeching around the curve of the road."

Kimmie Swartz revealed the horror she'd endured as a six-year-old child: "My mom liked to drive while she was drinking, and so there we were, tooling down the street in the pouring rain. The traffic was heavy, but my mother didn't care. Suddenly, we hit something, but my mother kept driving. I was in the front seat on the passenger side, and I noticed a piece of clothing flapping from the side mirror. Later I found out that my mother had hit a little old woman and crippled her for life. But my mother never stopped driving. She never even knew she had hit anyone."

"How do you like my new car?" grinned Mother proudly, stepping out of her new, buttercup yellow Cougar. The rest of us gathered around to admire it.

"I love it!" I exclaimed passionately. I was sixteen and had had my driver's license for almost a year. I pictured myself gliding coolly into the high school parking lot and casually stepping out with a poker face, as though driving a brand-new Cougar was the norm for me.

"When can I drive it?" I begged, slipping into the bucket seat.

The rubbery new-car smell was divine. In a state of ecstasy, I pushed in the clutch and slid the four-on-the-floor transmission into the different gears, feverish with excitement at the prospect of driving it.

"We'll see," said Mother. "Maybe when school starts this fall. But I want to break it in first."

A few days later, she said, "Ellie, I'm going into town to do some errands. Is there anything you want?"

"No, I guess not," I said.

"While I'm out, would you mind vacuuming the upstairs hall?" she asked.

"Okay." I watched the rear of the snazzy yellow car disappear down the road. It could not have been more than half an hour later that I glanced out the upstairs window to see the Cougar creeping slowly into the driveway. Mother's face came into view. It was flushed, and her mouth was pulled back in a grimace, as though she was crying. And there, behind the Cougar, followed an official black-and-white car. My heart dropped. I ran down the hallway and down the stairs, jumping the last three. In the shadow of the back porch, two silhouettes appeared at the screen door. The doorbell bonged. Mother, now heavily intoxicated, was half-standing, half-leaning, on the arm of the sheriff. Her unfocused, overflowing eyes were indignant as she shaped and spat out each word with effort, as though she was expectorating chewing tobacco.

"Ellie," she was saying thickly—but her voice still rose and peaked with resentment, "I've . . . been . . . arrested . . . for . . . drunk driving!"

My heart pounded as my mouth turned dry.

"Ah, I believe your mother needs to go upstairs and go to bed," said the sheriff in an exaggeratedly loud voice, for Mother's benefit as much as mine.

She leaned into his shoulder, her knees buckling. He heaved her up by *the elbow and repeated, while opening the screen door and edging her in,* "Why don't you take her inside, and we'll just forget about this, this time."

He winked profusely as he spoke, implying that Mother's drunken driving would be our little secret, that if I could just get her upstairs and off the road, the whole matter would be forgotten. After all, Dad was a prominent professional in our community; it would not be seemly for the good doctor's wife to cause any embarrassment!

The sheriff supported Mother's light frame as he walked her down the hallway to the base of the stairs.

She collapsed to the floor.

"Can you get her upstairs?" he asked me.

"Yes, thank you," I replied.

He turned and left, his large profile disappearing out the screen door. Mother lay in a heap. I took a deep breath and with effort, hoisted her up. Fortunately, she was light, so I was able to half lift, half drag her up the stairs, slowly, one by one. My arms ached by the time we got to the top. I pulled her down the length of the hallway, into the master bedroom, and let her fall onto the bed. She mumbled faint noises, but her eyes were closed, and she wasn't moving.

I looked at her and was suddenly filled with revulsion. I felt low and dirty and just wanted to get as far away from her as possible. Leaving the room, I closed the door and went downstairs. Then I called Dad at the office. He instructed me in his best professional voice not to worry, that he would take care of everything when he got home at supper time, and returned his attention to his current patient.

I paced the floor, mortified. Would this incident make the rounds of the high school gossip circuit? The sheriff's teenage son was in my class! My brother arrived home, and I told him what had happened. Together, we inspected the new car for damage.

"Look!" he said. Reaching behind the driver's seat, he pulled out a two-gallon jug of whiskey from the car floor. It was half empty.

"Come on," I said. Standing at the kitchen sink, we poured out the whiskey and watched the contents glug noisily down the drain. How *little we knew about alcoholics then! As if a simple ploy like that would make a difference!*

When Dad arrived home that evening—at the usual time—his mouth tightened, but Mother was still asleep, so there was nothing he could do now. Of course, when she emerged from the bedroom two days later, she had no memory of the incident. I had already learned that there was no point in trying to tell her. She wouldn't have believed me.

Many daughters of alcoholic mothers told us of their mothers' drunken escapades behind the wheel. Karen Campbell's mother would get sauced, take the car, and disappear for days at a time, with Karen's little sister and brother. She had several car accidents. Mia Mitchell remembers riding in the car with her drunken mother and being in many accidents. "She was once arrested twice in one week for DWI," says Mia. "One night when I was about nine, she was very drunk and wanted to go for more beer, so I took her keys from her, locked myself in the bathroom, and cried. I finally gave in, on the condition she take me to my grandmother's. She was arrested and thrown in jail that night for DWI." Diane Bryant cringes as she remembers the time her mother drove the car through the window of a convenience store. Later, Diane was teased at school.

Some of us were made into designated drivers when we were far too young. Morgan Landry, thirty-six, recalls driving at the age of ten when her mother was too drunk. Like Morgan, Angie Ferro also took up driving in order to save herself. "I learned how to drive when I was eight years old because I was terrified of my mom driving when she was drunk. I was in three accidents, almost more; no one was hurt, thank God."

Sharon's mother also was guilty of driving while drunk, and she was also guilty of injuring herself and others in accidents. Sharon recalls one incident that occurred when she was about fifteen, during a summer when her father was working out of state.

*   *   *

I was startled from sleep by the banging. Running to the door, I opened it to find my mother's drinking buddy Lottie Fae, whom my mother had gone to meet at one of the local bars several hours earlier.

"Your mama's been in a wreck," she told me. "They got her down at the hospital in Columbia, so I come back here to get you, since your daddy's not here, and take you to see her." I looked at the clock; it was well after midnight, which is when the bars closed. Quickly I woke up Sheila.

"Sheila, Mama's been in a wreck. I gotta go with Lottie Fae to the hospital to see her. You're in charge till I get back."

Sheila's green eyes flew open wide. "I want to come too! Wait, I'll get everybody up. We'll get our clothes on——"

"No," I told her sternly, in my strictest big-sister voice. "I don't want the babies woke up. I'll wake you up when I get back, and I'll tell you everything."

She wasn't happy, but there was no choice. It would be ridiculous to wake up three other children, two of whom were under five years of age. I had doubts that the hospital would even let me *in to see Mama at this hour, let alone the four others, all younger.*

I don't remember the drive to Columbia, which was about thirty miles from our home in Olla. I don't remember driving past Sam's Place and the Arkansas Bar, the two major drinking establishments——we called them "beer joints." I don't remember if Lottie Fae pointed out the exact spot where Mama's wreck had occurred; Mama had pulled out into oncoming traffic in front of the Arkansas Bar, I was told. She'd hit a man and his little boy; both of them were also hospitalized. Surely, if Lottie Fae had pointed and said, "This is where the wreck happened," I would have remembered that. Nor do I remember noticing the debris of wrecked vehicles. But it was night, I was shaking with the adrenaline rush of fear, and I disliked Lottie Fae so very much that I know I did not solicit conversation.

She parked in front of the hospital then turned to me and said, "We better go in through this side door, in case they try to stop us, it's so late."

I was happy to get out of her car, with its heavy cigarettes-and-beer stench. As we approached the door of the wood-framed country hospital, I was trembling, though the summer night was hot and airless.

Silently, we opened the side door—I felt vaguely guilty, as though I was trying to sneak in without paying—and then the smell of the ether hit me. Pushing past Lottie Fae back into the sandy yard, I dry-heaved beneath a mimosa tree. Impatiently, the older woman grabbed my arm and pulled me inside. The hallway was swimming in a kaleidoscope of green walls, bad lighting, and dirty white tile; I felt as though I was about to faint. This woman, Mama's so-called friend, scanned room numbers as I fought yet another wave of nausea. She pushed open the door marked WOMEN'S WARD. It was where poor women who couldn't afford private rooms were brought.

The room was large and almost dark. Several white-railed hospital beds, each headed by a small light, filled the space. Mama's bed was the first one on the left, nearest the door, but I began to walk past it because I did not recognize the woman in the bed. Lottie Fae stopped me, and it was only then that I realized that the swollen, bruised creature with bandages swathing her face and right leg was my mother.

I stood and stared, but she didn't speak to me. Her mouth, in the insufficient light, seemed different somehow. Looking closer, I could see that both her lips were cracked and swollen, huge and dark with blood. A white slash of bandages divided her face, setting off her green eyes like a veil. She had been watching me, glaring at me, accusing, not forgiving me for having seen her like this. I could smell the beer and the vomit, even over the smell of the ether, and I knew the smells came from Mama.

There was nothing I could do there. She was alive, only half awake, in a lot of pain. Lottie Fae drove me home through the darkness of the night, which seemed only half as dark as my thoughts.

Mama was released after a couple of days, as were the man and boy she hit. Her story—which she repeated to anyone who would listen, and especially to my father, who had had to interrupt his work out of state to rush back to Louisiana—was that she had never even seen the other car.

"That damn bastard didn't have his lights on, I know he didn't, or I woulda seen him!" she insisted. She was, however, the one ticketed for the accident, and a few days later, two men came and took the license plate off the back of my father's truck. There was no need to remove the plate from the undrivable wreck of my mother's car.

Sexual Abuse

Another type of abuse that most people don't associate with alcoholic mothers is sexual abuse. When sexual abuse occurs, the alcoholic mother's sin is usually one of omission—failing to prevent or stop the abuse—not of commission (though a handful of our respondents did report having been sexually abused by their mothers). When Mother is often absent, whether physically gone or lost in her alcoholic haze, daughters are left more vulnerable to others' demands and desires. If the father is still present in the home (and according to Ackerman and others, in nine cases out of ten, he isn't), he is often an alcoholic himself, subject to the boundary violations and lack of self-restraint that alcohol induces. He himself may be the abuser. If the mother has remarried or has boyfriends, these men may abuse her daughters. Even potentially abusive brothers, uncles, grandfathers, and various relatives and friends have more access to little girls when the woman who should be the foremost defender of her daughter's sexual safety is not capable of fulfilling that role.

Several of the women who participated in our research reported having been sexually abused by their fathers, grandfathers, stepfathers, brothers, uncles, and mothers' friends. Jackie McClain still has nightmares of her abuse, though she is now fifty years old, and she still blames her mother. "My mom would kick him out of the bedroom, and then he'd get in bed with me. He'd tell me that he was the only person who had ever loved me." However, Nichole Von Bergen, also middle-aged, forgives her mother for what she sees as her complicity in Nichole's father's sexual abuse: "My mother has a tremendous amount of guilt. My father sexually abused both me and my older sister, and I think most of my mother's emotional problems stem from that. I saw my father molest my sister on more than one occasion. Even now that we're adults, he's tried to molest us. I told my mother. She didn't deny it."

Psychologists such as Kristin Kunzman, who works frequently with women who have been sexually abused as children, report that family members constitute the "vast majority of people committing childhood sexual abuse." Kunzman also states, "It isn't the alcoholism itself that causes childhood sexual abuse, but it certainly plays a part in creating an atmosphere where such abuse will be more easily tolerated and rationalized."

Kunzman contrasts the alcoholic home with healthier homes, in which daughters may feel freer to report such abuse. Unlike daughters of alcoholic or dysfunctional mothers, they know that their mothers are *there* (mentally, physically, and emotionally), and that they are likely to take action against their child's abuser. In the alcoholic home, however, "parents . . . are emotionally distant, and their children do not feel free to tell of any personal hurts or episodes of confusing touches." Further, in healthy homes, the mother is herself less likely to have been sexually abused, but "[a] significant percentage of all females in chemical dependency treatment programs were abused as children," says Kunzman. Clearly, in a home with an alcoholic mother who was sexually abused as a child or teenager, the normal rules are broken.

According to a report issued in 1996 by the Center on Addiction and Substance Abuse at Columbia University, as many as 69 percent of women in alcoholism treatment were sexually abused as children. Abusers are often first the abused; study after study has shown the high correlation between being verbally, physically, and sexually abused as children, and becoming the verbal, physical, and sexual abuser as an adult.

Jo Ann Stills, at age twenty-six, remembers when she realized that her sexual abuser was also her mother's abuser. "I was molested by my grandfather, and I thought it was just me." Her voice lowers to a whisper. "Then I found out that my mother had been molested too and was still being molested, after I saw him put his hand down the back of her underpants. I didn't know what to think. Then I found out that he was doing the same thing to my baby sister. That's when I lost it."

This vicious cycle requires treatment and intervention, or it stands a great chance of being repeated in not just one but many subsequent generations, just the way it's being repeated with Sarah and Sybil.

Sarah and Sybil—The Abuse of Two Sisters

Sarah and Sybil are now in their forties. Sarah is older than Sybil by two years. Both are married with children. When they were young, barely entering adolescence, both these two sisters were sexually abused by an uncle, their mother's brother. He stole into their bedroom one night and crawled into bed with them.

"I was terrified," recalls Sarah. "I remember he touched my breasts—what little of them I had—and he ran his hands down into my panties and felt around my vagina. He tried to put his fingers into me, but I'd squeeze my legs together and pretend to be rolling around in my sleep."

The uncle finally fell asleep, and the next morning, the girls' parents found him there. Their father was furious, but their mother defended her brother, insisting that "nothing happened."

However, something had happened, not only on that occasion, but also on another, when this same uncle raped Sybil. She later miscarried the product of his rape. Her mother, drunk and passed out in another room as the rape occurred, would not believe Sybil when she tried to tell her about it. "You're lying. He wouldn't do that. You're just a slut."

Now, a generation later, the cycle is repeating itself. Sarah reports that Sybil is looking the other way while her second husband molests both Sybil's children from her first marriage, as well as his own son and daughters.

"Sybil *knows* what's going on," insists Sarah, "but she vacillates between saying, 'No, it isn't happening, and it never did,' to 'Well, it used to happen, but now he's stopped,' to 'Yes, it happened, and it's still happening, and I'm going to leave him.' But she doesn't do anything. It's like she's caught in this terrible inertia."

Recently Sybil's husband was arrested for his crimes against children, and Sybil's two grown children (among others) have come forward to file charges against him. Sybil, shocked at last into having to admit the truth, plans to file for divorce.

Becoming Our Mother's Caretakers

Many, many of us felt that we had to be our mothers' caretakers, since our mothers could not care for us. This is yet another form of both neglect and emotional abuse. "I always felt I had to watch over her when she was drunk, even when it put me in danger," says Meredith, a housewife from Kentucky.

Some alcoholic mothers were passive drunks, like the mother of three sisters—Lucy Clarke, fifty-one; Rebecca Farm, fifty; and Samantha Barnes, forty-two—who responded to our questionnaire. When they were growing up, the three of them took turns staying home from school on the day the Social Security check arrived, so they could pay bills and buy groceries.

"Still, there was never enough food to last the whole month, so I got a part-time job at age twelve," Lucy said. "When we'd come home from school, she'd just be sitting on the couch, doing nothing. She was pleasant, but she never *did* anything."

On the other hand, the alcoholic mothers who were anything but passive required even more caretaking from their daughters, as Ellie describes below.

* * *

When Mother was brought home drunk, I dragged her up the stairs, her limp legs thudding against each step. She was half-conscious, uttering garbled, nonsensical sounds as I moved her slowly down the hallway. With my arms around her waist, I half-carried, half-pulled her into her bedroom. With a sigh of relief, I let go, and she slumped forward onto the bed, facedown. I straightened her out, removed her shoes, and covered her with a blanket. Her skinny arm dangled over the edge of the mattress. Stiff white foam bubbled from her mouth. Her face was turned into the folds of the pillow, so I carefully bent down and listened for the sound of breathing. I feared she would suffocate.

I wanted to remove the pillow so she could breathe freely. At the same time, I did not want to risk awakening her. I stared at her small head, with its layered red hair, bright against the white pillow. She looked pitiful and vulnerable. I leaned over, pulled the pillow from beneath her face, and tossed it aside, angry that I always seemed to be the only family member at home when these events happened. But as sickened as I was by the whole fiasco, I also felt responsible for her well-being.

Diane Bryant will never forget the night she went out to a party with her boyfriend. They went back to his house, and because she was too tired to drive home, she stayed with him and returned home the next day about one in the afternoon.

"When I opened the door, all I saw was blood," recalls Diane. "Blood on the carpet, handprints of blood on the walls, a pool of blood in the kitchen, and the phone receiver lying on the floor. My mother had been drunk and had fallen in the bathroom, hitting the back of her head on the corner of the counter. She was bleeding and didn't know how to stop it. She struggled to the kitchen phone to call my grandmother, leaving copious amounts of blood along the way. My grandmother was eighty-one years old at the time, and it took her over an hour to arrive at my mother's. By that time Mom had lost so much blood she passed out. There were clots of blood on the kitchen floor. My grandmother called 911, and Mom was taken to the hospital and received a transfusion. When I arrived home—

no note, no mother, just an apartment covered in blood. I thought there had been an ax murder in the apartment. My first thought was she was dead, and it was my fault for not being there. I blamed myself."

Diane blamed herself for her mother's injury. She did not say, "If only she hadn't been drunk, she wouldn't have fallen." She said instead, "It was my fault for not being there. I blamed myself." Such thoughts as these are common to daughters of alcoholic mothers.

Laurie Wheeler, twenty-four, reveals that her mother's extensive drinking (a large bottle of wine each night) not surprisingly led to an accident in their home. "I had just started dating the man who is now my fiancé, and we were on the porch talking. Then we heard a huge thudding from in the house. We looked at each other, shrugged, and continued our conversation. A few minutes later we were going to get the dog. I was just stepping in the front door when I saw my mother cross-legged, 'butt naked,' sitting in a pool of blood. I asked what had happened. She said, 'I don't know.' Where did you fall from? 'I don't know.' I covered her and proceeded to put her in bed, all the while trying to stop the blood flowing from a one-and-a-half-inch gash in her head. No stitches were required, although she had a bruise the size of a football on her thigh. She had slipped at the top of the stairs and tumbled down one flight." Laurie adds sarcastically, "What a great first impression for my lover."

Emotional Abuse

There is a very fine line between neglect and emotional abuse, one that is almost impossible to draw. Emotional abuse goes beyond neglect; it implies willful action on the part of the mother. One such form of emotional abuse is our mothers' violation of our privacy, or boundary violations. Time and again, daughters describe mothers who read their diaries and letters, tore up their bedrooms, went through their closets and bureau drawers, and forbade their daughters to lock their bedrooms or even the bathroom.

Ellie poignantly describes one of her mother's habitual drunken behaviors—the trashing of Ellie's bedroom.

My bedroom door was open. I halted—like a bloodhound sniffing danger. Tiptoeing on the bare wood floor, I advanced quietly down the hall and peeked in. Mother's rounded derriere met my eyes. Wearing her usual tan shorts, she was bent over forward, sifting through a tangle of socks, bras, and underwear. Her bare legs, stiff and slightly apart, looked like white poles. An empty drawer, extracted from the bureau, sat nearby on the floor. "Goddamn, what a goddamn mess!" she muttered. Wearily, she stood up straight and moved toward the bureau, ready to pull out the next drawer and dump its contents onto the floor.

My sister Diana stood near the bedroom door, nervous but relieved that she would not bear the brunt of Mother's fury today. Meeting my eye, she held her fingertip to her mouth and waved me away. I nodded and backed quietly down the hall like some kind of fugitive escaping. Hurrying down the stairs, I ran out the screened back door and down the road, past the summerhouses that lined the lake on which we now lived in the new house my parents had built.

I felt so violated *again. Mother would become consumed with periodic and unpredictable urges to rifle through my drawers, and if my clothes weren't folded according to some sudden, arbitrary standard of neatness that was not applied to any other part of our house, she'd just pull out the drawers, dump everything out, and scream at me to put it all back neatly. But by the time I'd done this, she'd have forgotten all about it until the next round. As a teenager, I wanted some privacy. I needed to feel there were some physical and emotional boundaries over which no one would cross. Yet Mother felt free to go through my bureau drawers whenever the fit hit.*

I walked along the slate-rock shore of the lake for several hours. White sails rolled above the dark blue waves; the ferry crawled slowly toward the other side, full of cars and people. Rowboats tossed in the wakes of motorboats. Though this summer day was beautiful, and I even tried to enjoy it, fear ate at me. I knew Mother might be angrily looking for me right now. What if she was furious that I had fled? When the shadows grew long and the air cooled, I reluctantly started toward our house. As I walked, I passed the summerhouse of my best friend, Barbara. During the many dinners I'd enjoyed at her house, I'd always envied the peaceful atmosphere. I couldn't imagine Barbara's friendly mother even raising her voice, let alone overturning Barbara's bureaus in a rage. Barbara and her parents always conversed politely, without anger, tension, or fear. I would have gladly settled for that alone, but Barbara's mother also exchanged thoughts, ideas, hopes, and dreams with her! I couldn't fathom what that felt like. I tried to imagine having a mother who knew what my dreams were or who wondered enough to ask!

I stood at a cluster of trees in the distance and observed my own house. Even from a distance, I knew, as though by instinct, that it was safe to return. All three of us children had developed a strong ability to sense our mother's movements, actions, and moods, even from afar. Intuiting that it was safe to go in, I gingerly opened the back door and tiptoed nervously into the hallway. The silence told me right away that I'd been right. She was sleeping now. I picked up my clothes and jammed them back in my drawers. By morning, she'd forgotten all about it.

Ellie was not alone in feeling invaded by her mother's ransacking of her room. Virginia Mathew's mother used to throw all her clothes out onto the front lawn if she got angry.

Jackie McClain experienced a similar invasion. "She was manic. I mean *manic,* off-the-wall nuts. I'd come home from school in the afternoon, and my room would be torn to shreds. The sheets would be stripped, my mattress would be off the bed, my closet would be on the floor, my dresses would be on the floor, everything in the middle of the floor. I would have to redo everything, and then she'd come into my room and say it wasn't good enough, and she'd do it all again, maybe two or three times."

Sharon's mother did not turn her bedroom upside down—unless she was looking for something. She was constantly convinced that

Sharon was hiding something, anything, from her. Perhaps she was as hungry for an emotional connection to Sharon as Sharon was hungry for a connection to her, but her secret-hunting sweeps of her daughter's bedroom only caused Sharon to feel invaded and violated.

I'll never forget when she discovered my diaries, hidden carefully in what I'd hoped was the sanctuary of my bedroom, and started to decode them. What she found out was not how I felt about her and her drinking, but how I felt about a certain young man, a totally inappropriate man. He was tall, handsome, funny, and sweet, but very, very unavailable. He was not only a lot older and engaged to someone else, he was also a distant cousin. And he barely knew I existed, except as his slightly chubby relative, so much younger than he that I was merely a child in his eyes. His primary way of noticing me was to tease me in the same way he teased all the children.

Why I was enamored, I don't know. Maybe it was because he was a family member, and so he was "safe." Maybe it was because he noticed me at all, even though it was through teasing. Perhaps desperate in my loneliness, I had fixated on someone I knew well, rather than on one of the boys from my school. From them, I endured at best a casual dismissal and obvious condescension. (After all, who would be interested in the plump girl with obstinately curly hair, a girl who was forced to wear ugly rhinestone cat-eyed glasses? And even worse, who would want the daughter of the town drunk?)

I imagined myself to be madly in love and had filled my diaries with all my fantasies about him. But as soon as Mama had decoded enough of my diaries to realize the topic, she began to ridicule me. Whenever she was drunk, she'd mock, "Yeah, you think you know all about lo-oo-ove, don't you? And you can't even do any better than a crush on your own second cousin! You think you're so smart, with all those good grades, but you're really stupid and pathetic. I ought to tell your daddy . . ."

I figured she'd tell him eventually, no matter what I did. I was so scared of her! During most of my childhood, she'd used switches to stripe my legs, switches I had to pick myself, and they had to meet a certain standard—thin, limber, keen, capable of zinging through the air on their way to their target, my bare legs. She'd cut my legs up and down, leaving oozing, bleeding welts that for days stung like fire in the bathwater. As I'd gotten older, she'd stopped switching me and starting slapping my face. God, how I hated that! I would rather have had the switching—somehow it left me with a little more dignity than her handprint, plastered red across my face, with usually a nice cut or two where her rings would get me.

But even the face slapping was better than the verbal abuse. Her caustic words filled me with hatred and fear. It was as though she instinctively knew just what to say to tear my soul into shreds, to make me feel as though I barely deserved the gift of life she'd given me. She criticized my appearance—I was slightly overweight, with the usual dose of teenage acne and oily hair. She criticized my scholastic ambitions—"Yeah, like you think you'll get a scholarship in this town! Hah! I wouldn't count those chickens before they're hatched!" And now she was belittling my pathetic, imaginary love life.

I feared Daddy's disappointment in me even more than Mama's vicious verbal attacks. He had told me often that I was his golden girl, his hope for the future. I was the honor student, the one who was making the most of the education he'd worked so hard to provide for us. He himself had been pulled from school at age twelve to help support his widowed mother and baby sister. He did not want that to happen to his children. But my younger brother Curtis and sister Sheila were struggling in school and generally made poor grades. After all, given our climate at home, who would expect otherwise? I was a successful student for one reason: I'd figured out early in life that the only way out of that house and away from that kind of poverty-stricken, despairing, abusive existence was through college. I had to go to college, and the only way to get there was if I could get a scholarship. I would not stay in Olla, Louisiana, and become a drunk like my mother.

So I'd been working for a college scholarship since my first day of school, and Daddy had been working with me, getting up before dawn, *no matter the weather, to obliterate its silence and its trees with his power saw. Knowing of his sacrifices—so many and so hard—I felt even worse when Mama drunkenly blurted out my secret to him, as I'd known she would: "Oh, you think I'm so bad, don't you, Calill Cockerham? Well, you don't know what your precious daughter's been up to, do you? She's in lo-oo-ove, just a little white-trash whore!" Mama crowed, rolling her reddened eyes back in her head to indicate her disgust. She waved my diaries at me, victory twisting in her face. Now see who wins, she seemed to be saying. I could only stand there, white-faced, hating her.*

Daddy roared at her to shut up. I don't remember if he hit her; sometimes he'd knock her to the floor when he couldn't figure out what else to do to shut out her ugly words. He may have, because the rest of the kids scattered to whatever safety they could find, and I ran to my room. Later, after the house had gotten quiet, Daddy brought me my diaries.

It came to me then that, as he so often saved me from Mama's attacks, I was his savior too. I was the one he was counting on to remain unmarried so that I could get an education and make a lot of money to provide some blanket of security for his soon-to-come old age. Already I'd usurped Mama's former roles as cook, housekeeper, and mother to my siblings. Now I was also Daddy's confidante and his hope for the future. Looking at him sitting dejectedly by me on my chenille-covered bed, I saw Daddy for what he was—not a complex man, but a man to whom life had handed many hard burdens in his fifty-plus years. Nevertheless, he was also a man who dealt poorly with his complicated, much younger wife. Regardless of what she needed from him, he simply got up, went to work at whatever needed doing, and kept on expecting the world to revert to what it once had predictably been before Mama began to drink. It would not. And I could not make it so, not even for him.

Humiliating Public Behavior

Emotional abuse is confined not just to the invasions of our privacy and the blurring of the boundaries between what rightfully belongs to the daughter and what the mother can be involved in. Sometimes we feel that the greatest emotional abuse of all is the humiliation that we suffer frequently.

Sharon remembers how miserable she felt when the deputy sheriff's son, her classmate, would stare at her in class and then turn to his friends and whisper. They'd burst out laughing, and she would cringe in misery. She felt that everyone in their small town knew, but most of all, the son of the deputy sheriff, who had so many times brought her drunken mother to the door, surely knew more than most.

Many of us recall the painfully embarrassing moments in which we wished for the earth to open up and swallow us—moments during which our mothers were drunk in public, or behaved inappropriately in a sexual way, or wet themselves, or said embarrassing things to other people.

Jeanne Ebel says that her most significant, and most embarrassing, memory of her mother was of an event that occurred after Jeanne had started college. She was living at home and dating a man whom she liked. "We came home from a date," remembers Jeanne, now forty-one, "and she was passed out on the couch. I asked him in for a soda. While we were there in the kitchen, she got up, went to a loose-cushioned chair, lifted the seat cushion, sat on the supporting straps, and urinated onto the carpet."

Kitty Dellinger was humiliated when she returned home from out of town unannounced, bringing a friend with her. Her mother had been drinking for days and was still drunk. "She was still in her nightgown when she answered the door," says Kitty, an account executive from Maryland. "Later, she went out to the food market— in the same nightgown."

Emily Thompson cannot forget how her parents would yell, scream, and exchange blows right out in the front yard, for all the neighbors to see. Emily's worst memories are the ones of embarrassment when she tried to bring friends home from school. "I would always run in front of them and into the house quickly to check out the situation," says Emily, a beautician. "I never knew what I might find. I also remember I didn't want my mom to meet my friends' parents because who knows what condition she was in."

For Amanda Little, her mother's most embarrassing behavior occurred in a most public place—high school. "When I was in high school, I played volleyball and basketball. My dad would bring her to the games, and she'd be drunk. She couldn't get up the bleachers. She smelled of alcohol and cigarettes. I was very embarrassed."

For Antoinette Turner, the worst was watching her mother be straitjacketed and led away by her father's police-officer colleagues. When drunk, her mother would get out of control, and Antoinette would have to call the police department and ask for a car to come get her mother. Antoinette will never forget the humiliation of watching her mother being taken away in a straitjacket.

Bizarre Behavior

The bizarre or irrational behavior characteristic of alcoholics can strike fear in our hearts just as much as any burning cigarette or blows with fists and mop handles. Imagine how Joellen Weatherford, a Virginia travel agent, felt when she opened her Christmas gift from her mother—a nice new photo album, full of family pictures—only to find that the pictures had been mutilated with scissors. The heads and parts of the bodies of most people in the pictures had been cut out of the photographs. Joellen shivers at the memory.

Angie will never forget the day her mother strangled her cat. "I cried for hours," remembers Angie, twenty-four. "I did not speak to my mother for months. To this day, I never will forgive her. It was done out of spite and hatred, jealousy toward me."

Vickie Reaves's mother insisted on tape-recording a conversation they were having, so she could "prove" to everyone that Vickie did not treat her right. "She said, 'I am going to get this all down on tape so I have proof of how you talk to your mother. You will not lie about what you've said.' I was only trying to be honest about how her words and actions affected me, but she just kept telling me what a horrible, ungrateful, odious person I was. Then she called my dad, brother, sister, and husband into the living room and made them listen to the tape. No one said a word to back me up. I just cried.''

Susanna Moore, an Arizona secretary, is also bitter. She remembers her mother's bizarre behavior one Sunday morning as she, her father, and siblings prepared to go visit her grandmother. ''My mom threw herself in front of the car and dared my dad to run over her,'' she says. ''She broke off the radio antenna and started beating the windows of the car with it. We locked the doors, scared to death she would kill us. The whole time she screamed at us to get out of the car. The entire neighborhood must've heard her. How could she have been drunk at ten o'clock on a Sunday morning? I guess it's possible she had some 'hair of the dog' while we were at church, but her behavior was always so irrational to me when I was a child that I never really thought about it. That's just the way she was. Everyone said so.''

One perception held by many daughters of alcoholic mothers is that their mothers insisted upon being ''right.'' It seems to us that they would never concede wrongdoing and instead would blame everyone else for their problems. Carolyn Pridgen recalls, ''My mother always blamed my siblings, my father, and me for her drinking, depression, and destructive behavior. She would get very angry and smash things. Then, when she woke up or sobered up, she'd blame us for destroying her things.'' Ellie recalls that her mother behaved similarly, often castigating others for her own mistakes and not accepting that she was in the wrong.

Verbal Abuse

Dr. Grace Ketterman, author of *Verbal Abuse: Healing the Hidden Wound,* notes that verbal abuse has something in common with alcoholism: ''Verbal abuse,'' she writes, ''can accurately be defined as another type of addiction. It is an addiction to *power,* acquired at the high cost of denigrating others, and is repeated in predictable and definable ways over years of time." Verbal abuse, according to Ketterman's definition, is "any statement to a victim that results in emotional damage. Such damage limits his or her happiness and productivity for a lifetime." Obviously, most daughters of alcoholic mothers know what verbal abuse feels like—most of our respondents (three-fourths of them) indicated that they had been verbally abused by their mothers.

"I will never forget how devastated I was by my mother's comment about my appearance—'You think you're pretty, but you're not!'—when I was a teenager," says Sharon. "She also used to tell me my head was too big, and then she'd say, 'Little head, little wit; big head, not a bit,' to let me know that she certainly didn't think my large skull had any brains in it at all. My forehead is really high, and she was always trying to make me wear bangs to cover it up; she wore her hair partly over her own forehead to cover up her high brow, as though a high brow were ugly. I didn't learn to like my big head and high forehead until my foreign-born college roommate told me that in her country, those features were considered proof of intelligence. But I still don't think of myself as a pretty woman. I just can't. Every time anyone has ever said that I was pretty, my gut instinct is to think they were lying. After all, hadn't Mama already told me the truth? That I only *thought* I was pretty, but I really wasn't?

"Mama did the same thing to my two sisters. It was like she couldn't stand for us to think well of ourselves. She'd preach from the Bible about how vanity was a sin, and she'd deliberately keep us from practicing good grooming. Even though my hair was oily, she wouldn't let me wash it but once a week. Looking back, I can see how ridiculous it was that I'd have to sneak around in order to wash my hair! The primary way she kept us in line was through her verbal abuse, her constant belittling and insulting comments, which were always, always worse when she was drinking. Sober, she might say something like, 'Pretty is as pretty does' to keep us from thinking too highly of our appearance. Drunk, she'd cut to the bone and call us 'homely' or 'plain' or 'ugly,' in both appearance and in action.''

But appearance and body image are not the only things that our mothers criticized. They found other ways of stinging us with words.

"I remember my mother telling me," says Donna Cartee, "that if murder was not a crime, she would kill me."

Dale Waters recalls, "My mother was always very cold toward us. She wouldn't help us with our homework. 'You learned that in school today, didn't you? What are you, stupid?' was her most endearing quote!"

Marta Hendrix's mother would say, "No wonder you don't have any friends. Who would want to be your friend anyway, you slut, tramp, whore!" Marta, a straight-A student who did all the housework and never got into trouble, was crushed.

Our mothers did not even necessarily have to be drunk to become verbally abusive. June Godfrey's mother was "very negative, spiteful, and vindictive" even when she wasn't drinking. June, thirty-five, a collection agent, describes her as "a woman with a hurtful tongue, who doesn't care what she says to people—mostly inventions of her mind."

A few daughters have noted that their mothers were actually *less* critical when drinking. That was the case with Alicia Fortune, who remarks, "My mother was very nasty when she wasn't drinking. Although I hated her drinking, it subdued her. Sober, she would pick arguments and insult me." The same was true for Susan Steffan: "When she was sober, her temper got even shorter. She once broke a dining room chair by throwing it at my father. She became more depressed. It was like she could see everything that was wrong with her life, and it was our fault."

Like these two mothers, Charlene Harris's mother relied upon words to create a tempest that she seemed emotionally to need. Charlene, a payroll clerk from North Dakota, recalls, "My mother would create chaos, then storm out the door, which left us feeling guilty, knowing she would then drink. Creating the chaos gave her the permission to drink."

Culturally, we've been very accepting of someone's "need" to drink. How often have we heard, "Wow, I had a really bad day today! I need a drink!" In movies, on television, and in novels, when someone suffers a shock or great stress, helpful caretakers rush over with a brandy or some other intoxicant. As a result, it should come as no surprise that our mothers would create tumultuous situations in order to instigate a drinking situation; after all, they *wanted* to drink, and because they were addicted, they *needed* to drink. Consciously, of course, they probably weren't thinking, "Oh, if I can only create a major family argument, then I can have my excuse for reaching for the bottle," but in effect, that is exactly what many of them did. And they used their hurtful words to create those scenes.

Of course, we daughters weren't the only recipients of our mothers' verbal abuse; sometimes even strangers were. Deidre Goldblum recalls, "I was in the car with Mom and my sister Sara Jo, and somebody 'curbed' us, and we went off the road a little bit. It just sent Mom into a tailspin. The person stopped at a stop sign, and yelling and cursing, my mother got out of the car, ran up to their car, and as they were taking off, she grabbed onto the driver's door because she was planning to yank them out. Her hand got stuck, and so she was just running along beside the car. Eventually she got loose."

The telephone seemed to be useful to some of our alcoholic mothers when they felt the need to vent their rage against someone, as Rae Carlson can testify: "One of Mom's favorite things to do when drinking was to call people on the phone and rant and rave at them. She would call my sister and complain and 'bad-mouth' me, then call me and say things about my sister. She would also call former boyfriends or husbands (hers or ours) and harass them." Deidre and her sister Sara Jo remember that their mother would do the same thing; the family even installed a lock on the rotary-dial telephone just so their mother couldn't dial it. Sara Jo says, "She'd call the neighbors and say, 'Your tree is dropping leaves in my yard, and I'm going to cut it down.' They thought she was nuts."

As we have said repeatedly, most of us love our mothers, and we don't want to engage in a frenzy of mother bashing, either in this book or in our own personal lives. But the truth is that alcoholic mothers both cause abuse and allow it to happen. The truth is that daughters of alcoholic mothers have suffered sometimes irreparable harm because they were neglected, abandoned, insulted, cursed, ridiculed, slapped, scratched, pinched, choked, beaten, burned, and raped. It is small wonder that we have spent years trying to figure out what "normal" is and trying to create healthy adult lives for ourselves. We have low self-esteem, poor body images, frequent eating disorders, high divorce, depression, and addiction rates, and a painful emptiness, which haunts us even into adulthood.

One rare photo from Mother's past confirms that there was a lot I did not know about her life before she married my father. In it, she is a young woman, perhaps late teens or early twenties. Crowding around a restaurant table with two other women and three men, she smiles radiantly. A white flower adorns the top of her wavy auburn hair, giving her a girlish innocence, in contrast to her painted red fingernails. She clutches an empty glass; another empty glass sits nearby. One of the men at the table is raising his glass, as though in a toast. Everyone has already had a drink or two, for nine empty glasses are on the table.

She looks so happy in the photograph that I can't help wondering what had filled those empty glasses.

Her energetic smile continues in the photos of her wedding and of her early married days. In one picture, she sits like a pinup girl on a large boulder at the bank of the lake. She wears shorts, and her shapely bare legs are thrust out toward the water. Her sleeveless white blouse reveals firm, muscular arms. Her thick hair is barretted back from her forehead, but the breeze has blown a few stray locks loose. Her green eyes flirt beneath them. Energy and joy shine from her smile. She looks like a woman who loves life.

She became a mother nine months after her marriage, when I was born. In one photo, she cradles me in her arms and looks at me with a smile that is a mixture of awe and bliss. She holds me confidently, as though she is sure of herself as a mother. As a former nurse who once worked in the maternity ward, she had every reason to feel that way.

The months and years go by, and in the photos, she still smiles, but her face has lost some of its life force. Diana begins to appear in photos, then my brother. In one, Mother sits on the front porch with us three young children. It must be autumn, for the trees in the background still retain their leaves, yet it is cold enough for us to be wearing capes and coats. She smiles as she holds my wiggly brother firmly, but her smile has a tired quality to it—and who could blame her with three children four and under? She wears a checked pleated skirt and white sweater and no longer looks like a pinup girl.

I got a camera for my tenth birthday—just about the time Mother started to drink—and captured the family in pictures for many years. One photo in particular stands out in my mind, representative of the expression she wore during her worst years. We are on vacation in Washington, D.C., a terrible, tension-filled trip. Cold silence separates my parents. Nevertheless, since we're visiting the nation's capital, they feel obligated to make the best of it, so they take us to visit the sights. We walk around the downtown area, past the federal buildings. My camera clicks as Mother, Dad, Diana, and my brother walk up the slight incline in front of the FBI Building. A stranger would never, ever guess that these four people are together as they trudge wearily along, five feet apart from each other, each absorbed in their own thoughts. Mother's black, knee-length coat flutters in the wind, fanning out behind her. Her short, layered hair reveals more of the stiff chin jutting out, as though with determination. The eyes behind the clear glass of her cat's-eye frames are cold, the brows dark and frowning. She walks coolly ahead of my father, whose tan trenchcoat is buttoned up against the chilly air. His face is tight, his lips pursed. Diana and our brother keep a safe distance in the rear, far behind Mother and Dad and far apart from each other.

She stopped drinking when I was fourteen, and for a while, her smile reappears in photos. In one of my favorites, she stands in front of a high trellis of white flowers in her long-sleeved, tangerine dress. A shopping bag hangs over her left shoulder. Once again, her grin is in earnest, pushing her eyes up into happy crinkles. Her hair is still auburn, though more of a hairdresser-enhanced shade now. She looks older, as is to be expected. Her arms and legs are still thin, but her middle has thickened, and a hint of a potbelly shows.

This happy interlude lasted almost two years. Then, slowly, she slipped back into drinking.

What stands out to me the most about the last photo of her before her death is the resignation on her face. She faces the camera, stylishly dressed in a plaid suit, tangerine orange sweater, pearl beads and earrings, and a bracelet. The hair is still a youthful shade of red, but her complexion looks sallow. Her mouth is unsmiling. Most disturbing is the dull, flat look in her once sparkling green eyes.

I flip through the album and look at more pictures. The family history moves through the years, marked by college graduations, weddings, christenings, holiday get-togethers.

Mother no longer appears in any of the photos.

Part II

Chapter Four

Body Images

~

"*Whenever I look in the mirror, I sometimes see Mama's face looking back at me, and I just want to reach up there and claw it.*"
—*Serena Grail, thirty-five, church pianist, Austin, Texas*

"*My mother always told me that I was beautiful and that I looked just like her. I'd look at her after a 'drunk' and see ugly.*"
—*Nan MacGregor, twenty-seven, aerobics instructor, Winston-Salem, North Carolina*

~

The pear-shaped mirror, with its scrolled bird's-eye maple frame, reflected my image.

How I despised the ugly, thirteen-year-old girl with the blond hair and glasses who looked sadly back at me. Depression had settled into my whole bearing. My small, thin-lipped mouth had a natural downward curve, as though I'd been born to be sad. The droopy blue eyes, inherited from my father, also looked grave.

I was as tall as Mother now. My hips had widened and curved, my breasts were growing, and I menstruated regularly now. I was, in fact, beginning to look womanly, which frightened and depressed me. I hated my body. From the front, my frame was too wide; from the side, my expanding breasts made my profile look fat, or so I thought. To look thinner, I sewed the cups of my bra almost closed, flattening my chest, denying my breasts, perhaps in a pathetic attempt to regress to happier childhood times before Mother had started to drink heavily. Or maybe I

81

denied my breasts because on some subconscious level I was revolted at the thought of becoming a woman . . . in her image.

Until she had begun to drink, Mother had always been my primary role model for womanhood. Now, an entirely different woman had usurped her identity. This new woman, pale and skinny from too many skipped meals, stormed down the carpeted hallways, spewing sour breath, tears, and rage all over me. The house was saturated with a clammy, uncomfortable fear. When she slept the afternoons away in her darkened bedroom, I was grateful.

During the past year, terrorized right back to infancy by her rampages, I had suddenly started to wet the bed at night. Morning after morning, I would awaken with the horrible realization that my underwear was wet, the sheets drenched. I had tried to keep it a secret, but Mother couldn't miss seeing the wet sheets in the hamper.

One day, after school, she knocked furiously on my locked bedroom door, calling, "Open up! Right now!"

Reluctantly I turned the lock, and the door burst open.

"What's with the wet sheets?" she demanded. "Aren't you a bit old to be wetting the bed?"

I didn't know what to say, I was so mortified.

"At your age, I shouldn't have to wash and change the sheets every day!" she said contemptuously. "I did that for you when you were a baby!"

My poor body, over which I apparently no longer had any control, was betraying me in every possible way. Not only was I wetting the bed, which was reason enough to feel humiliated—and this went on for almost two years—but I was also developing those undeniable, conspicuous features of womanhood, a shameful confirmation that I was, indeed, turning into her. Therefore, I wore loose clothing to hide my curvy shape and used white lip base on my mouth, having decided that my lips' natural hue was too red. During these years, my father worked long hours in the city, building up his new private practice. He left on the 7:30 AM commuter train and returned on the 7:30 PM train. But even more than this, he had a classic case of denial (even shrinks aren't immune!), as though he believed (at this stage of our lives when she was beginning to drink heavily) that if he ignored my mother's problem, then maybe it would take care of itself and go away. Also, like many M.D.s, he tended to be somewhat dismissive of his own family members' ailments. If I had approached him about the bed-wetting problem, I'm sure he would have said, "Oh, is that right?" and then forgotten about it soon after.

I also began to chop my hair. Why not? It never looked right anyway. Even though I faithfully rolled it every night, following the explicit diagrams printed in hairstyle magazines, even though I slept uncomfortably with log-size curlers pressing into my head like iron pipes, it never came out right in the morning. It always looked lousy, uneven, limp. I didn't have any girlfriends who could advise me about style. Approaching my mother for advice was out of the question; in fact, I spent most of my time in my room praying she wouldn't seek me out for anything! So I began to trim it myself, a quarter inch here, a half inch there, clipping wherever I saw an unwanted wisp, hoping to even it out. I used the manicure scissors, which I carefully stole from my parents' bathroom medicine cabinet, despite Mother's repeatedly screeched warnings not to take those scissors. But as though addicted, I could not stop. In retrospect, I think I must have hated myself so much at the age of thirteen that I needed to inflict daily punishment upon my body. Chopping off my hair became a subtle form of self-mutilation.

Now, decades later, I'm a happy, middle-aged woman. I no longer hate myself or my body. But I've had to work at feeling that way. Even now, I search the mirror to see evidence of Mother's imprint on my face. I don't see it. The square jaw, the blue eyes, the thin, downturned mouth, are all Dad's. Or do I merely choose not to see it because it hurts too much? She was built differently than I; I am taller, larger framed and more buxom. She was always slender, almost bony, and had always joked that the only time she'd ever had any breasts was when she was pregnant.

A photo of Mother taken at a wedding in the late 1960s shows her looking elegant in a silk, jade green suit with a low-cut V neck. Her fluffy hat is covered with large white flowers with yellow and orange centers. She wears her usual strand of pearls and pearl earrings. The right hand, which of course holds a cigarette, is well manicured and polished. Her eyebrows are dark and perfectly shaped in arches; her lips are a perfectly shaped coral. In the photo, I, nineteen at the time, sit nearby in a simple, sleeveless dress, a plain pageboy hairstyle and no makeup, except perhaps pink lip gloss. Even today, I appear as a sharp contrast to her: she had elegance and style, I have a more natural, simple look. I'll confess: I don't know how to use makeup. Oh, sure, a little liner and shadow maybe, but beyond that, I don't have a clue, and I'm not even sure I want to at this point. I have grown comfortable (maybe too comfortable) with my uncomplicated look. One time a friend said, "Let's go to the mall and have makeovers, just for fun," and my first reaction was "No, thanks!" I admitted to myself, "I don't want a well-made-up face with perfect arched eyebrows, shaded in with pencil, a covering of foundation, powder, blush. I don't want eyelashes weighed down by mascara, nor do I want an outlined mouth filled with bright color." I sometimes wonder how much of my aversion toward learning better makeup skills is an indirect rejection of Mother?

Even women from healthy homes feel uncomfortable with their bodies and perpetually dissatisfied with their looks. Naomi Wolf points out in *The Beauty Myth* that Western culture has made most women harbor "a dark vein of self-hatred [and] physical obsessions."

But if it's that bad for females from functional homes, what is it like for girls from *un*healthy homes?

Judith Seixas and Geraldine Youcha report in *Children of Alcoholism: A Survivor's Manual* that daughters of alcoholic mothers are uncertain about their femaleness because they absorb "a confusing and often inadequate picture" of womanhood. As Nancy

Friday states in *My Mother/My Self,* girls are strongly influenced by their mother's self-esteem. "It is a deep-down good opinion of oneself that doesn't waver, and it is best given to a daughter by her mother," writes Friday. Far from detecting an unwavering, healthy self-esteem in our mothers, we daughters instead found pain, fear, depression, shame, and self-hatred. This was the role model for womanhood that we internalized.

Menstrual Stories

Puberty is a sensitive time of life, especially for girls. We are turning into women, but we're not sure how to handle it. Unfortunately, many of us daughters of alcoholic mothers felt very alone during this rite of passage. Our mothers may have been present in our homes, but they were usually too drunk, too sick, or too absorbed in their own demons to be guideposts for us.

An amazing number of daughters we talked to hid their periods from their mothers for times ranging from months to years. Danette Case, forty-seven, could not bring herself to tell her mother until she had gone through two cycles. Amanda Little managed to keep her secret for four or five months before her mother found out. Sara Oliver's mother did not know for two years.

Many of us hid our menstruations because we felt ashamed. For some of us, our mothers wouldn't talk about it at all, giving us the impression that menstruation must be something bad. Or our mothers may have insinuated that it was dirty, messy, and horrible, a curse. Or some of us may have been led to believe that it was directly connected to sexual behavior, which, we had also intuited, was dirty and disgusting. Susan Anderson, for example, had been told by her mother that menstruation only occurred after sexual encounters. As a result, Susan, still a virgin, was horrified and felt guilty when she began to bleed.

A further reason we did not want to tell Mother was because we sensed that she could never be discreet about it. In our homes, there were no physical or emotional boundaries. Mother rummaged through our drawers, read our mail and diaries, and listened in on the telephone. No wonder we felt uncomfortable sharing the news of our private bodily functions. Grace King learned the hard way.

Aware that her mother would tell the world, Grace tried to hide her menstrual onset, but her mother found out and immediately went to the phone and called a neighbor woman. "Grace's got her period!" she said. "Come on over." The friend arrived, and Grace's mother poured her a drink and another one for herself. Her mother held up a glass in a toast. "Here's to Grace," she shouted. The two women laughed and settled down to drink. The hours went by, and as they drank, their menstrual horror stories grew more powerful. "Oh, what hideous cramps I used to have!" laughed the neighbor woman. "Oh, hell, yes," said Grace's mother. "I used to be bedridden with them! But mostly I remember those awful rags we had to use. You remember those?" And the two of them proceeded to exchange explicit stories about buckets of bloody rags soaking. "I wished they would just shut up, it was so embarrassing," remembers Grace, now forty.

A last reason many of us kept our menstruations secret was because we were never sure what might set our mothers off. Even the onset of our cycles was fair game, so we hesitated, fearing her ridicule, indifference, anger, or bizarre reactions.

"When I started my period, my mother said, 'So what?'" remembers Rachel Addington.

"She made fun of me," says Charlene Todd.

"When I started my period, she was angry because I bled on her chair," says Jocelyn Pratt.

"She just got juiced one night and came into my room with some maudlin babble about blood and how I should tell her when it happened," says Nancy Codgill. "I was disgusted. I was at Grandma's when it did happen, and I don't think it was important to my mother at all."

"When I started, she said congratulations and told me to use condoms," says Penny McBride.

"My mother laughed at me because I was so concerned as to how much bleeding there was," says Diana Matthews, an LPN from Rhode Island.

Erica Zetterower was told on the day she started, "Shut up, and don't stop up the toilet."

"She laughed and said I would grow breasts and start having sex," says Iris Sheffield.

Nichole Van Tassell's mother was napping when Nichole began to menstruate. "She just yelled that everything I needed was in the drawer and to figure it out myself."

Recalls Cathy Taulbee, "My mother thought it no big deal when I started my period because it was my problem, not hers."

"She made me feel like it was a curse," admits Sherry Love, "like it was just going to be a huge chore. I felt stupid."

Maxine Caldwell was told that she would only be allowed to use napkins, not tampons. "She said it was evil to have something up your vagina," recalls Maxine. "She said it would take away my virginity."

"My mother's reaction to my first menstruation was to be shocked. She couldn't or wouldn't talk about it," remembers Leigh Vives.

Georgina Iler didn't get her period until she was fifteen. Prior to that, her mother's only instructions had been to hand her a box of Kotex and say cryptically, "Here, you'll need these someday." That was the sum total of the mother-daughter talk. So when Georgina first began bleeding, she was confused and afraid that something was wrong. She was scared enough to approach her mother even though she feared her anger. "I remember trying to tell my mother—now this is truly pathetic—following her around the kitchen with my stained panties crumpled up in my hand trying to get her attention to find out if it was what I thought it was," says Georgina, forty-one, an actress. "Would it surprise you if I said she was dismissive?"

Thus, our first impression of what womanhood was all about may have been sullied with negative associations. Our female bodies had done something embarrassing and shameful.

It had been a tense day. Traveling on the train for a family vacation, my parents, Diana, our brother, and I had been essentially trapped together in the tiny room that served as sleeping quarters. I had settled into a corner chair, terrified that my parents would begin another one of the arguments that had become more frequent in the past year since my mother had started to drink more heavily. The chilly tension between my parents felt almost tangible. Mother sat rigidly by the window, her cigarette glowing in her left hand. Dad opened up the Chicago Tribune, *lit his pipe, cleared his throat, and read the editorial page.*

Somehow, the hours passed uneventfully, and we went to the dining car for dinner, where Mother immediately ordered a martini. My heart contracted with grief that my family could look so fine from the outside but be decaying so rapidly on the inside.

These sad thoughts lingered as we returned to the room. I needed to use the rest room, so I stepped into the microscopic cubicle, pulled down my pants, and gasped at the sight of the large red stain. My first period! My initial joy was quickly tempered by the horrible realization that my whole family was outside that door, not five feet away. Blushing, I pulled toilet paper off the roll, wadded it up, and stuffed it inside my soaked underwear. Opening the door, I scanned the room and found my mother dozing on the top bunk, so I climbed the ladder and whispered, "Mother!"

"Huuhhh?" she started awake.

"Mother," I whispered urgently, "I've started to menstruate and my pants are covered with blood."

She let out a long, irritated sigh, which smelled faintly of gin. "No rest for the weary," she said.

I remember her anger as she and I squeezed side by side over the tiny sink in that tiny bathroom. Grumbling, she scrubbed the bloodstained underwear vigorously, angrily, with the white bar of soap, angry, oh so

angry, blaming me, lashing out. I wept loudly, shoulders heaving.
Again, I had done something wrong. No matter how hard I tried to be
good, I was always doing something *to make her mad! When we*
emerged from the rest room, I was doubly embarrassed, for not only was
my washed-out underwear now hanging inside the bathroom, on display
for all to see, but my face was red and swollen from crying.

Learning about Sex and Sexuality

A large number of us were either never told anything about sex or
were given inaccurate information. Both of these stances sent the
subtle message that femaleness was something secretive or forbidden.

"My mother gave me a booklet called 'Growing Up and Liking
It,' " remembers Crystal Inman, who is forty-nine. "After I read it, I
said, 'I'll grow up, but I'm *not* gonna like it!' That was the *only* time
this subject came up! I'm *still* waiting to know where babies come
from," she jokes.

"My mother chose a book, gave it to me, and said, 'Read it; if you
have any questions ask your sister,' " remembers Tanya Griffin,
thirty-four.

Some mothers delegated the job to their husbands. Louisa
McQuaid, a proofreader from Minnesota, learned from her father.
"My mother was drunk, so he sat us three girls down and said, 'You
know what "fucking" is?' Then he said, 'I don't want you doing it.'
I was in the third grade, and it could have been a dance, for all I
knew. I learned much more from friends and reading *Playboy*. It
made no sense to me to go to my mother, as I'd never come to her
for anything important."

When our mothers had an aversion to explaining sexual matters
to us, we were certainly not left with the impression that the female
body was anything to celebrate or enjoy. Whether their attempts
were halfhearted, inaccurate, or incomprehensible, we got the same
message.

Angie Ferro's mother was very drunk at a party when she decided to give Angie her only formal, albeit completely misleading, lesson about the facts of life. As usual, Angie and her brother had been dragged along to the party. Amid the music and laughter, Angie's mother lay down on one of the beds, called Angie over, and pointed to her own groin, saying, "Here are your ovaries, and if the man goes on this side, it's going to be a girl, and this side, it's going to be a boy." This was all she ever told Angie.

"My mother sat me down and half-assed explained it to me," says Susan Steffan. "I thank God my sister had already talked to me or I would have been scared to death."

"She said if a boy touched me, I could get pregnant," remembers Jill Palmer, forty-four, a Maryland office manager.

If the facts of life were a taboo subject for some mothers, birth control was too. Just as we learned about menstruation and sex from friends, books, or experience, many of us could not approach our mothers for advice on birth control. Ginny Durden confesses, "This is really bad and my husband would probably die if he knew I was telling you this, but I'm going to tell you anyhow. When we first started dating, it was *his* idea to go to the gynecologist and get me on birth control pills. I'd never thought about it. Nothing. My mom had never said anything, never a word about that kind of thing."

Our body images may have been further marred if our mothers implied to us, as many of them did, that sex and sexuality were disgusting and dirty. How could we feel proud of our femaleness if it inevitably meant bodily degradation? Many alcoholic women reveal contradictory attitudes about sex. Their sexual behavior may loosen up considerably when they've been drinking, and this leaves the misleading impression that they enjoy sex, when in actuality, they often do not. In truth, many alcoholic women feel reserved, if not frigid, about sex.

Caroline Knapp, a recovering alcoholic explains, in *Drinking: A Love Story* that alcohol and sexuality are closely connected: "Women . . . use alcohol to deaden a wide range of conflicted feelings—longing for intimacy and terror of it; a wish to merge with others and a fear of being consumed; profound uncertainty about how and when to maintain boundaries and how and when to let them down."

In other words, the conflicted feelings about sex are already there; alcohol merely masks them with false feelings of licentiousness. As we will talk about in the next chapter, it is theorized that women predisposed to alcoholism also suffer from social phobias and begin drinking to quell their anxieties, which may include a distaste for sex.

Sharon remembers the only facts-of-life talk she got from her mother.

" 'Sex,' Mama told me, 'is disgusting. Your husband will make you do these horrible things that you won't want to do, but you'll have to,' " Sharon recalls. "That was almost the full text of Mama's birds-and-bees talk. The other part was, 'Don't ever do it before you get married, because if you get pregnant, it'll just kill your daddy.' Maybe it would have. Combined with the daily shame heaped upon him by her drinking, maybe if I'd shamed him too, it would have been more than he could bear."

Other daughters remember their mothers' negative messages about sex. Rachel's mother told Rachel that it was distasteful and painful, though, as Rachel points out, her mother always had someone in her bed anyway. Maxine's mother said that sex was dirty and disgusting and only for procreation. Masturbation was also evil. Yet when drunk, her mother talked about sex all the time. Vickie was told by her mother that women did not like sex because it was too messy and dirty. Carlene's mother showed Carlene a picture of someone with syphilis and added, "Don't do it."

"My mother's attitude toward sex was that men were filthy, just like dogs, she said," recalls Regina Vickers, fifty-nine, a homemaker from Illinois. "When I began to ask questions, she reacted with disgust and wouldn't talk about it."

Alcoholic mothers' distaste for sex is also reflected in their paranoia about their daughters' alleged but often nonexistent sexual activities. A number of respondents mentioned that their mothers had falsely accused them of promiscuous sexual behavior. Maxine's mother was more than paranoid, she was obsessed. From the time Maxine was seven, her mother would accuse her of being sexually active, waking her up during the night and beating her violently and calling her "a little slut."

Maxine, a veterinarian from Alabama, recalls, "She'd be drunk; she'd take me out on this hill, and she'd sit there and tell me, 'I know you've been fooling around with such and such little boy down the road.' I was like, 'What are you talking about?' She said, 'I know you're not a virgin anymore, and unless you tell me what you did, I'm going to beat the hell out of you.' I couldn't tell her anything because I hadn't done anything. And she'd beat me and beat me. She finally ended up taking me to a doctor before she got off of that crap. And they told her I was still a virgin. I never understood how her mind worked. It was *sick.*"

Dianne Carlson's mother would accuse Dianne of being pregnant. One evening, Dianne, who was still a virgin, was standing by the sink washing dishes. She'd been out with her boyfriend earlier. Out of the blue, her mother asked her if she was pregnant. Shocked, Dianne said, "Of course not." Her mother replied, "Well, your legs look all swollen!" Dianne, weeping, said, "Well, I can't help it if I have fat legs!"

Mothers who accuse in this way may be projecting onto their daughters guilt about their own promiscuous behavior or guilt for having had thoughts about the "dirty" act of sex. Again, this contributes to the message that sex is "bad," which affects our attitudes toward our bodies.

Our body images may have been further damaged if we were sexually abused or if we learned about sex in unorthodox ways. "Unfortunately," remarks Kimberly Franks, "I learned the 'facts of life' from the sexual contact perpetrated by my father." Yvonne

Kenney agrees, stating that her early experiences involved "a couple of uncles who couldn't keep their hands off a child!!" Brandi Horan's sexual life "started very young when I was molested by my grandfather on my father's side."

"When I was around five years old, my mother's boyfriend sexually abused me," says Cathryn Silvers. "It lasted a few years, so my sexuality is totally screwed up."

We daughters may also have been exposed to our mothers' more open sexual activities with boyfriends or second or third husbands. Some respondents indicated that they were embarrassed and reluctant eavesdroppers to their mothers' liaisons in nearby rooms. "I walked in on my mom a few times," says Sam Jacobs, a nurse from Washington state. "She was very active."

"My mother didn't think twice about all the noise she was making with whomever she was with," adds Michelle Polinsky.

Their inhibitions removed, some alcoholic mothers may also have said things to us that were unfit for young ears. Katie Shyrock, thirty-six, recalls when her mother told her as a child that her father's penis was too small. Maxine's mother would go into graphic detail about her sexual relations with Maxine's father. "She'd sit there and tell me about her and my father. 'And he wanted me to put my mouth on it . . .' Stuff like that—to a seven year old child. 'Put your mouth on what, Mom?' You know? It was terrible!" asserted Maxine.

Susan Steffan's most important childhood memory occurred on the night when her mother, who was drunk, decided that Susan "needed" to know how to perform oral sex on her boyfriend. "She wanted me to practice on my dad!" says Susan with a shudder. "At first I thought she was kidding. When I realized that she wasn't I said no, then I screamed *no!* I ran to my room and locked and barricaded my door. This was in January, and for this stunt I was grounded until the middle of September. The subject was never brought up again, though. Needless to say, I associate a great deal of anger with this memory."

Through these unfortunate sexual experiences, we may come to associate femaleness with shame and degradation.

Feelings about Our Physical Appearances

Many of us received harsh criticism about our physical appearances. As we have learned during our research, alcoholic mothers tend to be much harder on their daughters than on their sons, perhaps because the drinking exacerbates whatever natural mother-daughter rivalry exists and opens up the floodgates for the free expression of it.

Beyond the fact that alcoholics are merely grandmasters—or in this case, grand mistresses—of the fine art of verbal abuse, a mother's denigration of her daughter's looks may reflect the mother's jealousy. Heavy drinking ages a woman fast. A woman who drinks, who is poorly nourished, who takes prescription and street drugs, who smokes, who keeps late hours, who loses sleep, and who lives the generally unhealthy lifestyle that accompanies alcoholism, will find her looks declining faster than normal. If, simultaneously, her daughter is coming into adolescence, that point in life "when youth and beauty are center stage," as Nancy Friday says in *The Power of Beauty,* any normal twinges of envy that a *non*alcoholic mother might feel are amplified and distorted for the alcoholic mother, causing her to release her fury upon her daughter.

Alicia Fortune suspects that envy fostered her mother's criticism of her. By the time Alicia was entering puberty, her mother was already fatally ill from drinking. "I think she was jealous because she was getting sick, and her looks had deteriorated terribly in a short time," says Alicia. "I would assume that it bothered her that I didn't look so sick or terrible."

The alcoholic mother's envy may go deeper. Despite her prolific protestations and denials about having any kind of problem, she very likely knows—at some level—that her own life *is* being damaged by drinking, yet she feels powerless to stop. Her daughter, on the other hand, is young, fresh, and just starting out. So, even as an alcoholic mother hopes for her daughter's wide-open future, she may also envy it.

A daughter may also be in jeopardy of her alcoholic mother's wrath because, as any good shrink knows, parents see their same-sex child as extensions of themselves. Chances are, by putting down her daughter, the alcoholic mother is merely revealing her subconscious contempt for herself. In her account *Drinking: A Love Story,* Knapp describes the inner pain and self-denigration that an alcoholic experiences: "Active alcoholism is such a demeaning state. Some part of you that resists denial, acts as the observer, quietly aware. I'd look at myself in the mirror some nights and I'd sense that observer staring back, loathing what she saw: a depressed, anxious, self-sabotaging thirty-four-year-old woman who could not seem to get out of her own way. Dark circles beneath her eyes, creases of worry across her forehead, those little burst blood vessels flecked across her skin. Sick and tired. A sick and tired woman."

The alcoholic mother who lashes out at her daughter is attempting to purge herself of her own self-hatred. The trouble is, as young girls, we often absorb that self-hatred and hold on to it.

Susan Steffan thought she was "the ugliest thing on earth" to begin with, and her mother never said anything to contradict that. Then, one day, her mother got drunk and chopped off Susan's very thick, curly hair with texturing shears. For the next few weeks, she yelled at Susan, saying that her unevenly cropped hair, now many different lengths but too short to be pulled back into a ponytail, always looked messy. A few weeks later, on Susan's thirteenth birthday, her mother punished her by cutting her hair even shorter, so she looked like a boy. "I was then called all kinds of names at school," says Susan. "Even today, I still hate the way I look. My friends tell me I'm pretty, and my boyfriend constantly calls me his 'beautiful lady,' but when I look in the mirror, I still see ugly."

Donna Cartee knows now from looking at photos that she was beautiful as a young teen. However, her mother always told her that the bangs she wore looked like "a roll of poop" on her forehead, and added that Donna's ears were too big for her to wear her hair behind them. "I believed her," says Donna, fifty. "Today, I still feel really lousy about my appearance."

Jackie McClain feels "terrible" about her appearance today "because she taught me I was ugly and stupid and would never amount to anything."

Jackie, fifty, continues, "When I think about my mother's verbal abuse, the first thing that comes to my mind is, 'You're not worth tits on a boar.' That was her favorite. Nice southern expression. 'You're useless, you're worthless, you'll never amount to a hill of beans, you don't have the sense God gave a rotten apple.' I was extremely ugly. When I was a kid, my mouth grew ahead of everything else. Actually, my dad was hardest on me about that, but she stood there and went along with it, you know? I was likened to a guy in town who was kind of the town jerk. He had this huge, huge mouth, which he never kept closed, it was always just hanging open. In my mind, I can see this pasty-faced guy with this really soft marshmallowy skin and these bi-i-i-g lips hanging open." Jackie became extremely self-conscious about her mouth and covered it often. Soon, she developed the habit of picking the skin off her lips until they bled, and even today she cannot stop doing this.

"I've never really gotten over that criticism," continues Jackie. "You know, men love my lips, love my mouth. But that makes me want to cover up even more. I feel horrible about my body now. Horrible. I'm with a man now who's just so in love with my body and my figure and my hair and my mouth and my face. He's teaching me that I'm okay, and he's helping me to learn to love myself. But I still see those flaws. I come back and I say to myself, 'It's okay. He really loves you, and it's okay.' But the thing is, I don't love it. I have an immense amount of shame about my body. My mother taught me a lot of shame about my body, and I've had a real hard time with it."

While we heard numerous stories of alcoholic mothers' overtly cruel put-downs of their daughter's looks, we discovered another interesting phenomenon. Those of us whose mothers were indifferent toward our looks, or those of us whose mothers were even complimentary, *still* tended to have exaggeratedly negative body images.

This is not too surprising. For one thing, the hallmark of an alcoholic personality is inconsistency. Mother's radical fluctuations of temperament, character, and behavior surely contributed to her lack of credibility. "Sometimes my mother would tell me I was beautiful," says Jana Ellis, fifty. "Sometimes she would tell me I was ugly. She mostly made me feel unlovable."

Furthermore, how could we believe someone whose own life was a web of lies and denial? How could she be telling the truth about our looks if she lied about so much else? Her very behavior nullified the sincerity of her compliments. Every day, in a hundred different painful ways, she sent out an unspoken but far more powerful message: "I love my booze more than you." Playing second fiddle to a bottle of alcohol was as much of a put-down as any well-aimed verbal barb she could fling.

Lorie Deal, a Pennsylvania telemarketer, was told that she was the smartest, most beautiful girl in the world, but she never felt that way. Nan MacGregor recalls, "My mother always told me that I was beautiful and that I looked just like her. But I'd look at her after a 'drunk' and see ugly."

Sometimes an added confirmation that our looks weren't valued enough was our mothers' willingness to drink away the limited family finances, which might have been used for our clothes, makeup, hair, or teeth. The money squandered on booze and, possibly, the added costs of wrecked vehicles, burned furniture, or personal injuries was money not available for our beautification. Again, the message came through to us as to where we ranked on the priority list.

Diana Matthews has two teeth that bother her today because her parents could no longer continue her orthodontry; she had her braces removed six months too early.

Victoria Brinson says that because her mother's drinking was a financial drain, "we never had clothes or food. My clothes were always torn. When we were young, we did not have new sneakers or shoes, everything was a hand-me-down or bought at the Salvation Army. As I grew older, I stole my clothes and makeup."

"My mother would lose money by hiding it when drunk and then be unable to find it when sober," says Charlene Harris. "Our clothes were either given to me used from a neighbor, or I sewed my own clothes. I also stole clothes by shoplifting. My self-esteem was very low. My teeth suffered from neglect too."

Mama chose my clothes for me until I began college, including my eyeglasses, shoes, and underwear, opting to pick, it seemed to me, the ugliest, cheapest things imaginable. For a five-day school week, I had three sale-rack or homemade dresses. As for underwear, I'd had to beg to get my first bra, and after that, I got two bras a year, the cheapest cotton ones she could buy, while she herself owned several expensive lacy ones. I had one pair of shoes a year, unless I outgrew them, which she considered a personal attack on the family's financial stability. When I had to have eyeglasses in ninth grade—for poor eyesight I had known about since fifth grade, but had been unable to convince her about—she chose for me the nerdiest blue rhinestone-studded-cat-eyed monstrosities that had ever existed. During my junior year, my friend Judy Moreau knocked them from my face accidentally one day at a pep rally; they fell twenty feet or so through the bleachers and broke. I was ecstatic; Mama was furious. Even though she always managed to scrape up enough money for booze and cigarettes, she resented the cost of my clothes and accessories.

For most of us, it hasn't come easily. We've had to work at appreciating our appearances, our bodies, our sexuality. Of course, this has meant focusing on our inner beings, which is the source of our negative self-perceptions. If we dislike our bodies and womanhood, it's because we really dislike ourselves. Some of us have built back our damaged egos through therapy; others of us have reached self-acceptance through the wisdom that comes from growing older. But overall, most of us have been able to develop more positive body images by discovering our own unique styles, by learning to accept ourselves the way we are—and by having a sense of humor.

"Well, thank God for hair straightener and Clairol, contact lenses, straightened teeth, and makeup," remarks Crystal Inman. "I'm happy with how I look. I still hate my nose, though. If I win the lottery, it goes first. I didn't inherit my mom's attractiveness. My mother was beautiful. Tall, slim, attractive. I looked awful: kinky hair, big nose, 'Coke-bottle' glasses, braces. (Thank God I went to an all-girls Catholic school. We all looked 'ugly': no makeup, and nuns who thought we needed humility.) I'm just lucky 'technology' in beauty has helped me along, although I'm still trying to 'regain my figure' (after the birth of my last child nineteen years ago). I'm down to a size fourteen from an eighteen and working hard to get to a ten-and-a-half."

Marta Hendrix's mother hated long hair and makeup and called Marta a slut from the time she was fourteen. "To this day my hair is long," says Marta. "I love makeup and I do everything feminine. I love the seductive clothing, the high heels, everything my mother never wore. I enjoy who I have become. I like my appearance. I would like to be a few inches taller and a few pounds lighter, but overall, I am happy."

"Once my clothes are on, I'm okay!" says Jody Macolly. "My stomach isn't flat, I have stretch marks, my boobs are too small, and my legs and hips are flabby. But I'm a strong person, a good mother, and a caring person."

"I've been blessed with a husband who loves me," says Sherry Love. "I have a great job, a home I love, two dogs that are like children to me. We have enough money to live nicely. I have lots of friends and like being a friend. I keep busy at home and have very few worries. I'm much happier now."

"I think I look damn good!" admits Susanna Moore, thirty-nine. "I hated myself as a teenager. I had very low self-esteem. My mother was very critical about my appearance. My body could use more toning, but at my age and after two kids, I'm comfortable with it."

Mary Starr, forty-three, says she has grown much more confident with age. Now that she's over forty, she knows what to do to stay in shape and feel good. She has also learned to handle stress and depression. "I didn't have a clue or any confidence growing up," she says. "When people would stare at me, I thought they knew my secret at home. I would have panic attacks. I never had anyone tell me I could be successful and be anything I wanted. I didn't realize it until my thirties."

"I am happy inside, so I feel it shows outside," says Summer O'Brien. "Growing up, I felt ugly, although I was told I was pretty. Now I am pretty and young-looking for fifty-four, although I would change my weight, and have a face-lift and liposuction to suck out the fat, and buy a new uplift bra!"

"My boyfriend, family, and friends think I'm just fine," says Lorena Gibson. "So do I, but if I had millions, boy what I would do!"

As adults, many of us have carved out a stylistic niche for ourselves and have found more important compensations in life than physical appearance. But let's face it, in a society that constantly promotes female physical beauty, we may have to work hard to overthrow our negative body images and reach a level of comfort. It's difficult to silence the voices from the past.

When I was about sixteen, I had recently read some romanticized history in which the heroine brushed her hair one hundred strokes each night. That seemed so elegant and romantic to me that I decided to try it. Seated with most of the family in the dining room, which is where we all generally gathered, I was brushing and brushing, feeling so mature and sophisticated. Occasionally, I'd stop and pick up the hand mirror to see if my efforts were paying off in shiny healthy locks.

Mama was drinking that evening, and when she drank, she avoided the family group, preferring instead her own lonely company in the dark on the porch. But on one of her forays into the kitchen to retrieve another can of beer, she saw my hair-brushing ritual and stopped to watch. I thought, mistakenly, that she was pleased, since she often yelled at me to take better care of my hair. Usually, Mama noticed me only when she disapproved of me. She seemed especially to criticize my appearance, and the arguments usually centered around my makeup or my hair. My hair was too long, it was too short, it was too oily, it was too dry, the style was too old, or it was too young. When a woman I admired, the school librarian, wore her hair a new way, and I tried the same style, Mama hooted with derisive laughter.

Mama had never taught me to wear makeup, though she herself wore it well. She'd carefully pencil in brown eyebrow color over her perfectly shaped but pale eyebrows, and she'd apply her foundation with a delicate hand, unlike some of the mothers in town, whose too-dark foundation ended along their jawlines, exposing throats that in contrast seemed too harshly white. Mama's lipstick was never a glaring color, but a delicate peach. I'd sneak around and get into her makeup, as most little girls do, but because I didn't have her coloring, it was never right on me. So I bought my own as often as I could—orangey tan foundation, glittery blue eye shadow that I wore into my untweezed heavy black eyebrows, black kohl eyeliner entirely encircling my eye, and mascara so thick you could do a handstand on it. It left greasy black streaks on my glasses. I favored either no lipstick (my lips were skinny, Mama told me, so I never wanted to draw attention to them) or else the popular white lipstick of the 1960s. In short, I usually looked like the "before" picture in the teen glamour magazines, never the "after."

Mama didn't teach me how to roll my hair either, saying that I had curly hair and didn't need to know how. But this was the late 1960s: curly hair was the social kiss of death; straight hair was in. Because her *own hair was straight and she permed it to add curls, Mama didn't understand that I needed to roll my hair in order to take curls out. When I went off to college, I learned from my roommate how to use orange juice cans as rollers so that my hair would be straighter. We even practiced ironing the curls and waves from each other's hair, but the starch buildup on the dorm irons usually made hair ironing a dangerous affair. I didn't get to have my first "good hair day" until the 1970s, when curly hair came back into style.*

But that night when I was sixteen, as Mama paused to watch me brush my hair, I thought maybe she was pleased, so I primped a little as she gazed at me through red-rimmed, swollen eyelids. Suddenly she said, her voice dripping caustically, "You think you're pretty. But you're not."

Chapter Five

Passing the Torch:
Anxieties and Addictions

~

"*I have made a promise to myself that I am going to do what it takes to stop the cycle in my family.*"
    —*Judy Cionotti, thirty-three, office assistant, St. Paul, Minnesota*

"*I know I would rather be dead than be like my mother when she was drunk.*"
    —*Maxine Caldwell, thirty-six, veterinarian, Mobile, Alabama*

~

My head was spinning. I was going to pass out. My tightened chest could not draw air. I knew I was going to die.

"What's the matter, Ellie?" asked my husband, who was driving the car.

"I don't know . . . I'm sick . . ." I breathed heavily. This suffocating feeling had come over me before, but never as bad as this. This time, I was really going to die! It must be a stroke or some sudden catastrophic event. A giant blood clot was lodging itself into a cerebral vessel. In just microseconds, my whole brain would explode. My hammering heart would seize up in a vice of unbearable pain. I was going to die! I felt nauseated and could already feel my bodily functions shutting down. I was fading away into the darkness. Death was coming. I didn't want to go. Twenty-seven years old is too young to die, screamed my fading inner voice!

My husband wasn't sure what to believe. He knew I was high-strung.

But what if it was real this time? As I bent over in the front seat, gasping for breath, expecting the curtain to fall, he detoured down Main Street and pulled into the parking lot of the hospital emergency room. For one who was dying, I did a pretty good job of staggering out of the car and hurrying inside the swinging white doors, with my husband at my side. Soon I lay on a stretcher in a small room, shivering in my sleeveless tank top. A kind young doctor pressed a stethoscope to my heart, read my blood pressure, beamed his light into my eyes and asked me a series of questions. Remarkably, I was already beginning to feel better—how embarrassing!

"Well," said the doctor, after reviewing all my vital signs, "I really don't see anything wrong with you. But you know, we're seeing a lot of this phenomenon nowadays, especially among women in their twenties and thirties."

"What is it?" I asked.

"It's called a panic attack," he replied. "It's not a real illness, as such, but the attacks themselves are very real, and they occur in people who get very stressed or depressed. Are you by any chance depressed?"

For the past year before that panic attack, I'd had several smaller events. A few months earlier, I'd had to leave work because the same horrible sensation had washed over me. The room was spinning. My feet and hands became numb. Terrified, with pounding heart, and certain I would keel over dead on the workplace floor, I'd managed to hide the fact that I was dying and told the boss in an almost normal voice that I thought I was getting the flu and needed to go home.

"It has to be a stroke," I thought as I hurried to the car, rubbing my numb hands together and stomping my feet on the ground. However, as I slowly coached the feeling back into my extremities and the "stroke" subsided, I was able to drive home and collapse in bed. How lovely it felt to lie down, alone, in a quiet room, covered with warm blankets, listening to birds tweeting softly on the pine branches outside. How lovely it would be if I could just stay right here for the next decade or so. But of course I didn't have the luxury of doing that.

Often during the past year I had not felt well. But I could never define exactly what was wrong; I could not have pointed to a specific pain and said, "Oh, I have such a throbbing in my left quadrant." I just felt a vague heaviness everywhere, as though my bloodstream was lined with lead. I could not shake the unwavering secret conviction that I was harboring some rare, asymptomatic fatal disease that would not be discovered until after I'd dropped dead, which I was certain would happen soon.

And now I was in the emergency room, very embarrassed at not having died, and the doctor was saying something about taking a very mild tranquilizer.

"Oh, no!" I replied, "I don't believe in pharmaceuticals." A vision of Mother's medicine cabinet, crammed with antidepressants, tranquilizers, and God knew what else, hovered before me.

"I know, I know," the doctor was saying, "But this is extremely mild." He turned and reached into the stainless steel cabinet, surveyed the rows of samples, and pulled out a small bottle. He tapped one pill into his white plastic-gloved hand and said, "One is not going to hurt you. Try it. It will make you feel better."

"Go ahead, Ellie," urged my husband. "It would do you good to relax a little bit for a change. You're much too tense."

So I swallowed the pill, and soon, a lovely warmth spread through my stiff muscles. I felt lighter, as though released from a body cast. Best of all, the dark thoughts retreated as feelings of peace and contentment flowed in. Had I ever felt this good? I filled the prescription the doctor gave me, used them and the two or three refills. A pleasant vacation from myself was just what I needed.

I didn't become addicted to tranquilizers, but I can surely understand Ohow easy it might be, how people who have experienced this mellow state of mind would never want it to end. But as much as I would have loved to walk on air forever, a part of me kept whispering, "Be careful! You're becoming just like Mother!"

None of us wants to follow our mother's example; addiction is, after all, a crucial woman's issue, not the least of which is the strong impact on the next generation. If we become alcoholics or drug addicts ourselves, we pass on to our children the same painful legacy we endured from our mothers. But as much as we do not want to be like her, we may have more in common with her than we realize. For a start, we may have inherited a predisposition to the depression and anxiety disorders that often prompt addictions in the first place.

Depression, Anxiety, Stress

In *Addiction: From Biology to Drug Policy,* Dr. Avram Goldstein writes that studies on alcoholism rates among identical twins and fraternal twins show that "identical twins do (or do not) become alcoholics with a significantly higher concordance rate than that of fraternal twins, suggesting a significant heritability of a predisposition to alcoholic addiction." At the risk of oversimplifying a complex phenomenon, this predisposition for alcoholism may include, as one of its components, a tendency to be anxious, fearful, or stressed. Dr. R. Reid Wilson states in *Don't Panic: Taking Control of Anxiety Attacks,* "The first centers affected [by drinking] are the inhibitory ones, so alcohol's first effect is usually the removal of tensions and inhibitions. This is the primary reason why people with anxiety, fears, or panic might turn to drinking." In *Children of Alcoholism: A Survivor's Manual,* Judith Seixas and Geraldine Youcha agree that "a supersensitive nervous system may be part of the inherited package that predisposes some people to alcoholism." In fact, two-thirds of the alcoholics in a study reported by Wilson had anxiety disorders, such as agoraphobia and other phobias. Another study revealed that the majority of phobic alcoholics had been phobic *before* they became alcoholics.

This may explain why such a large number of daughters who are not necessarily addicts themselves report depression, agoraphobia, nervous breakdowns, mental illness, and other maladies related to emotional sensitivity.

In fact, of the two hundred daughters who participated in our survey, well over half (57 percent) answered the open-ended question about the state of their physical and emotional health with reports of current or past depression, mental illness, anxiety disorders, high stress and/or emotional instability. They described a potpourri of conditions, including nervous breakdowns, bipolarity, multiple personality, depression, post-traumatic stress disorder (PTSD), emotional volatility, panic attacks, and agoraphobia. They also reported the use of antidepressants and therapy.

Some typical responses:

- "At times I am overemotional, cry easily over hurt feelings, and feel left out."
- "I am very depressed and have been for a long time. I am sad."
- "Mom died in 1976, and it took at least five or six years for me to recover from the stress of my life. I'm sixty-two now and feeling better than I ever have. I've also had about fifteen years of psychotherapy. I developed agoraphobia in my late teens."
- "I'm currently under psychiatric care for bipolar disorder."
- "Emotionally, I'm healing, although I have a long way to go. I'm fighting for me and my son."
- "I have had anxiety and nervous situational depression . . . that I believe to be directly tied to induced stress."
- "I've been on antidepressants for five years . . ."
- "I suffer from depression and PTSD."

I spent two years of my life as an agoraphobic. It began several years after I was married, during a really horrible patch in our lives that didn't improve until my older son was nearly four years old. Shortly after Stephen's first birthday, Doug's company had again transferred us, this time to Baton Rouge. We'd decided to buy a house, so Doug lived alone in a hotel room in Baton Rouge for six weeks while all the details of the house buying were worked out. That six weeks was lonely, problem plagued, and devastating. Stephen had started having nightmares, screaming and not sleeping unless I allowed him to sleep in my bed. I missed Doug, and I missed having help with our son. Naively, I hoped

*that when we moved into our lovely new home, everything would be
wonderful. That was not to be.*

*Doug, always a high-energy person, turned his feelings of inadequacy
as a husband and parent into a desire to be the Ideal Company Man. He
worked ten to fourteen hours a day, seven days a week. As a reward, the
company demoted him, reducing his salary to one we couldn't afford to
live on. So he changed jobs—twice. We sold the house, after having lived
in it only six months, and moved into a dirty, rundown duplex elsewhere
in the city. I became more and more afraid and insecure, seldom leaving
home.*

*Shortly after we moved in, I had walked outside to get the newspaper,
only to be addressed by a neighbor's child: "Hey, fat lady!" After that,
I hardly went outside at all. I didn't answer the door. I didn't answer
the phone. I stayed indoors with Stephen all the time, reading him his
favorite book* Where the Wild Things Are *several times a day. Doug
and I grew further apart. I often contemplated suicide, though I knew I
couldn't do that to Stephen.*

*Doug was after me to get a job, but I refused, fearing both to put
Stephen in day care and to face the cruel outside world. My weight
ballooned, and my self-esteem plummeted. Strangely, now that I'm past
that bad time and am able to look back, I have realized that both my
mother and my sister Sheila also experienced agoraphobia and depression. It has definitely been a "family" illness.*

Our high level of anxieties, depressions, and nervous disorders
may spring from the same biochemical culprit that fostered our
mothers' need to drink. As these daughters reveal below, many
alcoholic mothers drank to quiet their dark inner voices.

"My mother used alcohol to chase away the fears she had,"
remarks Anne Marie Cain. "Her esteem was low, and drinking
made her powerful, worthy, larger than life." Kitty Dellinger says,
"My mother drank to forget." Theresa Flynn states, "My mother
didn't feel she fit in with anyone and was always trying to say the

right thing to be liked. She needed to drink to lose her social anxiety." Polly Tyson adds, "She hated her life and her choices, and alcohol was used as an excuse for her behavior."

Given ours and our mothers' backgrounds, it is perhaps inevitable that there are many of us whose natural-born tendency to be nervous or depressed has led us—just as it led our mothers—to multiple addictions. The daughters in our study, in fact, seldom reported just one addiction.

Children of alcoholics may have a genetic predisposition for alcoholism. Daughters in particular are vulnerable. "Because of physiological differences, women become intoxicated faster than men and they feel the long-term effects of alcohol after a shorter period of time," says Kim Dude, director of the Alcohol and Drug Abuse Prevention Team and the Wellness Resource Center at the University of Missouri. And if it is in our genes to become addicted, our home environments do not help. When we grow up in alcoholic homes, the abuse damages our self-esteem, so we may be drawn to mind-altering substances to relieve the resulting feelings of anxiety and depression. "For female alcoholics, self-esteem is a significant factor," remarks Dude. Laura Lindsteadt, a therapist at the Arthur Center, adds that depression, more frequent in women than in men, often motivates women to drink. "We see a lot of women who come here for treatment who are suffering from symptoms of depression," she states. Not only is the stage for addiction set by our heredity and damaged self-esteem, we are also influenced by the examples set for us by Mother and the easy access to her addictive substances.

Audrey Moody, thirty-seven and an active alcoholic, used to drink with her mother. "Those were the best times I ever had," she says. Ironically, Audrey's mother stopped drinking seven months ago, but Audrey hasn't. Mickey Ballard, twenty-eight, began drinking at an early age too, "probably because of the easy access of it. There was nobody to tell me no. My mother didn't care. As long as she kept me out of her hair."

In addition to being influenced by our mothers, we may later be influenced by boyfriends and husbands. As we discuss in another chapter, daughters of alcoholic mothers frequently marry substance abusers, whose attitudes and habits may reinforce or precipitate our addictions.

Only 10 percent of our respondents reported that their mothers were recovering from alcoholism. Another 2 percent said skeptically that their mothers *claimed* to be off alcohol; another 3 percent said health problems and removal to nursing homes had forced their mothers to stop drinking involuntarily. Thus, the majority of our still-living mothers are active alcoholics; the majority of the deceased mothers died of alcohol-related causes. Ironically, however, the effects of our mothers' long-term alcoholism may be one of the reasons most of us daughters have been able to control the role of alcohol in our own lives.

To our question "Do you currently drink?" 57 percent of the participants responded yes. This group includes those who drink in moderation but are always aware of their risks, so they ration their intake; those who once had a phase of heavy drinking, but outgrew it without getting addicted; and those who sounded frightened because they think (or know) they *do* have a problem and don't know what to do about it. Forty-three percent of our respondents said they did not drink at all. Twenty-five percent of these nondrinkers volunteered that they were recovering alcoholics. (Because we did not specifically ask about recovery from alcoholism, there may have been an even larger number of recovering alcoholics among the nondrinkers.) Many other nondrinkers noted that they did not drink because they were terrified of becoming like their mothers.

Goldstein writes, "We have learned enough already to suggest that children of alcoholics might well be advised never to touch alcohol." Many of us have strong family histories of alcoholism. Not only did we have mothers who drank, we had fathers, grandparents, brothers, sisters, uncles, and aunts who were alcoholics. Later, even some of our children succumbed. Some of us are fearful enough of potential addiction to become teetotalers.

"I fear alcohol addiction and have no taste or desire for alcohol," says Gretchen, who has painful memories of being taken to bars and watching her mother urinate on herself before passing out.

"I'll not be like her," agrees Rachel, who does not drink. She remembers how her mother would stay at the bars until closing time, leaving Rachel and her brother unattended. Then she'd arrive home drunk, with some stranger. "She would sleep till ten A.M. and then start all over again."

Shawna is also a teetotaler because she realizes that, with an alcoholic father too, "My chances of becoming an alcoholic would be about seventy-five percent if I drank."

"I don't drink," says Heather McPherson, whose mother still drinks, smokes pot, and uses other drugs. "Because everyone makes choices—I choose not to be like her because I hate her. I wouldn't want to be hated by so many people. It would be a miserable life."

Others of us drink cautiously, in moderation, always aware of the possibility that alcoholism could creep up on us. Mia Mitchell says that the difference between her and her mother is that she, Mia, can stop after one or two beers, but her mother never could. Jo Ann Stills is also confident that she can keep her modest drinking under control. "I've seen what alcohol can do to a person, family, and society and I refuse to be a part of that destruction," she explains. As a child, Jo Ann knew all the bar phone numbers by heart because her mother was always at those bars.

Vickie Reaves, the only member of her immediate family who has not been committed to an alcoholism treatment program, says, "I drink but don't have the same taste for gallon jugs of Gallo Rhine wine as my mother did."

Many of us go through phases of heavy drinking and drug use but luckily have been able to stop as soon as we have outgrown it.

Cherry, thirty-five, now drinks "twice a year and on New Year's" but went through a drinking period for eight years. She stopped abruptly when her first child was born and now rarely drinks. "I would not do that to my kids," she explains. "I have two or three drinks a month," admits Jane Farrell, a Missouri bank teller. "I quit drugs four years ago. I once was very concerned about alcoholism but basically grew out of the need to be drunk or high."

Ellie went through a drinking phase too, as she describes below:

"Hi, Ellie, how's it going? Want a beer?"

Every Saturday night, we would all come together at one house or another for a long laughing evening of music, dancing, drinking, and pot smoking. Most of us were married and had young children, so we brought the kids along and shooed them off to play somewhere while we adults had a good time. I looked forward to these gatherings. Walking in the door, smiling, greeting friends, I would gravitate immediately toward the ice-filled cooler and pull out a beer. Gripped in my hand, the cold aluminum can felt good, reassuring, like a bottle of forthcoming confidence. I pulled the tab with a loud click and whoosh. Raising the can to my mouth, I would swallow that first cold sip. Aaaaah! The ritual itself was familiar and relaxing. Soon that warm feeling of community and connectedness would follow as my tension and self-consciousness evaporated, allowing me to be more open, flirtatious, and socially daring. I walked through the crowd of friends, beer in hand, conversing and laughing, maybe a little too loud. (When I mentioned to a friend who was not part of this crowd that when I drank, I became flirtatious, she burst out laughing and said, "You? I can't imagine you being flirtatious!" Maybe that sums up the way I was perceived by others when sober: serious, staid, boring.)

Several hours into our Saturday night parties, the pipe would begin making the rounds. After our beer highs were sufficiently enhanced, we'd begin dancing. Sometimes, we'd gather around the piano, and while someone pounded out a song, we'd bunch together, arm in arm, and sing heartily, swaying back and forth to the music. What I remember most from those days was feeling accepted, popular, desirable. Until the next morning, that is.

Inevitably, upon awakening in my own bed, I would review the events of the previous night. I would fret and agonize over every conversation, every comment. Had I been too forward, too foolish? My self-consciousness always returned, full force.

Fortunately, during these years, I never became addicted to alcohol. One day, after I'd decided to go back to school for an advanced degree, I stepped back and looked at myself. Realizing that I sought relaxation through beer just a little too much, I simply stopped drinking. I am thankful for whatever complex combinations of heredity, environment, and personality spared me from the same pain my mother endured. To say that my will was and still is stronger than hers is only partly true; to say that my genetic predisposition for alcoholism was weaker might be more true. Thank God.

Now, years later, having found genuine happiness rather than the false and temporary one offered by alcohol, I don't drink very much. Only on special occasions, perhaps. I can take it or leave it. I usually leave it.

Some of the daughters we heard from (18 percent of the group who drinks) sounded genuinely alarmed about their drinking. Predictably, these women seemed to have one common denominator, in addition to having an alcoholic mother: they were in emotional pain, with very low self-esteem.

"I drink to cover my pain and to cope with my life," admits Jackie McClain. "My health is poor. I have chronic fatigue, so I drink too much. Emotionally, I'm a wreck: I have blackouts from depression, a poor memory, and am generally suffering from post-traumatic stress disorder." Jackie has also struggled with smoking, anorexia, and bulimia.

Jane Howard swerves over curbs and flattens tires when she

drives, and her husband has asked her to quit drinking. She is worried about herself too but doesn't know what to do. "I'm out of shape, and I'm depressed, with low self-esteem," she explains. "I try to be a good mother and wife, but I'm very moody. I think I am a loner, isolated and paranoid. I have a steady job as a full-time nursing student, mother, and wife, but I am unhappy and never good enough." Jane, an ex-smoker, also describes herself as a compulsive overeater.

"I never want to be like my mother, but it's too late, and I don't know how to turn things around," admits Sherry Spence, who says she has a drinking problem. "More times than not, I wish I had never been born. Whenever I'm lonely, I eat and get high. I'm very much like my mother in the aspects that I don't do anything to change a bad situation only because I don't know how. I had no role models for good things."

Monique Perkins states that she has a drinking problem. "No matter how hard I tried, I was never good enough," she says. "My mother held the firm belief that if you tell someone they 'stink' at something, they will try harder to achieve. It didn't work for me. I just quit trying. I suffered a major depression and somehow managed to go back to college. I was awarded three academic scholarships which were announced in our local newspaper. Her comment was, 'Who would give a piece of shit like you anything?' "

Recovered Alcoholics

We were pleased and encouraged, however, to learn that at least 25 percent of the currently nondrinking daughters who participated in our study are recovering from alcoholism. Just like the respondents who fear they have a drinking problem, the recovering daughters also battle low self-esteem, but with the help of AA, therapy, or religion, they are beginning to strengthen their self-images as well as remain sober. "I am a recovered alcoholic, and I have many days where I can slip backward into my low self-esteem," says Caryl Brookins, forty-seven. "I have had to do a lot of work in this area, and I am working hard at loving myself as I am." Phyllis Torrence, fifty-five, has not had a drink since 1986; Carlene Wood, thirty-one, has been sober and clean for six years, Dorothy Groover, twenty-eight, has been sober for twenty months. They all say their lives are much better now. Dorothy, who still finds herself repeating some of her mother's parenting patterns, is particularly comforted by the fact that at least because of her sobriety she is able to see her own weaknesses as a mother, whereas her mother never did. Caryl, Phyllis, Carlene, and Dorothy are just a few of the many women who are recovering.

Many daughters told us how they were inspired to become sober by their love for their children. A turning point for Katie Shyrock, a counselor from Wisconsin, occurred several years ago when she entered detox. At the time, her youngest child was just beginning to talk. During a family visit, Katie, who was still struggling with addiction in the detox center, held her child on her lap, and suddenly, the baby spoke to her for the first time, saying haltingly, "I love you, Mommy." Katie mists at the memory. From that moment on, she knew she would never drink or take drugs again. And she hasn't. "I have been sober for four years and I haven't had a cigarette in six years," she says.

Cathryn Silvers is determined to "break the chain of screwed-up lives." Cathryn began to drink to numb the pain of having poor self-esteem, a problem that has hindered her personal growth all her life. Eventually, she slid into alcoholism. Now that she's joined AA, she has stopped drinking, and her emotional health is getting better, although she still has to work hard at not being verbally abusive to her children.

Jessica Orvis, forty-one, knew by the age of twenty-two that she was an alcoholic. "I couldn't believe I was becoming my mother, who I detested because of alcoholism. It scared me to look in the mirror and see her, since we looked so much alike." Jessica began going to AA and is now sober. She was also able to quit her twelve-year, pack-a-day smoking habit.

Drugs

Goldstein defines a drug as "any chemical agent that affects biologic function," so this technically includes alcohol, nicotine, and even caffeine. However, for the sake of clarity, when we refer to "drugs," we are generalizing about prescription medications, such as Valium, and illegal drugs, such as pot, cocaine, or heroin. Many of our mothers took pills that were legally prescribed by doctors. The problem was, our mothers usually didn't mention to the doctor that this was not the only bottle in their pharmacopoeias, nor did they call it to the doctor's attention that they would be washing these pills down with alcohol. In addition, some of our mothers used street drugs.

Just as a majority of us became drinkers and smokers, some of us also became drug users. On our survey, we did not ask any direct or isolated questions about drug use; information about that was voluntarily added to the questionnaire by 8 percent of the respondents, who wrote down that they had once used or currently use drugs. (There may have been more women who fit into this category but who did not mention it.) Rose Habegger, Maxine Caldwell, and Lorena Gibson are just a few ex-drug users. Rose has been clean for two and a half years, Maxine quit cocaine cold turkey by herself several years ago, and Lorena has been drug-free for four months. Brandi Horan, a twenty-two-year-old college student who has been off drugs for two and a half years, says she is "happy, positive and excited about life" now that she is clean. She is also engaged to be married.

Sharon's sister Sally has been addicted to prescription pills, as Sharon describes below:

* * *

The phone rings, and it's my brother-in-law, Arthur. I am amazed because he seldom phones me, so my first thought is, "What's wrong with Sally?" Sally, my baby sister, is ten years younger than I am, and I have always been her mother, her friend, and her sister, all rolled into one. I am the one she calls whenever anything is wrong.

This time, something is very wrong. Sally has been admitted into the hospital, not for the many health problems she's had since the accidental death of her eleven-year-old daughter in December of 1994, but for treatment of drug addiction. She is addicted to the prescription painkillers that doctors all over the area have been giving her. I feel guilty, reminded of the many times I've called recently, to find that her voice is slurred, too loud, too falsely cheerful. She'd be repetitive, telling me the same story two or three times. I knew that there was a problem, but I hadn't wanted to face it. Now I must face it.

"Sharon, the counselor wants to call you, if that's okay, to get a background on Sally's childhood," Arthur tells me. "Because you know better than anybody what went on." And when the counselor calls, I tell her everything I can think of—about our mother's drinking, our poverty, Sally's sacrifice of living with my aging, ill parents and caring for them until their deaths, and of course, about the death of Sally's daughter in a traffic accident. I tell her that Sally is the strong one in her marriage, carrying the burden of her husband's grief as well as her own.

As I speak to this faceless voice, it occurs to me, once again, that I am seven hundred miles away, caught in the middle of an intense semester in graduate school. I can't go to my sister, just as I couldn't get to her side immediately when Amanda was killed. My grief eats at me; my guilt is overwhelming. I should be there now, just as I used to be when Sally needed someone to tell her about her period, someone to help her buy school clothes, someone to sew her prom dress, someone to help her plan her wedding. I should be there.

Happily, within a month, Sally has been able to shake her addiction to the painkillers. They never worked anyway. Her real pain was and still is inside her heart, not inside her body—both she and I know this. But she was so busy being strong for everyone else that she has let her

pain push her into a place that both of us have sworn never to go—down
that same road to addiction that our mama once had taken.

Several daughters who contacted us admitted that they were still
using drugs. Sonya Graham, thirty-seven, from Atlanta, Georgia,
says she is a drug addict, a habit she picked up twenty years ago
when she lived overseas in a country where there was a lot of heroin,
and she thought she was snorting coke. "So I became a junkie," says
the former dental hygienist, now on disability. "It numbed my
feelings. I also take Lithium and Prozac and Mellaril and methadone, so I'm artificially chilled out. My self-esteem is very weak, very
low, yet, I know I'm smarter than most people because I was always
the best in my class except for math and science."

Georgina Iler, forty-one, says that she currently smokes pot. "I
know the stereotype is that you toke up and then sit around and
veg," she says. "Maybe this is true for some people, but this couldn't
be less true for me. I'm able to get a second wind and do more.
Instead of being pulled down by the negative voice inside my head
that is my mother's legacy to me, it helps me flip that switch in my
head."

Ellie, however, had a different reaction to marijuana. When one of
the men in her life introduced her to pot smoking, she went along
with it, convinced it was harmless because he and all his friends said
so.

"With my addictive personality, pot was a natural for me, right
along with alcohol and cigarettes," she states. "But over the long
run, it wasn't harmless for me. In retrospect, I can also see that my
life stagnated during the pot-smoking years. I went nowhere,
certainly not forward. That five- or six-year phase was like a
standstill. But like many children of alcoholics, I craved substances
that would calm my anxieties, numb my inner pain, and fill the void
of emptiness with artificial happiness. Then one day, I had what I
swear is a bad physical reaction, even though that's supposedly
impossible; pot is harmless, after all! Immediately after toking up

one afternoon, I rapidly began to feel very ill. I'll never forget it. I felt as though I was extremely drunk, only worse. Among other things, my vision blurred, voices sounded far away, my head pounded. This lasted for hours. It was very frightening. That day, I abruptly quit and have not touched it since, nor do I want to. Without pot, I began to make better choices, and I began to move out of stagnation, in a direction I wanted to go."

Smoking

Goldstein refers to tobacco as "a major addictive substance in the present century," one that has hooked many women since it became socially acceptable for women to smoke. He refers to smoking as "a low key high" which "alleviates stress and anxiety, reduces frustration, anger and aggressive feelings, and promotes a pleasurable state of relaxation." Smoking seems to go hand in hand with drinking: 85 percent of the alcoholic mothers in our sampling smoked. Sixty-three percent of the daughters were either smokers or ex-smokers. Feeling that they deserve one vice as a consolation for quitting drinking and/or drugs, many found smoking harder to give up than alcohol.

Lauranne Seiner smokes and considers that habit far less of a detriment than drinking. She says, "If I ever pick up a bottle, you might as well just shoot me dead. Just go ahead and shoot me because I want to be dead. I don't want to ever be an alcoholic. But I'm like a basket case sometimes, and I try to keep it together, so smoking is my release.'"

Susan Steffan, thirty-three, almost died from smoking after an asthma attack. She was in the hospital for six days, which really scared her. This forced her to quit smoking. But Susan admits that "when I get really upset I will have one cigarette." She justifies this by saying, "I used to be a speed freak. I used to freebase crystal, and to this day I know if it is put in front of me I can't turn away from it. I don't drink because I have developed a severe allergy to alcohol."

Therefore, she reasons, an occasional cigarette seems like a mild concession. Erica Zetterower, forty-four, a hairstylist, smokes two packs a day. When she tried to quit once, she "cried within hours."

Ellie describes how she got started smoking and the struggles she went through to quit:

Mother and I were driving into town. We were both very tense; she, evidently angry at my father; I, at some boyfriend. She reached for her pack on the dashboard and tapped one out; I watched the procedure, as I had thousands of times before. Sticking the cigarette between her pursed lips, she shoved the lighter into the control panel. When it glowed, she clicked it out and held it steadily to the end of the cigarette, drawing in deeply. Replacing the lighter, she exhaled with a long, deep, satisfied sigh. The tension in her face relaxed; her eyebrows unfurrowed slightly. Another puff, another long exhale and sigh.

Suddenly, on impulse—I don't know what in the world made me do this—I asked, "Can I have a puff?" Silently, she handed me her cigarette, her mind obviously miles away. I gingerly took a tiny puff. It tasted terrible, of course, but at the same time, a warm and unusual feeling surged through me . . . camaraderie! Here we two women were, driving along together, both angry at our men, martyrs together, smoking our cigarettes together, relieving our tension. That felt exciting! Never mind that the cigarette choked me and left a hideous taste in my mouth. The feeling of togetherness was powerfully seductive.

From then on, whenever I felt empty or lonely, I found a peculiar comfort in taking a puff or two from her leftover butts in the ashtray. Soon, I wanted whole cigarettes, and I didn't have to sneak them. If I felt like it, I could openly smoke along with Mother. She didn't seem to care. If I asked for one from her pack, she shrugged and tapped out one for herself too. Before long, I was hooked.

For the next fifteen years, my relationship with smoking was on-again, off-again. One of the times I quit was particularly difficult. During the first week of abstinence, I felt like I would surely die if I couldn't get just one little puff from somewhere. So I'd sneak around looking for one. Publicly, I would officially be smoke-free, but privately, I would grub around in ashtrays for butts, which I could stealthily light behind closed bathroom doors. I felt ashamed but justified because I had to have it.

The last time I quit, seventeen years ago, was the final time. It was horrid! But by then, I had learned a lot more about myself, and I knew a very important fact: I had to treat smoking in the same way an alcoholic treats alcohol. I could never take even one puff. Each time that I got rehooked on smoking, I had only intended to mooch "one little puff" from someone else's cigarette. From there, it had always accelerated right back to full-blown addiction. I understand what it feels like to be addicted!

Why We Quit Drinking and Drugs

We cannot explain why so many of the recovering daughters we spoke to have been able to quit their addictions, but one of the reasons they cited frequently was that they quit for the sake of their children. The big question and ultimate irony is, if *they* could do it for their children, why couldn't their mothers do it for them? Part of the answer lies in the population of the respondents—we probably heard from a more "recovered" segment of the daughter of alcoholic mother population. Women who were still weighed down by drinking or drug problems obviously were much less likely to participate.

Nan MacGregor's mother used to pour alcohol into the Kool-Aid to disguise her drinking. Nan noticed that her mother "was a bitch before she drank it, but when she finished drinking it, she was fine. I always felt terrible, and it seemed to me that what she was drinking made *her* feel better, so maybe it would make *me* feel better." So at the age of eight, Nan started drinking the laced Kool-Aid too.

Soon she developed a tolerance for alcohol, and by the time she was twelve, she was also smoking pot and snorting cocaine, which was easy for her to get where she lived in downtown Philadelphia.

"I took all these drugs until I was about nineteen until one day my little brother found me in the bathtub, sitting in water with my clothes on, snorting cocaine off the edge of the tub, with my face all bleeding from the overusage. I was taking way too much, and I just didn't want to stop this time. I was definitely out to kill myself because I just couldn't deal with my feelings anymore. I spent six months in rehab getting off of it. It was the worse six months of my life. I've been off of it for some time. I'm also a recovered alcoholic," continues Nan. "I still go to meetings."

When she was twenty-four and found out she was pregnant, Nan quit drinking and has been sober ever since. "It made me extremely depressed to get off of it," she states. "But then I started therapy and going to a counselor twice a week, and that seemed to help. And I'm going to AA meetings, and I have a great sponsor. It works. I'm a mother now, so no way would I go back on it! My daughter's so impressionable, and I don't want her around anything like that. So when we have friends over, I don't allow drinking in my house. No, I don't. Seriously."

Cherish West

As a child, Cherish West would hide in terror from her parents' violent fights. But around the age of ten, she started sneaking the alcohol so that she could put her feelings aside long enough to try to break up the fights. "Because I didn't want to *feel* anymore!" remembers Cherish, thirty-six, a wife and mother from Tulsa, Oklahoma. Soon, she began stealing her parents' vodka and replacing it with water, and her addiction became stronger.

"I got to the point where I was drinking Thunderbird wine. It's gross, but it was cheap, see. Oh, God. I did a lot of things." She laughs sadly.

For years, Cherish abused both alcohol and drugs. She was unable to stop even during pregnancy and gave birth to a child with fetal alcohol syndrome. This made her feel so wretched that she used drugs even more to quiet the guilt. Cherish became sober three years ago after spending some time in jail for theft. She turned to religion and found strength.

She says, "Every day when I wake up, I say, 'God, Your will, not mine. I ask him to help me stay clean and sober for *today*. Because all I have is today. I have a lot of guilt for everything I've done in the past, but I've had to say, 'Screw guilt. I have got to go on.' My two boys remind me of my past, saying, 'Well, you did it, Mommy. You did it,' implying that they can too. Yeah, but I don't do that today. There's right and wrong. It's really hard to be a parent who has gone through all that stuff, and you don't want your kids to go through it. I'm hoping because I'm three years clean and sober, because I love myself today, and because I love my children, I'm hoping that I broke the chain of alcoholism and drug addiction. That my children don't have to make the same choices I made."

Cherish's husband, also a former alcoholic, joined her in recovery, which has helped both of them remain sober. He has also been dry for three years. "We 'used' together, we lost everything together, we separated, then we got back together sober," she explains. "I'm more spiritual and happier inside and out than he is. I have God in my life. But he's still working on himself. He's very angry sober. But today, I have to love myself first, because I hated myself for so long."

Cherish works hard to be a loving mother to her children and make sure they receive the love she did not. Her alcoholic parents have also recovered. Cherish was the one to drive her mother to her first AA meeting fifteen years ago.

"Of course, I thought my mom had a problem, and I didn't. But I was just as sick as she was," she reflects. "But Mom was scared to go by herself. So I would get loaded, put her in the car, drop her off at an AA meeting, leave the meeting, go get loaded, and come back and pick her up. Like I knew that she had to get sober, but I didn't have a problem, because I was in denial at the time."

Cherish smiles. "If my friends from the past ever saw me today, they'd probably freak out if they even knew I was alive. I ran into the son of one of my mom and dad's friends. I went to school with him. He goes like, 'Oh, my God, you're still alive!?' He couldn't even believe it, and he couldn't believe that my parents were sober. He couldn't believe that I was sober. It blew him away. He had had a drug and alcohol problem, too, and he was sober. I said, 'If you ever run into any of our friends that we used to hang out with, please tell them I'm sober. Tell some good things about Cherish.' He goes, 'I will.' "

Why have so many daughters of alcoholic mothers been able to sober up and clean up? Maxine Caldwell, who quit drugs cold turkey, offers this insight: "Where did I get the strength to just quit a drug habit on the spot?" she asks reflectively. "It comes from having survived my childhood and having to fight for my life, all my life."

Early morning in Savannah is a favorite time of mine. The house is quiet. The day feels fresh and new and belongs to me, like an unopened present. I start the coffee while the dog (a "Scuppers the Sailor Dog" lookalike) springs vertically in three-foot leaps, overjoyed at the prospect of a walk. How lovely it is to wake up every morning with a clear head and a clear conscience . . . no cloudiness in my mind, no aches in my limbs. No morning-after anguish about whether I'd made a fool of myself at a social gathering or whether I'm popular enough. I put the leash on Pete and open the front door. Our cat, Gus, finishing his night shift, saunters in, purring and rubbing against my legs. Pete and I walk outside. It's still dark, and the Big Dipper sparkles clearly from above. By the time we get close to the marsh, the sky is royal blue, and the birds are awakening.

I particularly love it when the full moon is still shining down at dawn. As I walk along, I ruminate about whatever anxieties or troubles are plaguing me at the moment. One thing I've learned is that life is never free of difficulties; they just change forms and faces. But these days, I do not anesthetize them away with a beer or a joint or a tranquilizer.

If I am troubled about something, I just go ahead and feel *the pain and try to resolve it with a clear head. To do otherwise only postpones it.*

The horizon turns peach and birds flap overhead, crying loudly. I arrive back home, picking up the newspaper as I walk up the driveway. Inside, the house smells of fresh coffee. I pour a cup, sit at the table, and open the paper. Gus, always "full of sugar" in the morning after a night out, hops onto the table and settles down on top of the open editorial page, which I'm reading. He yawns and stretches full length over the letters to the editor, his claws mixing into George Will's column. "How could anyone say no to a face like yours?" I ask him, caressing his yellow coat. My coffee, sweet and creamed, tastes delicious. Sitting alone in the silent kitchen, awaiting the new day, I feel higher on joy and contentment than I ever did on pot or booze.

Chapter Six

"Weighting" for Love

~

"I was an obese child. My mother-substitute for food is love, plus my metabolism sucks, genetically, because both my parents had weight problems. When I was twelve, I starved myself and got down to about one hundred and thirty. Now I'm huge."
— *Sonya Graham, thirty-seven, Atlanta, Georgia*

~

The minute Doug left for work, I'd head for the ice cream. We bought it by the half gallon, always in my favorite flavor—chocolate! After I'd finished eating the half gallon, I'd walk down to this little store nearby and buy another half gallon, exactly like that one. Then I'd carefully scoop out the precise amount that he would remember was gone from the previous carton, and eat only that amount. That way, when Doug got home, he wouldn't go to get some ice cream and find that I'd eaten it all. I just couldn't stand to hear him ask, "What happened to all the ice cream, Sharon? I thought we had nearly a half gallon." If I couldn't replace the ice cream, and especially if we'd had guests, I'd lie and say others ate it. (After we had kids, I blamed them!) He caught me lying more than once, but that didn't stop me—the need was too strong.

I'd also buy things like cookies and candy and hide them all over the house. I'd leave some out for my husband, of course, but since I did most of the grocery shopping, he didn't know that I'd buy a dozen candy bars and tuck at least six or eight of them in my underwear drawer, or behind books on the bookshelf. For the first several years of our marriage, he worked nights, and I'd always been nervous alone after dark, so while he was gone, I'd eat and read and eat and watch TV and eat and eat and eat . . . It's no wonder I gained twenty-five pounds the first year of our marriage and another twenty-five during the second.

It took me a long time to realize that I was hiding food and compulsively overeating the same way my mother would hide booze and slip around from one hiding place to another in the house and get drunk. I was exactly like her, and the only saving grace was that my eating wasn't hurting anyone but me. Or so I told myself. It took me even longer to realize that as I got fatter, my self-esteem got lower, and as I sank in self-evaluation, my misery became contagious. I was more quarrelsome and negative and depressed. I constantly thought, "Just like Mama, I'm out of control!" My worrying about my weight carried over into my worries for my children as well. Like the Supermom I tried to be, I didn't want them to be fat and miserable too.

As the years passed, my weight went up and down, depending upon a number of factors. As long as I was "dieting," which I used to do pretty successfully, my weight would go down. Once I lost over one hundred pounds and got down to my slimmest adult weight— 132 pounds. I held that weight for maybe two weeks. Then, gradually, no matter what I did—I was living on eight hundred calories a day and exercising furiously—the weight began to creep back up.

Pregnancy, with all its weird effects on my appetite, certainly didn't help. Nor did the cruel comments that others made about my size. My doctors were the worst. The ob-gyn I saw when I was pregnant with my older son once said to me, "You're getting so fat, I'm going to have to examine you in the front yard! We won't be able to get you through the double doors." (This is the same pencil-thin jerk who later abandoned all his pregnant patients—and his wife—in order to run off with one of his nurses.)

I hit my top weight in the summer of 1996, right before I was diagnosed with mild diabetes. Since then, I've lost about forty pounds and have the diabetes under control with diet and exercise, mostly walking and stair climbing. Still, I am a very large woman, usually the largest in any random group. And that used to hurt so much. I was constantly looking at others and comparing myself to them, and of course, they were the winners and I was the loser—except in pounds. Then one day I realized that I had a choice. I could continue yo-yo dieting (which had contributed to the development of a thyroid condition), losing, regaining, and getting more and more unhealthy and miserable. Or I could accept the things I could not change and get on with living a happy life, regardless of my size.

Ladies' fashion magazines promise eternal slimness, if only one will follow their latest diet craze; such promises no longer hold credibility for me, for I have come to realize that I will never be a thin woman. With my genetic inheritance (both Mama—when she wasn't drinking—and my father had weight problems) combined with how my early environment wired my system, I don't have a prayer of becoming a thin person. That is not to say that I have "given up" on my weight. I haven't. What I've given up on is diets and unnatural means of size control, like pills or hypnosis or surgery. Instead, I will continue to do what I've been doing for the last year—eating right, exercising, and practicing feeling positive about myself.

It's the last one that isn't easy to do because the biggest obstacle for any fat person is not her appetite or her lack of willpower. It's the people around her—first her mother, who lets her know in no uncertain terms that she's a disappointment. Then it's the people who "helpfully" make cutting remarks ("You'd be rather pretty, if only you'd lose weight!"), or those who cuttingly make "helpful" remarks ("Oh, honey, I know just the right diet for you! Try it! You'll be amazed!"). I've come to look at my weight the same way I look at my height or my eye color. Yes, there are bizarre and horrible things I could do to become taller or shorter or to have different colored eyes, but why would I want to? Yes, it's true that I'd probably be healthier if I weighed 125 pounds. I'd also probably be healthier if I hadn't been born to a poverty-stricken, heavily smoking, alcoholic mother in the cancer-ridden state of Louisiana. But some things either can't be changed, or simply aren't worth the risk of trying to change them.

Besides, I've learned that my value as a human being is not based on what I weigh. I am intelligent, talented, kind to children, animals, and the elderly; and I think I'm probably both healthier and prettier than some of my students who are painfully anorexic, with their stick-thin arms and bulbous knees, their hollow eyes, and their dry, thin hair. I feel sorry, if truth be known, for people who can't or won't enjoy good food. Food is one of life's pleasures, and it should be enjoyed, not rationed out in tiny, tasteless bits. But the difference in my attitude toward food, between now and when I was younger, is that now I control food; it doesn't control me.

For example, I don't binge eat anymore, though I'll admit, I do still have problems at times with distinguishing between hunger and other emotions. Sometimes I'll eat when I think I'm hungry, but it won't be hunger; it'll be exhaustion, stress, frustration, or anger with something or someone. Or it will be loneliness. Loneliness is a big one. Ever since my childhood, when I didn't feel loved by anyone, I've felt alone, and it manifests itself like a giant hole inside me that I constantly keep trying to fill. I definitely have to battle reaching for the carbohydrates when I feel lonely, unloved, unappreciated—when I know what I really need to reach for is the company of my husband, or a friend, or a sister. But as any overweight person knows, other people can't always do it for us either. You can't expect other people to stop their lives and come hug you or talk to you, even when they live inside the same house with you. So when I can't get what I need emotionally from my own resources or from other people, there's still the carton of chocolate ice cream . . . but these days, it's sugar free and low fat!

"Children who grow up in families where one or both parents are alcoholic are especially prone to developing an eating disorder," assert Barbara McFarland and Tyeis Baker-Baumann, with the Eating Disorders Recovery Center in Cincinnati, and co-authors of *Feeding the Empty Heart: Adult Children and Compulsive Eating.* They note that not all adult children of alcoholics will develop eating disorders—and of course, many people with eating disorders come from other kinds of families—but the results of the authors' five-year clinical study suggest that more adult children of alcoholics will develop eating disorders than will adults who grew up in so-called normal homes.

Geneen Roth, author of *When Food Is Love* and other books on eating dysfunctions, expresses similar beliefs. Roth, who conducts compulsive eating workshops for thousands of people around the country, finds that over half the women in her workshops have alcoholic parents. Most of the participants come from dysfunctional families. "Yet," Roth adds, "they believe that food and weight are their biggest problems." She herself admits, "I grew up with a physically abusive mother who was addicted to drugs and alcohol; my father was often absent or emotionally unavailable."

To Roth, the connection between compulsive eating and the dysfunctional alcoholic home is based upon the lack of intimacy between parent and child. Poignantly, she writes that she has come to realize "I will never have a happy childhood. I missed it: the love, the acceptance, the feeling that I mattered. I missed it the first time around and I will never get the chance again." Her words will strike a familiar chord for the many daughters of alcoholic mothers who confessed to us that they have weight problems.

Nearly three-fourths of the women with whom we spoke reported weight problems: compulsive overeating, anorexia, bulimia, and self-esteem issues associated with being overweight. Further, many reported critical comments (as children, teens, and adults) from their mothers about their weight. (Our research suggests that the verbal abuse our respondents endured from their alcoholic mothers was often directed toward the daughter's appearance and size.) These women also experienced, as well, harshly controlling behaviors (such as locking food away from their children, or severely limiting the amount the children were allowed to eat). Mothers, feeling guilty over being unable to control their drinking, often inflicted their guilt upon their daughters by deciding that they *would* be in control—not of themselves but of their daughters, and of their daughters' food intake and body size. Such control, in place of unconditional love, led many daughters down the path of eating disorders.

Tellingly, research conducted for the book *Like Mother, Like Daughter* by nutritionist Debra Waterhouse indicates that "food is often a potent force in interpersonal relationships, especially the mother-daughter relationship." Many of the women interviewed for focus groups conducted for Waterhouse's research "noted that food was linked to sociability or that, in their childhood, it was equated to comfort or love." One of the most important findings from these focus groups seems to us to be the following: "The majority [of the women], however, recalled constant criticism [from their mothers] of their bodies and/or what they were eating. The daughters interpreted this criticism to indicate a lack of acceptance—not just of their bodies or their food choices, but of themselves as persons." If this link between food and self-acceptance is a problem in homes where the mother does not drink, it is an even greater problem in homes where the mother is an alcoholic, prone to ignoring boundaries and to verbally abusing her daughter.

There is also a connection between homes with alcoholic mothers and the availability, or lack thereof, of sufficient food for the children. In such families, chances are good that the father has abandoned or will abandon the home. (Robert Ackerman, who has written extensively on the alcoholic family, notes that only one in ten husbands remains with his alcoholic wife.) The ensuing lower standard of living means that less money is available for food. A number of daughters reported that their family's food stamps got traded for money to buy liquor, cigarettes, and drugs. Further, less money for food means that foods high in starches and fats will be chosen for the family to eat, rather than fresh fruits and vegetables and leaner cuts of meat.

Even if the family is not thrown into welfare or financial need by the father's absence and the mother's addiction, it has traditionally been the mother's responsibility to prepare meals for the family; but that is a task the alcoholic mother is often incapable of performing. Her children fend for themselves, frequently feeling both physically and emotionally malnourished as a result. Their experience will not be one of the intact family gathering around a happy dinner table to share stories of their day. More likely, the meal is something simple that the child can scrounge or that an older sibling can prepare. Even Ellie, who came from a family that could have afforded to hire a cook, notes, "When we were older, when my mother's drinking restarted, I was about sixteen, so we kids could easily grab something for ourselves. We all knew how to fry an egg or make toast! Maybe that's why even today I am content to just throw something together."

Even if the mother is trying to put meals on the table in a semblance of normalcy, mealtimes may become tension-filled: the child hurriedly eats in silence while the sullen mother, sometimes not eating at all, sits with her drink and her cigarettes. Sharon recalls, "Mama's place at the table wasn't hard to find; it was the one with the cigarette burn marks and the water rings. I remember many, many meals where she sat with us, maybe even picking listlessly at something to eat, but mostly just sucking on her Winstons and drinking Schlitz beer. Usually she told us she'd 'get something to eat later'—but she often didn't. I know for a long time during her heaviest drinking years, she was malnourished, living on beer and cigarettes, and because we kids were having to feed ourselves, we ate a lot of crap, food that could be easily prepared but was not very good for us, such as countless bologna or peanut-butter-and-jelly sandwiches."

Such an unstable, chaotic environment creates that sense of the "empty hole" that many daughters of alcoholics report feeling and trying compulsively to fill. Roth notes, "Compulsion is despair on the emotional level. Compulsion is the feeling that there is no one home. We become compulsive to put someone home." She continues, "Food was our love; eating was our way of *being* loved. Food was available when our parents weren't. . . . Food didn't hit. Food didn't get drunk. . . . Food became the closest thing we knew of love."

Dr. Ronald Ruden, author of *The Craving Brain,* theorizes that addictions of all kinds, whether they be addictions to drugs, alcohol, cigarettes, gambling, or food, have their origins in our brain's chemistry. It is his contention that both our genetic inheritance *and* our environment play a role in whether or not we will become addicted. Stress, for example, with its effects on brain chemicals, can affect the development and intensification of addiction. But while nature is affected by nurture, the equation is not perfect: individuals live lives of varying stress levels, yet only some people, and not necessarily the most stressed, will develop addictions.

Daughters of alcoholic mothers certainly seem casebook studies for such a theory. We not only have addicted mothers, and therefore a genetic predisposition toward addiction; we also have monumental stress, the kind that would drive anyone to seek relief. The brain chemicals dopamine and serotonin are the keys. When we are in pain (from hunger or loneliness, for instance), our brains release dopamine. Dopamine is necessary for survival. Without it, we'd be too apathetic to do anything about the pain. If the pain is not alleviated, though, we may become obsessive and begin to crave something that will stop the discomfort. We enter what Dr. Ruden calls the "gotta have it" stage. The answer to dopamine's "gotta have it" is serotonin, the "got it." Serotonin turns off the need. It "makes us feel safe, sated, and satisfied." The "fen-phen" diet medications, recently taken off the market due to their potential for harmful side effects, worked by raising levels of serotonin in the brain. These drugs have also been used to treat alcoholics and appear to stop alcohol craving in the same way they stop food craving.

Dr. Ruden's theory provides strong evidence for a biochemical basis for "food addiction," but it is not yet a widely accepted theory;

it certainly is not widely known or accepted among most people in our culture. Culturally, we persist in believing that excess weight is a matter of moral character: we overweight are called gluttons. Jokes are made about us. We are thought ugly and selfish. This seems an awfully harsh double punishment for women who are already fighting one source of shame—their mother's alcoholism.

One of the stresses that we face grows out of the effects of our mother's inconsistent behavior toward food, our weight, and our eating habits. Some of the happiest memories of our lives often are associated with our mothers who, when sober, prepared wonderful meals and snacks. Some of the worst are associated with our mothers who, when drunk, either prepared inedible or burned food, or who sat and drank as we tried to eat. Sharon recalls coming home from school one crisp fall day and finding that her mother was making spaghetti, something she did very seldom. "I sat in the living room and inhaled the wonderful aromas and thought how happy I was because she was cooking a special meal, one that I loved. The house smelled so good, rather than smelling of beer and cigarettes." Kay Browder, fifty, says, "My fondest memory was hanging out in the kitchen against the chimney talking to Mother while she cooked dinner . . ."

But most of us learned the hard way that such happy memories could change in an instant, in the time it took Mother to toss back a glass of wine. Then mealtimes could become horror stories. Grace King, forty, recalls behavior that will not seem unusual to many other daughters of alcoholic mothers: "On weekends my mother would make a big family dinner that often ended in someone running from the table in tears or stomping away in a rage. If my mother drank prior to the meal, we never knew if the meal would actually be edible. If it wasn't, and we dared to say something, she might force us to eat it or throw all the food on the floor in the kitchen and go upstairs. It was then our responsibility to clean up the kitchen and fend for ourselves for dinner."

Maya Renata, a poet and songwriter, sometimes uses her childhood experiences as inspiration. One experience is intimately connected to food: "When I started writing, I told my therapist that my mother would sit in the kitchen and smoke cigarettes and drink. She would fix us breakfast, and we would sit in the dining room and eat it. She would sit in the kitchen at this little table, like the hired help or something. I have a miserable image of her sitting there." That memory is so powerful for her that it is not surprising that Maya later developed problems with anorexia.

Leigh Vives, forty-six, who as an adult has a weight problem, fights many bad memories of her mother's "Jekyll and Hyde" personality. On the one hand, her mother was an excellent housekeeper who fulfilled her daily obligations. On the other, her mother's behavior regarding food was bizarre and controlling. She herself seldom ate because she was drinking instead; yet, believing that Leigh had a weight problem, she deprived her daughter of food. "Mother never ate with me because she always wanted 'one more' before dinner," Leigh says, describing an evening in which she had cooked a delicious meal that her mother did not eat. "I asked my mother to please join me. Of course, she wasn't ready. I ate alone and cleaned up." Leigh's mother told her to leave the food out, and she would eat and clean up later, so Leigh went on to bed, only to awaken about 2 A.M. "I could see the kitchen light on so I went to check. To my disgust and shame, there was my 'dignified, ladylike' mother eating out of the pots with her *hands!* Both hands going at the same time! I was so shocked! I just ran back to my room and sobbed myself to sleep in my pillow."

Leigh, who says she now has a weight problem, remembers that when she was a child, "My mother 'monitored' my eating, including locking the fridge. She put a lock and chain on the door. She had this thing about me gaining weight. I was the type of child who could gain weight very easily, and she just *hated* the fact that I'd gained five pounds." There was no financial reason for her mother's behavior; her only motivation was to deprive Leigh of food so that she would be thin. Hungry, Leigh began to steal food and hide the evidence in a vacant lot near their home. "Many times, I'd pray that she'd run to the grocery store or somewhere and leave me alone. While she was gone, I'd rush to the cupboard, get a can of corn, and gulp it down, or a can of green beans, just anything to satisfy me. And I'd pray to God that she wouldn't miss any of the cans, because a lot of times, she would count them. She'd say, 'Well, I've got six cans of corn.' After I ate the can of food, I'd run to the empty lot, and I'd dig a hole and I'd bury it. If they were to have an excavation, they would be amazed to see how many cans are buried there!

"But then she started counting how many slices of bread were left. I couldn't hide that fact, you know. It was too obvious when the loaf would get shorter and shorter." Leigh blames her current cumpulsive overeating on her mother's behavior. "As a matter of fact, a lot of times I'm not aware that I'm doing it until my husband points it out." Leigh notes that her mother is still controlling about food, providing barely enough food for single scant portions when guests come for dinner.

Such memories as these connect our mothers to food inseparably. Experiences with food, cooking, eating, and weight that are associated negatively with our mothers almost always come back to haunt us later on. Even the *good* memories, because they usually connect a *sober* mother to good food and happiness, imply that a *drunken* mother equates to bad food, no food at all, and unhappiness. Many daughters recall the miserable wars that they had with their drunken mothers over food. Like Leigh, others sometimes had to steal food in order to get enough to eat. It might seem strange to "normal" people, perhaps, how frequently some alcoholic mothers used food to control their children.

S. Jae Austin reports that her mother insisted upon controlling the family's diet—in the wrong way. While limiting the number of cookies all her daughters ate, S. Jae's mother failed to help her daughter learn to care for her diabetes's dietary requirements. "I was heavy all through school. And I never ate right. Mom refused to figure out my diet. It was *my* problem. Our favorite story, my three sisters and I, is when Mom would make homemade chocolate chip cookies. She would put them in one of these neat oblong Tupperware boxes and put it up on top of the refrigerator, and she would literally count how many she had made. And go in and check it every once in a while to see if there were any missing. We knew she would check only the edges, so we kept sneaking them out of the middle!" Remembering, S. Jae erupts in peals of laughter. "I'm amazed that I didn't wind up in a diabetic coma. I was never taken to the doctor or had my blood tested on a regular basis."

Even naturally slender Ellie had to deal with her mother's obsessive desire to control her childhood intake of cookies:

Mother's taste in food was different from mine. She hated sweets! She never ate them except for special occasions when she did not want to risk insulting a hostess. She loved fish and vegetables—not sweets. But her children were addicted to sweets. We had learned the joys of cookies, cakes, pies, and ice cream at Grandma's house, and of course had been bombarded with thousands of television commercials—which did not exactly promote fish and vegetables. "What's for dessert?" we asked every night after dinner. But Mother never prepared formal desserts for meals; she gave us ice cream.

When I was twelve, my addiction to sugar, as well as Diana's and my brother's, had grown to parallel Mother's addiction to alcohol. Sweets gave immediate comfort and filled up the bottomless emptiness that we were all feeling. I was fixated particularly on cookies; they did not leave any traces in my bedroom, such as crusted plates or bowls for Mother to find. Then one day Mother suddenly decided to put a stop to her children's addiction to sugar by mandating that the cookies would, from then on, be locked in a special cabinet in the cupboard; she would wear the padlock key on a chain around her neck.

It did not occur to her to simply stop buying the goodies. After all, if they weren't in the house, we could not have them. Perhaps she felt she was being charitable by keeping them in the house but doling them out at her discretion, her "discretion" these blue days being anything but rational. Maybe doing this made her feel in control; if she couldn't control her own addiction, she could at least control ours.

But we cookie junkies would wait until she fell into her usual deep alcoholic slumber. When we could hear her persistent heavy snoring, one of us would open the door to the bedroom, swallow hard, and tiptoe to the edge of the bed to check the location of the key. If she was sleeping soundly, unhooking the chain and sliding off the key was easy, as long as it had not become buried beneath her neck or the pillow. Then we'd run downstairs, open the padlock, and pounce upon the cookies, ripping open the cellophane package, fighting one another like hungry dogs at a garbage can. Then we'd return the key to the chain around her neck, or, if she had turned over, we'd leave it loose on the bed so she'd think it fell off on its own. Or we'd leave it in the padlock and lie to her, saying, "Don't you remember, Mother? You opened it just before you took a nap. Maybe you forgot and left it in there." We were no different from other addicts; we were willing to lie and steal to get our "drug."

After she began to suspect sabotage, she hid the chain and key while she took naps. But by then we'd found that the thin wooden divider between the junk food cupboard and the adjoining cupboard was weak. My brother found a drill and made a little hole in the sidewall, small enough not to be detected in the darkness of these lower cabinets, but big enough for our hands.

If the situation had been reversed, if we'd had the power to lock up Mother's alcohol and wear the key around our necks, I have no doubt that she also would have done whatever it took to gratify her addiction.

Ellie's younger sister, Diana, confirms Ellie's memory of stealing the key to the cookie cupboard, and adds, "I think Mother was probably trying to do it because our brother was very overweight.

That was part of the reason. Not that that was a good thing to do. She shouldn't have *purchased* it, you know? Back in that era, I'm not sure if that occurred to people, to simply not buy cookies, rather than buy them and then dole them out. Some people do that. They buy cookies and think it's normal that you should just have two. But I think she was honestly trying to help our brother and maybe not deprive the rest of us and let him only have a small amount."

But their mother's behavior has had an effect on Diana's eating behavior. "To this day, I do not buy stuff unless I plan on eating the entire thing. I don't really buy potato chips or cookies. Because I know I'll just eat them all, if given the chance. Sometimes I buy potato chips and eat them in the car—*all* of them. I would never just have a few and put them back. That seems abnormal to me."

Control and All-or-Nothing Behavior

Though of normal size, Diana is still engaging in all-or-nothing behavior with food; such behavior, epitomized in Diana's belief that she *had* to eat the whole package of cookies or potato chips, and not just a small amount, and in Sharon's need to eat an entire half gallon of ice cream, is not uncommon with daughters of alcoholic mothers. As Gravitz and Bowden suggest, "All-or-none functioning strongly influences the issue of control. Control is seen as either present (I am in control), or absent (I am out of control). I am either on top of everything or on top of nothing. Over and over, adult children of alcoholics admonish themselves not to lose control."

Issues of control affect almost all dieters. Many people with weight problems go on diets that are over almost as soon as they begin, because as soon as the dieter eats something not on her food plan, she feels like a failure. "Oh, I've blown it. I've lost control! I was doing so well until I just *had* to have those cookies! I might as well give up. I'm worthless." Sharon, a counselor for a major weight-loss business for three years (until she was "let go" for failing to keep her weight down), dealt daily with women who quit the weight-loss program the minute they ate even one "forbidden" food—even if they had eaten only a small amount! They were certain that they had proven to themselves—once again—that they could do nothing right.

Cherish West, who once weighed about three hundred pounds, has learned to recognize these destructive all-or-nothing tendencies. "I abuse food, I abuse sex, I abuse drugs, I abuse alcohol, I have an abusive personality. Everything. Gambling. Anything that comes into my life, I go to the limit. I don't half-ass something. I go all the way. When I get depressed, I eat a lot and get real full, and then I get depressed because I ate the whole thing."

These daughters may be affected not just by the psychological but also by the physical. According to Herbert Gravitz and Julie Bowden, authors of *Recovery: A Guide for Adult Children of Alcoholics,* it is not uncommon for adult children of alcoholics to suffer from "sugar imbalances or sensitivities which result in mood swings and 'sugar blues'." In fact, several women who participated in our research indicated that they were hypoglycemic, diabetic, or constantly craved sweets and carbohydrates. Morgan Landry, thirty-six, currently about fifty pounds overweight, says, "I remember specifically as a kid, when I started overeating, I would take my money and ride up to Jack in the Box and get hamburgers. And I've had this total passion for carbohydrates. And I still have to fight with that to this day because that was kind of my refuge. Sweets, and cakes and doughnuts, especially."

Deidre Goldblum and her sisters Sara Jo Kea and Molly Allen are hypoglycemic, as was their mother. Deidre relates, "It's hard to say if Mother was having a bad day and then had a beer and it just threw her blood sugar out into left field somewhere, or if she'd had a lot to drink. There were times when she hadn't had anything to drink and would slur her speech because her blood sugar just went way out of control. In a way, that was pretty stressful because her blood-sugar problem contributed to my never really knowing if she had a drinking problem or not." Deidre and her siblings also fight weight problems.

Over and over, family patterns emerge. Sharon and her sister Sheila are diabetic; their younger sister Sally is hypoglycemic. All three of them are, or have been, severely overweight. Their overweight maternal grandmother is diabetic, and their mother also was overweight during the periods of her life when she wasn't drinking much. "In the later years of her life, when Mama ate," Sharon remembers, "it was almost always sweets. She demanded them. She ate cake for breakfast and peanut-butter-and-jelly sandwiches for lunch. Supper was either a few bites of whatever my sister cooked for her, or it was cola and whiskey. She hardly ever ate vegetables or meat—her excuse was that her teeth were bad—but it was really because her out-of-balance system caused her to crave sweets and carbohydrates for that serotonin effect. I see similar behavior in my sisters and in me."

Recent research indicates that the cravings for sweets and carbohydrates reported by daughters of alcoholic mothers may indeed be biologically similar to alcohol addiction. The Medical Center at the University of Michigan reports, "Evidence also shows that people who are alcoholics metabolize alcohol differently than non-alcoholics, somewhat like a person with diabetes who metabolizes sugar differently." The center notes that one theory about alcoholism is that it is "an enzyme imbalance." Dr. Stephen J. Gislason, who uses nutritional therapy to help treat alcoholics, asserts, "We think the original problem in alcoholism is dietary." He calls alcoholic beverages "foods" and reports that drinking "is so closely linked to food selection, eating behaviors, and socialization that no consideration of diet and food-related illness is realistic without knowledge of alcoholic beverages." He points out that alcoholics trying to stop drinking often turn to heavily sweetened foods to satiate their cravings. Also reported is that the compulsive eater trying to control food binges will find herself caught in the same kinds of "recursive loops" as the alcoholic or drug addict trying to control drinking or drug use: "withdrawal, clearing, cravings, falling-off-the-wagon, bingeing, retreating, and clearing. This sequence repeats over months and years."

Diabetes and hypoglycemia, closely related illnesses, are, as our research has revealed, common among daughters of alcoholic mothers. Both diseases run within families, just as alcoholism also runs in families. If recent research is any indication, that connection may not be mere coincidence. Alcoholism, after all, is so common among hypoglycemics that it's actually listed as a major symptom in diagnosis. Since alcohol is a sugar-based product, it is one of the foods usually removed from or restricted in the diets of hypoglycemics and diabetics.

Like alcoholism, however, overweight is not only a biological issue; it is also a cultural and sociological one. A negative message about food's connection to one's body image is planted all too often inside the heads of daughters by their own mothers, contributing to all-or-nothing behavior in other areas of their lives. Dale Waters, thirty-eight, expresses that connection well: "I have tried to lose weight, but unsuccessfully. I find that I am my own worst enemy, and rarely do I ever complete a project I start and then I put myself down for it. I hear my mother's echos, 'You'll never amount to anything' and 'What are you, stupid?' And it kills me because I make her words ring true. It's like I'm afraid to succeed at something. My measurements were 36-22-32, yet I thought I was fat and homely. She always said, 'Pull that gut in!' Now as an adult, I am overweight by about thirty to thirty-five pounds." The authors of *Recovery: A Guide for Adult Children of Alcoholics,* Gravitz and Bowden, seemed to be seeing inside Dale's mind when they wrote,

> In terms of the issue of responsibility, adult children of alcoholics vacillate between feeling totally responsible or being totally irresponsible. If they decide they are totally responsible for something, they are also overwhelmed with guilt, because it is

usually something bad! . . . The guilt is all-or-none and genera-lizes into 'All I do is fail.' The result is chronically low self-esteem. Because of the rigidity of their thinking, they are either all right or all wrong, and the latter predominates. They rarely accept total responsibility for a success.

All-or-nothing feelings about food can easily lead to eating disorders, but these destructive messages can also send some daughters to thoughts of ending their own lives. Krista Mosely, forty-two, reports that she has recently gone from 316 pounds to 230 pounds through diet and walking. But "both physically and emotionally I'm drained. I've become a diabetic, overweight since childhood, with numerous hospitalizations. I've attempted suicide twice and feel very fragile. When I was a child, my mother kept telling me, 'You're such a beautiful girl, if only you'd lose weight!' Upon graduation, I weighed 250 pounds."

"I was told my mother originally tried to abort me," reports Sam Jacobs, thirty-seven. "My mom denies this. But from my childhood, I remember only a few good, happy times. Mom baking cookies, stroking my hair. Most of the time she complained I was too fat or something. I was always overweight. *Hated* myself! Didn't want to be like my mom. Now, at age thirty-seven, I weigh 245 pounds and am a Type II diabetic. I suffer from low self-esteem and depression. I would like to lose one hundred pounds. I have dieted and starved."

For Phyllis Torrence, fifty-five, who currently weighs 250 pounds, not even eight years of therapy has been successful at helping her overcome a negative body image associated with her weight and her mother's ongoing verbal abuse. "I feel quite good emotionally. But I am overweight, and I do not feel good about that! I've always felt fat. My mom has told me, ever since I can remember, that I was fat, but as I look back at pictures, I see I *wasn't!* I still feel and now *am* fat. I would love to be thin and lose my need for the comfort of food."

"My mother had me on a diet since day one. I took diet pills from various doctors since I was fourteen years old," says Erica Zetterower, forty-four. "As a teenager, I was pretty but was always weight watching." She smiles sadly. "I have few close friends. *Food* is my best friend." Melba Davison, thirty-eight, recalls, "I remember Mama making comments about my weight, and even today I can tell when she's drinking because she starts in about my weight." Such negative comments about our weight can have profound and lasting effects on our self-esteem.

Sending Contradictory Messages

Sometimes a mother's need to control her daughter's life, due at least in part to her own inability to control her *own* life, may mean that the mother may *force* her child to eat, leaving the child feeling helpless and out of control herself; or the mother may make comments about others' weight that let her daughter know clearly that one way to earn Mother's disapproval is to put on extra pounds. Diana Matthews's mother was one who sent the contradictory messages—eat, eat, eat, but don't dare gain weight. Diana says, "My mother told me I had to lose weight but *insisted* I eat everything on my plate! My weight is still a struggle."

Page Lafontaine fought and won a battle with anorexia, brought on in part by a boyfriend's infidelity with her best friend, and in part by her mother's simultaneous returning to heavy drinking and insisting that Page eat, eat, eat. After the betrayal of her boyfriend and her best friend, Page says, "I didn't really care whether I lived or died. I didn't eat or anything for about twenty-eight days. Then finally my mother said, 'Either you eat, or I'm going to put you in the hospital.' And so I said, 'Fine,' and I would eat and eat and eat and gorge myself, then I would go throw up. I was eating in front of her to satisfy her, but I was still throwing it up, so it didn't really make any difference. It was like a suicide attempt because I really didn't care. This was right after my mother started drinking again.

"My mother is a wonderful cook," Page continues. "In fact, sometimes it seemed she cooked better when she was drunk."

Thinking about what she's just said, Page suddenly realizes the contradiction: my mom is a wonderful cook who cooks better when she's drunk, and I throw up everything she makes me eat. "She was giving me this double message: on one hand, I was too fat, but here, have a cookie?"

Many alcoholic mothers criticized not only their daughters' weight and personal appearance, but also the weight and appearance of others. Erica Zetterower says, "Mother was a control freak. She was very self-conscious of personal appearance, and very judgmental of others' appearances." Joellen Weatherford, twenty-four, says about her mother, "She will just totally turn up her nose at somebody who's overweight, or who's sloppily dressed. I'm picturing this heavy woman who was at her apartment pool, and she wasn't wearing anything but a swimsuit. Mother said, 'She shouldn't be in a swimsuit at the swimming pool.'" The message that her mother sent to Joellen was that overweight people shouldn't be allowed to have enjoyable lives because they are ugly and undeserving; therefore, Joellen herself should not expect to have a good life if she is overweight. To be thin in a world that values thinness is a way to be "superior" and "in control," regardless of how that thinness is achieved. If it's achieved through not eating and living on cigarettes and liquor, then that's still better than being overweight, the outward evidence of being out of control with food.

When Mom Is Fat

Clearly, many daughters develop weight problems despite their passionate desire *not* to look like their overweight mothers. They associate their mother's weight oftentimes with her drinking; both become symbols of a woman who has lost control.

One of Sharon's childhood friends whose mother was an alcoholic once described her mother as "grossly overweight," though Sharon recalls, "I don't remember this woman as being overweight. She had a beer belly, that swollen abdomen that so many alcoholic women get, and she weighed maybe 130 pounds, with really thin legs and arms. It may be that what my friend *saw* was a reflection of how she *perceived* her mother, rather than the reality of her mother's body size."

If we really detest our mother's body, and we are desperately afraid of looking like her and therefore, by implication, *being* like her, sometimes we may overreact. Maya Renata even had surgery in order to change her body so that it would look less like her mother's body! "My mother had quite a large belly, and I was so worried about having that kind of figure that I went and had reconstructive surgery. Women in her family kind of sit back on their heels and have these huge stomachs."

Most of us don't go to such lengths to keep from resembling our mothers; all the same, we may consciously or unconsciously abhor our mother's overweight appearance. Ginny Durden says, "I have tried dieting, but I have no willpower and I have very low self-esteem." Ginny fears, more than anything, looking like her mother. "I fear I'll turn out to be an alcoholic, yes, but what I really fear is that I'll be real heavy and not good-looking. That other people will look down at me."

When Father Plays a Role

Other daughters with weight problems are the opposite of the women above: these women have mothers who, despite their drinking, were seen by their daughters as being attractive, elegant, stylish. How is it that overweight daughters are also likely to spring from mothers who are themselves attractive and slender and who are not reported to have actively demeaned their daughters' size and weight? As discussed earlier, there is the genetic influence, but another factor at work here may be the father's influence—fathers who either have weight problems themselves to pass on to their daughters, or who might be the ones doing the criticizing. After all, when we can't take out our anger upon the person with whom we are really angry, we tend to take it out upon someone less able to retaliate. Men who are angry with their wives for drinking may feel that they cannot criticize their spouses without repercussions, so their daughters can become easy targets. If the daughter has a tendency to be overweight—and few prepubescent girls escape their "chubby" period—then Dad may step in with inevitably painful "words of advice." Additionally, when men cannot control the behavior of their drinking wives, they may look around for some aspect of their lives they *can* control, and like Ellie and Diana's father, they may seize upon the weight or eating habits of their daughters.

In the summer of 1963, when I was fourteen, we moved back to Dad's hometown, in eastern upstate New York. The decision to move was an abrupt one, announced to us on the day we left for our annual summer vacation in Plattsburgh. As we gazed at the retreating Chicago skyline, Mother said sharply, "Take a good look, kids. Because we're not coming back."

Sudden as it may have been, moving seemed the best thing that could have happened to us. Our home life was dismal. Mother was depressed and drinking more. Dad was tired, working long hours and trying to cope with Mother's problems in the evening. They fought at night. I was doing poorly in school because I had lost interest. Diana had stopped eating during mealtimes, saying her stomach hurt too much. She and Dad spent much of dinnertime locked in a power struggle over eating. Diana would sit at the table, head bowed, tears streaming down her face, poking at the food on her plate.

Though he was a psychiatrist and did not intend to cause harm, Ellie and Diana's father no doubt found it easier to focus on the food that Diana was moving about on her plate rather than to focus on the bottle of ale that stood next to his wife's plate. Other fathers, less sensitive and less educated, may be much more overt with the harm they cause. "When I was growing up, I felt fat and ugly," says Janie Dailey. She describes a childhood that included a father's suspicions of his wife's adultery and of Janie's legitimacy as his child. "I was always bigger than the rest of the kids in the family. My father always told me, 'You're fat and you're ugly and you can do something about it if you want to.'" Her father's attitude not only caused Janie to see herself as fat and ugly; now she also has trouble with relationships, using her fat as a wall of defense. "I hide behind it; you don't have to deal with relationships when you're fat because nobody wants you; therefore, you can't get hurt."

For daughters like Antoinette Turner, whose alcoholic mother was no longer in the home, grocery shopping with her policeman father was one of the most pleasurable parts of her week—especially because her father would give her spending money as a reward for helping him. Antoinette would spend the money on candy and soda. Though her father did not criticize her weight, when she was in the seventh grade, she became the subject of cruel teasing from schoolmates: "Two-Ton Antoinette" and "Antoinette the Titanic." Shopping for clothes became an ordeal; only then did her father remark that she was outgrowing the chubbette-size clothing.

Antoinette, forty-four, who has spent a lifetime battling her weight, which ballooned following her father's sudden death when she was thirteen, reflects, "I agree with the theory that food equals love, up to a point. I think as a preteenager, you're searching for something, but you don't know it's that nurturing. You don't know it's that conversation with your parents. You don't know that you'd really just like to be held and rocked in a rocking chair. I think it's more like a pacifier because there's an emptiness there that you don't really recognize because your mental capacity and emotions are not developed that much. You're still trying to be a kid. You just know that something's wrong, and you realize that there isn't a mommy and a daddy, and the Sunday dinners that you were raised with are no longer there. You just wind up at the icebox. I'm more aware of it today than ever, that you go to the icebox because the icebox doesn't judge. It doesn't call you names. It makes no smart-ass remarks about your size. It's just there, with its door like semi-arms, open.

You take what you want. You're not the least bit hungry opening that door, but it diverts your mind from the pain of the situation or problem or anger that you don't want to face."

Antoinette adds, "I think children of alcoholic mothers search for all those emotions they miss. If they luck out and marry a spouse that can give them to them, praise God. But if they don't, I don't think any daughter will be totally satisfied, totally healthy, until they are able to have those needs met. They may even go to their graves with certain needs not met."

Competing with Mother's Beauty

Daughters with mothers who are attractive may feel that they cannot compete with their mother's beauty. Jeanne Ebel says, "As a teen, I thought I was too fat. The only way my mother affected how I felt was that she was very pretty, and I knew I'd never be pretty and thin like she was." Crystal Inman comments, "My mother was slim, attractive, and very youthful; a perfect size eight. She always looked perfect. She was often mistaken for a celebrity because of her looks and demeanor. She even did some modeling too."

Such beauty sets up so many conflicts: she's beautiful, and I love her, but she hurts me, so I don't want to be like her. She's beautiful, but she cares more about her appearance and her drinking than she does about me. She's beautiful and sexy, and men flock around her, and so I associate beauty with sex and with the pain I experience because of her neglect. She's beautiful, and I'm not, and so I'm a failure. Whatever the message—one of those, or one from any number of personal scripts—the result is often a daughter who is overweight and experiencing many problems in her life because of it, or even a daughter who is bulimic or anorexic.

Bulimia and Anorexia

"I used to be able to diet very successfully," says Donna Cartee, "but for the past seven years, I have not. Briefly, in 1980, I toyed with bulimia. My physical health is good despite the fact that I am extremely overweight, but I am very depressed and have been for a long time.''

Mina Calzone developed anorexia nervosa in her teens and almost died from the disorder. "I still 'watch' my weight," Mina admits, attributing her illness to her mother's behavior. "She drank virtually every weekend and most holidays. She made life *very* unpleasant.''

"Eating was my main way to cope as a child," says Morgan Landry. "My mother was always thin, due to *not* eating, but I ate! Then I had bulimia in college. I was thin then, but it was just because I would throw up what I ate. Antidepressants saved my life. Now, though I have battled my weight for years, I am currently fifty pounds overweight." Unlike many overweight daughters of alcoholic mothers, Morgan has developed a positive attitude. "I've accepted certain things about my appearance and don't obsess on one thing. Being healthy and fit is more important to me than 'thin' is!''

For daughters who have recognized a correlation between their weight and their mother's drinking, there is help. One source is Overeaters Anonymous and other AA-connected meetings. Another is workshops such as those conducted by Geneen Roth. The best starting place is to recognize that food is *not* love, even though the chemicals within certain foods can cause us to feel comforted and temporarily happy. Nevertheless, we will never get from a bar of chocolate, or from a pizza, or from all the cookies in the world, *any* of the love we did not get from our mothers. No doughnut, cookie, or pie will ever say to us, "Daughter, you are so beautiful! I'm proud of you. I love you.''

Part III

Chapter Seven

Mother Substitutes: Someone to Mother Me

~~

"I think I always wondered, as a child, why my mom didn't love me as I saw other mother/daughter teams loved each other. I thought it was because I didn't deserve her love. I always looked at other families and took refuge emotionally with them."
  —*Theresa Flynn, forty, office manager, Hartford, Connecticut*

~~

We buried Daddy on a Wednesday afternoon in autumn, and that night, I slept in the safest place I knew, the only place that had meant "refuge" for me in my childhood—Aunt Susie's house. Strange that I should need so badly to stay that night with her. I was, after all, a grown woman, thirty-seven years old, with a husband and children. I should have thought of them, or of my younger brothers and sisters, who might need me. Or even of my mother, now a widow. But I didn't. Like a baby instinctively reaching for the security of its comforting "blankie," I reached for the woman who'd been the real mother of my heart, my father's baby sister.

She was no longer a young woman. Widowed twice herself and the mother of four, Aunt Susie was, and is, a woman of great courage and strength. The second of her husbands had been an alcoholic, yet her children somehow made it to adulthood without the terrible psychological harm I see in my siblings and myself. Her children are strong because she is strong. They are secure because she is secure.

153

Each summer from childhood through adolescence, I'd spend at least two weeks at her house, and Aunt Susie's daughter Mary would, in turn, stay two weeks with me. We were the same age and wore almost the same size clothes. My aunt was a fabulous seamstress, and I adored getting Mary's hand-me-downs. Mary's hand-me-downs were always better than the things my own mother made for me. Mama's sewing was adequate when she was sober, but when she was drunk, the seams were uneven and the garment looked tacky and homemade. Sometimes it even had burn holes from Mama's ever-present cigarette, dangling, gravity-defying, from her lower lip.

My aunt, now in her eighties, still lives in the house she has always lived in, a small frame structure with a deep, cool front porch, from which we used to spit watermelon seeds. She has no air-conditioning and only one wood-burning heater for warmth. Two of her sons and their families live nearby, but she lives alone, keeping her own house, and until recently, doing her own driving. That house is not elegant; it is not even especially tidy, nor was it ever, because Susie always had better, more fun things to do. Those wonderful weeks at her house were full of blackberry picking, swimming, gathering eggs, playing softball, riding my cousin's sway-backed mare, or playing with the newest litter of puppies, sneaked into my cousin's bed. It wasn't all play; I helped Mary do her chores, but it wasn't like it was at home. No one was screaming at me to do something, or threatening me with a switch or a slap across the face. I remember clearly one scene from my early teen years, when Mary, without a word from her mother, cleared the table and began washing dishes.

"Let's do these later, Mary," I begged, wanting to get back to our more interesting endeavors—talking about boys, listening to rock music on Mary's old record player, and talking some more about boys.

Mary looked at me. "No, Sharon, if I don't do them now, Mama will do them."

I just stared at her, wondering what was wrong with that. I think Mary could sense my amazement because she patiently explained, "Mama's tired. She cooked that big meal, and she's not feeling very well. The least I can do is take some of the load off her by washing up these dishes."

Mary's love for her mother, her respect and admiration for her, were so obvious. I had never felt that way about my mother. But I did feel that way about my aunt, so without another word, I joined Mary at the kitchen sink.

As the years passed, and I became an adult, my love for my aunt did not waver. Though my dreams of my childhood at home—the few dreams I had—were usually nightmares, the good dreams, the ones full of happiness, love, and security, always were centered at my aunt's house. In all the years I watched my aunt single-handedly parent her four children, I never heard her yell and scream at them. I never saw her spank them, much less beat them. Whenever they needed her—if they fell or scraped a knee or had their heart broken—she was there, no chastising, no mean-spirited questions to belittle them. She just loved them, trusted them, and was happy to be with them.

Each night during those magical summer weeks at Aunt Susie's, we all went to bed about the same time, early, the way people do in the country. And each night, like the Waltons later were to do on television, Aunt Susie called out to each of her children, "'Night, Mary. 'Night, Ricky. 'Night, JohnDee. 'Night, Garland." And each of her children called back, "'Night, Mama. I love you." That was so different from my house, where any good-night calls coming from my bedroom were likely to be countered with, "Shut up, goddamn it, and go to sleep."

The night that I stayed with Aunt Susie, after we'd buried my father, I slept in Mary's old bedroom, and Aunt Susie slept in her room right next door. As I cuddled beneath her homemade quilts, I heard her call, "'Night, Sharon." And I called back, "'Night, Aunt Susie. I love you."

Children *need* mothers. They need their mother's love. And when it isn't reliably there, when Mother is too caught up in her own problems to give her children unconditional love, children don't simply stop needing it. Instead, they may turn to others for comfort and nurturing. Hope Edelman has addressed this issue in her book *Motherless Daughters:* "A mother surrogate unquestionably can help steer a girl through childhood, adolescence, and early adulthood. The single most important factor that helps children who grow up under adverse family or social conditions to become emotionally adjusted, competent adults is the active involvement of at least one stable adult who cares. A feminine mentor who's emotionally invested in a motherless girl's well-being can help her develop self-esteem and confidence as both a female and as an individual." Like Edelman, we found that daughters listed aunts, grandmothers, sisters, teachers, friends, and co-workers as mother substitutes. Other substitutes were also mentioned—friends' mothers, mothers-in-law, stepmothers, and husbands.

One pattern that began to surface as we talked to other daughters of alcoholic mothers was that those few of us who had had sober fathers (who often did double parenting duty) were the ones most likely to have survived Mother's drinking with the least amount of damage. Having one relatively "normal" parent seemed to cushion us from some of the pain, and we can look back upon our childhoods with relatively happy memories. So it came as no shock that about a fourth of the daughters indicated that their fathers (and sometimes even their stepfathers) functioned as "mother substitutes." One woman wrote, "My father played both roles." This nurturing seemed to be present whether or not the daughter lived with her father.

Another fourth of the women from whom we heard indicated that a sister or brother functioned as a mother substitute. The oldest daughter in the family, in particular, was often mentioned as a mother substitute. Additionally, grandmothers were frequently cited, as were aunts.

What seemed surprising was how often daughters of alcoholic mothers sought nurturing from nonfamily members: teachers, neighbors, friends' parents, boyfriends, girlfriends, and lovers. In fact, the category "boyfriends, girlfriends, lovers" was checked twice

as often as any other category of people to whom daughters of
alcoholic mothers turned for comfort. But daughters also listed such
people as stepmothers, employers, co-workers, foster families, house-
keepers, maids, even their father's girlfriends, and, of course, their
pets. Some cited therapists and pastors as their comfort-givers. One
desperate soul wrote in, "Anybody who will have me!"

When There Is No Mother Substitute

*When I was twelve, Mother had started drinking a lot. We had no
family close by, so I could not latch onto an aunt or grandmother as a
mother substitute. No teachers or other adults seemed accessible or
inspiring as mother figures. So I became attached to four men: the
Cartwrights from the TV show* Bonanza. *I escaped my pain through
fantasies. Not fleeting ones but carefully crafted, heavily detailed
scenarios, which I carried around in my head. Whenever I wanted to, I
could slip away from my own family to the sweet, safe Ponderosa Ranch.*

*The Cartwrights, such a normal, wholesome family, always met me
at the door with welcoming smiles and hugs. They took me in and
protected me, as they did everyone who wandered down their trail. In
every episode, they adopted some misfit or lost waif, so why not me? In
my fantasies, the cook, Hop Sing, served comforting meals, and Hoss
tucked me into the guest room bed at night. Meanwhile, Ben and Adam
sat downstairs in front of the fireplace, speaking in low, serious tones,
planning the ways they would right all the injustices I had endured.
Little Joe, with his quick temper, always had to be restrained by his
brothers to prevent him from galloping off to avenge me. Knowing that
someone cared about my pain was such a thrilling fantasy!*

*How revealing that I would select as my ideal family, my object of
adoration, my safe place to visit in my fantasies, an all-male family that
had no mother or wife figure!*

Like Ellie, not all daughters of alcoholic mothers had easily
available mother substitutes; in fact, some daughters deliberately

chose not to seek someone to help fill the nurturing gap—some out of loyalty to their mothers, some because they were too afraid of revealing the dreaded family secret. The punishment from even an accidental release of the secret can be too emotionally threatening for us to risk opening our hearts to someone. We may, for instance, be so fearful that we'll lose whatever suffices for our mother's approval and love that we'd rather continue our denial rather than speak openly to anyone about the problem.

Obviously, one can seek comfort, nurturing, "mothering," from someone without telling them the reason why, without actually *saying,* "My mother is a drunk. She doesn't pay any attention to me." But the secret is so close to the surface—it stains each action, each thought—that we sometimes feel that others will know it just by being near us. As Nancy Codgill says, "During the years of Mother's 'fulmination,' you kept your mouth shut about your 'trouble' at home."

Sadly, some daughters seek comfort from others only to find that they are met with blank walls, with grandparents or other relatives who refuse to intervene, who turn a blind eye or a deaf ear to our mother's drinking, or with neighbors who send us home, even when they can hear our parents screaming at each other and beating each other black and blue—abuse that we ourselves may be subjected to, once we enter the door. Pat Britt's grandparents refused to get involved. Pat, forty-eight, an administrative assistant, describes writing to her grandparents when she was only twelve, to beg them to help her stop her mother's drinking. "But they just ignored it. I asked them one time, 'Did you get my letter?' And they said, 'Yes, but honey, you're too young; you don't understand. Your mom doesn't have a problem, she's just sick.'" Pat adds defiantly, "That's the last time I saw them."

Pat believes that the secrecy of the times is what kept her grandparents from getting involved. "In those days, it was shameful. To my grandparents, it was just awful. And both of them, in their wills, asked for my forgiveness." Of course, by then it was too late.

Like Pat, some of us begin to fasten our hopes upon mother substitutes only to recognize early on that people cannot always help us; sometimes, of course, others simply don't understand. And sometimes other people are uncomfortable about getting involved in the problems of a dysfunctional home. Even if we had the courage to say, "Please love me. My mother drinks, and she leaves me alone at night, and I'm scared. Listen to me, pay attention to me," our pleas might be met with averted eyes and excuses. Honey Sanders says, "People in our small town and in our family knew about Mom, but no one intervened. *Nobody* talked about it." She attributes others' lack of involvement to her father's poor health—friends and family wanted to protect him—and to his prominence in the community. However, daughters from all sorts of families faced the same predicament.

Jackie McClain's voice breaks when she is asked whether anyone had served for her as a mother substitute. "No!" she cries, "and it makes me mad, because there *should* have been! I keep reading that if an abused kid has one good person in their life, one good reference point, that can make all the difference in the world. I do not know of one." Suddenly Jackie does remember one adult who cared enough to intervene. She relates the story of her stepgrandmother, who would come by her home daily to check on her when she was a baby. "She must have known something. She said she came every day to make sure I'd been changed and fed." Apparently this grandmother was aware that Jackie's mother left her unattended, in a lonely crib in the back bedroom, with the door closed, for hours on end.

Other daughters of alcoholic mothers fondly mention grandparents who helped them through the troubling lack of motherly affection. Ginny Durden says that she felt "normal" at her grandmother's house. "I never knew what a normal dinner was, or a normal dinnertime. The only time of normalcy was maybe at Christmas or Thanksgiving when we went to Grandma's. We were always shipped to Grandma's for the holidays. I enjoyed it."

Aunts, often cited as mother substitutes, can be great ones, as Sharon's story at the beginning of the chapter indicates. Sharon's younger sister Sheila, while also fond of their Aunt Susie, was equally fond of yet another aunt: "I loved Aunt Audie, Daddy's oldest sister, who lived about an hour or two south of us." Both aunts had homes full of cheer, love, good food, and patience, so unlike the girls' own home; both aunts always seemed welcoming, as though they genuinely *liked* their nieces and looked forward to their company.

Like Sheila and Sharon, Susanna Moore relied upon more than one aunt for mothering. They seemed ideal to her because none of them had daughters. "Any woman who was not my mother seemed like a safe haven to me. And if she was a relative, then so much the better because I felt like she *had* to take me in." Susanna turned to three different aunts, all the while filled with guilt because she felt that she was betraying her mother by loving and depending on these other women. She also found herself believing that her aunts were kind and caring only out of obligation. "This was the way it was supposed to be; they were acting that way because I wasn't their daughter. And that if I was their daughter, then they'd treat me the way my mom treated me."

Susanna also felt that these aunts felt pressured to care for the children who were "dumped" on them each summer. "My mother would farm all us kids out, and we would go spend weeks at someone else's house, a relative, you know?"

Happily, most daughters of alcoholic mothers found their aunts to be positive role models and loving nurturers, even if for only two weeks in the summer. Unfortunately for those daughters whose family structures had a pattern of only children, there were few aunts to perform the role of loving mother substitutes. These daughters of alcoholic mothers turned to nonrelatives as mother substitutes.

Some of us found mother substitutes within our husbands' families, often coming to love our mothers-in-law as much as, if not more than, our mothers. Despite the many stories that abound about bad mothers-in-law, Dianne Carlson found comfort with hers: "I loved my mother-in-law. She was a lot like me; we got along well. In fact, I felt closer to her than I did to my own mother." Dianne adds sadly, "She's dead now."

Sharon also found a wonderful friend in her mother-in-law:

One of my favorite wedding pictures is one in which my new mother-in-law is hugging me. I knew she wasn't especially excited that her nineteen-year-old son was dropping out of college and getting married, and she probably was worried that the little family whispers of "She's gotta be pregnant" were true. (They weren't!) In addition, and this is very important in the South, she didn't know my family. (If she had, she might have enlisted the National Guard to prevent the wedding!) She even paid for a lot of the wedding, which was held in her house. I'm sure she wondered why my parents weren't doing it. But I never felt anything less than accepted and loved by her, not then, and not now.

My mother-in-law's favorite book is Gone with the Wind, *which doesn't surprise me, because she's just like Scarlett O'Hara's mother, Ellen. She is quiet, strong, uncomplaining, stoic, forever patient. If anything, she errs on the side of doing too much and complaining too seldom, enduring when she should be fighting. Yet I can't imagine that I would admire her so much if she were more openly emotional. My mother's emotions were plenty for me, since they ran the gamut from hysteria and rage to self-pity. From my mother-in-law, I've learned that, unlike for my mother, love doesn't come with a "payment due" notice attached.*

It took a long time before I had the courage to tell my mother-in-law about my mother's alcoholism, but she has been very understanding. In addition, I've found myself talking to her about all the things I'd always thought a woman could talk to her own mother about. In many ways, she has been closer to me than Mama ever was, possibly because her own mother died when she was only a small child, and she can understand how unmothered I've always felt. If she were ever to need me to care for her, I would do it gladly—I feel like I owe her so much. She taught me to at least act like a lady, even when I never felt much like one.

And, since Mama's death, my mother-in-law has become even more important to me. I think of her not only as a second mother, but also as one of my best friends. I've teased my husband often, telling him, "If we ever get a divorce, I'm keeping your mother!"

Because of the high divorce rate in families in which the mother is alcoholic, daughters of alcoholic mothers are not infrequently raised by stepmothers. In her research on daughters of deceased mothers, Hope Edelman finds that stepmothers who "replace" deceased mothers can be problematical and can cause even more damage to children than even the death of their mother did: "It seems that inadequate mothering *after* a mother dies or leaves, rather than the mother's absence per se, is the missing link between mother loss and a daughter's later depression." She adds that some daughters of deceased mothers attribute "their lack of confidence, their low self-esteem, and their pervasive loneliness" to being stepmothered. Daughters of alcoholic mothers, however, may not share that feeling. After all, motherless daughters may, by idealizing a dead mother, see a stepmother as anything *but* perfect. As Edelman also notes, daughters may be angry with their mothers for dying and resultingly displace that anger onto their stepmothers. That does not seem to be the case with daughters of alcoholic mothers. Because our mothers are usually living—and their flaws are very, very obvious—we may find sanctuary in our stepmothers, who may exemplify for us all the good that we remember and hope for in our own mothers.

Janie Dailey is one of many who found a more-than-adequate substitute in her stepmother. Janie says, "My stepmom was my primary mother during my growing-up years. My dad remarried, and God bless her, I don't know how she dealt with it."

Our immediate and extended families frequently do not provide a suitable mother substitute, and so we reach outward, to women who are willing to nurture us though they are not tied to us biologically. "Many of the great mothers have not been biological," writes Adrienne Rich, in *Of Woman Born*. "For centuries, daughters have been strengthened and energized by nonbiological mothers." For Gabriella Chandler, that "nonbiological mother" was a house-keeper her father hired after her mother's departure. "The house-keeper that I loved came in when I was twelve. It took a year to find a good one. We had gone through a bunch of really unreliable ones and ones that just didn't come back the next day, and just didn't like working there . . . so we finally found one who was interested in us as *people*." Gabriella notes that during this beloved woman's interview for the position of housekeeper, she focused her questions on the children's needs, likes, and dislikes. "She talked to us like we mattered in some way. She was very special, cared about us, and after this became a mother substitute, if not a mother herself to us. She had a lot of good values. Her warmth and unconditional acceptance of us was important, because we'd never had that from our mother."

Teachers and people from church, while not as intimately involved with us as a relative or even a housekeeper might be, can also play important nurturing roles in the lives of many daughters of alcoholic mothers. For Mickey Ballard, it was a strict male teacher who made the difference. "He was the reason I even graduated from high school. He kind of did the 'tough love' thing with me. He took the time to make me do what I had to do." Apparently Mickey was fond of cutting class, but "if he saw me trying to leave, he grabbed me. He had a desk in his office that was mine; that's where I sat and did my work. I went back and saw him one time, and he remembered me. I was thankful for that. I was tickled."

Abby Giles notes that the women in her church seemed ideal mothers to her: "They had it all together, women I wanted my mom to be like, people who made cookies and stuff. Like a substitute mom. And I always wondered, why doesn't my mom do that?"

Sally Joiner, Sharon's younger sister, remembers the influence of an elderly woman who lived on their street. "I don't know why Mama let me go to church with Miss Stewart, but I'm thankful for that. I have really high thoughts of her even today, even when I pass Pine Hill Cemetery, I glance out in the direction I know she's buried in. Because she did make a big impression on my life, and I appreciate that."

Other daughters of alcoholic mothers have found mother substitutes in older friends and in the mothers of friends. For Brandi Jones, a special nurse became that mother substitute who made a difference in her life. Brandi says, "I called her Ma-ma. She died a year ago in October. And she was my 'mother.' She didn't adopt me; I adopted her. I think her most qualifying attribute was unconditional love, with that look of 'You fucked up again, but I still love you.'

"At her funeral, there were many, many wounded children who had learned how to live life on life's terms through the care and guidance of this woman. And many, many children of those children. She was always very active and participative with my children. She was their grandmother."

Maxine Caldwell, a lesbian, searched for a mother substitute in the lover she chose when she was sixteen. "I was looking for that mother figure. And I treated her like Mommy. She didn't want to be Mommy, she wanted a lover. But she was Mommy to me." Maxine describes how she would push her lover to abuse her. "It was the only way I knew to get attention. I'd push her, and when she'd hit me, she'd feel so damn bad about it, and then I'd get my way. But she left me. And I don't blame her. I'd have left me too. Her walking out on me was the best thing she could have ever done for herself."

When Sister Means Mother

"I was and still am the caretaker! I was the mother, the cook, the driver to extracurricular activities, the listener, the advisor, the friend, the

comforter, the sister, the protector, the mother. Now I am the sister, the worrier, the friend, the advisor."
　　　　　　—Beth Petrie, twenty-six, insurance agent, Columbus, Georgia

〜

Daughters of alcoholic mothers not only seek mother substitutes; frequently, they *become* them, particularly for their younger siblings. In fact, no one was mentioned as a mother substitute more often than the oldest daughter of the family.

"Have you heard what old lady Tannehill told Coach McCarty about taking his football players out of her English class?" I asked Janis, my best friend. I was sitting on the floor in the hall, the heavy black telephone cradled between my puffy red ear and my shoulder. I'd been on the phone gossiping for at least an hour because Mama wasn't home to yell at me; she'd left a few hours ago to go Christmas shopping. As the oldest, I was, as usual, baby-sitting my younger brothers and sisters.

Suddenly Sheila, the second oldest, burst in. Angrily, I cupped my hand over the receiver and hissed, "Get out of here! I don't want you listening in on my phone conversations. You're too much of a tattletale, and you'll just try to get me in trouble with Mama!" But Sheila didn't go away. In her hand, she was clutching a rectangular silver can.

"Sharon, Delmer drank this can of lighter fluid! We gotta make him puke!" she screamed.

Janis heard her. Both of us had just taken a first-aid course as part of our P.E., and she yelled into my ear, "No! Read what it says on the can first!"

"I'll call you back," I said and hung up.

Snatching the can from Sheila, I read, "Do not induce vomiting."

I hastily dialed the number of our next-door neighbor, my cousin Edna Mae.

"Edna Mae, Delmer drank lighter fluid, and we need somebody to take us to the hospital!"

Within a matter of a few minutes, Edna Mae's brother LaVee, who was at her house visiting, pulled up in our yard. Throwing coats and sweaters onto my brother and me, running, carrying him, I got into the car.

At the hospital, the one in which Delmer had been born less than two years ago, we rushed into Dr. Mauterer's office. "He drank lighter fluid!" I cried as Delmer was taken from me and rushed into an examining room. I sat on the bench near the door to wait, uncomfortably aware of the horrible noises coming from inside the examining room. Delmer was screaming and gagging. After a long while, a nurse came out. "They're pumping his stomach. Sharon, where's your mama at?"

"My cousin went looking for her. She's supposed to be in town somewhere, doing some Christmas shopping."

More time passed. Minutes? Hours? The noises in the examining room abated. The nurse came out again and told me, "They're just about done. Have they found your mama yet?"

As I opened my mouth to say, "No, ma'am," the big front door opened, and in a whoosh of beer-scented air, Mama and my cousin walked in. I could tell immediately that Mama was drunk. She was radiating drunk—her eyes, her posture, her voice. My heart began to hammer; there would be a scene, I knew there would be a scene. But somehow, no one else seemed to notice that she was drunk. She hadn't yet started screaming in that garbled, irrational way that was growing so familiar to me.

The doctor emerged, peeling off his gloves. "Oh, there you are, Ora. Your boy's going to be fine. He just drank himself about half a can of lighter fluid is all. But we've pumped his stomach, and he's going to be all right, thanks to Sharon getting him here as quick as she did. Y'all can take him on home now."

But I was not getting up. Instead, limp, I was sliding off the bench onto the floor, my lips cold, the room spinning.

The oldest daughter of an alcoholic mother often bears a special burden. She is the caretaker. Her own needs frequently are sublimated by the more pressing needs of her family. Her younger siblings need a mother. They need someone to cook for them, help them do their homework, wash their clothes, kiss their boo-boos, get them ready for school. They need someone who is emotionally available when they're sad, or frightened, or their feelings are hurt. They need someone who is willing to stand between them and the neglect and abuse they've come to expect from their mother. If the father is still a part of the home, he needs someone he can depend upon to keep the home running while he works. He may even shift that need to even greater extremes, expecting his oldest daughter to be his confidante, his friend, and sometimes even his sexual partner. This caretaking daughter feels that her presence is critical to the survival of the family; such pressure can make her—or break her.

Not surprisingly, the view from the top looking down is much different than the view looking up from the bottom. The caretaker and the one cared for don't always agree on the amount of nurturing that has occurred, nor on the competence of the caretaker. As Francine Klagsbrun points out in *Mixed Feelings,* the caretaking sibling (almost always the oldest girl, whether or not she is the oldest child) is often angry not only toward the parents who have forced her into this position, but also toward the siblings who need her care. She may feel as though she had no childhood, that she had to be a substitute mother instead. She may feel guilty that she just couldn't do enough, and even guiltier when she finally escapes the family home, leaving the younger ones to fend for themselves.

However, the younger children also feel cheated, Klagsbrun adds. After all, someone who is still a child, albeit a child older than they are, is probably not an adequate substitute for a grown-up mother or father. Further, because feeling angry at the parent who has opted out of her responsibilities is so often futile, if not downright dangerous, these younger children may turn that anger toward their older sibling, as if the problems of the parent were somehow the older child's fault. It is no wonder that siblings in these families have such difficult relationships both as children and as adults—there is so much unresolved anger.

For an older daughter, who has probably already spent many years taking care of her mother—lying for her, putting out her lit cigarettes after she passes out, taking away the car keys when she's drunk, putting her to bed when she can't get there by herself—doing her mother's job by raising her mother's children is just another one of the many burdens.

Because the perspective of the older daughter can be so different from that of her younger siblings, we have given her first voice. (As older sisters ourselves, we can already imagine the choruses in the background of, "You're older, and so you always get to go first! No fair!")

Life as the Caretaker

Jo Ann Stills, twenty-six, the oldest of three children, found herself being mother to the other two at a young age. "I don't have what I think is a typical brother-sister relationship, and it's more or less because I've always taken responsibility for them, taken care of them." Jo Ann explains that they moved often; and though they sometimes lived near other relatives who helped out, when they didn't, the responsibility of mothering fell onto her young shoulders.

"I took care of them in ways that a mother would have traditionally cared for her children. Oh, the things I did that my mother should have!" She laughs. "I remember times when my mom would go away for a couple of days. And I would just have to cook and clean and get my sister up for school. When my brother and sister would screw up, I would get angry with them just like my mother would."

Though Jo Ann's mother usually did not leave for extended periods without taking the baby with her, Jo Ann, still a child herself, had to care for her infant brother often. "There were many nights where she was out at a friend's, or out at a party, or out at the bar, that I was up at two in the morning doing the bottle, changing the diapers, and doing that sort of thing. Fortunately, she was usually around in the morning when I got up for school."

Like many other oldest daughters, S. Jae Austin, thirty-nine, says, "I was the parent, consoler, confidante to both my younger sisters and my mother." She bemoans her current lack of closeness with her sisters and attributes it to their unreal expectations of family life. "We had only television-based ideas of what a family was supposed to be like. Those expectations were dashed long ago.

"Now Beverly's thirty-seven, Jill's thirty-four, and Beatrice's thirty-two this year. But when we were kids, I was their substitute mother. I was basically responsible for every need. I don't think I ever changed Beverly's diapers, but I know I changed Jill's and Beatrice's." Even though S. Jae was perhaps the one child who needed mothering most—she has had Type I diabetes since childhood and is now legally blind from the complications of her disease—she had to care for the needs of her mother and three younger sisters.

June Godfrey says, "I was the eldest and the only girl. It was hell. I was doing everything moms were supposed to do. Though I didn't end up sleeping with my father, he did frequently call me by my mother's name. Nevertheless, no one had any respect for me for what I did, or they didn't realize what I did, or didn't care."

Like many caretakers, Susanna Moore resented her additional responsibilites for her younger brothers and sisters and could hardly wait to get out of the house and away from the burden. She relates an incident from one Christmas during her childhood. "It was about turning on the Christmas lights at night. Everybody took a turn. And I went outside and told my brother Justin it was his turn. And he apparently thought I said it was time, so he went inside and turned them on. My mother had a fit, and I said, 'Well, I just told Justin it was his turn. Justin thought I said it was time.' So she stood there, beating us for half an hour at the top of the stairs to the basement." Susanna describes how she, on a stair lower than her brother, kept trying to keep him from being knocked down the stairs, while he thought she was trying to push him into the abusive hands of their mother. Both of them were convinced that their mother was trying to kill them.

Desperate to escape her mother, Susanna recalls, "When I left for college, there wasn't a second look back. I didn't give those guys another thought. It was like I was out of there, and I had no more responsibilities except to myself. My sister says that, after everybody left, and she was the last one there, she felt like we abandoned her. I told her, 'I'm sorry you feel that way, but . . .' I felt like I had to get out of there to survive. There's no way I could have handled staying there any longer."

Sometimes the relationship between an older caretaking sibling and her younger one becomes even closer than a sibling relationship; sometimes the older child will take steps to legally care for her brother or sister. Such was the case for Brandi Jones, who sees her relationship with her sister-daughter quite differently from how the younger woman sees it.

A Caretaker's Story

Brandi, now thirty-seven, admits that she "kidnapped" her sister, Mickey Ballard, now twenty-eight, and then legally adopted her when she herself was only fifteen, following their parents' divorce and bitter custody battle. The father, also an alcoholic, won custody from the mother, who then more or less disappeared. A few years after her parents' divorce, Brandi left home and began a harsh life on the streets, occasionally stealing from her father's house to stay alive. She also kept returning in order to bask in the unconditional love she received from her baby sister, Mickey. "She always loved me. Even when I spanked her, she'd turn and she'd hold me and she'd say, 'But I love you.' And it was so important to me to have that. So—I just *took* her." When her father caught Brandi inside his home stealing both his food and his younger daughter, they began to argue. "After the end of it, I said, 'Fine, I'm going to take her so she doesn't turn out like me.'" Brandi laughs at the irony of her remark. "Finally, he said that I could keep her if she stayed in school, so I kept her for a couple of years.

"When I was fifteen, he drew me into court to have me emancipated, because I had three more years to legal adulthood, and he was financially and morally still responsible for my actions. I took advantage of the situation and told him that I wanted to legally adopt Mickey. That if he thought I was old enough to be an adult, and the government was going to okay this, then by God, I ought to be able to keep her."

Brandi describes the complex legal maneuvering involved in her successful case—she was, after all, an emancipated minor adopting another minor—and her concerns about her baby sister's reaction to the chaos. "While this was going on, Mickey was having a really tough time." Mickey was caught in the tug-of-war between her sister and her father. "And she would go back and forth. She'd be with me three, four, five months, and then she'd be with him about that."

After Brandi married, her life with her sister-daughter became somewhat more stable, except for the addiction problems shared by the two of them. The two sisters' relationship is now shaky. They seem unable to move from the mother-daughter relationship to a more equal sister-sister relationship. Brandi admits that that is true, but adds, "My personal opinion is, anytime it starts to be that, she stops it. I think she's scared to go there. I'm not sure how to go about getting us there. There've been some developments recently that have not been happy for me. But she's come a long way, despite her humble beginnings. I love her a lot. Oh, I do. And she loves me a lot, I know."

A Younger Sister's Story

Mickey Ballard, twenty-four, says of her caretaking sister, "My mom, the one who is in my life the most, is my sister by birth. She adopted me, and she helped give me the ability to show that I *had* feelings, period. Had she not been able to give that to me, I totally wouldn't be able to share my feelings with my kids now.

"Her being a child herself, it was very hard. We lived at my dad's for a while, and then she got married, and I moved into her home. And it bounced back and forth. We've never had a sister-sister relationship, because she was always the adult figure in my life."

Regarding their current relationship, Mickey says, "She's still my mom. We tried to have a sister-sister relationship at one time. We did attempt it. It did not work. There are things you can tell a sister that you can't tell the authority figure in your life. That was the reality of what it was. She and I are not very close anymore."

Yet Mickey is clearly aware that she has a special relationship with this caretaking sibling; she knows that Brandi sacrificed her childhood to raise her. "What did she give up to raise me? She asked me that question, too. She didn't have a child when she started raising me. So she gave up being a child herself. And then when she did have a kid of her own, she still had the responsibility of me. I don't know. I would think she had to give up a lot to raise a kid. I know to raise someone else's child, you have to. I know she's only human, but sometimes she can still. . . ." Mickey describes confronting Brandi for the first time recently about the troubled years. "She actually listened and accepted it and admitted guilt to a lot of things that I'd never thought that she would."

Complicating the relationship is that both Brandi and Mickey are working on their own recoveries from drug and alcohol addiction. Brandi is quite active in her recovery group, causing Mickey to feel that even in their recovery efforts, Brandi is trying to "mother" her. Only time will tell whether these two sisters, the caretaker and her "child," can work into a more comfortable relationship.

Life as the Cared For

Other younger sisters also report troubled relationships with their caretaking sisters. One of these is Joellen Weatherford, twenty-four, a travel agency trainee from Richmond, Virginia, who tells this story about her sister Tiffany, eight years her senior. "My sister was sixteen, and I was eight when our parents divorced. She argued with Mom over drinking and taking care of me—which I never knew. My sister stayed until she was eighteen, and then she moved out . . . leaving me alone with Mom."

Joellen continues, sadness tingeing her voice. "Now Tiffany's just showing all the symptoms that our mother has. She talks like her, her morals are turning like hers, and I can hardly stand to see this happen to my nephew."

Part of the two sisters' current trouble, Joellen acknowledges, is jealousy. She admits that her parents provided more for her financially than they had provided for Tiffany, something that Tiffany seems now to resent. Joellen evidently has her own reasons to feel jealous—Tiffany had more of her mother as a sober mother. Still, when things got bad with their mother, Joellen would move in with Tiffany.

Joellen's story clearly reveals Tiffany's protection of her, including taking her in, illegally, to keep her safe from her mother's neglect. But still a child herself, Tiffany couldn't do everything a mother should be doing; for example, she didn't send Joellen to school regularly. And, in Joellen's mind, Tiffany abandoned her by having a social life when Joellen was a child. Now that Tiffany is fighting alcohol addiction, Joellen feels even more abandoned. She empathizes strongly with the feelings of her nephew, Tiffany's child. Tiffany, deprived of her childhood, has turned to the only thing she knows to anesthetize her pain—drinking.

Janie Dailey tells a similar story. "My mother had technically been around during the time while I was growing up, but yet she *wasn't* around because she was always in the bars. So my big sister was really my mom. I can remember times when I hurt myself, cried

'Mommy!' and ran to my sister. So I remember knowing that my mother wasn't there for us. I didn't run to my real mother; I don't think I knew any different. I probably thought that was the way it was supposed to be."

Nichole Von Bergen is the younger sister in her family. Nichole says, "My sister was very maternal toward me. She taught me how to do many things like read and tie my shoes. I looked to her for protection and advice. We often discussed how our parents behaved, and we felt somewhat parentless because our parents were so immature and absorbed in themselves.

"But my sister has always thought Mother was partial to me. And as a result of that, my sister has always resented my mother and me to some extent. Because she thought I had a special relationship with Mother, and she came second. But my sister was like the mother. She took care of me. She was the one who'd help me find my shoes, or teach me how to do things, or read to me at night. My mother didn't read to me before I went to bed, my sister did." Now adults, the two sisters maintain a usually loving relationship. Nichole says, "I'm real close to her. But we always end up fighting at some point."

Perhaps not surprisingly, considering the complexity of the emotional ties, many younger sisters report estrangement from their older caretaking sisters. For Jane Farrell, her relationship with her older sister is marked by the family secrets that her much-older siblings continue to keep. "My sister played 'mommy'—she was the oldest—and took more care of me than my mother. My relationship with my mother was basically nonexistent. I have tried to learn as much as possible about my mother, but my sister does not want to share the 'deep, dark family secrets.' She says that she is 'protecting' me."

Sometimes it requires unusual compromises to make the older caretaker-sibling/younger sibling relationship work. For Tina Avery, the youngest child in her extended family, that compromise was baby-sitting her nieces and nephews. "My older sisters felt they were forced to baby-sit me all the time because my parents were busy running a restaurant. I didn't develop relationships with them till I was older. It was difficult because I felt their resentment and jealousy of my being the baby and being spoiled. It wasn't until I began baby-sitting for them and becoming independent that I earned respect from them."

Sharon, the oldest of five children, knows only too well what it is like to be the caretaking sibling. From the time her sister Sheila came into the world less than two years after her own birth, Sharon was charged with the responsibility of caring for younger brothers and sisters. It was a burden that she did not always accept graciously, yet it is one she knows she's now having trouble relinquishing. "I just can't let go and keep my nose out of their business. I worry constantly about all of them, especially my two sisters, even though they are grown, with families of their own. But if I know that one of them is having some kind of problem, I want to rush to their side and take charge. And they resent it. Of course they do! They *should* resent it. But it's hard to just suddenly stop feeling like I'm always the one who gets blamed if something goes wrong."

It's the morning of my fifteenth birthday. I awaken early, toss aside the sheet, and hurl myself happily out of bed. Daddy is not home, which is one thing that would have made me truly happy; he's out of state working. Mama is still sleeping off last night's beer, and the younger kids are in their rooms. But I don't care if I'm alone; it's my birthday! And somehow, being fifteen today means magic. I am young, strong, healthy, and very sure that today will mark a major change in my life. Today, Mama won't drink or go out, leaving us alone for hours. Today, I think, with a shiver of excitement, I am old enough to date! (Okay, nobody is waiting in the wings to whisk me away, but there is possibility in the wind!)

I go into the kitchen and make coffee. The house is not yet hot, though July sunlight is pouring through the open windows. I take my coffee into the living room and sit there on the old red plastic couch, with its cigarette burn holes and rips, through which stuffing appears, turns gray, and is torn out. I don't care, for once, how ugly it is. Today I want to just sit, drink my coffee, and bask in the joy of being this special age.

Suddenly I hear the splatting sound of small flat feet, coupled with another sound—whining and crying. It's my little brother Delmer. He's not quite two years old, and he is walking around in the kitchen and dining room. I don't want him to wake up Mama, so I call to him softly, "Come in here, Delmer. I'm in here." He pads into the living room. Brown liquid is running down both his skinny legs. Diarrhea. It's everywhere. He has been walking all around the house, with puddles forming at each step.

I feel like crying with anger and despair. Such a stinking mess! But I know better than to wake Mama over this. She'd merely look at me through her swollen red eyes and ask sarcastically, "And what's wrong with you, Miss Priss? You think because it's your birthday, you're too damned good to clean up a little shit?" Then in addition to cleaning up after my brother, I'd just have to put up with her nasty mood all day.

So first I delicately remove the oozing diaper from Delmer and put him in the bathtub. After a quick wash, he gets a clean diaper and a pair of heavy-duty rubber underpants. Then I stick him in bed with my sister and tell her not to let him get back out, while I hustle to fetch the mop, the mop bucket, and the detergent. After mopping the kitchen, dining room, living room, and two bedrooms, I wash out the mop and mop bucket with bleach water. Then bending over the toilet, I rinse the excess from the diaper and put it in the diaper pail. But the diaper pail is full, so I start a load of diapers to wash—hot wash, hot rinse, extra bleach.

When I've finally cleaned everything, I realize that over an hour has passed since I'd gotten up so full of joy. Now everyone except Mama is up and about. The house still smells like Delmer's sour stomach, though, so I pour out my cup of cold, unfinished coffee. A refill seems unappetizing at this point. Besides, no one has even said "Happy Birthday" to me.

Chapter Eight

Men: Our Romantic Relationships

~

"Usually the nicer the men were, the more I disliked them."
—Theresa Hale, twenty-nine, medical transcriptionist,
Oakland, California

"I attract drunks and fat dogs. Ha! I have been celibate for seven years
and it works for me."
—Evelyn Collins, fifty-one, Birmingham, Alabama

~

Absently, from force of habit, I burst into song as I walked through the
house.

"Geez, Ellie," he remarked with a critical laugh. "Your voice is
awful! Please don't sing around me."

Oops, I'd forgotten again.

Singing had been a lifelong pleasure for me. Over the years, I'd sung
in many church choirs and school choruses simply because singing felt so
exhilarating! I discovered my love for it in elementary school music
classes, then later started piano lessons. As I'd sit at the piano, playing
selections from musicals, old ballads, contemporary rock hits, spirituals,
cowboy songs from the Old West, Irish lullabies, it didn't matter—I
sang my heart out. I may not have been great, but I felt alive, exuberant,
and joyful, transported somewhere over the rainbow.

He criticized my singing voice right from the start.

"Augh," he would groan whenever I sang. "Please! You can't carry a tune. Your voice is so off-key." And he would laugh.

What had first attracted me to him was his powerful stage presence. His voice, his stride, his self-assurance, filled up the room. He resonated confidence, an attribute that I both admired and lacked. At once, I felt safe and taken care of. Strong-willed and opinionated, he was the leader I had yearned for. So I became a willing follower, and slowly, I was pulled into the undertow of his personality.

I missed singing, all those years I was with him.

It is no secret that in our romantic relationships, we daughters of alcoholics tend to have poor track records. Though we know of no research that has focused specifically on the marriage patterns of daughters of alcoholic mothers, it is known that daughters of alcoholics often marry alcoholics. Judith S. Seixas and Geraldine Youcha, authors of *Children of Alcoholism: A Survivor's Manual,* report that "one estimate is as high as 60 percent . . . in some women this pattern is so strong that they divorce one alcoholic husband and marry another, often very quickly. They fall into the trap unconsciously and in spite of firm determination never to become involved with another alcoholic man." Claudia Black, author of *It Will Never Happen to Me,* states that she is "aware of the tendency of daughters to marry alcoholic men." Herbert L. Gravitz and Julie D. Bowden agree. In *Recovery: A Guide for Adult Children of Alcoholics,* they note that children of alcoholics are indeed at risk for marrying alcoholics. And a partner's alcoholism may be just one component of a larger behavioral package that includes drug use, the need to dominate, and perhaps physical and verbal abuse. Although we think of "abuse" as behavior that is dramatic, loud, or physically violent, it can also take the form of subtle psychological dominance, which can be just as degrading, perhaps even more, because it is so much less obvious than outright blows and curses. It can build up so slowly that a woman is barely aware of it. Chances are she is underconfident and unsure of herself to begin with, so it is easy for him to chip away at her self-esteem and subtly gain control over her.

In *Perfect Daughters*, Ackerman writes, "Of all the problems that I have heard from adult daughters about their relationships, being in a relationship with a very controlling male was at the core of most of the problems . . . regardless of the type of male, whether alcoholic, abusive, or emotionally distant, these males had one thing in common: They were very controlling."

Many of us marry young as a way of escaping unhappy homes. If a daughter of an alcoholic meets someone when she is "at [her] lowest emotional point," writes Ackerman, she may envision him as a savior who will emancipate her from the unhappiness at home. She may feel "instantly and totally attracted to the first person who gives any emotional support. This person usually was not the best, but was the first," he concludes. This needy feeling, plus the desire to get away from home, may lead to an early first marriage. Many of us, insatiable in our hunger for love, and rightfully dissatisfied with our choices of mates, move through multiple relationships and marriages in our never-ending quest to find a partner who will make us feel whole. Of the daughters in our project who had been married, half had been divorced one or more times. Though they were not asked, many volunteered that their past or current lovers or husbands were alcoholics, abusers, or just plain losers.

Sara Oliver, forty-eight, a loan officer from Flagstaff, Arizona, has been divorced three times because "I have never been able to trust anyone to stay or to take care of me." Currently, Sara is involved in four different relationships. "One is an alcoholic and wants to get married," she confides. "I won't unless he stops drinking. The second is much younger than I am. The third is much older than I am. The fourth is a family friend and younger than I am."

A stormy relationship with an alcoholic mother may be one of the driving forces behind a daughter's poor romantic choices. Dr. Carole Leiberman and Lisa Collier Cool agree in their book *Bad Boys* that women often seek to re-create their childhood turbulence through their partners: "Bad boys may hold a fatal attraction to you because you have an overpowering need to replay a disturbing drama from your childhood in your adult love affairs. . . . Even though you risk excruciating pain from these relationships, you secretly hope that by reliving the trauma that wounded you as a girl—over and over, if necessary—you will eventually figure out how to give the story a happy ending. Your fantasy is that, with the right rogue, you'll finally heal, and be able to move on."

Donna Cartee is a perfect example. "I married a man exactly like my mother," she says. "After thirteen tortured years I divorced him. I have missed a lot of opportunities in my life because of my lack of self-confidence."

"My perception of love was colored by my relationship with my mother," agrees Susanna Moore. "All my relationships have been tainted with anxiety, distrust, and constant worry about love being yanked away—my mother's love was *extremely* conditional."

Poor Judgment

For years, we daughters look forward to leaving our chaotic homes. Marriage seems like a nice, respectable escape. Why, then, do we often make such bad choices of mates? Shouldn't we know better than anybody whom *not* to choose? Yet we are so often drawn to men who are not good for us.

"The scary thing is," confesses Emily, forty-eight, who has been divorced twice, "that alcoholic guys are *still* more attractive to me— at first. The difference is that now I know intellectually they're not good for me. But—they do get my attention!"

Even when we do find a potentially suitable partner, we may not give ourselves to him emotionally as much as we would like because we often fear intimacy—even while we crave it. Janet Woititz, author of *Adult Children of Alcoholics,* refers to this struggle as the "push-pull, approach-avoidance, the 'I want you—go away,' the colossal terror of being close, yet the desire and need for it."

Of course, there are many of us who manage to enter healthy romantic relationships, get married, and stay married. Fifty percent of the daughters in our sampling, after all, had married only once and had not been divorced (though some volunteered that they were "struggling" to stay married). But when we daughters do end up in poor relationships, it may not be just our own happiness that is at stake, although that in itself is an important consideration. We daughters often hold the key to either repeating or breaking the destructive cycle for the next generation. When we end up marrying abusive, addicted, or unfit partners, we prolong the destructive family pattern. Even more serious, the type of men we tend to be drawn to may hurt our children in a more tangible way, either by physically or verbally abusing them, or introducing them to undesirable lifestyles. Susan Steffan, a teacher from Montana, says, "I put up with being hit and with his affairs, but I left when I found out he had hit and choked my daughter while I was at work."

Shannon Nichols is aware of her ex-husband's negative effect on her child. Her son got high for the first time at a very young age and was hooked on drugs from that moment on. Who introduced him to drugs? His alcoholic, drug-abusing stepfather.

Ackerman points out in *Perfect Daughters* that daughters of alcoholic mothers "have different issues than do daughters of alcoholic fathers." These include problems with sexual and feminine identity; trust; and the willingness to want to please others at our own expense. Obviously, problems in these areas could contribute substantially to troubled romantic relationships. First, our mothers were not positive and consistent enough gender role models, so we feel unsure about how to relate to men. We are confused, in other words, about what a "normal" woman is supposed to be—as if this wasn't confusing enough to begin with, given the social upheavals in recent times. In addition, as we discuss elsewhere, many of our mothers conveyed to us the attitude that sex and sexuality were disgusting and degrading, which could also complicate romantic relationships.

Trust is another issue. As Ackerman states, many daughters do "not feel comfortable trusting their own feelings and believing that they perceived things accurately."

The real problem is: how can we evaluate men intelligently and weed out the losers if we have no confidence in our own judgment?

"I can totally relate to this idea of not trusting my own feelings," says Ellie. "Often, I could not accurately gauge my feelings about a man because I could not trust my own judgment. My ability to see things clearly had fuzzed forever on that day I first confronted Mother about her drunkenness, and she had *insisted* I was making it all up. How could I later trust whatever feelings I thought I had toward a man? How did I know they weren't just another 'illusion,' like her drinking?"

Jo Ann Stills, twenty-six, was married for six years to a man she didn't really love, even at the altar. But because she felt she *should* have loved him, she went ahead with the wedding. "I would hear my family and everybody say, 'Oh, he's just such a wonderful person. Oh, he'd make such a great husband. He just loves you so much,'" explains Jo Ann. "I thought something was wrong with *me* for not loving him. So I thought, 'Well, then, I'll learn to.' I'd never seen a healthy relationship, so I didn't know what one was supposed to be like or feel like."

Trying Too Hard to Please

Our people-pleasing ways can also set us up for unhealthy relationships. According to Ackerman, adult daughters "shared that they often felt emotionally trapped because they admitted they tried to please someone who caused them anger."

Ellie agrees. "One important lesson I learned at my mother's knee, so to speak, is 'Don't be yourself or express your true feelings. You'll make somebody mad. Then they won't like you anymore. Or, you might trigger an argument.' After bearing the brunt of my mother's illogical and inconsistent responses to me, I was never sure what might light her fire. Therefore, to be safe and to avoid her capricious reactions, I stifled my true feelings; I became very careful about what I said or did. It became habitual. This carried over into relationships with men. I always hesitated to spill out any truths about what bothered me, what needed fixing, or what my unmet needs were. I kept those bottled up, for fear that he would either drop me immediately or blow up. And, of course, I could not have dreamed of engaging in the type of violent quarrels that my parents had engaged in! It was much safer to avoid disagreement altogether. In my mind, *all* disagreement automatically led to loud, cursing altercations. I did not learn until much later that there is a middle ground between silence and violence."

Desperate for Love . . .

Dogged by low self-esteem, hungry for love and affirmation from an outside source, we bond too quickly with anyone who throws a few crumbs of affection our way. We daughters are clearly at a higher risk for seeking love—or what we naively interpret as love—from partners who would use us in varying degrees. Not only are we always searching for affection and attention, we are usually overly grateful when we receive it.

"In my relationships with men, I become too needy," says Diana Matthews, forty. "There's a part of me that dies and takes on the other person's needs and interests. I threatened one man by sending a funny 'suicide' card saying 'If you ever leave me, I'll—' "

Shari Lynn Curts, forty-nine, lives in Eugene, Oregon, with her third husband. The six-year marriage, she admits, is not satisfying. "I guess I'm just in it so I have someone. I *hate* to be alone."

Shy and dateless in high school until the end of my junior year, ashamed of Mama's drinking and fearful that everyone knew of it, I had gone outside my school district for my first boyfriend. We'd made a good couple, I thought. Glenn was tall, fair, and blue-eyed. The summer we met, I had been working in a diner next door to the gas station his father owned. Outside my hometown and in my work uniform, I could be just like anyone else. No one had to know that I was the oldest daughter of a poor man and his drunken wife. It was like a fairy tale, Cinderella with a twist.

When he dropped me, the loss was not only of my love, but of my identity. The big ring on my finger announced to the world that I was somebody, a girl who was desired by a boy. For the rest of the school year, I went dateless. No one wanted the morose, bespectacled, plumpish daughter of the town drunk. I sensed that even Glenn, to whom I'd never told my secret, felt that I was one of the untouchables, the lowest caste. He had been right to ditch me, I told myself. After all, what if I turned out like Mama, as my cruel high school yearbook had predicted: "Girl most likely to become a barmaid at Sam's Place"—Mama's favorite watering hole. Later, I found out that he'd dumped me because he'd met another girl. He later married that girl—but not before he came back to me long enough to cheat on her with me. I let him make love to me even though he was engaged to be married in only a couple of weeks.

We are also often drawn to the types of men who love us and leave us, as the saying goes. Janie Dailey, a single mother, says the father of her child "disappeared when the state began to hit him for the first time for child support." Diane Bryant's boyfriend of four years dumped her as soon as he found out she was pregnant. "Now he doesn't want anything to do with his baby." Diane, a college student, is due to have her baby soon.

. . . But Fearful of Intimacy

Despite our yearning for love, we may fear physical and emotional intimacy. At first glance, this appears to be a contradiction, but it is really not. On the surface, we desire love because we feel a great emptiness inside. We seek romantic love as a cure. But often we are too quick to substitute a handsome face and a good line for true intimacy, because the charms of a dynamic, unavailable "bad boy" are often so intense. We feel instantly filled up with emotion and excitement, which temporarily obliterates that empty feeling. But if we meet a "nice" guy whose merits unfold more slowly, a man who seeks true emotional intimacy, we may feel oddly scared and push him away, dubbing him "boring."

Dallas Whitaker admits that she has never related to any of her four spouses on as deep a level as she should have. "Because it's like you have that inner self that you nurture, because you've nurtured it for so many years, that you just don't trust anybody to go there," she explains. "It's like your own space in life. I don't know if normal people are able to let their loved ones into that space or not. But I've never been able to. Maybe what I'm afraid of, about letting someone in there, is that everybody who's gotten even close to that place has turned around and hurt me. Nobody gets in there again, it's too painful."

Kitty Dellinger, forty-eight, who has been divorced twice from the same man, has had trouble with emotional intimacy. She has had many significant romantic relationships but ends them because she fears abandonment. "Today, I walk away from relationships when I sense closeness, or I withdraw and make myself unavailable without explaining why," she says. "It's easier to walk away than to risk pain. Yet I relive moments and restage fairy tale outcomes. I'm still pining away for a man I left in 1976. These men are ever with me in my mind."

Mia Mitchell, thirty-two, admits, "I had a lot of meaningless relationships prior to meeting and marrying my husband. I sought out the worst type of men, men who used me. I ended the relationships with anyone who got 'too close.'"

Cathryn Silvers, forty-four, has entered many relationships because she is terrified of being alone. But once she's with a man, she begins to resent him. If he proves himself reliable, she finds him boring and leaves him. She has been divorced twice and is "ready to do number three."

Choosing unavailable men is a common ploy for avoiding intimacy.

Caryl Brookins, forty-seven, has never married but has been involved in four significant romantic relationships. "Three of the men were married, and I was tired of waiting," admits Caryl. "The last person just couldn't commit to the relationship."

Honey Sanders has been involved in three significant romantic relationships since her divorce. "These men were unavailable," says Honey. "Poor choices on my part. One was an alcoholic and two were married. I ended the relationships because they were unable to commit."

Our Nurturing Instincts at Work

Sometimes we are attracted to men whom we wish to "cure" of their problems. Because the mother-child relationship was often reversed in our homes, we have learned to be responsible for others' needs at the expense of our own and may be automatically attracted to partners who need some kind of "rehabilitation."

Sonya Graham describes her contradictory feelings toward the men in her life: "My boyfriends are usually totally devoted to me, and I take care of them. I tend to go for males I can mother—if not financially, then emotionally and physically. Then I start to lose respect for them, because I need a strong man."

Felecia Purvis, thirty-nine, who has been divorced three times, describes herself as "exhausted. I feel that I have fixed them up— and what's left of me?" she asks.

Cindy Rebstock says that "even when my relationship is really bad, I tend to cling to them. I pick lousy men and try to help them solve their problems."

Our Need for Drama

Excitement and upheaval, even of the negative sort, is a pattern we became used to as we grew up. We adult daughters sometimes have trouble feeling comfortable when life gets too routine. We may be driven by an inexplicable need to shake things up periodically. What better way to do this than to ally ourselves with "dangerous," unavailable men?

Janie Dailey says, "The men I tend to be attracted to have drug problems or alcohol problems. It's the bad-boy thing. I can't think of a guy I've ever been involved with who *didn't* have an alcohol or drug problem. Actually, though, I *can* think of one who didn't . . . and I threw him out really quick." She laughs. "He was too boring! It was awful! I was like, 'Honey, let's go out and do something,' and he'd say, 'What do you want to do, go to McDonald's?' and I'd yell, 'Nooo! That's not what I want to do!' I had quit drinking by then, yet I still wanted to say, 'I want to go out to a bar and get trashed!' But, no, that's *not* what I wanted to do! It's still really hard for me to find a man because I look at the guys in church, and I'm like, 'Well, that's what I *should* be looking at, but you know what? I like *that*— out *there*. Even though I know better now, I'm still real attracted to that bad-boy thing. Like I keep saying, 'If you can just find me a Christian biker, okay! I'll take that!' "

Beth Petrie, twenty-six, agrees. "I get bored a lot," she says. "Relationships must be full of excitement, and if not, I move on or move away. I also don't want to have to share my secrets," she adds, admitting that she is relieved that there is little time for quiet talking with the men she chooses.

"I certainly fit the marital profile of the typical daughter of an alcoholic mother," says Ellie, who has been divorced twice and remarried for the third time. "Many of the men in my life— husbands and otherwise—have tended to be 'colorful' or 'different' in some way . . . in other words, never boring. But at the price of being inappropriate, controlling, devious, or unavailable. However, my low confidence probably helped to foster those behaviors in men. Maybe they'd have been completely different with another woman."

Our Inability to Recognize Addicts

We were amazed that many daughters we talked to had had no idea that the men they were marrying were active or latent alcoholics or drug addicts. We daughters apparently have the uncanny ability to hone in on men whose addictive personalities seduce us even before we know what the addictions are.

Punkin Johnson, fifty-two, says, "When I got married, I did the classic thing. I married my mother. He was a drug addict, it turned out, more than an alcoholic. He kept it very carefully hidden from me until after I was married. I took my marriage vows very seriously and planned just to stick it out, since I had a kid and, well, I was seven months pregnant when I found out about the drug addiction. Then apparently he was also a sociopath. After about a year and a half, it became dangerous for the baby and me to stay close to him. So I picked up my marbles and left. That marriage was over in three years. Short and sweet. I realized what I'd gotten myself into, and that I couldn't do anything to help him. He was actually about to do something to hurt us."

Shannon Nichol's second husband turned out to be an alcoholic and drug addict, a fact she also was not aware of before taking her vows. "Did I have any idea before the marriage that my husband had these tendencies? Goodness, *no!*" she exclaims. "No, I really, really didn't. Because he was *so* attentive, and so kind and very generous, and he acted nice to my son. I didn't know that he had a drinking problem. Nor did I know that he had a drug problem."

Betty Buxton, fifty-four and a college professor in Arizona, is intelligent, witty, and has a great sense of humor. A turning point occurred in her twenty-three-year marriage when she was apart from her husband during a one-year sabbatical. She didn't realize until she was separated from him that he was an alcoholic. She laughs self-deprecatingly.

"I had no insights whatsoever about the fact that I had selected a mate who reproduced the old emotional turmoil of my childhood," she says. "Here I'd picked a man who was really a wonderful composite of my mother and my father, who were both alcoholics, a man who was clearly an alcoholic himself. I should have known that on the first date! But I didn't."

He was charming, he was talented, and he was handsome. Betty married him after a ten-day courtship and spent the next twenty-three years in "a relationship from hell."

For years, Betty had been depressed—sometimes seriously, sometimes mildly—and she assumed that because of this, she needed him more than ever to bolster up her mood.

"Because here I was, this pathetic person who was always on the verge of depression. I couldn't see that he was someone who was probably fundamentally *causing* a lot of it. So the sabbatical provided this opportunity to get off the merry-go-round. And all of a sudden, I started feeling . . . really *good!*" laughs Betty.

During their separation, her husband became increasingly insecure and anxious about Betty's being on her own and began to drink even more. Meanwhile, she was drinking less and mellowing out. "It was looking better and better without him."

Then she met a man who served as a catalyst for her breakup. They had a brief but passionate affair.

"We just sort of fell into each other's arms and had"—Betty bursts into laughter—"a fabulous three weeks. It was just a big, big wake-up call for me. First of all, there was something called the possibility of a wonderful life." She realized she could never go back to her marriage in its current state and hoped counseling would help. She and her husband went together, but when the counselor suggested that he stop drinking, he refused.

Betty then decided to turn her life around, with or without him.

She divorced him, went into therapy, and began to read self-help books. Mainly, she tried for the first time in her life to take care of herself and her own needs. She reflected on the past twenty-three years and concluded that her own insecurities and lack of confidence had kept her in this destructive marriage.

"I also had the realization," continues Betty, "that I shouldn't turn taking care of myself over to anybody. My own well-being needs to be stuff that I engineer, not what I expect somebody else to do for me, because that's fraught with peril."

Betty has recently met another man, "and even with him now, I can see some potential problems if I'm not kind of careful. I used to tell my therapist that first year, that I truly must have a sign on my back: 'If you have an addiction, please come to me. I love men with addictions.' Because that's what I was attracting," she says.

Her new beau does not drink much, but Betty is wary of his pot-smoking habit. He is very mellow and not too ambitious. He has admitted to her that he smokes "probably too much" marijuana. Betty sighs and says dryly, "That gave me some pause." She plans to think carefully about this new relationship, adding that talking about her romantic history has given her insights about her new boyfriend that "I need to have, I think."

"It's very hard to find healthy men," she concludes. "At least I find it's very hard to find someone who is not an alcoholic or not a drug addict or not a sexaholic or not a workaholic. In other words, it seems like everyone I meet, most everyone I meet, has been in some dependent relationship with *something*. The healthier I get, the more I realize, I'm *not* going to be propping somebody up. I'm not going to be getting into a relationship like that again."

Portraits of Our Relationships

Below, we present stories told to us by daughters of alcoholic mothers. We hope that in reading these examples, other daughters will recognize themselves and realize that they are far from alone in their experiences with husbands or partners. To be sure, many of us have had unsatisfactory relationships, sometimes many. But the good news is that most of us have gained wisdom from them and are actively working to break the old romantic patterns.

Karisa Pickett

Karisa Pickett, twenty-four and the mother of three children, is a secretary from Wichita, Kansas, who describes herself as "a caring person who helps anyone who needs help." Fifteen when she met her first boyfriend and thinking she was in love, she latched onto him, got pregnant, and moved out of her mother's house. Soon he became abusive and controlling.

"Whenever it was a full moon, I got knocked around," says Karisa. "I would always think, 'Well, it will be okay, the baby's not hurt, and I didn't have any pain in my stomach,' so I didn't pay any attention." Her boyfriend would not allow her to receive prenatal care because he was jealous and fearful that she might flirt with the doctor. He told her what to wear and he would not allow her to put on makeup.

"If we drove down the road in the car, I couldn't look out the window," says Karisa. "I had to look at the floorboard or the dash. If I looked out the windows, and it happened that a guy might be riding by on a bicycle or something, he'd say, 'Oh, you're just looking at him because you want some new dick.'"

Predictably, Karisa discovered that he was cheating on her. She had picked up his photos from Wal-Mart and found, in the collection, a picture of him and another young woman, half naked. When she gave him the photos, he asked if she'd looked at them, but she said no. Later, he brought the pictures out for her to see, and the incriminating ones were missing.

She gave birth to a son, and for a while, her boyfriend stopped hitting her. Soon she was pregnant again. Then he began beating the little boy, who was now six months old. "He got where he would pick my son up, out of the playpen, by his foot, like a rag doll and beat his butt until literally the diaper tapes would pop off," says Karisa. "Then he'd throw him in the playpen like he was some kind of stuffed toy."

Taking the baby, Karisa left him. With the help of some men friends to protect her, she returned the next day to pick up her clothes, which he had not allowed her to take. He had also stolen $21,000 she had received as a settlement for a childhood accident.

"The guy took me for every penny of it," Karisa says. "He never did a good thing for me except produce a beautiful child."

Now her boyfriend is pressing her to start seeing him again. He swears he has changed. But Karisa is older and much wiser now.

Virginia Mathew

"I was seventeen years old; what did *I* know?" exclaims Virginia Mathew, referring to her first marriage. Virginia, forty-six, a well-spoken college professor from Albany, New York, was swept off her feet by the good-looking young man who drove a Jaguar. Besides, marrying him was a way to get out of the house.

"I was so miserable with my mother *I just wanted out,*" she asserts. Her husband, a politician, had a large ego and a low tolerance for anyone who could not further his career. Virginia was not exactly happy in the marriage, but she lived in a nice house and drove a nice car. Besides, she worried that if she left him, she might end up with someone even worse. "So you stay in it because it's comfortable even though it's not good," she admits.

Her husband was a backstabber who used and dropped people heartlessly. This bothered Virginia. In fact, she lost all respect for him. But she still could not bring herself to leave him even though he "stabbed his way all the way up and tried to prevent me from seeing the people he didn't think were suitable. Oh, yes, he was very controlling. But I trusted him; this was the person who loved me, who wouldn't do anything to harm me, of *course,* he *loved* me," she says wryly.

Virginia halfheartedly stayed with him for nearly eleven years. But then the problem was solved: he ran off with her best friend. As the old joke goes, Virginia was grief-stricken—because she missed her girlfriend so much.

Nan MacGregor

Nan MacGregor, twenty-eight, has been married and divorced four times and is now living with someone. "Oh, God. Oh, God. You're probably going to laugh," she warns as she tells her story. Her first husband, at age forty-four, was quite a bit older than she was. Their marriage lasted one month. Nan feels it was her alcoholism that broke them up.

"I'd sit there and I'd just boldfaced *lie* to him and say, 'No, I'm not drinking.' You know? He just got tired of it and said, 'I want a divorce,' and I said, 'Fine.' At the time, my alcohol meant more to me. Okay, the next one . . . who was it?" she muses. "The next one was just to get out of a bad situation. You know what I mean? The rebound husband. We were married for about two years, but I left after about two months. What was wrong with him? He was a wife beater. Husband number three. Man, he was a trip. My daughter's father. He was older; he's almost fifty now. He's an ass. But, oh God, how do I explain him. He looked like James Dean when we got married. We got divorced about two days before my daughter was born. Then, husband number four, he was just *pathetic.* I married him because I thought he was just everything I ever wanted, everything I ever dreamed of.

"What did I dream of? I wanted somebody who was going to love me and care for me for *me,* not for what I could do."

The last marriage was strained by the presence of Nan's mother-in-law, who spent a lot of time at their house. Also she fought a lot with her husband over money. "I wasn't happy," she said. "I'd keep getting confronted with something, like I spent too much money, and I'd get all defensive, freak out, and start yelling and screaming. That was it."

Nan, who is now a recovering alcoholic and drug addict, has been living with someone for a year, but she describes it as "not real good." A stepchild complicates their relationship, plus the two adults are constantly engaged in power struggles.

She explains, "He wants things done a certain way, you know, 'Life According to Him'? For example, he says I've got to do the dishes in cold water, and I'm like, 'No, you don't; you've got to do them in hot water.' He says, 'No, you don't.' We'll sit there and argue and fight over the stupidest little thing.

"But," adds Nan thoughtfully, "I think all these relationship problems are because of me too, because I am so picky. I was always by myself, from the time I was just a *kid;* I was four when my brother was born, and I was changing his diapers, I was feeding him, and I was on my own. I guess I'm just so used to doing things *my way* that it's either my way or the highway. I was forced into early responsibility and missed my childhood, so I want things my way now."

"I don't think this relationship is going to work either. I think I just need to be alone," she admits. "My relationships are like a sick pattern. You know, I'm looking for Mr. Right in all the wrong places. What *is* Mr. Right? A more important question is, am I okay with *me?* Because if I'm not okay with *me,* I'm not going to be okay with anybody else. But I really love the man I'm with, I really, really do, and I know there are some things about me that I need to change. You know, I need to lighten up a little bit. I need to learn how to do that."

Jackie Llaneza

"We don't really count marriage number one because I was only seventeen, and it only lasted a month," says Jackie, twenty-nine, a day care provider from Alabama who has been divorced twice and remarried for a year. When her first husband became violent very soon after the wedding, she left him and went home.

"It was a stupid teenage mistake," she explains.

Two years later, she met her second husband, an alcoholic. But of course, she did not recognize this at the time. Being only nineteen, she found it exciting to go out with him and his friends to drink.

"I went from taking care of Mom to taking care of him, so it was very, very, very natural," she says. During their courtship, Jackie's mother began attending AA meetings. Sometimes Jackie would go along with her, and in so doing, she became better informed about alcoholism.

"I was just starting to become aware of what alcoholism was all about and how it had affected my life," she says. "Yet I went ahead and married my second husband anyway and stayed for about four more years in this abusive relationship before I got out.

"Denial is a great thing!" She laughs. "He was going to quit; I just knew it. He even went into treatment, the same program my mother went into. He did whatever he thought he could do to make me stay. But he became a very pathetic alcoholic, and it just didn't work anymore. I had thoughts of suicide. I would say my husband's drinking affected me in that aspect. Twice I tried to overdose."

Another difficulty in the marriage was the presence of two stepchildren. "At the time that I met their father, I was very young and because I was so codependent, it was perfectly natural for me to take on a man who had two young children," says Jackie. "Being the motherly type person that I am, it was a challenge." She raised them for four years and became particularly close to the younger one. The older one, on the other hand, was closer to his father. After observing his father abusing her, he also began to treat her poorly.

"He saw his dad abuse me and bad-mouth me, so he picked up on it and thought, 'Hey, it's okay to treat her this way,'" she says.

Her husband's drinking accelerated, and he became abusive

toward his children as well. She could not bear this. She knew she could no longer stay with this man and have children of her own with him.

"Knowing this made it very easy to turn around, walk away, and say, 'I don't want to have a family with you,'" she remembers. "I had gotten to the point where it was either make *their* lives better or make *my* life better. I chose to take care of *myself* at that point."

Her mother's recovery taught Jackie a lot about alcoholism, and she is grateful to her mother for her efforts to become sober.

"I'm very thankful to my mother for stopping the chain reaction that is so common in so many families. When you were raised that way, and you marry somebody that way, and you live that way, it goes on that way. Your kids are brought up that way. I'm very thankful that when I raise my children, drugs and alcohol don't have to be part of the lifestyle that I live. Hopefully, my children will not live through what I have lived through as the child of an alcoholic.

"I remarried a third time," she continues. "I was thoroughly surprised, in the relationship I'm in now with my new husband, that he drinks less than I do, and I don't drink much at all. So that, to me, was a sign that I've progressed forward in my life, as far as what kind of partners I pick. I learned my lessons from the first two. That is encouraging. I think Mom's getting treatment opened my eyes and got me out of the bad situation I was in, and instead of going back into that same type of situation, I chose a different kind of person. So that was encouraging to me. That's what I told my husband, 'Third time's a charm.'"

Shannon Nichols

Shannon Nichols, forty-eight, a veterinarian from Pennsylvania, has been divorced twice and is now remarried. Typical of many daughters of alcoholic mothers, she was young and pregnant when she married the first time. Her mother made her get married because "she was ashamed," explains Shannon. "She used that word a lot. I should be *ashamed* that this was a horrible, terrible thing to do to the family.

"Was I in love with him?" Shannon contemplates the question, and then responds, "Yes, in a teenagey sort of way, I was in love with being able to please somebody. I thought that pleasing somebody was what I was supposed to do. I had *no* idea who I was at that time."

Two years later, her husband left her, and five years later, she remarried.

"I married this man who I thought was going to be the cure-all of every problem I'd ever had, not knowing then what I know now," she says. Her second husband, who turned out to be an alcoholic and drug user, cheated on her frequently. She describes how her ex-husband's mother would even accommodate his infidelity.

"My mother-in-law would come and visit us, and while I was off at work, my husband would bring home his girlfriends to meet his mother. And she would cook for them!"

When he left her, she was not heartbroken. In fact, she felt rather relieved. "But I said to myself, 'Okay, look at yourself now, Shannon, you've been married twice; you'd better take a look at what's going on.' I had never taken a look at what was *really* going on, which was the alcohol. I, too, had become an alcoholic by that point. Then I moved to another city, and I stopped drinking. I read all the information about sobriety, and it said, 'Don't date for a whole year after you've stopped drinking.'"

So Shannon spent some time alone working on her recovery. Then, in 1989, a friend said she had a man she wanted Shannon to meet. The first question Shannon asked was, "Does he drink?" The friend laughed and said, "You two are about the same. Because the first question he asked about you was, 'Does she drink?'"

Shannon laughs. "We both had stopped drinking. We met, we married a year later, and we're still together. What do I know now

nd relationships that I didn't before? After my second
de myself a list of prerequisites for a husband. I had
veral other men, and I asked them the questions on my list,
just in general conversation, and if I didn't get the right answers,
then I would say, 'I don't think you and I can see each other
anymore.' The first question on my list was, 'Do you believe in
God?' The second was, 'Do you believe in prayer?' 'Are you
embarrassed to pray?' 'Would you pray with me?' 'Would you pray
out loud with me?' I also was a very young grandmother—I'd had
grandchildren in my life since I was in my thirties—and I wanted to
know how grandchildren would impact upon the relationship. I
needed to know how the man felt about children, how he would
treat children. Were they important people? Because my grandchildren were becoming really important to me. I felt at that time that
grandchildren were gifts from God to grandparents because they let
you do it better the second time. I also asked questions about
temperament: 'What makes you angry, what do you do when you're
angry, do you raise your voice, do you go into a rage?' I asked
questions about fidelity."

Shannon went through the list with the man who is now her
husband. Obviously, he passed the test.

"When I stopped drinking," she concludes, "it was really
important to me that I change everything that I could in myself.
What I realize now is that alcoholics will always seek other
alcoholics. It's the old adage, 'Birds of a feather flock together'
because we know how to survive in each other's environment. One
important question I would recommend that a woman ask of a
potential husband, if he was brought up in an alcoholic home or is
an alcoholic, is 'How much work have you yourself done to deal with
your alcoholic upbringing? How much work have you done on
yourself?' "

Leigh Vives

Leigh Vives, forty-six, lives in Cincinnati, Ohio, with her second
husband. Her first marriage, at the age of twenty-one, was "just a

way to get out of the house." Leigh's mother is a particularly violent and abusive alcoholic who has struck Leigh in front of both her husbands.

"It turned out that my first husband just wasn't man enough to help me stand up to my mother," she says. "He just never said anything when she slapped me in front of him. But my second husband would not put up with my mother slapping me. He put his foot down and said, 'You don't slap my wife!' My mother would say, 'Well, she's my daughter!' and he'd say, 'I don't care; she's my wife!'"

Leigh's second husband has been instrumental in helping her break away from the destructive relationship with her mother. Four years ago, Leigh and her husband helped her mother move from a house to an apartment.

"My husband bent over backward; he was a sweetheart to help her pack and move her furniture," declares Leigh. The two of them worked all day to help her mother move in July heat that "was hot as blue blazes and she still didn't have her power turned on.

"That night, all hell broke loose. We had everything moved out of the house except the mattress that Peter and I were sleeping on, and the love seat that she slept on that night. And she got so *drunk* that night! And she got belligerent. Oh, so belligerent! She came in and cussed Peter out for all he was worth. So Peter grabbed the keys to the U-Haul that he was driving, and he said to my mother, 'Here, you know how to drive it? You move yourself!' Four-letter words were flying out of her mouth to him, and it was just unbelievable. So he and I packed up in the middle of the night and left. Since then, my mother and I have been estranged. Of course, she told everybody that we left her high and dry and all that."

Leigh is grateful to her husband for helping her see the light about a no-win relationship.

"Even before that incident, whenever I'd go to see my mother, I'd be in tears when I left. Just sobbing my heart out. Peter usually said,

'I can't take this anymore. If you want to be a glutton for punishment, then you're going to have to go on your own. I will not be a part of it. It's either me or it's *her.*' And I kept saying, 'But I can't; she's my mother, she's my mother! I can't forsake her. I'm supposed to love her.' But then we had that big blowup the day of the move, and we have not seen my mother since. My husband brought me out of the gutter, so to speak. I've found out now that I've been gone from her for four years—that I'm a better person."

Sharon

I am one of the exceptions to the profile of daughters of alcoholic mothers: I have been married to one man for twenty-six years. Once I fell in love with Doug, it was all over with any other man I was seeing. As maudlin as it sounds, I knew almost immediately that within this skinny young man who couldn't match his shirts with his pants was another piece of me, the one that had been missing for so long. Everything in me that was broken, I trusted him to heal. All that anger, sadness, fear, and loneliness—he could handle it. That is such a huge burden to dump on the narrow shoulders of an eighteen-year-old boy who couldn't even get his acne to clear up. It was, and is, an unfair burden. At times, he's faltered beneath it. But Doug and I somehow have made a marriage.

Nevertheless, the first year was almost the last year—because I so desperately longed for something different from the pulsing pain of Mama and Daddy's marriage and because, being addicted to reading, my idea of marriage fell awkwardly between Who's Afraid of Virginia Woolf? *and sappy, happily-ever-after romance novels. Doug, in turn, had parents who believed it was unwise to disagree with each other in front of the children. They also thought it was tasteless to show emotion in public. So Doug was reserved, not prone to talking about his feelings, and totally unaware that a married couple could disagree without bringing an end to their relationship.*

Twenty-six years of marriage haven't completely cured either of us from our worst sins against each other. Though we have had problems, we have learned to accommodate each other's strengths and weaknesses. He hasn't always been understanding of my struggles to cast off Mama's legacy; how could he be? One thing Mama was always careful to do was to be as sober as possible in his presence. Even at Mama's drunkest and most verbally abusive, she never criticized him, so he has only the testimony of Mama's children to convince him that his gentle, quiet mother-in-law could be a sadistic, vindictive, violent person. It has been difficult for me to realize that he has a right, even a need, to see her differently from the way I do.

Even though I speak casually of Mama's drinking to many people now, I haven't even told Doug everything her drinking put me through. He has carried my emotional baggage for me so many times when I just could not carry it for myself that I know he knows there's a lot of pain there.

Ellie

I married for the third time at the age of thirty-seven. Older and wiser now, I was no longer a starstruck young girl looking for a fairy tale. What first attracted me to him was his warmth and expressiveness. They filled up the room. He loved to laugh, but he was also not ashamed to cry. He was kind and considerate to everyone, he had intellectual curiosity and a broad knowledge of history, politics, and current events, yet he also loved hearing the juicy, gossipy, trivial details of my workday, my trips, my conversations with other people. He was the best friend that I had yearned for.

One day, years after we were married, I accidentally burst into song. "I didn't know you had such a nice singing voice," he remarked.

Chapter Nine

Relationships with Female Friends: Learning to Trust

"Since recovery, I've learned how to love a woman, something I did not know how to do before. Women were competition. They had nothing to offer me. But my world was empty without them, and I didn't know it."
—Brandi Jones, thirty-seven, saleswoman, Topeka, Kansas, who took her current job to be surrounded by men rather than women

May 1989

When the phone rang, my husband picked it up. "Oh, hi, Sharon's right here. Oh! Okay." He sat down next to the telephone, and as I approached, he waved me away. I returned to the living room where I could still hear his conversation. However, there was little to hear because he was doing much more listening than talking. Finally, he said, his voice tight with anger, "Thank you for calling. I appreciate your concern."

"What was that about?" I asked.

"I'd really rather not talk about it right now."

"Well, at least tell me who it was," I wheedled. "You sure sounded mad."

He frowned. "It was your friend Janis."

I was startled. Janis and I had had breakfast earlier that day, talking nonstop as we usually did. In fact, she had seemed to be especially warm and comforting that morning as I'd confided my misgivings about my family's upcoming move out of state. She knew that my father had just died, my mother's health was failing rapidly, my sister had just had major surgery, and a number of other friends and relatives were growing older and beginning to ail. As the "responsible" oldest child in the family, I was fearful of leaving these people behind, knowing how hard it would be to make an emergency trip home from seven hundred miles away. She had listened intently, offering support and encouragement. She knew, as I did, that this move was necessary in order for my husband to begin work at his first academic appointment, and she had expressed how much she personally would miss me.

After all, we had been friends for over thirty years. We'd been each other's lifelines during our childhoods with our alcoholic mothers, with Janis always taking the more dominant role in our friendship. Worshipfully, I'd gone along with almost every suggestion she'd made. As adults, I'd been her maid of honor at her first wedding. She'd been with me the day my older son had been born and had been my staunchest supporter in my efforts to breast-feed him.

My mother had never liked Janis, which had not bothered me; in fact, that had been a point in Janis's favor. But other members of my family and other friends seldom liked her either. Most importantly, Doug had never liked her, which had always bothered me. I had to know what had occurred to turn Doug's mild dislike into this cold anger.

Finally he told me, "Janis called to tell me that she thought you were in serious need of therapy, that your fears about this move are abnormal, and she is afraid that you are suicidal. She thinks I should have you seen by someone right away."

"What?! You've got to be kidding. Why would she say that?"

"I don't know, but she did. In fact, I'm beginning to think that there's a lot you overlook about Janis."

"Such as?" I demanded.

"Well, for one thing, she sort of flirts with me. She even called recently and hinted that she would like for me to escort her to a play. She was sure you wouldn't mind, though she was careful not to ask me in your presence."

"Well, did you take her?" I had to ask, trying to remember if there

had been any evenings unaccounted for. As graduate students at different schools, both of us spent large amounts of time away from each other, during which we could have been studying—or cheating.

He glared. "Of course not. But to be honest, I've never been comfortable around her. She looks at me like I'm a piece of meat she's planning to eat."

Suddenly, thoughts that I'd uneasily suppressed for years began to flood my mind. My first boyfriend, with whom Janis had flirted frequently; the story I'd written in high school, which she'd torn up and called "vulgar"; the many critical remarks she'd made about my weight, the warnings she'd offered "in the spirit of friendship" regarding my husband's potential infidelity if I didn't lose the extra poundage . . . And now she was trying to convince my husband that I was insane, or at the very least, on the verge of a major breakdown. Only with my mother had I ever felt more betrayed and manipulated. Janis had been my oldest and dearest friend, but suddenly I realized I'd never be able to trust her again.

Lies, broken promises, betrayals—such behavior is par for the course in many homes with alcoholic mothers. The alcoholic mother may not *mean* to lie to her children constantly, but she often does. Her many promises to stop drinking are, of course, broken. The plans we made weeks ago are canceled at the last minute because we are forced to stay home instead and baby-sit our younger siblings while she parties or sleeps it off. The secrets that we confide during her sober, seemingly trustworthy moments are spread to everyone in earshot once the drink begins to flow. Is it any wonder that we learn to distrust our mothers, the very women that our culture insists we should be able to trust with our lives?

Carmen Renee Berry and Tamara Traeder, friends and co-authors of *Girlfriends: Invisible Bonds, Enduring Ties,* state that for some of us, our lack of trust in our own mothers leads us to a mistrust of *all* women. Some of us even imitate our mothers, becoming the women other women can't trust, believing that it's best to do unto others before they do it to us first. Some daughters close the emotional doors, trusting no one at all, forever hiding beneath a hard shell of suspicion, keeping our own counsel and none other. Still others of us trust too easily, too willingly, and often too foolishly, always hoping that at long last someone will love us unconditionally; then we are forced to suffer the consequences of having trusted women who may be as damaged as we are and who may have no remorse about using us and betraying us. Some of us find, to our dismay, that if we have developed any degree of strength and self-esteem, we are sought out by "emotional vampires," women whose needs drain us and leave us feeling angry with them and with ourselves. Some of us *are* those emotional vampires, desperately hoping that someone else's fortitude will be sufficient for us as well. Some daughters even turn to pets or imaginary friends in lieu of human friendships.

In fact, friendships with other women may seem so problematic that we hesitate to form them or, almost as bad, find that we are unable to open ourselves up to healthy relationships with women who are indeed worthy of trust. Whichever is the case, many daughters of alcoholic mothers go through life never able to savor the joys of having close female friends. Of the women who participated in our study, 21 percent stated that they now prefer or once preferred male friends, and only 13 percent expressed a strong preference for female friends. Some daughters, in fact, expressed dislike or distrust of other women, or in some way were extremely restrictive of the kinds of women they would befriend: "I'll only be friends with women who are married." Fortunately, others of us *have* somehow managed to find true and lasting friendships early in life and depend upon these women friends for much that we could not and did not get from our mothers. There are those of us who learn much later, perhaps after therapy of some sort, how to develop positive relationships. We then can finally enjoy something that we may have longed for all our lives. Better still, we can learn how to *be* a positive, healthy friend.

Our Mother's Secret

In many of our homes, our mother's alcoholism is kept secret. Since our mothers can appear so charming and believable to outsiders, we even begin to doubt our sanity: "I see her as a vicious drunk, but my friends see her as a fun, happy-go-lucky, ideal mother. If I can't see those positive things, then I must be crazy." Our friends may refuse to believe that our mothers have problems, especially if their mothers don't, and may even accuse us of exaggerating or of failing to "grow up."

When experience teaches us that others won't understand, the message of secrecy is again reinforced. Ginny Durden comments on how difficult it is to confide to friends that our mothers are alcoholic: "I don't talk a whole lot about my family to my friends, only to real close people now. To tell my friends that she was an alcoholic was very hard, and I just, within the last five years, have told close friends. Some were shocked. They couldn't believe it. Because, 'How could you have a mother like *that?*' "

Over and over, keeping the secret of "Mother's little problem" erodes our self-esteem and our ability to rely upon the testimony of our eyes and ears. And because society itself seems so obstinately determined that mothers aren't, can't be, alcoholics, and if they are, they are relatively harmless, we are even more betrayed. We cannot say with credibility, "My mother is an alcoholic, and she made my life a living hell," because the world around us, in conspiracy it seems with our own family and friends, is so bent upon convincing us otherwise.

Donna Cartee learned early that she could not depend upon her friends' seeing through her mother's false front. "If I say something about my mother to a friend of mine, she'll say, 'Oh, she's just getting old,' or, 'Oh, this' or 'Oh that,' and I say, 'No, you don't understand. This is the way it *always* was! It's not that she's getting old; it's that she is who and what she is.' And I'm sure that lots of times, people think, 'Let go of it, grow up.' " Other daughters of alcoholic mothers know exactly what she means. Most of us find it very frustrating to try to reveal the secret of Mother's drinking to others who simply never saw the painful moments of our lives at home. Because it was so hard to explain and so humiliating, and because we often weren't believed *anyway,* we simply avoided having friends come into our homes. Outsiders may not have even understood what they saw and heard within. Some of our friends have been more than happy to misinterpret the alcoholic's "jovial" demeanor as being merely that of an outgoing person. (They may also be envious of the free flow of drugs and alcohol and the constant "partying" within our homes.)

The secrecy in our house may have affected us in other ways. Like many other daughters of alcoholic mothers, Antoinette Turner felt that one obstacle to her making friends when she was a child was the fact that she had been taught so well to lie. She'd learned to lie to many people to cover up her mother's drinking, so when it came time to cover up her own mistakes and problems, lying came naturally. She tells the story of having broken a basement window at her friend's home, and when the friend's mother asked about it, she lied. "I formed up this big lie about how this boy had thrown a rock and it had bounced off my shoulder and hit this window," says Antoinette. "I still remember the lie! We went inside, and she made us hunt for the rock that was never there. Ginny's mother finally confronted me and said, 'You're lying about this.' I wound up in tears saying, 'No, I'm not.' I was afraid that I would lose Ginny's friendship. I couldn't confess. My lie cost me a girlfriend. She knew I lied. I knew I lied. She may have told her parents later that I lied. She wouldn't be my friend again."

Our Mothers' Friendships

We are affected by the examples our mothers set for us with their own friendships. Were her friends real ones, supportive people who loved her and perhaps tried to help her escape her addiction? Or did those friends gradually disappear, to be replaced by "drinking buddies"? How did they interact with Mother? How did they relate to *us?*

For Page Lafontaine, constant alcohol and drug abuse surrounded her when her mother's friends were visiting. "I can remember sitting in a room with my mom and her friends, and them smoking marijuana and passing it around. They tried to pass it to me. I didn't really realize how I felt about that until probably a year ago, when one of my mom's friends came back into town." Page describes a woman who, having become a born-again Christian, wanted to make amends. "I said, 'Okay, what do you want?' And she said, 'Oh, Page, how are you doing? When you were a young child, I was so worried about you.' I responded angrily, 'Well, if you were so worried about me, then why did you do all the things you did in front of me?'"

Sharon says, "Mama was always saying to me, 'If you want a friend, be a friend.' But then she didn't show me how to be a friend. Our closest next-door neighbor, Edna Mae, was a relative who, for a long time, was practically Mama's *only* friend. These two would meet together daily at one house or another to have coffee and a brief visit and would get along well, until suddenly they'd have a fight over absolutely nothing at all and not speak to each other for a year or more. We lived next door to each other and were the only two homes on our block! It got worse after the drinking started—then they became drinking and fighting buddies. I once told my sister Sally that I didn't learn how to be a friend from watching Mama; I learned only what *not* to do. I learned what caused pain to other people. And I'd say to myself, 'I'm not going to do that.' Yet often I have found that my mother's antisocial nature has affected me deeply and that when I feel crowded by someone in a friendship, I become just as bitter and angry as Mama was with Edna Mae."

Ellie recalls, "I remember a period of time when my mother's formerly close relationship with my grandmother, her mother-in-law, soured. Mother, who had resumed drinking after a two-year respite, had become jealous of my father's frequent, fifteen-minute stops at my grandmother's house on his way home from work. 'Here's a grown man, stopping by at his *mother's'*—she spat out the word with great contempt—'every day of his life!' My parents had many arguments about this, and my mother became increasingly bitter toward my grandmother, who phoned my mother every day, probably to check up on her. She went to great lengths to evade her phone calls, even devising a telephone signal known only to us. I picked up a damaging message from Mother's imagined rivalry with her mother-in-law and her dramatic overreactions to my father's daily visits. I was taught that even female relatives, from sisters-in-law to stepdaughters, were supposed to be my rivals."

"I Can't Let My Friends See Mother Like This . . ."

For many of us, our difficulties in developing friendships go back to our childhoods and teenage years, when we were thwarted in our attempts to make friends by our mothers' behavior. Too frequently, we would invite friends over, only to have them witness some horrible scene involving our mother's drunkenness. As Sally Joiner, a florist in Louisiana, recollects, "It was always terrifying when I knew Daddy was coming home. I would see him coming down the road, and I knew that Mama was drinking. It was especially terrible if my friends Lisa and Sandra were over playing. It was always really embarrassing for me when we'd see Mama go sailing out the back door because Daddy had just kicked her down the steps. My heart would go out to Mama in one way, and in another sense, I'd wish I was kicking Mama out the door too at the same time, for being drunk and embarrassing me in front of people."

"Isn't it a beautiful day?" smiled Maria, squinting up at two thin jet streams gliding across the sky. The late afternoon sun shone through the gold and orange trees that arched over the sidewalk, as we walked past manicured lawns toward my house.

Outwardly, I feigned casual cheerfulness—but truthfully, my stomach was in knots. I was terribly afraid of how Mother might be when we got home. I desperately wanted our family to be normal again. I figured if I just played along as though everything was normal and invited Maria home with me from school, like other normal seventh grade girls did, then maybe everything would be normal.

"Oh, Ellie, your house is so pretty," remarked Maria as we turned down the walk.

She followed me in the front door. We moved through the dark entrance hall into the foyer. The mahogany woodwork, the ivory walls, the royal purple carpeting, and the pump organ with its open sheet of music gave the house a churchlike atmosphere. That, and the silence.

Then I heard the sound of Mother's bare feet hurrying toward us from the dining room. A bad omen. I was, as usual, attuned to the subtle signals. Then Mother charged around the corner wearing her shorty nightgown, the one that revealed every inch of her white legs.

"Why the hell did you leave your room in such a goddamn mess this morning?" she screamed, moving closer with raised fists. "You knew Rosa was coming to clean today, and she couldn't vacuum your room because those goddamn magazines and papers were all over the floor!"

I cowered, terrified, as she continued on and on. I hardly heard her words; I was only miserably aware of Maria in the shadows behind me. Suddenly, Mother reached over to a nearby table and picked up a large dictionary. Raising it high above her head, she slammed it down smartly upon my shoulder, again and again, like a drumbeat emphasizing her words.

"Jesus Christ, I have told you [thump] every day of your life [thump] that you have to pick up the floor of your room [thump] on Thursdays when Rosa is here . . ."

Maria, whose mouth had been momentarily frozen into a big O, let out a scream as I tried to shield myself from Mother's blows. Then Maria disappeared out the door. When Mother had vented enough of her anger, she paused, breathing heavily. I tore upstairs and flung myself into bed.

I didn't see Mother for the rest of the evening, but the next morning, she encountered me in the hallway as I was leaving for school.

She said quietly, "Ellie, I . . . just . . . want to say that I'm sorry about yesterday. You see, when you came into the hallway, I was furious, and while I was hitting you, I thought I saw someone else out of the corner of my eye—but I didn't realize that one of your classmates was there until it was too late. I'm sorry I did that in front of her. If I had known she was there, I wouldn't have done it."

This was a first! And, as it turned out, a last. It was the only time I can ever recall that she remembered the hurt she had inflicted upon me and had acted remorseful.

In fact, I was so moved by her apology that it wasn't until later that I realized that she was only apologizing for whacking me in front of Maria—*not for whacking me in the first place.*

Other daughters of alcoholic mothers tell similar tales of their mother's violence in front of their friends. Maxine Caldwell, who has known she was lesbian since childhood, craved simple friendships with other girls, something her mother's actions denied her. She recalls one incident when, at age fifteen, she had brought home a school friend, only to be met at the door by her violent drunken mother. "I walked my friend in the door—and that woman was *fried.* She came at me and she went, 'Who is this *slut* you've brought home? Who is this *friend?* Is that one of your *queer* friends?' And it wasn't. The people in high school didn't know I was gay. This was just a friend. I was embarrassed. I was trying to be friends, trying to be *normal* like everyone else." Her mother began to push Maxine, daring her to hit her back. "She said, 'Bitch, I know you want to hit me.' My friend was standing there, and I was totally embarrassed. She says, 'Come on, hit me!' And—whack!—I decked her."

I Can't Trust You

Because of her childhood experiences, Abby Giles learned never to trust others at all. She says, "Anyone who lies to me, I can't trust.

I think a lot of that comes from growing up and hearing, 'Oh, I won't drink anymore, I promise,' and then she'd go and do it again. I think that experience has a lot to do with the way I feel. If somebody lies to me, I detest that person. I won't have anything to do with them until they can prove to me they won't do it anymore, or I never trust them again, never." Abby's comment is typical of the all-or-nothing attitude that many of us develop. When the issue is trust, it's either "I can trust you totally" or "I can't trust you at all." As Abby pointed out, when the trust is broken, even once, even over a small matter, then it is lost. To avoid having to go through that painful experience, many daughters of alcoholic mothers simply choose not to trust other people at all. We've just been so hurt, repeatedly, that it seems too frightening to open ourselves up to people who might hurt us once again.

Turning to Men as Friends

Those of us who have trouble making friends with other women sometimes choose to befriend men instead. Women who prefer men as friends may do so for a variety of reasons. Morgan Landry reflects one viewpoint: "It's never been important for me to have a deep friendship with a woman. It's just more effort than I want to put out." She laughs and adds, "That sounds so rude! Maybe it's just easier to be friends with men because men don't expect intimate emotional exchanges."

Virginia Mathew has rationalized the preference for men this way: "If you get with a person who recognizes the power that they hold to hurt you, some people abuse it, and they keep you down because of it. I think women tend to do that a little bit more than men do because most women don't have the kind of relationship with men in which they get real personal, the way women talk to women, and tell their deep dark secrets." In other words, because women are more likely to exchange confidences with other women, they are more likely to hurt each other; whereas, if women are associating mostly with men, they are less likely to be doing that kind of intimate confiding.

Many daughters of alcoholic women have been taught to see women not as friends but as competitors. Judy Cionotti recalls, "I had mostly male friends all of my life. I have lots of female friends, but I always seem to judge myself when with them—i.e., 'She's much prettier, skinnier, sexier, etc., than I am.'"

Some daughters feel that other women try to "get into their heads" and manipulate them more than men do. For instance, Marie Willow notes, "I get along better with male friends than females. I don't like anyone trying to change me, but to accept me, and females tend to try to change people." Shari Lynn Curts likes men as friends better "because they don't play games. You don't have to worry about petty stuff."

Other daughters openly admit that it isn't that they prefer *men;* it's that they hate *women.* Dallas Whitaker, for one, deliberately limits her female friendships: "I dislike feminine women. I get along better with men." Sandra Peabody puts it more bluntly: "Generally, I do not like women." Cathryn Silvers finds herself troubled by her dislike of other women and is working to change that. "I hesitated to form relationships with women. I didn't trust them. I am trying now to work through that. I don't know why I basically hated everything about women."

The women who describe having moved from primarily male friendships, to more female friendships, see it as a positive, healthy move, one associated with maturity and stability. Kimberly Franks notes, "I used to have more male friends than female, but it's been balancing out as of late. I have learned how to develop female relationships. I tend to choose women who are similar to myself in values and experiences."

These women are probably on the right track. As much of the literature on alcoholism suggests, many children of alcoholics have grown up associating emotional closeness only with sexual closeness. As Judith S. Seixas and Geraldine Youcha note in *Children of Alcoholism: A Survivor's Manual*, "In looking for the love and closeness they missed as children, some people confuse physical contact or sexual involvement with emotional warmth." To be friends with men and not with women may be evidence that we are still caught in the trap of feeling that someone with whom we can be sexual is also someone with whom we can be emotionally intimate. Or it could be as simple as preferring men because we are avoiding emotional closeness, which in itself is not healthy. While men are, of course, capable of emotional intimacy, many of us have bought into the stereotype of the genders—that men are willing to talk about football and women want to talk only about feelings. Emotional intimacy can be very threatening to a woman who has spent a lifetime trying to suppress her feelings, or who has learned that revealing her feelings to someone else is far too risky. After all, don't most of us remember what our mother did when we told her how we felt about something, anything? We were ignored or punished. Mother's feelings were important; ours weren't.

Damaged Friends

Unfortunately, because of our backgrounds, many daughters spend a lifetime trying to create friendships with other damaged women—alcoholics, addicts, abusers, betrayers, and desperately needy "emotional vampires." We feel more at home with what we already know, regardless of how harmful it is, than with what we have not experienced, regardless of how healthy it is. So we sometimes allow ourselves, even willingly seek, relationships with people who will betray us and undermine us.

Betty Buxton was asked whether she had ever found herself making friends with women who undermined her. As though a nerve had been struck, she responded, "Yes! Yes! Oh, yes! And I just recently figured all that out. Apparently, in my female relationships,

I was being attracted to strong personalities, but they were often very competitive and very controlling. I've had a lot of frustration with certain close female friends over the years who were putting me down.

"For a while, I used to be so hurt by people who would be subtly critical or belittling, and I would say, 'What is the matter with *me?* What is the matter with *me* that these people would want to make me feel so bad?' "

Betty has finally come to terms with her selection process for friends and has developed insight as to these women's motivations. "These people are doing the best they can do. That's kind of a cliché, but from their own insecurities, they are doing their shit. And it might be dumped on you. I no longer internalize it. When somebody does something that's pretty hurtful, I pull back, and I realize, okay, I'm not going to be *around* for them to do that."

Betty describes a friendship she has had in which, as she's grown healthier, the so-called friend has grown more attacking. "We were very close for about two years, but then suddenly I realized that as I got healthier and healthier, she got more and more toxic to me. Because I think it worked better for her when I wasn't healthy. And so, when I was no longer the malleable tonto that she needed, then she became more and more negative toward me."

Betty's experience illustrates a point that Berry and Traeder make in *Girlfriends:*

The friendships we value most are those that have a natural rhythm of give and take, shared vulnerability that is mutually beneficial to both women involved. However, sometimes what may look like a friendship, initially, turns out to be something else, something out of balance. Perhaps this woman is a mentor, a guide, or a caregiver but, sadly enough, she is not a friend. She does not have that unspoken appreciation of what we are experiencing, the ability to be there without being asked. And in that disappointment, we experience the sting of betrayal and regret.

Befriending Other Daughters of Alcoholics

Some of us may find that we are drawn into friendships with other children of alcoholics; the old adage "misery loves company" may be at work here. These friends know what we've been through. However, other daughters of alcoholic mothers may be alcoholics themselves. As we discussed in chapter 5, offspring of alcoholics are at higher risk for becoming alcoholics. Fifty-seven percent of the participants in our research reported that they currently drink. Of the nondrinkers who responded, 25 percent volunteered that they were recovering alcoholics. As we ourselves enter recovery, either as the adult child of an alcoholic or drug addict, or as someone trying to stop drinking or using drugs, choosing our friends from among other women in recovery is certainly better than continuing to pal around with people who are not getting help or who are still "using." We cannot comfortably continue to befriend people who are still drinking or using drugs, or are simply too badly damaged to be trustworthy friends.

As a child, Louisa McQuaid was attracted to friendships with other children of alcoholic mothers. "I just basically had one friend who I could bring home, and her mother was also an alcoholic. So we had that basic unspoken understanding. If my mom was having a bad day, she understood. No biggie." Louisa laughs, but no doubt as a child, it wasn't quite so funny to her. She may have felt, as many of us have, that she was limited in her choices of friends, that she *had* to pick another child of an alcoholic in order to avoid humiliation and betrayal. Such a motive may be at work within us even after we arrive at adulthood.

For Linda Hanson, befriending other daughters of alcoholics who had healed from the damage was evidence of her own emotional health. "When I moved out here to Oregon, I think I started sort of creating an alternate family. A collection of people I spent holidays with, who knew what I was worried about, and who I could rely on. By that time I had read enough and found friends who had one or more alcoholic parents."

Needy Us, Needier Them?

Part of the "wound licking" that daughters of alcoholic mothers do is to help nurture others who are needy, or to seek others who can nurture us if we are needy. Again, this is not necessarily healthy— and many daughters know it and react negatively to it—but it seems to be common, as though in being drawn to others like us, we know we must somehow give strength or borrow it.

Deidre Goldblum is one who felt the need to share strength with another, even during a time of crisis in her own life, her divorce. "During my marriage and after, I started to make friends with this woman out in West Texas. She was very family oriented, and she sort of adopted us, and we adopted her. Then I found out that the guy she'd been living with had been beating the crap out of her. I think that her self-esteem was just so horrible. She felt like she was unattractive, and she felt like she weighed too much, and all this other stuff. And that's what I talked to her about. I felt like I was coaching her."

But some daughters see needy women as being too much like their mothers—simply sending out false signals in order to get others to do for them the things they should be doing for themselves. Morgan Landry says bluntly, "As an adult, I have a real problem dealing with needy women. I've had a few friends, acquaintances, who are really needy, needy people. They're like a sponge. I cannot deal with that. I will run the other way as fast as possible." When asked whether these needy women reminded her of her mother in any way, she reflected a moment and said, in surprise, "I guess that could be it, yeah. Boy! I don't want to deal with that again, because I've done that with my mother." She adds, almost in relief, "I've always thought that something was terribly wrong with me for not having that desire to be friends with other women."

It will surprise no one that we ourselves can be the needy partner in the friendship, the one that others try to help or maybe even the one others run from. We begin feeling needy in our childhoods—after all, the one woman who should have been able to meet our intimacy needs, our mother, just wasn't there for us. Sometimes our loneliness means that we can't bear to spend an evening in our own company. This is a problem that Joellen Weatherford speaks about candidly, attributing it to her isolated childhood. "I can't stand to be without people. I like people around me. I don't do 'alone' very well. I'm learning how to now, but there are a lot of times I still get up and go stay at a friend's house. I won't stay alone."

All too often, friendship can mean that we want others to put their own lives on hold for just a little while and tend to *our* needs. Sharon describes such an instance in her own life. "I was living in Georgia, and my closest friend from my master's program, April, had moved to Texas. She was in the middle of getting a divorce, she had two little kids, she was developing health problems, and she was in a doctoral program, so she was very busy. But I was also having problems, both at work and with my children. I kept writing her one insistent letter after another, demanding to know why she wasn't answering my letters. Finally, I got this letter from her that was just *rabid,* full of obscenities and anger. No adult woman since my mother had used such language with me, and I was crushed. It didn't occur to me that I was just pushing too hard, being too needy, and that I'd finally just driven her to this anger. I wrote back to her, ending the relationship, and for years we didn't write or phone. Only recently have we started gently edging our way into resuming our friendship, and I think we're both still a little bit wary of each other. For my part, I don't plan to push to get the closeness back. If it returns, I'll be very happy. But I know now that I was being too needy and that April felt overwhelmed with having to handle her own problems and being burdened as well with mine. I won't do that to her again.''

The Bad Friend No One Wants

Sometimes we daughters of alcoholic mothers find ourselves ''buying'' friends by being generous to them, flattering them, going the extra mile, often for people who would not do that for us in return. But for Cherish West, who learned to drink and use drugs in her parents' home when she was only a child, her current generosity is a matter of atonement for past selfishness. Cherish says, ''I'm a real giver. I would give my last dime. I try to treat people exactly the way I would want to be treated. But I've gotten hurt quite a few times. You give an inch and they'll just take a mile from you. You know, you're being really nice, and they'll just walk all over you and stab that knife in your back a little bit farther, and you're like, 'Why are you doing this to me?' ''

What Cherish is feeling—betrayal—seems poetic justice, considering her treatment of others when she was younger, which she admits was selfish and cruel. ''Girls at school wouldn't hang around with me much. I was actually very mean. The alcohol and drugs made me into a very controlling and directing and unloyal friend. I would lead you on and probably steal the shirt off your back. It got really ugly. I would take my girlfriends' boyfriends away, and I would give them drugs and alcohol and have them carry my homework. I totally controlled them. Told them what they were going to do. And I did it with the drugs and alcohol. They probably don't like me even today.''

A person who treats us as Cherish treated her friends in high school is certainly a hurtful person, not one that we can healthfully call ''friend.'' But even that kind of abusive friend pales in comparison to the adult women we call friends who prefer the company of our husbands instead. Such a double betrayal occurred to Virginia Mathew. "My first husband ran off with my best friend. The only real woman friend that I've ever had that hurt me was the one who ran off with my husband. I trusted her . . . When the marriage broke up, I missed *her* more than I missed him!" Virginia's voice grows tight. "I'd leave her standing there in *my* kitchen every morning after she dropped her kids off, and I'm going off to work, and they're having a cup of coffee. That's how much I trusted her."

Setting Up Rules for Friendship

In self-protection against negative relationships, many of us set down rules for friendship, clearly defining what characteristics we want in a friend, which is what Gabriella Chandler has done. "I avoid certain types—superficial, manipulative types. I tend to listen too long ('listen' as in 'let them talk') to the wrong types of people for me. I need to take some time to realize they may be manipulative or negative-attitude people."

Ellie also has established some guidelines: "If I leave a conversation or an encounter with a friend and feel diminished, I don't waste time analyzing it. I trust my instincts. If I *feel* put down or disparaged in any subtle way, that's good enough for me. That person very likely *does* have an unconscious, hidden agenda, and it's not my imagination or oversensitivity on my part. Years ago, I probably would have given that person the benefit of the doubt over and over again, or blamed myself somehow, or worked to improve myself so I could win that person's approval. No more. I don't have room in my life for friends who don't like me just the way I am."

In an effort to avoid hurtful people, some daughters of alcoholic mothers decide that older women are likely to be wiser and more trustworthy—which may seem strange, given our experience with our mothers. But what we are hoping for is to re-create our relationship with that "first friend"—our mothers—and this time, it will be right. This time, this older, wiser woman will be there for us, will listen to us, provide sage advice, love us unconditionally.

Perhaps this is the sort of relationship that Jo Ann Stills is looking for. Jo Ann admits, "Most of my friends were and are a lot older than me. My friends have been a lot older because of my mental age and because of my work environment." She thinks about it for a moment. "I may be looking for an ideal mother figure. Either that, or it's just because I relate to them because I feel that that's where I am in my mind-set."

Successful, Healthy Friendships

Developing healthy relationships with other women is not just desirable, it is a necessity for our own mental well-being. At the very least, it is the best way of showing our children, especially our daughters, how to be good friends themselves. Of course, it isn't always easy for us to work our way through the distrust in order to get to that place within ourselves that can be opened to friendship. Nevertheless, many of us have managed it and have glowing stories of happy, well-adjusted friendships to relate. Donna is an example. "My women-to-women friendships are for the most part open, close, and honest. I can tell my best friend just about everything."

Most of us hope to develop such healthy friendship choices. One way is to find good friends who share lifestyles in common with us, which is what Lynn Clifton has done: "The women I choose are solid, spiritual people who have similar values and their heads screwed on straight."

Grace King also has such a friend. Though some of her friends are not healthy for her, she says, "I have another friend who knows all my history and loves me anyway. She frequently tells me she loves me and we enjoy doing things together; she is very optimistic. We share our feelings and try to help each other."

S. Jae Austin says that her ability to make strong friendships is because she herself fills her own emotional needs now. "But it's my friends who hug me, tell me 'I love you.' If it weren't for my friends, and being able to talk frankly and argumentatively and without

222 ~ MY MAMA'S WALTZ

conditions, oh, man, I'd be a basket case. Each of my friends loves me in a different way, to a different degree, and it's a different kind of support system. It's really neat. I love them each in their own separate way. It's pretty interesting when you think about it. My friends have turned out to be the supporters, the family, and they know it."

We wish we could all say that we have wonderful, supportive, loving friends who supply all our missing needs. Realistically, we know that is not the case. Brandi Jones, a recovering alcoholic and drug addict who has been fighting—and winning—her way back into relationships with other women, perhaps says it best: "The women that I have in my life today, it's been a guarded relationship, there's no doubt about it. I still have a very difficult time sharing my life with them. I can share my experience, and I can share my strength. And I can share my hope. Since recovery, I've got women friends today that I didn't before, and I have forgiveness for people, and I have such tolerance that I never would have dreamed of."

These days, Janis and I continue to send occasional Christmas cards, but both of us know that the friendship, if indeed it could ever have been called a true friendship, is over. I don't trust her not to hurt me again, and I feel that she doesn't respect me. I know I shouldn't have been so angry when she thought I needed therapy, but it just struck me as being so underhanded and deceitful. If she really felt that way, why didn't she say it to me, not to my husband? I can only presume that she didn't trust me either.

What's weird is that even after that incident, it took me a long time to realize that, for years, she'd been closing down our relationship. For instance, when we were in our twenties, she didn't bother to tell me she had cervical cancer until after she'd had surgery and she knew she'd be okay. When we were in our thirties, she didn't bother to call and tell me her grandmother had died, though I knew the woman well. I only found out because I'd called to chat, and she mentioned it. Her grandmother had been the woman who was, for all intents and purposes, Janis's mother. (Janis didn't tell me when her birthmother died either.) In fact, looking back, I realize that Janis seldom told me about anything important that was happening in her life, though we'd been very, very close in high school and for years afterward. Or so I'd thought.

Why didn't I realize what she was saying to me, which was obviously that she no longer felt close enough to be my friend? Part of it was that I couldn't imagine why she would have wanted to end our friendship. Thinking about it now, I suppose one reason could have been a form of jealousy. Though when we were growing up, she'd had so much more than I, I'd married well and happily, to an intelligent, charming, faithful man. She, on the other hand, had been divorced and in and out of relationships with men who were okay but certainly not the caliber she deserved. (Though, to give her credit, she is now married to a wonderful older man.) Maybe her inability to understand what it was that made my marriage happy was behind her desire to distance herself from me. I don't know. She didn't tell me that either.

Because of this sense of betrayal from this relationship, which has intensified the lack of trust of other women that I already felt because of my mother, I find myself being really hesitant to trust other women, even Ellie, who now knows more about me than almost anyone alive. I get so suspicious over things, that Ellie once said to me, "I'm not Janis. You can trust me." And I want to. I really want to. But that little voice keeps nagging me, saying, "If you open yourself up to anyone, you'll be hurt. You'll be rejected."

Chapter Ten

Becoming Mothers Ourselves: Recapturing Lost Love

$\backsim$

"I think my kids taught me everything I know about love."
—Maya Renata, forty-seven, poet and songwriter,
Dayton, Ohio, mother of two grown daughters

$\backsim$

I looked down at the packet of birth control pills; there were still several left to take for the month. In fact, the next one, today's, was in my hand; the glass of water stood ready next to the bathroom sink. Suddenly I turned and threw the little yellow pill into the toilet, flushing it.

My God, what had I done? My heart began to hammer.

Doug was not going to understand. How could he? I didn't understand it myself. We were only twenty-two, married for two years. I couldn't explain to him that I was overwhelmed with emptiness, drowning with the need to have a baby of my own. Perhaps it seemed so important because so many of my friends and relatives already had babies. Perhaps the desire went deeper than envy; I think it did. Looking back, I think I needed a baby so that someone would love me unconditionally and would need me totally. I didn't really examine the need that drove me; I just continued to flush the pills, one by one, each day.

My period came late that month. Overjoyed, I told Doug that I might be pregnant and confessed what I'd been doing. He was furious, of course. No, he did not understand—or maybe he understood only too well. At any rate, I kept trying to explain it to him.

"I love being married to you, but you are so reserved, self-sufficient, self-contained. You love me, and in some ways, you need me, but you have never needed me or loved me as much as I love you. I always feel empty inside, like I have this giant hole in me," I pleaded.

"Sharon, no one could fill a hole like that," he said, holding my hands in his. "You're expecting a baby—and me—to do something that no one can do for another person."

He was right; not even a child of my own could fill that empty place in me, though at the time, I felt sure that one could. I thought that the emptiness was there because I needed a child, but I was wrong. The emptiness was there because I hadn't been a child. I had gone from infancy to adulthood overnight, it seemed, never allowed to be needy, never having a mother fill me with love. Like many children of alcoholic mothers, I was all too often my mother's mother, trying to be and do whatever she wanted, taught to ignore my own feelings and to put aside my own desires. Still, I was just sure that having a baby of my own would be the magic it would take to make me whole again.

Motherhood—that moment in our lives when we come closest to re-creating our own mother's patterns and actions—is not surprisingly one of the most emotional and troublesome periods in the lives of daughters of alcoholic mothers. We are terrified: "What if I screw it up as badly as she did?" Yet we are determined: "I *won't* be as bad as she was!" Surprisingly, despite the lack of a good role model, the majority of the daughters who participated in our study believe that they have turned out to be pretty good mothers.

Baby Hunger

Like Sharon, many of us begin to feel "baby hunger" gnaw at us at quite a young age; in fact, it is not uncommon for us to deliberately get pregnant in our teens, not only because we, like most girls with low self-esteem, are easy marks for the charming "bad boys" who want to bed us and then leave us, not only because we need an excuse to escape from our dysfunctional homes, but because deep down, we've wanted babies all along. We want to experience the intense and consistent mother-child love that we feel we missed. Nichole Van Tassell, twenty-eight, is the mother of three children. "I had children at a very young age, and I did it because of the relationship with my mother," she explains. "I felt that if I had a child, our relationship, I swore, was going to be different, and that child was going to love *me*. This was something my mother and I didn't have."

Like many daughters of alcoholic mothers, Diane, a twenty-one-year-old college student, found herself the victim of "baby hunger," although she says, "The pregnancy was an accident. I was on the pill and it didn't work. So, yeah, it was an accident. Yet I had a really strong urge to have a baby," she admitted. "I tried to put that feeling off. But I know that feeling of baby hunger." Diane used to teach preschool and loved it. The children, she said, brightened her day.

"I would never give up my child," asserts Diane. The father of her child, a boyfriend of four years, dropped her as soon as he found out she was pregnant. He advised her to give the baby up for adoption, reminding her that her estranged family, including her alcoholic mother, would be of no help. Diane replied emphatically, "I *am* the baby's family, and if you're not going to be there, that's your choice, but I'm still going to be its mother."

Ellie, too, remembers the feeling of baby hunger.

Long ago, when I was a slim and smooth-skinned young mother, with one thirteen-month-old son toddling around our tiny two-story wooden house in Massachusetts, I was already yearning for a second baby, the sooner the better. Six months earlier, my alcoholic mother had died in her sleep after years of battling the bottle and those prescription drugs that many middle-class housewives of that era popped regularly. I can see now that my amplified baby hunger may have been connected to this loss. All those years of our stormy and painful relationship, I had been denied that spirit-strengthening flow of unconditional Mother Love. Now that my mother was prematurely dead, all hope that she would be miraculously cured of alcoholism so that we could have a normal relationship was forever quashed. My heart cried out for another baby. If having one child was joyous, then having two would be sublime. Right? Besides, I needed a girl.

Gender

For many daughters of alcoholic mothers, feelings about gender preferences go to opposite extremes. Some of us are terrified of giving birth to a daughter and re-creating a mother-daughter relationship; others of us long for a daughter—for the same reason.

Janie, the mother of a little boy, feared having a daughter of her own. "When I was pregnant, I was concerned about how I would relate to the child if it was a girl," she admitted. "When they said, 'It's a boy,' I said, 'Wheeww!' Because I don't think I'd know how to raise a daughter."

Alicia Fortune, on the other hand, wanted a girl but recognized that her reasons for wanting one may not have been entirely healthy. "I think I wanted a girl so I could have this relationship that I never had." But after having a son, Alicia realized that "I just had this unrealistic expectation of having a daughter."

It is true that many of us want a daughter so that we can have a shot at experiencing a real mother-daughter relationship—even if it's from the opposite perspective. As Sara Jo Kea says, "It's the strangest thing. I don't know what it is exactly, it's almost like a superstition in some way, I always feel like I will have a daughter, and that that daughter will be a cipher—a replacement, a sidekick—for me in the same way I've become a cipher for my mother." Yet as Ellie describes below, we often don't realize when we first set out to be mothers that a child's gender can be the very least of the considerations that we'll have to deal with.

"I have two generations of children—all of them boys!" says Ellie. "What's interesting is how I changed in my attitude toward gender between my first generation of sons and my second go-round with motherhood. In my first two pregnancies, I wanted a daughter. I probably believed that having a girl would give me that 'second chance.' I didn't get a girl, but I loved my sons so much it didn't matter. When I became pregnant with my 'second generation' child—the older boys were teens by then—I actually wanted another son! For one thing, I'd gotten fond of being the mother of sons. Second, I had learned over the years that gender doesn't matter as much as individual differences. There was nothing I couldn't do or talk about with my sons that I could have with a daughter."

Becoming Mothers without Role Models

Because we did not have good mothering role models upon which to rely, we often have to guess at what is "right" or "normal" in parenting. As Yolanda Blake-Bergin, fifty-eight, remarks, "If I had had a mother there for me when I first became a mother, I think I would have known more what to do; I don't think I would have questioned as much why I did things or why I felt the way I did. I wouldn't have been as insecure."

Linda Hanson, mother of an eight-year-old daughter, is aware of her conflicted feelings. "Sometimes I feel angry at my child, and that's a troubling sort of feeling. While I don't *drink,* I do sometimes lose my temper, and I realize that that must be frightening for her. It's probably not nearly as frightening for her as I imagine it to be because I know other mothers lose their tempers too. That's one of the hardest things, trying to figure out what it is to be a 'normal' parent," she says. "Because I have no models at all."

One thing we daughters do know for sure, though, is that being beaten or verbally abused, as we were, is *not* normal. This is one aspect of our mother's parenting that we are most eager to dispense with in our own approach to childrearing.

Ellie says, "After I had my first baby, motherhood stirred up in me some angry retroactive feelings toward my mother. Now that I had my precious baby and had experienced mother-child love, which saturated my every pore, I thought back to those nightmarish times when Mother had punished Diana and me by knocking our heads together or whipping us with the yardstick because she was frustrated with *her* life. Now that I was a mother, I felt that I could never inflict that cruel, out-of-control punishment on *my* child."

Susanna Moore, the mother of a ten-year-old son and a four-year-old daughter, says that when she first became a mother, she vowed that she would never strike her children. "I was afraid I would cross the line," she explains. "I was afraid that there was too much in me like my mom, so just in case, I made this rule, and I never have hit them."

Alicia Fortune adds, "I still can't imagine how my own mother could have treated me the way she did. I just don't know how. I realize now, our mothers must have been very *sick* to do and say the things they did because it's just not in a *mother* to be so abusive!"

Sharon has also felt insecure as a mother, even after twenty-two years of motherhood, because she still has doubts about what normal maternal behavior is:

Every time I have a problem with either of my sons—maybe I feel that Stephen is not being very respectful, or that Daniel is pushing the envelope with his curfew—I am filled with self-doubt and anger. I don't know if it would have been easier to be a mother if I'd had a good example, but I suspect it would have been. I see how easily and comfortably my husband handled things when the boys were younger. If our sons misbehaved in any way, he didn't blame himself—he simply said, "Straighten up, guys. You know better than that." He was confident. *He has hardly ever spanked them—and that was only when they were little. And the spanking was just a brief whack on the posterior. He never went berserk and screamed, "Off with their heads!" which, to be honest, I feel like I have done. I know that I have a thousand times questioned whether I ought ever to have had children.*

Showing Affection

Another thing we do to break the destructive cycle is to make sure we touch, hug, kiss, and have physical contact with our children. We try to say "I love you" frequently, something our mothers had trouble doing with us.

Page says, "The first thing I tell my daughter every morning is that I love her. I say, 'Good morning, Sunshine. Mommy loves you.' Every single morning."

JoAnn Sills has also been demonstrative with her daughter, telling her daily how much she loves her. Now her daughter comes out of her bedroom at odd times just to say, "I love you, Mommy." JoAnn replies, "I love you, too, honey."

Shannon Nichols recalls how she always showed affection to her son, from the moment he was born. "It was important to me that I touch him; I remember that was really important to me, to touch him and keep telling him, 'I love you, I love you.' Because I felt I didn't get that from my mother. That's why I said to myself, 'One thing that this kid is always going to get is touching and 'I love you.'"

Controlling, Overprotective Mothers

It is well established in alcoholism literature that adult children of alcoholics are often control freaks. Janet Woititz explains in *Adult Children of Alcoholics:* "The young child of the alcoholic was not in control. In order to survive when growing up [a child of an alcoholic] needed to turn that around. . . . This became very important and remains so. . . . As a result, [adult children of alcoholics] are very often accused of being controlling, rigid, and lacking in spontaneity. This is probably true." In addition, Robert Ackerman points out in *Perfect Daughters,* "Many adult daughters stated that they wanted to be there for their children because their mothers were not there for them." If we have any faults as mothers, one of them is our tendency to overdo our "perfect" mothering. We are often a bit too strict, frequently overprotective, and sometimes too involved in our children's lives.

JoAnn Sills has set rules for her daughter and sticks to them. If her daughter breaks any of them, she faces consequences. "I just can't stand to be out of control," JoAnn admits. "I have to always be in control of everything. I try to watch myself when it comes to my daughter's chores because I have found that she'll say, 'Oh, Mommy, come look, my room is clean!' I'll look, and some things are kind of piled in a basket and not put on the shelf as I think they should be. I'll praise her, but I almost have to bite my tongue to keep from criticizing. It is very hard to stop myself from going into her room and changing things or fixing things."

Conflicted about Motherhood

We know we want to be better mothers than our mothers were, and we are quite likely to approach motherhood with the unrealistic expectation that, for *us,* perfect motherhood can be achieved. For *us,* motherhood is going to be this idealized Mother's-Day-card scenario. And of course it isn't. It can't be. The burden of our need for love is far too great for a child to carry, and we ourselves aren't usually healthy enough not to place such a huge emotional load on our children. "Rescue me from my loneliness!" we beg of them. "Love me unconditionally!"

But because of our backgrounds, sometimes our mothering expectations and experiences aren't without conflicts, as Ellie describes in her account of her first pregnancy:

*　　*　　*

The day loomed ahead of me like a gray void. Young, married, and pregnant for the first time, I spent my days alone in a third-floor apartment on an ugly corner block. We had just moved to a new city so my husband could move up in his job. I didn't mind; I was ready to retire into pregnancy and motherhood. Or so I thought. Before, when I was working long, tension-filled hours as a newspaper reporter, I imagined being a stay-at-home mother as cozy, safe, and relaxing. Before, when I was working, I had imagined all the things I wanted to do when I had the free time. But now I just didn't feel like doing anything. *After seeing my husband off to work each morning, I'd close the homemade red-and-white-checked curtains and turn around to face the silent living room. I'd manage to pour myself yet another bowl of cornflakes and milk and eat it while staring halfheartedly at the pile of wrinkled shirts in the corner, which I fully intended to iron—someday.*

"Ellie, you are depressed!" I told myself. Although I was vaguely looking forward to having this baby, eons in the future, and my middle was beginning to bulge, in those days before sonograms, amniocentesis, Lamaze classes, and the romanticization of childbirth and children, I was simply not able to bond with this unknown future child of mine. This baby growing inside of me was a concept, a dream, an idea, but not a human being yet. The women's magazines I'd read all my life—ever since I'd begun reading the confessional obstetrical and gynecological articles in my mother's Ladies' Home Journal, *when I was eight—had always promised the joys of marriage and motherhood. Obviously being a housewife and mother had not been good for* my *mother—but that was because she was flawed as a person. Wasn't it? Or, I wondered, as a belated epiphany hovered tentatively on the brink of my consciousness— had Mother become "flawed" because of housewifery and motherhood? But I pushed that uncomfortable thought away.*

I felt very conflicted about my impending motherhood. At first, I had wanted to get pregnant. I had hungered desperately for a baby—a girl baby. She would adore me; I would adore her. And the hole in my heart would slowly regenerate itself, and I could be normal again. Yet now as I sat, alone and lonely in this quiet apartment, unable to get a job because of this pregnancy, I felt angry. I was restless and knew that in order to save my sanity, I had to get out and do something. But potential employers, as soon as they saw my condition, advised me that they could not hire a pregnant woman, since I would no doubt quit as soon as the baby was born.

I had a college degree and work experience. I was smart, responsible, and earnest. But now this bulge on my belly, this baby, was thwarting any opportunities for me to get out of this bloody apartment a little bit and interact with the world of humans. My feelings were mixed. I resented this baby, even as much as I wanted it. And I couldn't help wondering: had Mother ever felt like this?

I realized then I would not be good at full-time motherhood. Even before the baby was born, I could already see how much of my former self had been subjugated to this higher purpose of Motherhood. In spite of the newly launched women's movement, most mothers of small children did not work. But as soon as my baby was born, I began forging a career. Not because I needed money. But because I needed assurance that I would have something for myself.

I kept thinking about Mother in the years of her young motherhood, slim and elegant in short shorts and a blouse. Pretty and healthy, she read to us, cut out paper dolls with us, frosted birthday cakes while we licked the spatula and bowl, set the dining room table with paper plates, balloons, and favors for birthday parties, and schlepped us across town in the green Plymouth to dentists, lessons, children's houses. Then I remembered her in the later years; I could see the half-finished mug of ale on the bedside table, the rumpled sheets on the unmade bed where she lay snoring in the afternoon, the unmitigated fury that so often flashed from her watery green eyes when she was awake and looking accusingly at all of us . . .

Much as I wanted to be a mother, I did not want to end up like my mother.

Alcoholic Grandmother

Even though we become good mothers ourselves, most of us feel cheated out of having a responsible, loving grandmother figure for our children, not only to guide us with her wisdom but also to adore our children as much as we do. Many of our mothers show less interest in our children than we'd like, and they certainly cannot be trusted as reliable baby-sitters. Some of them even become jealous of our relationships with our children.

Diane, who is pregnant, does not plan to tell her mother "because eventually when I have this child, she's not going to be able to touch it. She's one of those people who's so shaky right now, you know, from being an alcoholic, I wouldn't want her around the baby."

Susanna Moore says of her son's relationship with his grandmother, "He knows there's a problem, but he gets along with her pretty good, and I keep an eye on her. I don't think she'd really hurt my children physically. I'm more concerned about the emotional aspect; she's very condescending to everyone in her family, and more so to children, and I don't want my kids to be around someone who's criticizing them. In fact, I would never let my mother baby-sit them."

Jody Macolly, twenty-two, the mother of a little girl, is getting married in May. She plans to go on a short honeymoon, but who will take care of her two-year-old? Her mother has offered, but Jody does not trust her. As a solution, she approached her father, who is still married to her mother, and made him promise that he would do the real child care.

"If I had to pick anybody to leave my daughter with that I trusted with her life, it'd be my father," says Jody. "The drawback to that is my mother! My parents, even my mother when she's sober, are excellent with my daughter. They take her for walks, things like that. But I told my father, 'I'm totally trusting my daughter with you, and I don't want my daughter alone with my mother *at all*. The whole time.'

"The sad thing," continues Jody, "is that I know how much my mother loves my daughter, but I also know what her priority is. Drinking. I know that if she is alone with my daughter and gets that urge, she has access to keys and the car, and she'll take her. Those thoughts just keep running through my head. I'm terrified. Even if my father took her car keys away, my mother would call a cab and ask them to go to the liquor store for her. They have in the past. Or I can just imagine her saying, 'Well, I don't have a car seat, but the child will be okay in the backseat; I'm just going up the road,' and then she'll be off the road in a tree somewhere. So this is frightening to me, but I know my father. I said, 'The only way I'm going to leave my daughter with you is if you swear that you will not leave her alone with Mom,' and he said, 'You have my word; if I have to go anywhere else, I'll strap the kid in the car and I'll take her with me, but I won't leave her with your mother.'"

Jody adds, "I wish my mother could just be a normal person, a normal grandmother I could drop my child off with."

In addition to being unreliable, many alcoholic grandmothers are just as uninvolved with their grandchildren as they were with us. Morgan Landry says, "My mother chooses for my boys to call her 'Pam.' She doesn't like little children especially. She's definitely not a baby person. She's never really made an effort to be close with them. The last time she baby-sat, we just walked in the house, and she was drunk and passed out. We could not wake her. So that was the last time she baby-sat."

It is also not at all uncommon for alcoholic grandmothers to be critical of their daughter's parenting and to feel jealous of her relationship with her own children. Dianne Carlson, forty-five, has two children, a son, nineteen, and a daughter, seventeen. "I have a real good relationship with my daughter; we're very close. But my mother does not like Kelli; she treats her awful. I think it's jealousy, because she is jealous that Kelli and I have a real close relationship, which is something my mother and I don't have, and we've never had. Unless it's jealousy, I don't understand why she treats her so mean."

Healing through Motherhood

Seventy-three percent of the daughters in our study were mothers. The vast majority stated emphatically on the questionnaire that motherhood had brought them joy. Most also believed that they were very good at mothering. Although children cannot cure our emptiness entirely, they allow us to love in a way that we never would have imagined—which almost makes up for the absence of mother love in our own lives.

Sharon says, "I think of the many happinesses my sons have brought me—how my heart felt full for the very first time when I looked down into my newborn son's dark blue eyes as he nursed at my breast. How beautiful they both are to me, even now that they're hairy, deep-voiced men who pat me on top of my head and laugh at my ignorance of computers, cars, and sports. One of the best things is that they love each other without condition, with no jealousy, not like in my own birth family, where my sisters and brothers and I barely dared to love each other at all, for fear Mama would notice and set us against one another. My sons are honest, intelligent, funny, likeable men, and surely, I had some small part in that. I would like to think that with my own children, I have broken the chain that began as far back, and maybe even further, as my mother's father's alcoholism."

It is not just for the kids that we work so hard to be wonderful mothers. We do it for ourselves too. Alicia Fortune says, "I'm a good mother—the one thing I've really ever thought I *was* good at. It's something that I don't want to mess up. It's really fulfilling for me. I'm happy about it. I think it's been a big step in putting the past behind me."

Janie, the single mother of a child, says, "He's the best thing that ever happened to me. I would have more children in a heartbeat." She sighs with bliss. "He is *everything*. He is amazing. Even in his worst moments, I would never give him up."

"My daughter is the most important thing to me," says Page Lafontaine, twenty-eight, a single mother. "When I was growing up, my mother was never there. I remember having to go to school for the school parties and having no one there for me. I can remember Christmases that she was nowhere around. I don't care if I have to take off work, whatever, I will be there, no matter what it takes."

Morgan Landry, whose three sons are thirteen, twelve, and seven, is having a childhood *with* them—the one she never had. "I never got to enjoy being a child. I was always worried about my mother being passed out somewhere, or driving somewhere. In a lot of ways, I'm kind of on my sons' level. It drives my husband crazy." Morgan giggles. "I laugh, and I laugh at inappropriate things, like little boys do. I have fun, I try to enjoy myself. I don't even have to try, I just do."

Sharon's sister Sally has endured more hardships than most mothers, yet her heart is full of love and joy. This is her story:

Sally

As my oldest child was being born after an extremely difficult, prolonged labor, my cervix collapsed around her chest and collapsed her lungs. The doctor worked with her for forty-five minutes before she drew her first breath. Lying on the delivery table, I prayed with all that was in me, then with no more words to pray, I began to sing "I Need Thee Every Hour." At that moment, my daughter took her first breath. After two weeks in neonatal intensive care, she finally came home.

Her dad and I dedicated her to the Lord on her first Sunday in church.

I've always been very active in my church, my haven from the storms of life. And that's where, even as a child myself, I knew I would raise my children. My girls haven't been sent to church. I've taken them. I was standing beside my oldest daughter when she gave her heart to the

Lord. I was also standing beside her when she was lying in a hospital bed in ICU on life support after a car wreck that took her from us. The nurses honored my request and moved her over so I could get into the bed with her and "snuggle" one last time and sing to her a song that she had loved since she was a baby. And I cherish every sweet memory of her and look forward to the day when I'll get to be with her again.

My second daughter was born after less than six months of pregnancy; she lived only nine and a half hours. I know that she also awaits me in heaven. I pray God will grant me a few thousand years just to rock her and snuggle her in my arms.

My youngest daughter Amber is now five years old and has cerebral palsy. She is a joy to be with. She has a radiant smile and a personality that wins every heart that she comes into contact with. She is learning to walk with a walker and uses a wheelchair at home and school. Already, she sings "specials" in church.

Yes, sometimes it's a struggle, and often I'm down with my back. At the end of a day, we are both thankful it's finally time for bed. But when Amber is grown and leading a full life, I'll know I've done all a mom could do.

Mama probably did the best she knew how with us, but her mother didn't have a mother most of her life, so she was not mothered adequately herself. That, along with the alcohol, probably affected her in ways I'll never understand.

Every sacrifice as a mother has been worth it because Amber is a winner with a faith and determination that I will never match.

I salute my daughters, each one. Because of them, I'm who I am today. Through it all, still, I am blessed. Thank you, Lord Jesus, for the blessing of being a mother.

Letting Go

As women who have actively worked at being better mothers than our own, we may find it challenging, if not painful, after so many years of parent-child closeness, to step back and let go when the time comes. After all, children do grow up and develop personalities of their own.

My second son, Daniel, was born to be a comic. No joke goes untold, no comedy routine unpracticed. He amuses us by the hour. It's better than living next door to Robin Williams. With his shoulder-length blond hair and baggy "gangsta" clothes, it's easy to size him up for the marching-to-the-beat-of-a-different-drummer musician that he is. He actually has dreams of becoming a bounty hunter. Ooo-kaaay . . . Since he's the kind of really bright kid whose picture is in the dictionary next to the word underachiever, *he has made no plans to go to college (yet). Still he's adamant that he won't be one of the millions of other minimum-wage earners who have had to make a career out of asking, "Would you like fries with that?"*

The hardest thing with Daniel has been loving him in spite of himself. He's always had a problem with his attention span, and he used to be hyperactive, but those we could live with. The hard part is watching him do poorly in school even though we've had him tested— he's well above average—and we know what he could *be doing. But unlike my mother, I'm not going to put a price tag on my love. I'm not going to say, or even think, that I would love him more if he did better in school. I will continue to love Daniel and be proud of him—even if he* does *become a bounty hunter!*

Because we tried so hard to be supermothers and did everything "right," we may feel surprised when our children grow up and have minds of their own. Some of our children also develop problems for which we blame ourselves and feel terribly guilty, when we shouldn't. As Yolanda points out, "I think a lot of it has to do with decisions *they* make, and the friends they choose. It's real easy to feel responsible, but you can't. They make their own decisions. They know the consequences. You have to let go, which is hard."

One of the hardest things for a mother to acknowledge is that one or more of her children has an addiction problem. For daughters of alcoholic mothers, it is especially difficult because no one knows better than we do what a profound and harmful effect addiction can have on the family unit. Still we don't stop loving our children, just as most of us didn't stop loving our mothers. But at least we are in a far better position to seek help for our children; as children ourselves when our mothers drank, we were all too often impotent. One mother who is currently dealing with a child's addiction is Antoinette Turner, forty-four, who has two daughters, ages twenty-six and twenty-five. "I was compelled to be all the mother my mother wasn't," explains Antoinette. "That was a driving force. I was going to be the best mother I knew how and do all the things that my mother didn't do well. Of course, I went apeshit the other way. And now, my younger daughter is fighting with alcoholism and trust and lying."

Shannon Nichols's son committed suicide a year ago; he was twenty-nine. She had been only eighteen when she gave birth to him. "You know how some folks say, 'I never want to be like my mother'? I will do everything I can not to be like my mother. When my son was younger, I worked very hard at not being like her. I made sure that I touched him, I made sure that I hugged him, I made sure that we made eye contact, I said 'I love you' . . . those are things I concentrated on. In my quest to concentrate on those, I missed some of the other areas—and ended up being like my mother!" She laughs at the irony.

"In some areas, I may have been too nice. In other areas, I ended up being just like her, with the work ethic. My son and I were alone for many years, and I thought that I had to work three jobs . . . You know, hindsight is so beautiful. If I had only known then what I know now, I wouldn't have done that. We would have done without a few things and we would have been together much more. But when I was seventeen and just married and pregnant, I couldn't rely at all on my mother to give me advice on any of these events."

Unfortunately, Shannon's second husband was an alcoholic who introduced her son to drugs. Like many mothers of addicted children, Shannon was uncertain just how much help she should give her son. She knew that money would be spent on drugs. Yet she couldn't simply abandon him; instead of money, she sent him words of wisdom.

"I wrote him a letter that it was important that he become responsible for himself, just for himself. So I prayed about him. And what I came out with was, 'Look, you can't control him, so you give him over to God.' What I'm dealing with right now is that I turned him over to God and he died. Still," Shannon muses, "if I had given him money when he wanted it, he may have ended up doing the same thing anyway—maybe even sooner."

How young and naive I was in those golden days of early motherhood, as I hungered eagerly for the babies who would fill up my empty soul. I was going to be a perfect mother and raise them according to my values. They would all love British literature, musicals, and museums! Little did I know then that children are born with personalities and minds of their own. My babies are now twenty-six and twenty-four and eleven, and all three of them are as different from each other as they can be. One thing they do have in common, though, is that none of them particularly wants to read E. M. Forster or Charlotte Brontë. My oldest son, an engineer, has wiry brown hair with a slightly receding hairline, hazel eyes, and an olive complexion. His glasses give him a serious look, but he has a wonderful sense of humor. And he always remembers my birthday. The middle son, an artist, has a lion's mane of thick auburn hair hanging to his shoulders, ocean blue eyes, aristocratic features, and a gentle, self-assured smile. He tends to stay out of touch. My youngest son, who has auburn-glinted mahogany hair and brown eyes, is very intense and quick to express his emotions. I love them all very much, but guess what? I did not turn out to be a perfect mother, after all! I have gained a much better understanding of my own mother, and I sympathize with her.

I often wonder . . . with all the conflicting feelings I've had about motherhood, I, at least, have always had a separate life of my own, outside motherhood and homemaking. What in the world was it like for my mother, a smart, attractive, well-educated woman who had dropped out of medical school to become a housewife and raise three children? What was it like for her *to be alone in that big, empty house, now cleaned by maids who commuted out to the suburbs every Tuesday and Thursday? What was it like for* her, *with no career, with her kids growing up and becoming independent, and her husband far away in the city, shrinking depressed women's heads ten hours a day?*

Maybe that's why she became an alcoholic . . .

Part IV

Chapter Eleven

Mother's Aging, Illness, and Death

∽

"I miss her very much. I often wish she were here to see her grandchildren and the life she missed out on. I loved her very much even though she made my life a living hell. I understand now as an adult that the booze is what took her life over."
— Victoria Brinson, forty-one, office manager, Chicago, Illinois

"I surprised myself by crying at her funeral, because I always said I hated her. But I cried because of the wasted life she had."
— Ronda Davidson, forty-four, Union, New Jersey

"Driving to the hospital the other night, I kept praying that she would be dead by the time I arrived. It would have ended both our miseries."
— Donna Cartee, fifty, sales representative, Canaan, New Hampshire

∽

August 13, 1972: Dannemora, New York

On Saturday night, Mother went to bed as usual. The next morning, my father found her dead. He'd brought coffee into their room, he told me. I'm sure he was in his customary morning mode of sunshine and song. I can see him now, a youthful-looking forty-nine, with wavy blond hair, striding cheerfully into the carpeted bedroom with the two steaming cups. In his happy morning voice, he goaded and teased her to wake up and smell the coffee. But her auburn head did not turn toward his voice. She lay on her side, facing the opposite wall, her white shoulder bare above

245

the satin sheet. Placing the coffee on the bedside table, Dad sat down on his side of the bed and gently shook her. No response. He got up and walked around to the other side of the bed. He saw that her fingers were blue.

Sad to say, alcoholism is a one-way journey to an early grave. Statistics show that of the small percentage of alcoholics who attempt to dry out, an even smaller percentage succeeds. Avram Goldstein, M.D., notes in his book *Addiction: From Biology to Drug Policy* that many alcoholics join recovery groups, but "many drop out, and . . . long term abstinence rates are low." Complicating this is the fact that female alcoholics often try to hide their alcoholism and avoid seeking recovery until the disease has taken a stronger hold on them. "Male alcoholics tend to reveal themselves earlier," states Curt Kresbach, senior counselor at Boonville [Missouri] Valley Hope Treatment Center. "Women who admit to a drinking problem risk attracting the stereotype of being weak, inferior and sexually promiscuous. Because female alcoholics require more initial recovery time than men, this is harmful to their recovery from the disease. Generally, when a woman decides to seek treatment, she has more severe medical problems than her male counterpart." This grim reality was reflected in our sampling. According to the more than two hundred daughters we heard from, only fifteen had mothers who had recovered for any significant amount of time. The rest had either suffered untimely deaths from alcohol-related causes or were on the decline.

Alcohol contributes to rapid aging, health problems, and almost inevitably, untimely death. We feel the tug of guilt as we watch our mothers' abused bodies begin to fail, as alcoholism and its frequent sidekicks, heavy smoking, poor nutrition, and too many Valiums, begin to take their toll.

The Aging Alcoholic Mother

Old family photographs of Mama show a vivacious blond, trim of figure, animated of expression. Then the photos start to change. Her face grows more worried, the figure gaunt. After the drinking has taken over, her belly starts to bulge, her eyes look slack and hostile, her mouth frowns. Photos of her from different periods feature a heavier woman, her skin roughened and illuminating the scars from a car's tearing metal and from skin cancer. Her eyelids have drooped into a permanently suspicious squint. Her mouth has lost its allure, pulled down by its ever-present cigarette, slackened by the alcohol. Her figure has changed. Her buttocks hang flaccidly, her once firm breasts sag. She has stopped being active, no longer doing housework or gardening. Her days of sitting in one spot, drinking and smoking, have stretched into years. The wooden dining chair she constantly sat in has grown to look like her, and she like it. Photos of her just before she died in 1993 show a very thin, wrinkled, elderly woman with dreamy, unfocused eyes.

Angie Ferro says, "I know alcohol will be the death of my mother. She's aged quite a bit from drinking. You look at her in one picture and then you see her five years later, and it looks like she's aged twenty years or so." Joellen Weatherford's mother smokes "constantly when drinking," says Joellen. Her mother's nose is red and her face scarred from her drunk-driving accidents. "I fear her death will be related to drinking," sighs Joellen. "I think I'm prepared for the phone call." Katharine Deng, twenty-six, describes her mother as "always sick. Something is always severely wrong. She has protruding ribs and emphysema from smoking a pack a day." Mary Garfinkle says that her mother, who smokes a pack a day and takes sleeping pills in addition to drinking, "starts about 6 or 7 A.M. and quits when she goes to bed at 7 P.M. She shakes constantly and can barely walk some days. Her memory is gone. She is depressed, embarrassing, meddling, rough. She knows she has ruined her brain and body."

Mama had such severe lung damage that she remained connected day and night to an oxygen tank. She could barely walk from the bedroom to the bathroom. One night, my sister Sally called. Mama, at home in bed, had almost stopped breathing. Sally and our brother Delmer had been taking turns staying up all night, listening to her breathe, frightened that each struggling gasp was the last. Finally, they could stand it no longer. Delmer told Mama that he was going to physically pick her up, carry her to the car, and get her to the hospital, and that unless she wanted to go in her nightgown, she'd better get dressed. (For the last several years, Mama hadn't dressed in anything but nightgowns and robes.)

She went. They hospitalized her. Her lung X rays showed that she had barely a flicker of air getting in. The doctors insisted that she stop smoking immediately or die. For a while after Sally and Delmer brought her home, she began to recover until finally she had regained enough strength to be able to get out and about again. The first place she headed was to buy booze and cigarettes.

Depression, Mental Illness, Alcohol-Burnt Brain

Not only does drinking add to the physical health problems of our aging alcoholic mothers, but it also affects their mental well-being. Of course, depression frequently accompanies alcoholism, both as a cause and later an effect. We daughters have always had to deal with this, but it gets worse over the years.

Prolonged drinking muddles the mind permanently. We heard quite a few stories from daughters whose mothers had suffered from some degree of alcoholic dementia, a type of insanity caused by persistent overdrinking. Dallas Whitaker's mother, who had heart disease, congestive heart problems, and emphysema, died just recently. Dallas, forty-five, a contractor from Long Island, New York, says that her mother prior to her death became a total recluse and "lived like these people you see on the ten o'clock news that they haul out of their houses after twenty years." Dallas describes her mother's living conditions: "She had shit stacked up in every dang corner, and the cats! She insisted on having those stupid cats! I love cats, don't get me wrong, I have a bunch myself. But she would not take care of them, and they would shit in the laundry baskets. She would pee in her clothes and wouldn't change them. She would go like that for weeks.

"Once," continues Dallas, "I ended up having to take her down to a doctor, because I came home, and I hadn't seen her in a year, and her toenails had grown over the ends of her toes, almost to the floor, and there was absolutely no way that you could cut them because it was so painful for her. They had started attaching themselves to the end of her toes. So we had to take her down to the doctor. She had to go back three or four more times before they could ever get them cut back. They were still misshapen, and they would never go back to where normal toenails were supposed to be. Her fingernails grew almost like a bird's, with an arc to them, and they were all yellow from smoking. The woman was hideous, absolutely hideous."

Donna Cartee doesn't remember a time when her mother didn't drink. Now her mother's fading mind complicates their already rocky relationship. "I have a very difficult relationship with her because I think she's so *nuts* at this stage of the game," sighs Donna, who meets her mother for dinner once a week and can barely have a conversation with her. "She's ornery, nasty, and negative, and she doesn't see beauty in anything. I find myself just sitting there biting the inside of my mouth, or kicking myself under the table and just agreeing with her because it's so much easier than disagreeing with her. If you say, 'Mom, I think you're wrong,' she gets annoyed and angry"—Donna mocks her mother's hissing voice—" 'Let's just not discuss it!' So it's just easier to sit there and be a puppet."

Leigh says her mother's mental health "is shot. Alcohol has just messed up her brain. When I phone her—I don't see her anymore although I'm only thirty minutes away—she has to dig it all up again. Everything I have done from the time I was born."

"My mother lives in a filthy, dirty house, and drinks every day," says Karisa. "She's been with the same guy off and on for seven years who beats her up. She never pays her bills, and she writes hot checks."

Accidents

With increasing age also comes the likelihood of more alcohol-related accidents, especially when we daughters are no longer in the home to provide twenty-four-hour surveillance. Although fathers or other siblings may still remain at home, we still feel responsible for her well-being, especially if we are the oldest child. Dianne Carlson, whose alcoholic mother lives in the same city, says, "I worry about her setting the bed on fire smoking. A lot of times, she has little burn holes in her furniture. Although I don't think she gets out that much when she's drinking real bad, she does drive under the influence. Recently, we were supposed to go to a banquet, and she was going to drive both of us. By the time I got to her house, she was already drunk. I didn't really realize it until we were already on the road. She got lost and she was going off the road. I was scared to death. We never did get there; we ended up going back home. It really worries me."

Angie adds, "My mother gets clumsy; she falls a lot. She has a gash on the side of her face where she fell down on the step and hit the corner of the television. She's hurt herself a lot when she's been drunk."

Helpless Observers of Her Slow Alcoholic Suicide

The last time I saw Mother alive, our weekend visit was going well. Then, out of the blue, on Sunday, just before my husband and I were going to leave, Mother wobbled into the kitchen. Her pale, skinny legs showed beneath her knee-length tangerine dress as she moved unsteadily toward us. Her layered auburn hair was tousled. She frowned, as though in concentration, except that her cloudy green eyes were unseeing, like those of a sleeping person whose eyes have flickered open momentarily. Her mouth hung open, and when she talked, her jaw muscles made exaggerated movements to shape the words, which she produced slowly in a high-pitched, slurred voice. I couldn't understand anything she said. Anger gripped me.

"Why do you still keep on doing this?" I shouted at her, openly disgusted. "How can you do this to us?"

But she was so far gone that she couldn't even take up the gauntlet, unlike earlier years, when she would have raised holy hell at my accusations. Instead, she looked right through me with her watery eyes, mumbling jabberwockian sentences as though she were talking to an invisible person next to me.

It is harrowing to watch our mothers decline. We daughters often feel guilty that we are unable to halt the destructive process before it is too late. With each passing year, our faint hope for her recovery, which we have never been able to entirely abandon, diminishes more and more. Yet many of us repeatedly try intervention.

Page Lafontaine, twenty-eight, now realizes that her mother will never stop drinking and will die an alcoholic. "She doesn't eat but maybe one meal every two days," reports Page. "To her, drinking her Coors Light is about as important as other humans drinking water. On Sunday morning around eleven o'clock, she goes and gets a case, and it's gone by the evening. She also smokes four packs of cigarettes a day. Two years ago, the family doctor told her that if she didn't quit smoking, she'd be dead by the time she's fifty. She's forty-six now and has had one lung collapse on her. Once, she went on a sobriety kick for about fourteen months. She was like the mother that everyone would dream for. Then one day she came home and was just totally teecocked, and from then it just got worse."

Last Chance for a Reconciliation

On her eighteenth birthday, Page confronted her mother about her drinking. Her mother only laughed in her face and said she did not plan to stop. Seeking advice, Page called her father's psychiatrist. She phoned the local detox center. "They both told me exactly the same thing. They said that until she's *ready* to stop drinking, she ain't *gonna* stop drinking. And she will just flat out tell you that she does not have a drinking problem!

"When she dies," continues Page, "I'll probably be really, really upset because I never had a mother. But on the other hand, I'll be relieved because I won't have to deal with her anymore. I can get on without having to worry where she is, who she's with, or whether she's drinking and driving and is going to kill somebody that day. The last time she wrecked her truck, she didn't even remember how she'd wrecked it."

Jo Ann, twenty-seven, has also confronted her mother, in hopes that she can become sober before it's too late. Her mother wept and said she was "trying" but it was too difficult. Jo Ann explained— once again—the steps that her mother needed to take to get her life in order. Recalls Jo Ann, "It was, 'Yes, yes, I'll do that,' and 'I love you so much,' and 'I promise, I promise, I promise,' and of course as soon as I was gone and not there to enforce it and to be in control, she was back to drinking, not working, and everything else."

She adds, "I always hope for my mother's recovery. The last time she stopped drinking, I was very happy and I thought, 'Good! She can start being, if not a mom, at least a good friend who *knows* me, knows my background, knows me for me.' One day I was talking to my grandmother, and I said, 'Grandma, if Mom were to die today, I would not care. I don't think I'd even cry. I would almost be relieved that she wouldn't be a burden to anybody anymore and cause anybody any more pain. It's not like I wouldn't be sad, so much as I wouldn't feel like I had lost anything. It's not as though I would lose any future relationship with her. Because I just don't see one."

Angie says that the thought of her mother dying "kind of scares me because I have so much hate for her now. I wish I could resolve it, but I know I can't because I can't talk to her. I know. I've tried."

Julie Lee-Jones, fifty-one, says that when her mother dies, she too will regret the fact that she and her mother have never been close. "I wish we'd had the affection. I missed that. The really good mother-daughter talks. I know that I love my mother, but we don't have a relationship because I can't talk to her. She gets really up on a high horse and just says, 'Stay out of my way; I'm not talking to you anymore.' She gets really bent out of shape for the very slightest thing you say. I don't know how much her dying is going to hurt."

Dianne still wants to try to make peace with her mother before it is too late. However, their relationship has been troubled for so long that she is not optimistic. Even when she was a child, her mother would not kiss her good-bye before leaving for work. "I would think, 'What if something happens to her, and I never see her again? And she didn't even kiss me good-bye,'" remembers Dianne. "I'd just cry. Now I don't spend that much time with her anymore. There are times when I've gone over there, and she'll keep going in the kitchen cabinet and getting it, pouring it, and drinking it down, and she keeps getting drunker and drunker. I just don't want to be around her, so I'll leave. When she dies . . . I feel like . . . I don't know." She hesitates. "I don't know how I will feel about it. I'm not real close to her. But I want to make peace with her; I really want things to be different. I don't want her to just die."

Death by Alcoholism: Not a Pretty Sight

As we attend our mothers in their final days, we cringe at the mortal damage that has been inflicted upon their bodies and minds.

Virginia heard her mother speaking to a nurse from her hospital deathbed: "If I had known this would be so awful, I would never have taken that first drink." Though it has been nearly thirty years now since her mother died, Virginia remembers that statement vividly. While writing this book, we heard numerous sad stories about alcoholic mothers' drinking-related deaths.

Samantha Barnes, forty-two, a day care provider from Ellsworth, Kansas, remembers the phone call in February, twenty years ago: her mother had been found dead in her apartment. "Her death was the most horrible thing that ever happened to me in my life," says Samantha. "It was all so sad. When I was in eighth grade, the courts said that she was an unfit parent, so I lived in a foster home for nine months. She had to stop drinking in order for me to live with her again. She did it, and I went back home to her. I was home a few months when she started drinking again. I lived with my sister awhile, then went back home. My sister and I put her in the hospital to dry out quite a few times. She would go for a while without drinking—and then start again. Once when I was shopping with her in the grocery store, she went into convulsions due to not having had any alcohol in her system for a few days. It was so scary for me; I didn't know what was happening. She was hospitalized in December. My husband and I picked her up on Christmas Day, and we all went to my sister's house for Christmas. She was pretty sick. The doctor told her if she drank any more, she'd die. One week after that, she was drinking again. Then it happened. The police called my sister the first week of February saying that her landlord had found my mother dead. On her death certificate, it says 'Acute Hemorrhagic Pancreatitis,' which means her pancreas had ruptured. The doctor explained to me when your liver is no longer working, your pancreas takes over the liver's job. I stayed with her all day at the funeral home for the viewing. It was so hard for me to leave. Her death seemed so sudden, I was unprepared."

Meredith Rushing says that her mother and father went out on a Thanksgiving night drinking binge. The next morning, her mother turned up dead on the living room floor. "Apparently she had a seizure, landed on her back, and drowned in her own vomit," says Meredith, thirty-nine. "She haunted my dreams for years, appearing like a zombie."

Marie Willow lost her mother when she was only seventeen. Her mother, fifty-seven at the time of her death, not only took prescription drugs while drinking but also smoked three packs a day. "She was ill a lot, with vomiting and seizures," remembers Marie. "I used to have to hospitalize her starting when I was eleven years old until I was seventeen. She would pass out into comas. She was also a diabetic. When she died, at first I missed her dearly. But now, as miserable as she was, I know she's better off at peace with the Lord."

Maxine's mother died when Maxine was seventeen. "She had cancer," says Maxine, now thirty-six, bitterly recalling that time. "It started out in the ovaries. A lot of it was because of her drinking. She was always drunk. She'd lie on the couch and bleed from her rectum. There would just be blood everywhere, and she'd be screaming, 'I've got cancer! I know I've got cancer!' and she just let herself waste away. She never ate. All she'd do is drink. She didn't seek help. She knew she had it, but she wanted to die."

"Mama died in my arms," says Pat Britt softly. "It was a *horrible* death. She died of drinking-related causes. She had been overweight, had extreme high blood pressure, and fluid on her heart, not to mention depression. She had come and spent Christmas with me, and it was a wonderful Christmas. However, my father had recently divorced her, and he took someone else on a vacation with him, and after that, everything went downhill with her from there. She lost all her drive. Then she died. She had a massive cerebral hemorrhage. She bit the end of her tongue off, blood came through both ears, through the nostrils, and sort of welled up into the eye sockets. She really was not conscious, but when I called her name, her eyes would roll, and she could squeeze my hand. Of course, she was virtually dead within a minute. But to save my life, I couldn't get rid of that memory of her dying moments. For a long, long time, I couldn't get rid of remembering that fight she made. I couldn't talk about it."

Ronda comments, "Mother died at fifty-two and looked seventy-two in the casket. She literally drank herself to death. She was bleeding internally at the time of her death. Her mind was almost gone. She'd have tremors and her mouth would go up and down. It was horrible. I surprised myself by crying when she died, because I always said I hated her. But I cried because of the wasted life she had."

If watching our mothers decline and die isn't bad enough, we are often not prepared for the waves of ugly, frightening, and contrary feelings which ebb and flow after her death. We're supposed to feel grief-stricken, and we do, but not for the usual reasons. Our minds are full of conflicted emotions.

The Guilt of Having Wished for Her Death

"Ellie, I've got some awfully bad news for you, and I don't know any other way except to go ahead and tell you," my father said. His voice was oddly deep and steady, the professional voice that he used in his work as a psychiatrist.

This sounded serious. My knees weakened.

"Your mother is dead."

I was unable to speak, breathless with pain, as he continued.

"She died in her sleep last night. When I couldn't rouse her this morning, she was taken to the hospital and pronounced dead on arrival."

"I don't believe it!" I gasped at last. My mouth had turned to sand.

"I don't believe it either." Dad's voice was muffled. Was he crying?

The bleak gray sky and torrential rain served as an appropriate backdrop for the five-hour journey home to my mother's funeral. As though the sky was crying right along with me, the rivers of rain flowed down the car windows like endless streams of tears. This was surely an ironic analog to all the tears both Mother and I had wept over the years.

Although I had worried and half-expected that she might harm herself in some way during her bouts of drinking, her mysterious and unexpected death had still come as a shock. I cried as my husband navigated the rain-flooded interstate. I wept with loss and guilt. As much as I had feared or hated my mother over the years, I had also loved her. Somewhere deep down, I had always imagined that she would finally overcome her problems and be okay. All our old conflicts would be resolved. We would become good friends, a close mother-and-daughter pair, and live happily ever after. But now those hopes of reconciliation were forever quashed.

"I feel so guilty," I confessed to my husband through my tears. "Sometimes, a part of me wanted her to die."

How we wish we had known earlier how common it is to want our alcoholic mothers dead. This guilty thought flickers through our minds most often during our years at home when we feel most powerless to stop her from drinking, yet are too young to leave.

Grace tells about a night years ago that she still remembers vividly: "When I was a teenager, my drunken mother took a particularly nasty tumble down the stairs. She fell from about the second or third step from the top. My sister and I had plenty of time to get to the hallway to see her crash her head into the solid wood front door. The noise was unbelievable. We were convinced this would kill her. She had actually broken the wood on the door with her head. She lay on the slate floor, blood coming from her head and her nightgown up around her waist, exposing her, as she was wearing no underwear. She came to, we helped her up, and she raged how it was our fault and my father's fault that she had fallen. Her head had a gash and a huge lump, but she would not seek medical help. That night I prayed she would die in her sleep. She did not and was very angry for a week or so."

Donna Cartee's mother was recently rushed to the hospital in an alcoholic seizure. When the paramedics arrived, she had no heartbeat, but they revived her and got her to the hospital. Donna says, "A brain scan shows that she has atrophy of the brain from alcohol consumption. She is emaciated because she starves herself. I have thought for a couple of years that she is anorexic—she has this bizarre pride over how thin she is. They are replenishing her body with electrolytes because her potassium level was very low, and they are medicating her with Ativan and Haldol to keep her calm and to relieve any 'coming down' symptoms. She is totally out of it. So this coming week I have to find a nursing home to place her in when she gets out of the hospital. Driving to the hospital the other night, I kept praying that she would be dead by the time I arrived. It would have ended both our miseries."

Sharon states frankly, "When I was a teenager, especially, I used to hope that Mama would die. It seemed that my life, and the lives of Daddy and my siblings, would be so much better and easier if she weren't around to constantly be torturing us. Whenever I'd get angry with her, which was almost daily, I'd plot ways of getting rid of her. A high school friend, also burdened with an alcoholic mother, used to help me compile a List of People to Send to Siberia. Heading that list were our mothers. At least at that time, my friend no longer lived with her mother. Mine was always there, passed out in her filthy bed, stained with old menstrual blood, or setting fire to the cracked red plastic sofa with a forgotten cigarette, or stumbling through the kitchen, screaming, with her cup of bitter instant coffee slopping all over her and the floor."

Penny McBride, twenty, describes very passionately in one of her diary entries how much she wishes her alcoholic mother would die. In addition to drinking, her mother smokes several packs a day and uses heroin, methadone, and marijuana.

"I hate you Mom, I hate you," writes Penny. "So much I could kill you. Bitch. I hate you so much. This weekend I'm running away. I hate you, vodka-bloated woman . . . Pump more Smirnoff into your system. You Asshole, you obvious Asshole. Do you know what you're doing to yourself and me and your son and your family. You're ruining our lives, not only your own. I hate you, maybe you'll die soon like your father. Maybe I'd be a happier healthier person without you, Bitch."

Cathy Taulbee, forty-eight, states bluntly, "I hate her as much now as I did when she died. In fact, I had her cremated and threw her ashes in the gutter in front of her favorite bar."

Monique admits that her mother's death "would be the only way now to deal with the pain and lies I've had to deal with." Her mother is still alive and drinking, smoking a pack a day. "My mother denies everything in her life," adds Monique. "She lies, and I think she believes her lies. She's very unhealthy, very thin, constantly coughing, her feet are swollen, and so is her face, and she is always shaking."

Susanna is frank when she says she wants her mother to die. Her mother has been drinking for as long as Susanna can remember and is a "volatile and vicious" alcoholic. "For as long as I can remember, fear was the most important feeling I associated with her," confesses Susanna. "I remember lying in bed and praying she would die. Since I've become an adult, I have lived for the day she'll be on her deathbed."

"Killing Her Off" Emotionally, Long Before Her Death

Some of us have spent so many years mourning our mothers prior to their deaths that our grief is largely spent when they actually *do* die. "My mother's death was sad—but overdue," admits Lucy Smith. Having already mourned sufficiently during our mothers' living years, some of us have taken the final step of severing all emotional ties with our mothers in order to save ourselves. Thus our mothers have already "died" long before the real event.

June Godfrey laughs comfortably, without guilt, when asked about how she will cope with her mother's death. "I will probably go to her funeral just to make sure they put her twelve feet under instead of six because the closer to hell she is, the faster she'll get there! I've been so angry with my mother. One time, in my late twenties, I made out a death certificate with her name on it and sent it to her. I haven't necessarily wished her dead, but I've made remarks to the point of, 'I don't have a mother.' "

"My mom—to me—'died' when I was around sixteen, and I just recently emotionally buried her," says Diana Matthew, forty, an LPN from Providence, Rhode Island. "She has not been a mom in any sense of the word. She is not even a grandmother to my kids. Oh, yeah, she sends money in a card, but there is very little communication with us. She lives forty minutes away. In December 1995, she and I had 'words.' I told her she was an alcoholic, and I was not responsible for how she felt. I said, 'The drinking must be talking now—did you have one or two today?' She got really mad then. I have asked her since if she thought she had a drinking problem, and she replied, 'No, I don't, but other people have told me I had a problem. But no, I don't.'

"Then I knew. She may never get it," she explains. "Never, until she's dead and buried. My mother refused me access to my grandmother (her mother, living with her sister). We had more words and four weeks later my father called to tell me Grandma was in the ICU dying. It was the blizzard of '96, so I was unable to see her. Instead, I called! I told Grandma that I was trying to get to her but had to wait until the weekend, due to the ten feet plus of snow. She said to take care of my children, forgive my mother, and take care of my husband. I'm trying real hard to do all three. I did not hug my mother at the funeral. A year has now passed. My love for her is nonexistent. She has a right to see her grandchildren, but I am not connected to her in any way. It's hurtful to think I buried my mother and grandmother weeks apart, but I did. My mother's gone—but still lives. It's very sad."

Dallas did not cry at her mother's funeral because her mother had already died in Dallas's heart long before. "I know that not being able to cry at my mother's funeral is something most people look at in horror because they just can't imagine that you can't love the woman who brought you into this world. But they don't realize that

that woman died when I was in junior high. At the funeral, this metamorphosis was *not* my mother, and I knew it."

Susie Abell, thirty, whose mother is still alive and drinking, "buried" her mother years ago, as a way of coping. "I loved my mother very much," says Susie. "But the woman I knew has been dead to me for years. When I needed her the most—as a sixteen-year-old with a baby—she wasn't there for me, and after my brother died, she totally disappeared. I grieve for her all the time and pray that the woman she is now will pass away and her pain will end."

Marla Venerable, whose mother died many years ago, admits, "I left home at nineteen and never looked back. Even all these years later I have almost all negative feelings for her. It still hurts! She died nine years after I left home, when I was approximately twenty-eight. A good friend of mine saw my mother's obituary in the paper. She knew where I was because we would send Christmas cards back and forth, so she called me on the phone to tell me that my mother had died. I have a little bit of regret, but mostly none. For me to leave my mother when I was nineteen was a life-or-death situation. I had to go."

An Ending to a Sad Tale Begun Long Ago

Mama's death was more like an ending to a tale begun long ago—no shock, no overwhelming grief, just a sense of sadness because she never loved life or embraced it. In the intensive care unit, with a respirator tube down her throat, Mama could not talk. Instead, she'd scratch out messages: "I love you." Each painfully written note told us she was offering them as talismans against the inevitable. We took turns staying at the hospital with her. One morning, when it was my turn, I was told that Mama must have a tracheostomy because the breathing tube was causing so much damage to her throat and vocal cords. If she survived this episode and ever needed to be connected to a respirator again, it would be much easier if she could be connected via the trach opening. Mama would not sign for the surgery. Terror contorted her swollen face into a mask each time the doctors mentioned it. I was standing by her bedside when they asked once again whether she would agree to the surgery. She shook her head violently and pointed to me.

"Do you want me to sign for you, Mama?" I asked. She nodded, relieved. So I signed, my handwriting as shaky as her own was.

"We'll call you when we're ready to do the surgery," they told me. "It will probably be about four this afternoon."

Because the doctor who was to do the surgery became involved in an emergency, they did not call me down from the hospitality suite until one o'clock in the morning. I sat alone in the waiting room. I'd been told that the surgery would take about thirty minutes. I was terrified about the seriousness of Mama's condition. During the next hour and a half, I sat, dizzy and nearly fainting, in one of the many chairs in the large, empty room. My heart hammered within my chest. I cried. I prayed. Even though I'd hated her at times, I didn't want her to die. I wished desperately for someone to be with me. When someone finally came to tell me that I could go in to see Mama, I was near hysteria.

Numbly, I followed the nurse into Mama's ICU cubicle. Mama's draped body was arched over a bed that had been arranged to bend somewhat down at the head, for purposes of drainage. Very pale and motionless, she looked dead. But, once again, she had fought and won.

A few days later, after she had stabilized, I had to walk into the hospital room and pretend to be brave and cheerful. I told Mama that it was time for me to return home. Then I broke down and began to sob.

I said, "I don't want to leave you, Mama. I'm so sorry I have to go. I love you."

Through my tears, I could see the pain on her face. It was one of the few times in my life that I knew that she was hurting for me, not for herself. That made it even worse. I must have cried all seven hundred miles back to Georgia. I wanted to stay with her, and guiltily, I was so very glad not to have to be there anymore, listening to the hiss and gasp of the machines.

After a few more days, Mama was moved to a special convalescent facility that cared for the extremely ill. I called her and talked to her occasionally, but it was difficult to talk for long because her voice was so weak and raspy. In October the day came for her to be released from the center. She was so happy to be going home that my sister Sally, who had been her at-home caretaker, did not bring up the subject of a nursing home. Knowing what Mama's reaction would be, she dreaded mentioning it.

Losing most of her voice had not substantially altered the fact that Mama's worst abuse of her children was verbal. All of us dreaded Mama's anger and tongue lashings. Somehow, she seemed to know the right words to use to inflict upon us the most painful humiliations. Sally, though rightfully fearful of Mama's reaction to going into a nursing home, had secretly placed Mama's name on a waiting list. In the meantime, she cared for her with almost no help except for a home health nurse whom Mama objected to but accepted only because she seemed to understand that Sally just couldn't do it all anymore.

Mama's creditors called almost daily wanting money. She had run up huge sums on credit cards that charged outrageous amounts of interest. Her purchases were limited to alcohol and cigarettes, but in the quantities that Mama consumed, they were still very costly.

Then the blow fell. I received some tragic news about my niece, Amanda, Sally's eleven-year-old daughter. A few days after Thanksgiving, on December 3, I was sitting at my kitchen table grading final exams, when the phone rang. It was late, so my first thought was "Oh, God, something's wrong with Mama." When I heard Sally's voice, I knew it for sure: "Sharon, I've got some real bad news." I felt sure Mama was dead. If only that had been the news. Instead, what Sally had to tell me was that Amanda had been severely injured in a car accident and was not going to live.

Eleven-year-old Amanda was pronounced dead before we could make the fourteen-hour drive back to Louisiana. The hysteria that enveloped our family was not unexpected, nor was Mama's reaction. I sat with Mama for a long time. It was hard for her to cry with a tracheostomy, so with the buildup of fluid, she was having trouble breathing. With something like shame, she told me, "I loved that little girl. I know I *ought not to admit it, but I loved her even more than I did my own kids."*

Mama could not go to Amanda's funeral. She did not feel that she could handle it, but she wanted to say good-bye, so we brought her to the church before the funeral began. My brother rolled her wheelchair near Amanda's white coffin. I could tell that Mama was almost afraid to look at her, but when she did, a terrible crumbling, followed by a longing, seemed to etch her face. She reached out her hand and touched Amanda's. "Baby, Mamaw will be with you soon." She repeatedly told us, "It should have been me. Why wasn't it me?" After the funeral, she said, "Amanda is in heaven with Papaw, but he can't take care of her. She needs me. I'll be with her soon."

Amanda's death seemed to change Mama's fear. If Amanda could be brave enough to go before her, then couldn't she be brave enough to follow?

We had buried Amanda on Tuesday and returned home on Wednesday. That Saturday night, when I called and talked to Mama, she told me that she was there alone. I couldn't believe it. I called Sally's mother-in-law, who told me that Sally and Arthur had had to take their baby to the hospital because she was running a high fever. A neighbor was to have stayed, but Mama sent her home. I could tell that Mama was having trouble breathing, and I figured that she was probably going to need to return to the hospital before long.

I went to bed that night, and though I was worried, I was extremely tired and forgot to switch the telephone ringer on in the bedroom. When I arose the next morning, the light on the answering machine in the living room was blinking furiously. Mama had died shortly before dawn, and everyone had been trying to call me. She had been found dead at about five that morning by my brother. His wife, catnapping in the next room, had been getting up every half hour or so to check on Mama, but finally, exhausted, she had slept about an hour before waking. Delmer had been working his usual graveyard shift and, worried about Mama, left early. He got to the house and looked into her room. He didn't see her, but he also didn't see the long trail of respirator tubing that followed Mama,

*connected as it was to her. Mama was on the floor where her body had
rolled, probably following the relaxation of muscles after her death.*

"Grief?" remarks Sharon thoughtfully. "I'd already been grieving
for three decades *before* she died. Strangely, before she actually died,
my primary worry was not how I would feel but whether her death
would interrupt my school year. That sounds selfish to say, but
there's not a selfless way to be selfish. Whenever someone said
anything about Mama's ill health, all I could think of was, 'I hope
she dies during summer vacation.' She didn't; she died during
Christmas vacation. But I got my wish. Mama didn't interrupt the
school year. I got to have that nice little holiday break in which to
deal with the business of grieving."

While many of us, like Sharon, may feel well prepared, our
mother's death may pack more of a wallop than we imagined. At
first, we may feel little or nothing, perhaps because the unusual
potpourri of highly mixed and buried feelings toward her and
toward her death may be too much for some of us to absorb right
away. The impact may hit later. Pat Britt was twenty when she lost
her mother. "For eighteen to twenty years, I suppressed everything
about my mother," recalls Pat. "I couldn't visit her grave for about
ten years without my own feelings of depression. I felt abandoned. I
hadn't learned enough about being a female, how to cook, or things
like that. In November '89, on Thanksgiving, my father died at my
house, and his last days brought Mother's death to a surface that I
had apparently buried for years. My grief over Mother hit me very
hard even after all those years."

Maxine blocked out her grief about her mother's untimely death
"for a very long time." Her mother died when she was seventeen,
and at first, Maxine felt nothing. "I didn't go to her funeral," she
says. "I didn't want to go. I felt at that point that I didn't care. She
had a little black cat that I had given to her for her birthday, and
after she died, I took that cat. I think what happened was that in my
mind, I still had that cat, so I had her. Then the cat got hit by a car.

That was it. That's when I lost it. I was really upset, crying, destroying things, hurting things just to hurt things. You see, I'd never grieved. Any grieving I did, I did when that cat got killed."

Unfinished Business

Our relationships with our mothers all too frequently end on a sour note. All the differences between us, from yesterday's petty quarrel to a lifetime of conflicts and unspoken feelings, die along with her, unresolved. The unfinished business stands as a chaotic barrier between us and a reasonable sense of closure. When she departs, it is as though the last chapter of an unfinished book has been ripped out just as we have turned to it.

"I feel so guilty that my last conversation with her was recriminating," states Louisa, whose mother died at the age of fifty-seven when Louisa was thirty-three. Their last conversation took place three days before her mother was hospitalized for the last time. Louisa had just found out that her mother had been vomiting blood and was unable to eat.

"So I lashed out at her for not telling me. Then my father called me twenty-four hours later to tell me she was now in a coma. He was pretty acrimonious about my last conversation with my mother and how much it upset her. She and I never got to resolve that."

Linda Hanson, now forty-nine, was a twenty-year-old junior in college when her mother died suddenly. Their last words to each other, several months earlier, had been yelled in anger. Linda had come home for Thanksgiving break when an argument erupted. She recalls, "It was a fairly stormy five-day Thanksgiving break. My parents were going to get divorced, and I think she felt somehow as though I had sided with my father against her."

Her mother yelled, "I don't want to see you again!"

"Fine, that's fine with me," Linda yelled back.

Linda came home again for Christmas. By this time, her mother had moved into her own apartment. She invited Linda's sisters to come over to see her, "but she made it very clear that I was not to come," remembers Linda. A few weeks later, Linda returned home to her father's house for semester break. There she received a phone call from her mother's sister. Aunt Ruth said, "Your mother's in the hospital."

Linda told her, "Aunt Ruth, the last thing she said to me was that she didn't want to see me again; if she's sick enough to be in the hospital, it's probably not going to help her if I go in."

Aunt Ruth said, "Linda, if you ever want to see your mother alive again, you'd better go to that hospital."

"What do you mean?" asked Linda.

"She's not going to live."

Linda hung up and hurried to the hospital.

"Her liver had just stopped working," explains Linda. "I'd had no idea. At all. I'd had absolutely no idea whatsoever. The last time I'd seen her, at Thanksgiving two months before, she'd seemed fine. But I don't know enough about cirrhosis. The color of her skin was the color of that yellowish mustard. I went and visited her two or three times, and then she went into a coma. Two or three days later, she died. During those final days, she and I certainly didn't argue. The one thing that's very sharp in my memory was that she said, probably the first time I visited, 'Nobody's brought me flowers.' Of course it never occurred to me, in the context of her dying, to bring flowers. I also have this very strong memory of talking about very mundane things: the dog was going to have puppies; Jill and Julia were doing fine at school; this is what we were going to have for dinner. So I suppose in some ways, this was an overture toward making peace. But I was still very angry, I think, at the *whole* situation. I felt scared that somehow I was never going to shed all the baggage that came along with being in an alcoholic family. I do feel a deep sadness that she never got to see me grow up or meet her granddaughter. I also wish I had someone to ask 'mother' questions of. I remember vividly how she looked when she was dying: jaundiced, bloated, and so alone."

Guilty Relief

Yet if we're really honest, we may also be a little bit relieved when our mothers die. We are so tired of *worrying*. As we were growing up, worrying had been a full-time preoccupation for us. We were always tuned in to where our mother was and what she was doing. We knew when to avoid her and when to look in on her. Our eyes and ears were always on alert. Even after we leave our mothers' homes, the anxiety may diminish but does not disappear. Thus when she dies, we don't have to do that anymore. A burden has been lifted.

Betty Buxton's mother drank heavily until she died at the age of sixty-nine. She smoked two or three packs a day and took tranquilizers. "I have really been relieved by her death," states Betty bluntly. "I was out of touch with her during her last years of illness. I had no love for her and found her intolerable—sober or drunk. I am sorry she never tried to help herself. I am sorry she couldn't have been a loving parent to me or my sisters, or a loving wife."

Sara Jo Kea's mother died this year at the age of sixty. She had been drinking since Sara Jo was a child and smoked a pack a day. "I am devastated about my mother's death," reports Sara Jo. "At the same time, I feel almost free—there is no need to care for her, worry for her, or feel guilty about not giving her enough attention. I miss her very, very much, but I know she's at peace."

Camille Robbins, who was twenty-eight when her mother died, remembers waiting in the hospital room where her mother lay unconscious. "When she died, I was relieved the battle was finally over, no more fighting and hating each other."

Susan Anderson's feelings are similar. "I'm not sorry she's dead. It's a lot easier for me not having to deal with it. She was a weak person. She had no courage."

"Her death was the only answer to her failing physical and mental health," says Lynn Clifton. "Although I grieved her death, it was also a relief to have her suffering ended."

*   *   *

During calling hours for Mother, some of our hometown friends and neighbors couldn't resist gently probing. "Was Jess's death a surprise, or had she been ill?" asked Cousin Marilyn. "Completely out of the blue," asserted my father. "Probably a heart attack," he added vaguely. Pamela Roberts, well intentioned even as she was chronically blunt, took me aside and whispered consolingly, "Ah, dear me, it's such a shame. I know how sad you must be. You know, on that Sunday morning when they brought her into the hospital, my husband Randall was on duty there. 'Oh,' he said, 'even though she was dead, Jess looked so natural, so good.' And you know, dear, Randall and I had invited your mother and dad for dinner on that Saturday night, but they couldn't come." She sighed heavily. "I can't help but think that if they had come for dinner, things might have been . . . different." "You mean," I thought to myself, "she might not have gotten drunk that night and perhaps suffocated in the pillow in her own bedroom?"

Did Pamela know? After all, she and Mother had been friends. How could she not know? How many, I wondered as I stood in the receiving line shaking hands with a trail of familiar and unfamiliar people, how many of these people had known about Mother's drinking and prescription drug problem? We had tried so hard and so long to put up the front of a "normal" family, hiding behind the closed doors of our "happy" middle-class life. How many outsiders had known or suspected? That such things were not proper funeral parlor talk did little to dissuade some of the more persistent.

Maude Cornwell, my grandmother's heavyset elderly friend, appeared to harbor a certain secret delight in funerals. She asked, "Were you at home that night when your mother was taken sick?"

"She was never sick," I responded defensively.

The curious stares continued during the funeral service. A sea of people turned their wondering faces to the four of us, Dad, me, Diana, and my brother, sitting in the front pew. As the grieving family, we were first to follow the coffin down the church aisle when the ceremony ended.

Out of the mob of people, one face came into focus as I hurried down the aisle, eager to escape the limelight—the face of Patricia Ford. She stared at me intently from her aisle seat. Long ago, I had dated her son, Dan. His family had been civil to me, but a trace of faint disapproval had always hung in the air. On one occasion, after I had started college, Patricia had prevented Dan from riding with my mother to pick me up. When my mother arrived alone, I asked, "Where's Dan?" Mother, calm and sober that day, explained that she'd had a phone call that morning from Patricia, informing her that Dan was asleep and wouldn't be coming with her. At the time, I had been furious at Patricia for once again thwarting the limited time Dan and I had together, and I had been even more furious at him for not also being furious with his mother. However, as I followed Mother's coffin down the church aisle, the insight flashed that perhaps Patricia had known about Mother's "secret" problem and had not wanted her son to ride with a potentially drunk driver.

I had tried so hard to protect Mother's reputation and make us seem to the public like a normal family. Now I would no longer have to do that. Guiltily, I felt very relieved.

The If-Only's

Although this feeling follows any loved one's death, it is particularly poignant when the departed one appears to have had some choice in the matter. *If only* she had not started drinking, we agonize. *If only* she could have stopped. So often we are haunted by what might have been if she had not started down that alcoholic path from which few return. When she dies, we grieve not so much for the loss of the woman she had become, but for the loss of the woman that she might have been and the relationship that we might have had.

Samantha was only twenty-two when her mother died, and even now, twenty years later, she feels cheated. "I think about my mother every day. I was eight months pregnant with my daughter at the time. I wish so much that she could have seen my daughter. The only child my mother saw was my oldest son, and she loved him to death. He's twenty-four now."

Rebecca, Samantha's sister, adds, "I'm very sad that a person with so much to offer the world never had much of a chance to do so."

Louisa agrees: "When my mother died, I was sad about the waste of a person who had so much potential."

Virginia Mathew, whose mother died several decades ago, talks at length about the regrets she and her family feel: "It just seems like such a shame," she says with anguish in her voice. "I think about my mother's not being around and missing out on all the accomplishments I achieved. Her approval meant a lot. I was happy to have my father there when I graduated from graduate school, but I *really* wish that my mother had been there. It's such a shame that she missed out on all of this. I wish that it had been a different time period, where there were places to go to get help. Back then, there weren't. It's a shame that we didn't have one of those family intervention deals. Then she would have been around to enjoy retirement with my father, and they would have done all the things they wanted to do. My father owned part of an island, and they were going to build a house. He ended up just practically giving it away because it was too painful for him to keep, because that had been their dream. I watched my father go through twenty-something years without her. He waited until their anniversary to die. He loved her till the day he died."

After Mother's death, I vividly remembered the conversation my husband and I had as we returned home from that awful last visit with her. We had talked about what could or should be done for her.

"I keep wanting to believe that she's okay, that somehow she's been transformed into a 'normal' mother. I keep hoping that she'll get better," I told him.

From afar, when her letters and phone calls had often sounded so normal, I always managed to convince myself once again that there never had been a problem, that maybe I had exaggerated the situation. Inevitably, though, during visits I was proven wrong. This last visit had been no exception.

"I think your father should have her involuntarily committed to some kind of institution," my husband said.

"But Dad says she has to want to be cured first," I replied, thinking uncomfortably about how Dad seemed to do nothing about her alcoholism. I also suspected that he was prescribing various antidepressants and tranquilizers for her, such as the routine Valium. I had challenged my father about it before.

"Honey," he told me, as he always had, "if she doesn't get it from me, she can get it from someone else."

I thought of the medicine cabinet that was always filled with bottles of prescription medicines, and of the bedside table upon which my mother's mug of ale seemed a permanent fixture. Had it been there when Dad found her?

 I thought about the irony of Dad's position as a successful psychiatrist. His framed academic and medical diplomas filled the walls of his office. Over many years, dozens of patients had looked into his droopy blue eyes and poured out their deepest fears, secrets, and troubles, while he listened in solemn silence, puffing his pipe, making direct eye contact. At proper intervals, his soothing voice offered guidance and reassurance. At the end of the session, he wrote out any necessary prescriptions, signed his name followed by a large "M.D.," and said warmly, "See you next time" to one more person whose shaky life he was now getting back on track. At the end of the day, he packed his briefcase, rode home, and walked into our house.

The moment the door shut, he was instantly transformed from competent psychiatrist to helpless spouse of an alcoholic.

All his years of medical school and psychiatric training, all of his work with the state hospitals, all of his experience treating patients, had still not prepared him for what he faced at home. Alcoholism is indeed *the great leveler—psychiatrists and lay people alike are equally powerless to "make" the alcoholic stop drinking.*

In the early years, when Mother first started to drink, Dad appeared to be oblivious to it. At the time, I assumed he had the power to "make" my mother change and simply chose not to. But now I know that, psychiatrist or not, he was just as much at the mercy of her alcoholism and just as bewildered about it as any untrained spouse would be. He must have struggled with some secret feelings of inadequacy: he was the psychiatrist who could cure everyone but his own wife.

Over the years, he tried different tactics. He confronted her. "This has got to stop!" I could hear him demand during their violent nighttime arguments. That didn't work.

He sent her to other psychiatrists; that also didn't work.

We moved. She had been very unhappy in Highland Park, Illinois, where she felt so snubbed and excluded by the cliquish women who lived there. So we moved back to my father's hometown in upstate New York, which helped for a while. But slowly, she slipped back into drinking.

Finally, he threatened to leave her. Although she still denied having a problem, she did what she had to do to keep him. She stopped again. I remember the day my parents came to visit me at my college. Mother appeared unusually upbeat. Dad took me aside and whispered, "Don't worry about your mother anymore. I've gotten her straightened out once and for all," he said triumphantly.

That phase was short-lived.

Maybe I could have done more to help Mother. Why had I abandoned her?

"I always knew something like that was going to happen to her," Diana had said blackly after the funeral as we rode darkly ensconced in the backseat of the limousine.

The Aftermath

The aftermath of our mother's death is often painful and guilt-ridden as the unresolved issues hover in the air around us like angry ghosts. Suddenly, after a lifetime of waltzing, we are left standing alone on the empty dance floor, unsure of what to do next. We have strong, almost violent feelings about their deaths.

Though on the surface, it may appear that the daughters who told their stories for this book were consumed only with hatred and disgust for their mothers, the majority of daughters still loved them and felt bad about their deaths. Maxine Caldwell is a good example. Maxine, who endured severe abuse from her mother and described her as "violent, abusive, pitiful, and scary," surprised us during the interview when she stated, "I loved her! God knows, I loved her." Perhaps the instinctive love a daughter has for her mother is an enduring one that does not die easily; perhaps for some of us who no longer feel it, it has merely gone into hibernation.

Mama's funeral was held exactly a week after Amanda's. Relatives I hadn't seen in years were there, including former spouses of relatives. I was somewhat surprised that so many came. Mama had been such a recluse for so many years, first with Daddy during his three years of being bedridden and then with her own poor health, that I felt sure everyone would have forgotten her. Ironically, the funeral included some words that were terribly untrue—about the unfailing love a mother has for her children, and how she will put her children before everything else.

Mama was buried next to Daddy, allowing us to finally put up the double headstone that she had adamantly and superstitiously fought against after his death. Their graves are at the foot of my father's parents' graves. That small cemetery is, in fact, full of my relatives on Daddy's side, some of whom died in the Civil War. Mama and Daddy face a forest of tall pine trees, and on their double gravestone is a nature scene, which would have pleased them both: Daddy because he worked outdoors all his life, and Mama because she preferred to sit indoors watching television nature shows.

I have set myself a goal that Mama would never have understood or approved: getting my doctoral degree. Each positive change I have made seems a little less threatening now that I don't have to face explaining it to Mama, who so feared and dreaded change. Revisiting and reliving her death has been good for me, though. That final act of separation has enabled me to know that in many ways, some of which I have to fight against, I am much like Mama. In others, I know myself to be far stronger than she.

It is important for us to let go of the guilt. We may be haunted by the feeling that it was in our power to persuade our mothers to quit drinking, and if only we had been better, smarter, stronger, more convincing people, we could have done *something.* But chances are we *did* do everything that we could. We daughters tend to feel overly responsible for everyone around us, a long-engrained habit that can be traced back to our childhoods. This exaggerated sense of responsibility makes us feel that we failed when our mothers continued to drink and then died. We have to learn to let go of this old, old habit. We are not responsible for other people's actions. Only our own.

In addition, is it so wrong to feel some relief? Never again will we have to worry about whether she will get smashed and plow into some innocent family while driving her car. Never again will we have to worry about whether she will collapse at the mall. Never again will we have to worry about how much it will hurt when she strikes us with fists or words.

At the same time, we remember Mother at her best, the mother who held us when we cried in first grade because the kids at school had laughed at us, the mother who stayed up all night making us special costumes for a school play, the mother who helped us with our homework. And we weep, even now, at what might have been.

"I do miss Mama," admits Sharon. "I miss calling and talking to her on Saturdays, which I had done for years. I miss her laugh, which sounded, as she aged, so much like her own father's. Unlike him, though, she didn't laugh often. I don't miss her vicious verbal abuse. I wish I could. It follows me in my life in every decision I make. It affects who I am and what I do. It ruins my ability to experience joy and accomplishment. I wish I could silence that wounding voice and hear only her deep-throated chuckle."

For years, I had dreams in which Mother appeared, sober and solemn, dressed in her heather green angora sweater and skirt set. Very serious, with her eyebrows furrowed slightly, she would lean over toward me across the kitchen table and carefully explain that there had been a terrible misunderstanding and that she was not really dead after all. She had merely been away on an extended trip to her ancestral country, Scotland, where she had been visiting relatives. In the dream, she even seemed a tad irritated that any of us believed her to be dead. Over the course of the twenty-five years since her death, however, that dream has slowly drifted away.

However, I still have my fantasies, particularly on holidays and on my children's birthdays. She did not live long enough to meet my second two sons, now twenty-four and eleven, and she only knew my first son for eight months (he is now twenty-six). I fantasize that Mother arrives at the house, just like the Mother of my childhood, though now a sweet, gray-haired grandmother, overflowing with warmth and adoration for her grandsons. She is happy, smiling, upbeat, healthy, and completely sober, of course. She gives my sons presents, hugs my husband, and then turns her attention to me. We tell each other everything. She leans forward to hear every word I say. She praises my accomplishments. She is interested and supportive. We are overjoyed to be together!

The fantasy ends abruptly, like an expanding soap bubble popping into mist.

Chapter Twelve

Building Happy Lives

⌒

"*It's* hard work *to be happy!"*
   —*Shannon Nichols, forty-eight, veterinarian, Philadelphia, Pennsylvania*

"*I have a* tape *that thinks I'm irreparably broken and therefore unlovable, but
I have a* brain *that knows I'm very capable."*
   —*Jocelyn Pratt, fifty, consultant, Norfolk, Virginia*

⌒

*Am I happy? Yes, most of the time. I've fought depression—crushing,
blackening, soul-stealing, mind-numbing, energy-robbing depression—
and I've conquered agoraphobia. Almost. I still have a tendency to
dislike going places, especially alone. I fear driving sometimes, irration-
ally, and I fear flying—which I personally consider pretty rational. But
I do it. I have a weight problem that used to ruin my life. I kept waiting
for life to begin when I lost weight. I don't do that anymore, because
that's what my mother did—she died without having lived, still
waiting. In her case, drinking robbed her of her enjoyment of life. I won't
let excess weight rob me of joy.*

*I am now forty-six years old. When my mother was forty-six, she'd
been a full-blown alcoholic for at least fourteen years. She'd been
married for thirty-one years. She had five children and three grandchildren, with another two grandchildren on the way. For all of her life,
she'd been poor. She was a heavy smoker, with early emphysema, and she
didn't eat right. She hadn't been to a doctor in years, even though she
had a huge skin cancer on her cheek.*

I've been married for nearly twenty-six years—the one way in which

I'm similar to Mama. We marry young in our family, and we generally stay married, for better or for worse. In my case, it's been for better. He's a wonderful, kind, hard-working man, and he's been a good father to our two sons and a good father-in-law to our daughter-in-law. We have a comfortable life together.

I have friends who keep me active mentally, and I have good relationships with most of my family members. My youngest sister and her little girl are very, very important to me. Sally is more my daughter than my sister, and Amber (and her sister, our beloved lost Amanda) are my grandchildren. Additionally, I look forward to having grandchildren from my two sons.

I'm doing well academically and hope to find an academic appointment when I'm done with my degree. But if I don't, I know that I'm not a one-trick pony. I can paint, I can write, and if I need to, I can sell vacuum cleaners. My life is full of can, *not* can't, *as my mother's was. She was always telling us not to use* can't *because "Can't never could do nothin'!" Yet she lived bound by* can'ts *and* don'ts *and* won'ts *and* shouldn'ts. *I choose to live a positive life instead, though I'm not always successful. Far too often, I hear Mama's voice in my head, criticizing, nagging. But I've learned to talk back to her in ways I dared not in real life. "Mama," I tell her now when she interrupts my dreams, "I loved you, but I didn't like you very much. You tried to make all of us into emotional cripples, and now that I know I don't have to be one, I choose not to be. So shut up." (She can't slap my face from the grave!)*

I know that many people would envy me my life. Sometimes my good fortune is still surprising to me. I keep waiting for something bad to happen; it's superstition. Somewhere, deep down, I suspect that I'm supposed to pay for each joy with an equal amount of misery. Rationally, I know that that's hogwash, and I can't really pin that on Mama. She wasn't an especially superstitious person. But the belief that each good will be negated by a bad is something that is deeply ingrained in me somehow. Such a belief may have come from my childhood experiences, when the woman who loved me most was able to hurt me so deeply. The hugs that turned into slaps may have become the joys that turned into disappointments.

Do I have any advice to other daughters of alcoholic mothers for living happy lives? Yes. One day about ten years ago, as I was coming out of a prolonged depression, I realized that happiness is an inner thing, not an outer one. No one can give you happiness. All of us have the seeds for it within us, and all we have to do is let them bloom. If you keep waiting for a man to make you happy, or a child to make you happy, or a job to make you happy, or losing weight to make you happy, or stopping drinking or using drugs to make you happy, then you're going at it backward. You have to make yourself happy. Then everything else will be better. No guarantees that you'll get the guy or the job, or that your addiction will end, or that your child will suddenly behave, but you will be better. Your life will become better. You just have to trust yourself, trust that you have sufficient inner resources for happiness. Because you do.

Like Sharon, many of us have come a long way. Outwardly, almost all of us are reasonably functioning women who hold jobs, raise kids, meet friends for coffee, keep our lives together. But under the surface, most of us will always grapple with irrational plunges in self-confidence and sometimes serious waves of depression. There is no cure for the lifelong repercussions of being the daughter of an alcoholic mother, and we do not pretend to have one. Thus when we talk about how to build happy lives, we take it for granted that daughters who are reading this book understand there is no magic wand that can wave away the scars. However, many of us have learned to be genuinely happy to the best of our ability. As Shannon Nichols points out, "You know, it's *hard work* to be happy! It's *work* not to get sucked into these little things that can foster negativity. But clearly there are things that make me happy. I didn't know how to be happy until I got cancer. Through group work and some individual therapy, I found things that I could be happy about.

Before that, I was absolutely petrified of happiness. Because I was sure that if I was happy, all I had to do was wait for the other shoe to drop."

The Snake in the Woodpile

We daughters are at high risk for depression. Not only may we have inherited whatever depressive tendencies our mothers had— which may have lured them to drinking in the first place—but we "are a special population with special needs," according to Claudia Black in *It Will Never Happen to Me*. Most of us have hurtful memories of neglect, abandonment, abuse, violence, and humiliation, which have laid the groundwork for potential depression later, whether we have the genes for it or not. As Judith S. Seixas and Geraldine Youcha state in *Children of Alcoholism: A Survivor's Manual*, in alcoholic families, "alcoholism is found more frequently in males and depression more frequently in females."

Depression comes in varying levels. Serious, prolonged depression, of course, requires medical attention. Even those of us who have never been clinically depressed still tend to be dragged down by shorter, smaller bouts of despair, including dark anxieties, shame, self-loathing, emptiness, inadequacy, and longing, which can creep in like an evening fog, graying our outlooks and self-perceptions. There is a lot we can do to be happy, but most of us will never entirely eradicate that "snake in the woodpile," no matter how well things go for us.

"The snake" is a metaphor for those melancholy feelings. The creature lies quietly in wait, hidden in the recesses of our minds, waiting to strike at unpredictable moments. Without warning, and often without reason, the snake can symbolically poison even the sunniest moments of our lives with its unwelcome presence.

Although Margaret Laskin has moderately good self-esteem and "big confidence in my ability to do about anything I'm physically able to do," she admits, "sometimes at night, I hate myself because of the hurt I have caused. Inside, I'm a lost person that loved and protected my children fiercely but was not the best mother I knew how to be." Gail Ricker, forty, an attorney from New York City, reveals that while she appears to be "strong and successful to the outside world, taking on life on my own terms," on the inside, she is "sad, lonely, and confused." These women have not quite learned to identify and tame the snake.

"I decided to treat 'the snake' like any other type of handicap," says Ellie. "First, I became familiar with it, learning as much as I could. Under-confidence is common among women in general, but daughters of alcoholic mothers have, at their core, a more persistent struggle with self-loathing because they have internalized the distaste and anger they feel toward their fallen role models. I started to observe the 'snake's' patterns and noted when it was most likely to strike. One would expect it to appear more frequently during bad times, times of rejection, failure, letdown. However, my 'snake' will also strike during the happiest times, such as when I've had a professional accomplishment or a personal triumph. Something nice happens, and I feel on top of the world, but then, out of nowhere, the snake bites, and my jubilance is sullied by shadows of doubt. This feeling is very common. As children, we became so used to having promises broken, happy times ruined, and good moods demolished that now, as adults, we still have trouble trusting happiness; we think it inevitable that it will end without warning. Also, in spite of all rational evidence to the contrary, we often feel inferior and perhaps undeserving of life's rewards."

Documenting the snake's patterns, knowing when it might appear, and being prepared to shoo it back with a mental broom can be a triumph of our wills over our emotions. Most of us do have strong wills as the result of our childhood experiences, and we can use that mental strength to our advantage. As Jocelyn Pratt says, "I have a *tape* that thinks I'm irreparably broken and therefore unlovable, but I have a *brain* that knows I'm very capable."

Understanding Alcoholism

Although we may think we've had far more exposure to alcoholism than we'll ever need, many of us benefit from learning more about the disease. Some of us may be convinced that drinking or not drinking is entirely a moral choice and a matter of willpower; after all, alcoholism, especially in women, has always been considered a fall from grace. But natural brain chemistry also plays a part, as we have noted in an earlier chapter. Alcoholics feel a physical craving for the chemicals in alcohol, which relieve the discomfort of those depleted circuits, but the end result is the opposite of what drove them to drink—they become *more* depressed, not less.

Knowing more about the chemical nature of this disease does not erase the pain, anger, guilt, shame, or emptiness that we may feel for past and present injustices, but it may help us understand why our mothers' willpower or good intentions were simply not a match for the powerful chemical hunger that drove (or still drives) them to choose drinking over us.

Understanding Ourselves

In addition to understanding Mother, we need to understand ourselves. There are many self-help books on the market to educate us about the typical characteristics of adult children of alcoholics and to assure us we are not alone in whatever quirks and neuroses we harbor. (See the bibliographical list at the end of this book.) In addition, many of us have been helped by therapy or by joining groups such as AA, Al-Anon, Ala-teen, Adult Children of Alcoholics, and others. Through them, we can learn the important truth that Mother was (or still is) the one with the problem—not us. The negative messages that overflowed onto us as we were maturing were manifestations of the chemically altered reality *she* lived in, *her* reality only. We are separate beings, with separate lives.

"I came to see that she was sick, not me," says Rachel Addington.

"I know I can't change her at this point, nor do I really want to. I need more work on myself. Now, after many years of browbeatings, I like myself—and so do a lot of people."

Lynn Cliffton joined Adult Children of Alcoholics after her mother's death thirty-six years ago. Her mother, who had blackouts, hallucinations, and frequent falls when drinking, died of alcohol-related causes when Lynn, the oldest of two children, was twenty-three. Lynn never fully realized the degree of emotional abuse she endured growing up until she became an adult and a parent herself. Although she feels that she is an attractive warm, outgoing, enthusiastic woman, she says that the pain and scars of her childhood abuse continue to surface. "The alcoholic family is a life sentence that must be dealt with daily in a positive way," she explains. However, unlike her mother, she feels that she has control over her choices and actions. She thinks of her adversities as "a maturing adventure" and is grateful for her blessings: a husband, children, grandchildren, friends, a career, good health, a sense of well-being, and faith in a higher power. "Sometimes I cope with my feelings by turning to prayer, listening to quiet music, or quickly getting back on track by counting all the blessings in my life."

Linda underwent private therapy. She remembers the session that was a breakthrough. One day, she was telling her therapist about her alcoholic parents and was startled when her therapist said, "That must have been awful." Linda remembers replying, "Nah, I lived through it." Then the therapist said, "Listen to yourself . . ." That moment was a revelation for Linda: she realized how much of a wall she'd built around her pain. "I remember the therapist saying, 'It must have been awful.' That was the first time anybody had ever said to me in a kind of empathetic, sympathetic, supportive way, 'Wow, that was awful—I'm sorry it was so awful.'"

Sandra Peabody, twenty-nine, has attempted suicide three times. She confesses, "I used to go out and shop and so forth when I felt lonely; I would do anything to get away from it. But I have been in counseling since age sixteen, and a member of ACOA for eight years.

Now, if I feel lonely, I just sit there and sometimes think or read or—just go with it. I know I will not die from it."

Three years ago, Rae Carlson had a tumor removed from her uterus. She firmly believes her illness was caused, in part, by a lifetime of stress and repression. Therefore, she sought professional counseling and has been in a weekly support group ever since. Rae, forty-five, explains the positive impact: "I am learning new, healthy ways of dealing with life; I'm reaching out to people more, taking more risks, and doing many of the things I'd always wanted to do but was too fearful to try. Now that I've joined the support group, I've been taking a lot more responsibility for myself and am less critical of myself. I care less what others think of me. I take more risks, speak out more, am more visible to the world."

No More Secrets

Another thing we daughters need to do is to talk about our family histories more openly, even outside of formal therapy or group sessions. Thankfully, society is far more open than it was when we were young. In the past, we, like most daughters of alcoholic mothers, worked hard to hide our families' problems; we would never have told others about our mothers' drinking. (We could barely acknowledge it to *ourselves!*) Previously, there was less social awareness about alcoholism's damage to the drinker and to the family. There were no hot lines, no talk-show discussions, no public service announcements encouraging children of alcoholics to seek help. We felt completely alone. And if any other kids' parents were alcoholics, we didn't know about it—they had learned to hide it as well as we had! But nowadays, women can feel much freer to bring it out in the open, and they should. Secrecy only feeds the snake in the woodpile.

Brenda Burton discovered by accident that talking about the problem to outsiders helped her feel better. It happened while she was teaching an adult Sunday school seminar, part of which dealt with alcoholic parents. The group watched a videotape, but after it was over, Brenda felt that it had not explored the subject deeply enough. Spontaneously, she told the group about being raised in an alcoholic home.

"So I got up in front of this whole group of people after the video, and I said, 'What the speaker said on there is true, but she's touching the tip of the iceberg with what you go through as the child of an alcoholic,'" Brenda recalls. "I started telling them that both my parents were alcoholics and that you just never knew what you'd come home to, you just could never guarantee what you'd find when you walked in the door, you never brought friends home, you never trusted your parents to even answer the phone. All of a sudden, I started seeing some recognition in some faces. After this class, a couple of people came up to me, and they said, 'Boy, that's exactly what I went through.'" When Brenda told her sister that she talks to others about their life in an alcoholic home, her sister, shocked, said, "You *do?*" Brenda told her, "'You've *got* to talk about it.' She said, 'Oh, God, no, I can't talk to anybody about this.' I said, 'No, you *have* to talk about it. *You* did nothing wrong. In order for you to heal yourself, you've got to talk about this and try to help other people who need to be healed.' And she said, 'Oh, I could never do that!' I said, 'There's nothing to be ashamed of. I've always just talked about it, and I treat it like the disease that it is. Unfortunately, it affects many people. I'm more comfortable talking about it now than I was five or six years ago. *I've* done nothing wrong.'"

Writing about It

As teachers of writing, we cannot say enough about the therapeutic value of writing. All human beings are born with the intense desire to communicate, and we know from experience that daughters of alcoholic mothers will benefit from writing down their thoughts and memories. We authors—who thought we knew ourselves—learned even more by writing this book. Faded memories and stunted feelings came bubbling to the surface like buried treasure loosened by an ocean current. As we sat writing at our respective computers hundreds of miles apart, we both cried—sentimental, sad, angry—as we revisited our pasts. But the long-lasting psychological rewards of the process have been immeasurable.

We urge all daughters of alcoholic mothers, if they are not already doing so, to write about their experiences and feelings, whether for a private daily journal which no one else will see, or as a story to share with others. Many women who responded to our lengthy survey, in fact, wrote us additional notes—sometimes *pages* of their memories—telling us that the process was indeed restorative, if painful. Marsha wrote, "Answering your queries even provided the opportunity to heal (again) as I found myself referencing (again) the troubled alcoholic (again) and permitting myself (again) to 'feel' (again) those many references (again, again, and again!). It is both painful and pleasurable."

(Note: At the back of this book, we have issued an invitation for interested readers to write to us about their experiences.)

Cutting Off Contact with Mother

Severing ties with our mother may be the hardest thing we have ever done—she is, after all, our *mother*—but our own emotional survival may depend on it. Some of us have had to cut off all contact. Jill Palmer, forty-four, once listened in agony as her mother said, "I'm going to drink until I die." Jill replied, "I don't have to watch you," and left home at the age of thirteen and never returned. Jill now says, "The mother that I knew and loved died a long time ago—the one that was loving and caring died when she started drinking."

Patricia Frink, twenty-nine, has not seen her mother for eleven years. Although Patricia still has bouts of severe depression, she has made the conscious decision never to give up, as her mother did, to be a "victor" in life rather than the victim that her mother was. Having learned more about alcoholism, Patricia now understands her mother's illness better and also realizes that she herself has "the choice not to do it."

Sometimes, it is not logistically possible to end all contact with our mothers, but some of us, if we *must* see her, make the decision to end our emotional connections. Heather McPherson, twenty-nine, left home when she was seventeen, but still feared her mother from afar for years. Her mother, who had a horrible temper, once knocked Heather's head through a glass door. She also used to threaten to place Heather in a mental institution or foster home if she didn't behave. As a result, Heather never talked back or stood up for herself. Even after leaving home, she felt controlled—until one life-changing night. "I found myself hiding *in my own house,* in my closet, pregnant with my daughter, while my husband politely lied to my mom that I wasn't home. That's when it occurred to me that now I have the power and control. I won't let her hurt me anymore! I love her, but I don't like her. And I don't have to."

Confrontation

Even after we've left home, some of us find it therapeutic to confront our mothers about the past. This can be a cathartic experience, though most alcoholic mothers will still deny having a problem and may become outraged or abusive. The process, however, can be a relief for the daughter.

Susanna Moore was thirty before she worked up the courage to tell her mother off. Always silenced, Susanna had learned to hold her feelings inside and never to cross her abusive mother. Now, years later, her hands shook and her stomach tightened as she joined her siblings in confronting her mother for the first time. "Liars! You're ganging up on me!" responded her mother angrily, denying that she had a problem. Remembering little from the past, her mother was convinced that her children were lying out of spite. She could not fathom why they were all so unhappy. However, by speaking out and breaking away emotionally, Susanna feels set free from the past. Although she cannot forget what she endured, she has been able to forgive her mother. When her mother was diagnosed with a potentially fatal disease about two years ago, Susanna no longer cared. "I feel as though I'm stuck on a plane next to a very annoying fellow passenger, and just nod and smile politely while she goes on and on about her illness," she says. "While I'm sorry it's happened (it's a terrible illness), it doesn't affect me, and there's nothing I can do about it. It's almost as if it's happening to a total stranger."

Susanna's life has improved, not only because she refuses to participate in the destructive relationship with her mother any longer, but because she has also made the conscious decision to have a positive outlook on life. Previously negative and paranoid, always thinking everyone was out to get her, she has forced herself to reconstruct her way of thinking. Her husband and happy family life have helped. Now Susanna describes herself as "an incurable optimist" with high self-esteem.

Nurturing and Caring for Ourselves

Many of the daughters we talked to have become advocates for their own health and mental well-being. That's good news because we daughters tend to be self-sacrificial, a behavior that was learned in our childhoods when much of our lives revolved around taking care of, covering for, or avoiding our alcoholic mothers. Many of us never had the chance to nurture ourselves, or if we did, we felt guilty about it.

"I know I could be a good candidate for emotional problems, so I take care of myself better than I do any other family member," says Mary Starr, forty-three. "I am determined to live a much healthier, fuller life. I don't smoke; I watch what I eat; I walk off stress; I don't even drink a glass of wine except occasionally." Like many of us, Mary had a rough upbringing. The youngest of four children, she received physical and verbal abuse from her manic-depressive mother, who had been drinking and using prescription drugs for as long as Mary could remember. Her mother's addictions had a major negative impact on the family finances. "We were evicted from lots of apartment units and grew up on financial aid."

Still Mary considers herself a winner. Her self-esteem is generally high, she says, but "it took me many years to feel this good. I had to learn to survive my childhood, and I used humor. I thought if I kept Mom laughing, it would all be okay. I still act immature for my age, but humor helps me cope. I love making people happy, but it doesn't rule my life. I accept myself now, and let people know *me*."

"I have had to do a lot of work on accepting myself exactly where I am," says Caryl Brookins, forty-seven. "I have many days where I can slip backward into my low self-esteem, so I am working hard at loving myself as I am. My mother feels sorry for herself and victimized by the world. She always needed to be the one taken care of instead of being the caregiver. I have worked hard at *not* being a victim."

Finding Fulfillment through New Challenges

For many of us, our sense of self is linked to our accomplishments. With our weak self-esteem, we often find ourselves working to prove *and* improve ourselves. If approached in the right spirit and for the right reasons, seeking new goals can enrich and make life brighter.

Virginia Mathew, now a law professor, returned to college at the age of thirty to complete the undergraduate degree she missed out on by marrying young. Disliking her life as a stay-at-home wife in her first marriage, Virginia decided after her divorce that she wanted to do something fulfilling and challenging. She thought to herself, "I'm not stupid—I'm going back to school." From there, she tackled graduate school. "Everybody kind of gives it this mystique, as though it's just people with 'superior ability' who can go to graduate school, that it takes high intellect. Instead, it takes hard work. You have to put your head down and focus for a certain period of time. For a while, you have to give up other things that you would like to do. I try to encourage anybody who shows any interest in doing *anything*. If that's what you want to do, don't let anybody tell you that you can't do it. You just need to go into it thinking, 'Well, I'm going to have to sacrifice for this amount of time,' and you can do it!"

Maxine Caldwell, a veterinarian, is proud of her achievements and says her inner strength is a result of having had literally to fight for her life during her childhood with a violent, abusive mother. Because her mother's drinking prevented her from holding a job, they were desperately poor, so Maxine was motivated to seek financial security. "Today, if I want something, I get it. I've worked like hell to get everything that I've got, and I don't expect anybody to give me anything. I work seven days a week, twelve hours a day. My work is an extension of what makes me most happy in life: animals. I've always turned to animals. They are an addiction. I couldn't live without them."

New Places, New People

I was scared to death on the day that I, a graduate teaching assistant, and now supposedly the authority figure, taught my first college class. I'd always wanted to teach others—I'd just never had the guts to try. I envied and admired others who taught and wondered how they had the courage to stand before twenty-five or thirty students and lead a discussion. I cringed at the thought. I knew I wasn't good enough. Or was I?

The six or seven years following my mother's death had been a tumultuous time for me. Mother's sudden departure had been like the grand finale of unfair abandonment. A gloom that I could not shake had settled into me. While consulting a therapist, reading a lot of self-help books, and thinking things through on my own, I began to understand why I was so haunted by feelings of inadequacy.

The result of that troubled turning point was that I made a conscious decision. If I expected to have any kind of happy or productive life, I would have to ignore the inner voices that told me how inferior I was. They could not be easily quieted no matter what I did, so I would have to plug my ears, keep my eyes on the prize, and keep marching forward. I applied for admittance to the master's degree program at the university. They accepted me and gave me free tuition and a small teaching stipend in exchange for my services as a teacher. Now my work was about to start.

My heart was pounding as I entered that classroom. I placed my books on the desk, adjusted my glasses, and looked up unsmilingly at the baby faces of the twenty-five students seated in their chairs. Though I'd spent a week memorizing my introductory speech, my throat tightened as they waited expectantly. The room was deathly quiet. Nervously clearing my throat, I introduced myself.

A heavyset guy in the first row shot his hand up. "Are you a graduate student?" he asked sarcastically.

What could I say? Of course I was a graduate student, and my awkward inexperience obviously showed. But somehow, heart racing, I proceeded, reminding myself that a thousand-mile journey begins with the first step. Although the fifty minutes seemed like five hundred to me (Lord knows how long it felt to them!), I got through it without any major blunders. When the time was up and the students hurried out of the room, a little spark of pride flickered.

I had done something that I had feared!

Although I didn't know it at the time, that first day of class was indeed the first step in a thousand-mile journey, from the Northeast of my birth, to Louisiana, to Georgia, a journey that led through a master's, a Ph.D., and eventually to tenure.

Visiting or moving to new locations is scary, but it can also be an enriching, healing experience, for it helps us to further transcend the unhealthy realities we grew up in. It's not that we can run away from ourselves—the ghosts will always follow us wherever we relocate—but by exposing ourselves to as many new and different environments as possible, we are reminded that a great big world out there awaits us, with countless options, opportunities, and people who see us with unbiased eyes. Surrounded by these, we may feel reborn as new and better women.

Linda Hanson taught in China when she was in her thirties. Until that point, she had made "safe" career decisions, and though her current job provided her with a living, it wasn't intellectually interesting. Whether her feelings of discontent were based upon a late rebellion or an early midlife crisis, Linda isn't sure. All she knew was that she was haunted by the feeling of "Is this all there is?" She was "between husbands" and had enough vacation leave, so she jumped at the chance when told about the opportunity to teach abroad. Linda remembers asking herself, "What am I doing?" and then quickly answering, "Who cares? I'll take a leave of absence and come back."

"It was wonderful—although it wasn't for the first few weeks," she recalls. "I remember thinking, *What* have I done to myself?' I couldn't figure out a lot of the ground rules for running the class, so I thought, 'I'm in over my head here.' I felt almost immobilized for a week or ten days. Then I woke up one morning and thought, 'There are planes out of here twice a week. You can get on a plane and go home, if you want.' At that point, it became a choice, not a sentence, and I had a great time."

Dead armadillos lined the highway, stiff little legs sticking pathetically skyward. I had never seen an armadillo before in my life, had never really thought about them. I'd always assumed they inhabited outer Pakistan or something. Apparently, they lived—and died—right here in Louisiana. Here I was, a lifelong Yankee, driving along the thruway toward Baton Rouge, where I would live for the next four years while I worked on a Ph.D. This was the first time in my life I'd ever been in the Deep South. As I drove along, the hot air blew onto me through the open car window. (Of course, my northern car didn't have air-conditioning.)

This new country was flat, hot, and swampy, with a hazy white sky. Instead of the tall maples and pines that I'd been used to in New England, this land was covered with sprawling live oak trees, whose wide crooked branches sometimes brushed the ground. A barge chugged along on the brown Mississippi River, which was lined with people of all ages and colors holding fishing poles. It all seemed so unfamiliar to me, and when I pulled up to the address of the cheap campus housing that I'd rented, sight unseen, I wept.

"Oh, I hate the South!" I sobbed, homesick and exhausted from the long trip. I felt like a kindergartner on the first day of school who wanted to go home to Mommy. Of course, in my case, there was no more "Mommy"—she had been dead for nearly a decade.

I got out of the car and walked around the campus. It was three in the afternoon. A jet black cloud slid rapidly in overhead. The sun retreated. A drop of rain splashed on my head, so I took cover near the front door of the student union. Suddenly, the heavens opened up and with a whooooosh! emptied its entire contents onto the earth below, as though a housewife in the sky had tossed a basin of wash water out a second-story window. A blinding sheet of rain pounded the ground while thunder boomed and lightning flashed. I had never seen the likes of this! Within moments, rivers were rushing along the streets, swirling and hissing into gutters; minilakes were spreading across the grass, and brooks were coursing along the sidewalks. Water blew sideways through the air, splashing torrents on the people huddled under temporary shelters. Then—just as suddenly, it seemed—it was over. The hiss of rainfall softened and died. One or two random drops ping-pinged onto car tops. The sun and birds reemerged.

How dramatic the rain was here in the South! When it rained in the North, it usually rained slowly and patiently for hours. Here in Louisiana, I discovered, a black raincloud moved in every afternoon at three and got it over with in ten minutes.

That first day I hated the South. A sick feeling formed in my gut, telling me that I'd made a terrible mistake. I phoned my sister, Diana, sobbing. She advised me to give it twenty-four more hours, and if I still felt the same, to return. The next day, I still felt the same, but I postponed a decision for another day. In the days that followed, I felt physically sick with longing to go back to the North, to the terrain, the climate, the friends, the culture that I was used to, and kept promising myself that tomorrow I would return. Forget the Ph.D. program. But for some reason, just like an alcoholic taking it one day at a time, I kept postponing my departure. My rational mind was struggling valiantly with my emotions, reminding me that I was here to accomplish a goal that I hoped would give me a much-needed direction.

Sad and homesick as I was, I made an effort to appreciate this new country. Climbing the grassy levee by the Mississippi River, I watched the choppy water flow swiftly along, carrying boats, barges, logs. The sandy bank was dotted with tiny, well-sculpted holes, which I later learned were the homes of crawfish (in the South, pronounced "CRAW-fish"), a culinary staple. An elderly black man sat in a folding chair near the bank monitoring three or four fish lines. He greeted me with a smile, revealing a gold front tooth. As the days passed, the people I met seemed very friendly. When I began my teaching assistantship, I found that the college students were different from the ones I'd been used to. They politely addressed me as "Ma'am" and listened respectfully. My initial impressions were that the young women wore heavy makeup, curly hairstyles, and plenty of perfume, in contrast to the straight-haired, natural-looking northern girls. The guys were clean-shaven, clean-cut, and short-haired, unlike their long-haired, bearded counter-parts up north. They referred to their parents as "Mama" and "Daddy," they went to family reunions every weekend, and attended church regularly.

For a long time, I felt homesick and out of place. But slowly, the South charmed me. It was not so bad after all. In the summertime, the velvet twilights smelled of honeysuckle. The mild autumns lingered into Thanksgiving when the leaf-bearing trees finally turned into muted yellows and orange-browns. The winters were short and snowless. About once per decade a few snowflakes swirled through the sky and melted, prompting the governor to order the closing of all schools. As a Yankee who had never known anything but freezing winters with six-foot snowdrifts, I rejoiced in the respite. I hadn't realized before how much of my energy had been spent on anticipating, preparing for, and enduring the long winters. Now, for the first time, I did not have to buy a heavy-duty car battery or snow tires. Nor did I have to order five hundred gallons of home heating oil. Nor did I need new boots or gloves. Best of all, the green winters were morale-boosting. Birds still sang, plants still grew. In the springtime, which came early, the landscape exploded in pinks, whites, reds, and purples as the crepe myrtles, camellias, dogwoods, azaleas, bougainvilleas, and wisteria blossomed everywhere.

I took steamboat rides on the Mississippi, visited New Orleans, tasted pralines, went to crawfish boils. I got used to the friendliness, the accents, the ways of thinking and living. I met more people of color and of different nationalities. The separation from my own region, although immensely painful at first, enabled me to reinvent myself within a new culture. It forced me to consider other belief systems besides the one I'd been raised with. Best of all, it gave me an opportunity to reexamine those old family scripts in the new and different light that separation can offer.

Moving to the Deep South turned out to be one of the best things I ever did for myself—though I didn't think so at the time. Now it frightens me to think how much I would have missed, how little I might have grown, if I had packed my bags and left Louisiana, as I wanted to.

Letting Go of the Past

Many of us have found happiness by creating our own families. Though 50 percent of the daughters who participated in our project have been divorced one or more times, many have learned from earlier marital mistakes and have settled into satisfying relationships. Also, 73 percent have children. A lot of the daughters we talked to attribute their current satisfaction with life to the nuclear families they have created.

"My husband is just perfect; he has effectively undone much of my emotional destruction from my childhood," says Bonnie French. "He has allowed me to show more of my true self over the last eight years. Overall, my emotions are usually okay, other than feeling a little insecure at times or lacking self-esteem, but my husband really helps me with this."

Mickey Madigan is now happily married after three divorces; she has an active life, which includes seven children and many grandchildren. "I have a wonderful, hard-working husband. After those earlier bad marriages, I thank God for the good things in my life."

Finding the Joy in Life

As Shannon Nichols stated at the opening of this chapter, being happy takes work. In other words, we have to *look* for things to be happy about, to make a conscious effort to appreciate the joys and laughter in life. Sometimes comparing our present lives with our past can provide an uplifting frame of reference.

"I feel that I've rediscovered the happy child that I used to be before Mother's drinking started," says Ellie. "I'm sure that maybe some of my colleagues at work think I'm sickeningly exuberant because I usually do feel very upbeat. But I can't help it. It's partly biological, I suppose; my father was usually happy, a characteristic that I think aggravated the hell out of my more depressive mother. In fact, I think that's one of the reasons she seemed to inflict her anger on me the most—I was the child who looked and acted most like him. My happiness is more than biological, though. Every day, I feel so grateful that I can wake up and be myself without having to worry about making somebody mad if I say or do the wrong thing. My home is no longer a place where I must tiptoe around someone else's irrational moods and needs. I am free to do and say anything I want. It's *my* home. I feel grateful that I don't have to live in fear anymore. Also, in recent years, I have had a spiritual awakening, and see life in a different light—literally—than I did during my youth. I believe in a Higher Power and an eternal order to things. This has shaped my vision of the world as an exciting place with endless wonders and possibilities. So I may seem childish to others . . . So what? If it makes me happy to enjoy life to the fullest, who cares what anyone thinks?"

"I feel emotionally healthy for the first time in my life," states Crystal Knight, thirty-seven. "I've had several years of counseling that have helped me deal with having grown up with an alcoholic mother. Though it helped me to understand both my mother and myself much better, it can't erase the scars that were left behind. But I also realize I'm a stronger and better person since these wounds have begun to heal."

She adds, "I miss my mother because she was my mother; no one can replace her. I miss the good times that we shared when she was sober. I miss what only a mother can give a daughter in her life. I wish she had lived to see her grandson. With her passing, I think she finally found peace and, to an extent, so did I.

"I don't think parents realize how much of themselves they pass onto their children," she says. "I see a lot of my mother in me—the way I was from early childhood up until the time I started receiving counseling. I've dealt with my demons in depth. Where it was once important to be liked, loved, and accepted no matter what I had to sacrifice, now my feelings and well-being are more important than others'. I believe that low self-esteem is a lack of love for oneself, so I learned to love me."

Am I happy? Yes! In a few months, I will be fifty, the same age Mother was when she died. Drinking robbed her of her life. Now, as I get "up there" (as the eye doctor said just the other day), I know that added birthdays are "supposed" to upset me, but they don't. They have the opposite effect. Perhaps this is because my mother's life—and her early death—provide a frame of reference that always reminds me of how much I have to be thankful for. Outwardly, she seemed to have it all—intelligence, a good education, a handsome, prosperous husband, three lovely children, financial security, a nice home. But something must have been missing. What, I don't know.

If my mother could return from the beyond for a second chance, don't you think that she would have made different choices and would have enjoyed being fifty-one, fifty-two, fifty-three, and very much looked forward to sixty, seventy, one hundred? To be honest, it irritates me when I hear women whining, "Oh, dear, I'm going to be forty next week! I feel so o-o-old." What do they think the alternative is? Even more important than the duration of life is how much it is enjoyed. Drinking robbed my mother of much enjoyment that she could have had.

Like so many of the wonderful daughters I have met and talked to during the writing of this book, I have gained something from my painful experiences. During my formative years, I was forced to turn inward for strength and comfort, to find solace in books, in music, in my imagination and dreams. I learned to enjoy my own company and still do. Very early on in life, I began to see life as a treasure trove of learning experiences—maybe because the financial security with which I grew up seemed irrelevant, considering it was not much of a substitute for a close, comforting family bond, which I yearned for.

Maybe that's part of the reason I've spent my adult life pursuing occupations and experiences that were meaningful rather than lucrative. In my early twenties, I worked as a newspaper reporter and feature writer because it stretched my mind and introduced me to new events and new people. Next, I "lived off the land" for five years in a log cabin in Maine and learned invaluable lessons about life. After that, in my thirties, I sacrificed immeasurably to go to graduate school because it was rewarding, though definitely not from a financial point of view. After graduate school, I became a full-time college professor. For years now, I have listened to and read about the thoughts, experiences, and dreams of thousands of young adults as they have passed through my classes as one of the many stops on their journeys through life. I have learned as much or more from them as they have from me. Maybe that's why I feel spiritually rich today.

Do I have any advice to other daughters for living happy lives? No pat formulas, no, because it's different for everyone. We're all dealt a different hand, so to speak. All women must search inside themselves and learn what that particular hand is, and how to make the most happiness from it. Instead, I think the most important message I can give to other daughters is to tell them this: just continue to be strong.

A Letter to the Reader

If you are the daughter of an alcoholic mother, how has this affected your life?

If you are the husband, boyfriend, partner, sister, brother, child, or parent of a woman who is the daughter of an alcoholic mother, how has this impacted upon your relationship with her?

Share your story with us, no matter how long or short. Send it with a self-addressed, stamped envelope to:

Eleanor Agnew and Sharon Robideaux
c/o Pocket Books
1230 Avenue of the Americas
New York, NY 10020

Notes

⌐⌐

Preface

xviii Robert Ackerman, author of Perfect Daughters, estimates . . . :
Robert Ackerman, *Perfect Daughters: Adult Daughters of Alcoholics*
(Deerfield Beach, FL: Health Communications, Inc., 1989), 6.

xviii Ackerman found that 40 percent . . . : Ibid., 12.

xix As Alan Leshner, director of the National Institute on Drug
Abuse, has said . . . : Tippi Nicole Thole, "Women Abusers
Need Different Treatment Than Men," *Columbia Missourian* 21
April 1996, 1G.

xx For instance, Curt Krebsbach, a counselor . . . : Ibid.

Part I

Chapter One: Introduction

15 Throughout history, in fact . . . : Mark Lender and James Martin,
Drinking in America: A History (New York, The Free Press, 1982)
20, 99, 117.

15 Women who get drunk . . . : Amanda Smith, "The Plight of
Women Alcoholics," *The Eagle* 30 Sept. 1992, 13.

16 Elizabeth Ettore, author of *Women and Substance Abuse* . . . : Elizabeth Ettore, *Women and Substance Abuse* (New Brunswick, NJ: Rutgers UP, 1992), 38–39.

16 As Jean Kirkpatrick explains . . . : Jean Kirkpatrick, *Goodbye Hangovers, Hello Life* (New York: Atheneum, 1986), xvii.

16 The film industry has also gone a long way . . . : Norman Denzin, *Hollywood Shot by Shot: Alcoholism in American Cinema* (New York: Aldine de Gruyter, 1991), 70, 71.

16 As Judith Seixas and Geraldine Youcha observe . . . : Judith S. Seixas and Geraldine Youcha, *Children of Alcoholism: A Survivor's Manual* (New York: Harper & Row, 1985), 4.

16 Linda Tschirhart Sanford and Mary Ellen Donovan . . . : Linda Tschirhart Sanford and Mary Ellen Donovan, *Women and Self-Esteem* (New York: Penguin Books, 1984), 70, 91, 86.

17 More women than ever are drinking . . . : "Drug Use by Women, Girls on Rise." *Columbia Daily Tribune,* 5 June 1996, 12A.

17 Laura Lindsteadt, a therapist at the Arthur Center . . . : Thole, "Women Abusers Need Different Treatment Than Men," 1G.

18 Although the number of women in the workforce . . . : Dorothy Schneider and Carl F. Schneider, *Women in the Workplace* (Santa Barbara, CA: ABC-CLIO, Inc., 1993), xi.

18 Susan Faludi, author of *Backlash* . . . : Susan Faludi, *Backlash* (New York: Doubleday, 1991), xiv.

18 Linda Sanford, a licensed psychotherapist . . . : Sanford and Donovan, *Women and Self-Esteem,* 66.

19 As Signe Hammer asserts . . . : Signe Hammer, *Daughters and Mothers: Mothers and Daughters* (New York: Quadrangle/New York Times Book Co., 1975), xi, 1, xiv.

19 According to a 1991 study . . . : Lynn Prowitt, "Ninja Turtles or Little Mermaids?" *Ladies' Home Journal,* September 1992, 134.

19 Further, according to a study . . . : Nancy J. Perry, "Why It's So Tough to Be a Girl." *Fortune* 10 August 1992, 82.

20　The guru of child care . . . : Benjamin Spock, *Baby and Child Care* (New York: Pocket Books, 1976), 15.

20　According to Francine Klagsbrun . . . : Francine Klagsbrun, *Mixed Feelings: Love, Hate, Rivalry, and Reconciliation Among Brothers and Sisters* (New York: Bantam Books, 1992), 270.

21　As Sanford and Donovan note . . . : Sanford and Donovan, *Women and Self-Esteem*, 70.

22　As Klagsbrun notes about alcoholic . . . : Klagsbrun, *Mixed Feelings*, 201.

Chapter Two: Mother at Her Best

28　As Ackerman notes . . . : Ackerman, *Perfect Daughters*, 8.

28　As Ackerman adds . . . : Ibid., 9.

29　Seixas and Youcha state . . . : Seixas and Youcha, *Children of Alcoholism: A Survivor's Manual*, 5.

29　Janet Woititz, author of *Adult Children of Alcoholics,* confirms . . . : Janet Geringer Woititz, *Adult Children of Alcoholics* (Deerfield Beach, FL: Health Communications, Inc., 1983), 5.

29　Woititz points out . . . : Ibid., 5.

Chapter Three: Mother at Her Worst

40　In *Perfect Daughters,* Ackerman notes . . . : Ackerman, *Perfect Daughters*, 41–42, 50.

51　One area that concerns not just the children . . . : Joey Kennedy, "Drunk Driving Makes a Comeback." *Redbook,* May 1997, 90, 130.

58　If the father is still present in the home . . . : Ackerman, *Perfect Daughters*, 50.

59　Psychologists such as Kristin Kunzman . . . : Kristin Kunzman, *Healing from Childhood Sexual Abuse: A Woman's Recovery Guide* (Center City, MN: Hazelden Publishing & Education, 1989), 5, 9, 10, 11.

59　According to a report issued in 1996 . . . : "Drug Use by Women, Girls on Rise," 12A.

71 "Verbal abuse . . ." : Grace Ketterman, *Verbal Abuse: Healing the Hidden Wound* (Ann Arbor, MI: Servant Publications, 1992), 14, 205.

Part II

Chapter Four: Body Images

84 Naomi Wolf points out . . . : Naomi Wolf, *The Beauty Myth* (New York: Doubleday, 1991), 10.

84 Judith Seixas and Geraldine Youcha report . . . : Seixas and Youcha, *Children of Alcoholism: A Survivor's Manual,* 87.

84 As Nancy Friday states . . .": Nancy Friday, *My Mother/My Self* (New York: Dell, 1987), vi–vii.

90 Caroline Knapp, a recovering alcoholic . . . : Caroline Knapp, *Drinking: A Love Story* (New York: Dial Press, 1996), 73.

94 If, simultaneously, her daughter . . . : Nancy Friday, *The Power of Beauty* (New York: HarperCollins, 1996), 216.

95 In her account *Drinking* . . . : Knapp, *Drinking: A Love Story,* 210.

Chapter Five: Passing the Torch: Anxieties and Addictions

106 In *Addiction: From Biology to Drug Policy* . . . : Avram Goldstein, *Addiction: From Biology to Drug Policy* (New York: W. H. Freeman & Co., 1994), 93.

106 Dr. R. Reid Wilson states . . . : R. Reid Wilson, *Don't Panic: Taking Control of Anxiety Attacks* (New York: Harper Collins, 1996), 97.

106 In *Children of Alcoholism: A Survivor's Manual* . . . : Seixas and Youcha, *Children of Alcoholism: A Survivor's Manual,* 133.

106 In fact, two-thirds of the alcoholics . . . : Wilson, *Don't Panic,* 98.

109 "Because of physiological differences . . .": Tippi Nicole Thole, "Women and Alcohol Equal Danger," *Columbia Missourian,* 21 April 1996, 2G.

109 "For female alcoholics . . .": Thole, "Women Abusers Need Different Treatment Than Men," 1G.

110 Goldstein writes . . . : Goldstein, *Addiction: From Biology to Drug Policy,* 98.

116 Goldstein defines a drug . . . : Ibid., 2.

119 Goldstein refers to tobacco . . . : Ibid., 102, 111, 113.

Chapter Six: "Weighting" for Love

129 "Children who grow up in families . . .": Barbara McFarland and Tyeis Baker-Baumann, *Feeding the Empty Heart: Adult Children and Compulsive Eating* (Center City, MN: Hazelden Publishing & Education, 1988), 3.

130 Geneen Roth, author of *When Food Is Love* . . . : Geneen Roth, *When Food Is Love* (New York: Plume/Penguin, 1992), 3, 4.

130 To Roth, the connection between compulsive eating . . . : Ibid., 3, 4, 123.

131 Tellingly, research conducted . . . : Debra Waterhouse, *Like Mother, Like Daughter: How Women Are Influenced by Their Mothers' Relationship with Food—and How to Break the Pattern* (New York, Hyperion, 1997), 193.

131 Robert Ackerman, who has written extensively . . . : Ackerman, *Perfect Daughters,* 50.

132 Roth notes . . . : Roth, *When Food Is Love,* 18.

133 Dr. Ronald Ruden, author of *The Craving Brain* . . . : Ronald Ruden, *The Craving Brain: The Biobalance Approach to Controlling Addictions* (New York: HarperCollins, 1977), 18–19.

133 We enter what Dr. Ruden calls . . . : Ibid., 19, 18.

139 As Gravitz and Bowden suggest . . . : Herbert Gravitz and Julie Bowden, *Recovery: A Guide for Adult Children of Alcoholics* (Holmes Beach, FL: Learning Publications, 1985), 66.

140 According to Herbert Gravitz and Julie Bowden . . . : Ibid., 93.

141 The Medical Center at the University of Michigan reports . . . : University of Michigan Medical Center. "Health and Medical Library: Substance Abuse, Alcohol, Drugs." Internet. 21 Oct. 1997. Available: http://www.med.umich.edu/1libr/subabuse/alcol02.htm.

141 Dr. Stephen J. Gislason . . . : Stephen J. Gislason, "Alcoholic Beverages and Alcohol Abuse." Internet. 21 Oct. 1997. Available: http://www.nutramed.com/zeno/alcohol.htm#Alcohol.

141 Also reported is that . . . : Environmed Research. "Alcoholic Beverages and Alcohol Abuse." Internet. 21 Oct. 1997. Available: http://www.nutramed.com/zeno/alcoholism.htm.

142 The authors of *Recovery: A Guide for Adult Children of Alcoholics* . . . : Gravitz and Bowden, *Recovery: A Guide for Adult Children of Alcoholics,* 67.

Part III

Chapter Seven: Mother Substitutes: Someone to Mother Me

156 Hope Edelman has addressed this issue . . . : Hope Edelman, *Motherless Daughters* (New York: Dell, 1994), 185–186.

156 Like Edelman, we found that daughters listed aunts . . . : Ibid., 186.

162 In her research on daughters . . . : Ibid., 187, 189.

162 As Edelman also notes . . . : Ibid., 187, 189.

163 "Many of the great mothers . . .": Adrienne Rich, *Of Woman Born: Motherhood as Experience and Institution,* 2nd ed. (New York: W. W. Norton, 1986), 252.

167 As Francine Klagsbrun points out . . . : Klagsbrun, *Mixed Feelings,* 205, 206–07.

167 However, the young children . . . : Ibid., 206.

Chapter Eight: Men: Our Romantic Relationships

178 Judith S. Seixas and Geraldine Youcha . . . : Seixas and Youcha, *Children of Alcoholism: A Survivor's Manual,* 82.

178 Claudia Black, author of *It Will Never Happen to Me,* states . . . : Claudia Black, *It Will Never Happen to Me,* (New York: Ballantine Books, 1981), 194.

178 In *Recovery: A Guide for Adult Children of Alcoholics* . . . : Gravitz and Bowden, *Recovery: A Guide for Adult Children of Alcoholics,* 4.

179 In *Perfect Daughters* . . . : Ackerman, *Perfect Daughters,* 146.

179 If a daughter of an alcoholic . . . : Ibid., 133.

179 Dr. Carole Leiberman and Lisa Collier Cool agree . . . : Carole Leiberman and Lisa Collier Cool, *Bad Boys: Why We Love Them, How to Live with Them, and When to Leave Them,* 6.

180 Janet Woititz, author of *Adult Children of Alcoholics,* refers . . . : Woititz, *Adult Children of Alcoholics,* 40.

181 Ackerman points out . . . : Ackerman, *Perfect Daughters,* 43.

182 As Ackerman states . . . : *Ibid.,* 48.

182 According to Ackerman . . . : *Ibid.,* 48–49.

Chapter Nine: Relationships with Female Friends: Learning to Trust

204 Carmen Renee Berry and Tamara Traeder . . . : Carmen Renee Berry and Tamara Traeder, *Girlfriends: Invisible Bonds, Enduring Ties,* (Berkeley, CA: Wildcat Canyon Press, 1995), 137.

214 As Judith S. Seixas and Geraldine Youcha note . . . : Seixas and Youcha, *Children of Alcoholism: A Survivor's Manual,* 80.

215 Betty's experience illustrates a point . . . : Berry and Traeder, *Girlfriends,* 40.

Chapter Ten: Becoming Mothers Ourselves:
Recapturing Lost Love

230 Janet Woititz explains . . . : Janet Geringer Woititz, *Adult Children of Alcoholics,* 46.
231 In addition, Robert Ackerman points out . . . : Ackerman, *Perfect Daughters,* 47.

Part IV

Chapter Eleven: Mother's Aging, Illness, and Death

246 Avram Goldstein, M. D., notes . . . : Goldstein, *Addiction: From Biology to Drug Policy,* 133.
246 "Male alcoholics tend to reveal . . .": Thole, "Women Abusers Need Different Treatment Than Men," 1G.

Chapter Twelve: Building Happy Lives

280 . . . we "are a special population with special needs . . .": Black, *It Will Never Happen to Me,* 110.
280 But as Judith S. Seixas and Geraldine Youcha state . . . : Seixas and Youcha, *Children of Alcoholism: A Survivor's Manual,* 134.

Bibliography

Ackerman, Robert. *Perfect Daughters: Adult Daughters of Alcoholics.* Deerfield Beach, FL: Health Communications, Inc., 1989.

Berry, Carmen Renee, and Tamara Traeder. *Girlfriends: Invisible Bonds, Enduring Ties.* Berkeley, CA: Wildcat Canyon Press, 1995.

Black, Claudia. *It Will Never Happen to Me.* New York: Ballantine Books, 1981.

Denzin, Norman. *Hollywood Shot by Shot: Alcoholism in American Cinema.* New York: Aldine de Gruyter, 1991.

"Drug Use by Women, Girls on Rise." *Columbia Daily Tribune,* 5 June 1996, 12A.

Edelman, Hope. *Motherless Daughters.* New York: Dell, 1994.

Environmed Research. "Alcoholic Beverages and Alcohol Abuse." Internet. 21 Oct. 1997. Available: http://www.nutramed.com/zeno/alcoholism.htm.

Ettore, Elizabeth. *Women and Substance Abuse.* New Brunswick, NJ: Rutgers UP, 1992.

Faludi, Susan. *Backlash.* New York: Doubleday, 1991.

Friday, Nancy. *My Mother/My Self.* New York: Dell, 1987.

_____. *The Power of Beauty.* New York: HarperCollins, 1996.

Gislason, Stephen J. "Alcoholic Beverages and Alcohol Abuse." Internet. 21

Oct. 1997. Available:
http://www.nutramed.com/zeno/alcohol.htm#Alcohol.

Goldstein, Avram. *Addiction: From Biology to Drug Policy.* New York: W. H. Freeman & Co., 1994.

Gravitz, Herbert, and Julie Bowden. *Recovery: A Guide for Adult Children of Alcoholics.* Holmes Beach, FL: Learning Publications, 1985.

Hammer, Signe. *Daughters and Mothers: Mothers and Daughters.* New York: Quadrangle/New York Times Book Co., 1975.

Kennedy, Joey. "Drunk Driving Makes a Comeback." *Redbook,* May 1997, 89+.

Ketterman, Grace. *Verbal Abuse: Healing the Hidden Wound.* Ann Arbor, MI: Servant Publications, 1992.

Kirkpatrick, Jean. *Goodbye Hangovers, Hello Life: Self-Help for Women.* New York: Atheneum, 1986.

Klagsbrun, Francine. *Mixed Feelings: Love, Hate, Rivalry, and Reconciliation Among Brothers and Sisters.* New York: Bantam Books, 1992.

Knapp, Caroline. *Drinking: A Love Story.* New York: Dial Press, 1996.

Kunzman, Kristin. *Healing from Childhood Sexual Abuse: A Woman's Recovery Guide.* Center City, MN: Hazelden Publishing & Education, 1989.

Leiberman, Carole, and Lisa Collier Cool. *Bad Boys: Why We Love Them, How to Live with Them, and When to Leave Them.* New York: Dutton, 1997.

Lender, Mark Edward, and James Kirby Martin. *Drinking in America: A History.* New York: The Free Press, 1982.

McFarland, Barbara, and Tyeis Baker-Baumann. *Feeding the Empty Heart: Adult Children and Compulsive Eating.* Center City, MN: Hazelden Publishing & Education, 1988.

Perry, Nancy J. "Why It's So Tough to Be a Girl." *Fortune* 10 August 1992, 82–84.

Prowitt, Lynn. "Ninja Turtles or Little Mermaids?" *Ladies' Home Journal,* September 1992: 132+.

Rich, Adrienne. *Of Woman Born: Motherhood as Experience and Institution.* 2nd ed. New York: W. W. Norton, 1986.

Roth, Geneen. *When Food Is Love.* New York: Plume/Penguin, 1992.

Ruden, Ronald. *The Craving Brain: The Biobalance Approach to Controlling Addictions.* New York: HarperCollins, 1977.

Sanford, Linda Tschirhart, and Mary Ellen Donovan. *Women and Self-Esteem.* New York: Penguin Books, 1984.

Schneider, Dorothy, and Carl F. Schneider. *Women in the Workplace.* Santa Barbara, CA: ABC-CLIO, Inc., 1993.

Seixas, Judith, and Geraldine Youcha. *Children of Alcoholism: A Survivor's Manual.* New York: Harper & Row, 1985.

Smith, Amanda. "The Plight of Women Alcoholics." *The Eagle* 30 Sept. 1992, 13.

Spock, Benjamin Spock. *Baby and Child Care.* New York: Pocket Books, 1976.

Thole, Tippi Nicole. "Women Abusers Need Different Treatment Than Men." *Columbia Missourian* 21 April 1996, 1G.

———. "Women and Alcohol Equal Danger." *Columbia Missourian* 21 April 1996, 2G.

University of Michigan Medical Center. "Health and Medical Library: Substance Abuse, Alcohol, Drugs." Internet. 21 Oct. 1997. Available: http://www.med.umich.edu/1libr/subabuse/alcol02.htm.

Waterhouse, Debra. *Like Mother, Like Daughter: How Women Are Influenced by Their Mothers' Relationship with Food—and How to Break the Pattern.* New York: Hyperion, 1997.

Wilson, R. Reid. *Don't Panic: Taking Control of Anxiety Attacks.* New York: HarperCollins, 1996.

Woititz, Janet Geringer. *Adult Children of Alcoholics.* Deerfield Beach, FL: Health Communications, Inc., 1983.

Wolf, Naomi. *The Beauty Myth.* New York: Doubleday, 1991.